Oddly Enough

Tales of the Unordinary (volume one)

Kim M. Watt

Buy the book. Gift the book. Read the book. Borrow the book. Talk about the book. Share the book. Just don't steal the book.

Book thieves will have sock monsters and demons of minor inconvenience wished upon them.

But never underestimate how weird - and coincidental - life is.

For further information contact www.kmwatt.com

Cover design: Monika McFarland, www.ampersandbookcovers.com

Editor: Lynda Dietz, www.easyreaderediting.com

ISBN this edition: 978-0-473-61065-4

ISBN KDP ebook: 978-0-473-61067-8

ISBN IngramSpark paperback: 978-0-473-61068-5

ISBN ePub: 978-0-473-61066-1

First Edition December 2021

10 9 8 7 6 5 4 3 2 1

Contents

To you, lovely people.
The ones who see the weird side of things.
The funny side too, sometimes.
But mostly the weird.
These are your stories.

Before We Begin

Hello lovely people.

Thank you so much for stopping by. I don't normally go in for forewords, or introductions, or prefaces or preludes or any of that stuff that happens before we get to the good bits. I mean, it's not like anyone reads them, right? So I'm likely talking to myself here, but as I think that's a pretty good description of writing in general, we may as well continue.

Herein are a few notes on what to expect from this book:

Chickens! Rubber ducks! Demons! Sea monsters! Pies! Apocalypses! (Apocalypi?)

But you already probably expected that, so let's talk a few details.

If you've been around the newsletter and blog for a while, it's likely you'll have run across some or even a number of the stories in this collection. I've given them a dust off and a lick of polish, straightened their collars and brushed their hair, but many of these have appeared online previously. However, a number of readers have asked about having them in book form, which I completely understand. After spending all day staring at words on a screen, I'm definitely a fan of not reading online, but rather on a page, or at least a different screen. A nice ereader-type one.

So here we have nineteen older stories, some familiar, and some not. And we have five brand new ones, all shiny and startled-looking. And I hope you enjoy every single one of them.

Unfortunately, it appears I've written more short stories than I thought, so in order to stop this turning into an impossibly hefty tome I've not included all of them (and have, in fact, added an extra downloadable one at the end, just for you). I apologise now if your favourite didn't make it this time, but I do plan to do another collection in a year or so, so I promise to include it then. Jump to the website or social media and drop me a message if you want to make sure I don't miss it!

As for how this book works ... Well, a Twitter poll (because this is the only way to gauge public opinion, obviously), convinced me that readers like to know a little about where each story came from. Or where I suspect it may have come from, as stories are their own strange creatures, full of erratic life, quick and slippery as fish in the night. But I have included notes, and please feel free to ignore them or read them as you wish. You don't need them to enjoy the stories.

And finally, please read these stories any way you fancy. They're in no way sequential or chronological. Devour them in one gulp, first to last. Read them backwards. Read odd numbers today and even ones tomorrow, or choose them based on star signs or days of the month or how many seeds were in your watermelon. Dip in and out. Keep the collection handy for when you need a quick read while waiting at the dentist's or bus stop. Do whatever you will with them. They're your stories now, and I only hope that you enjoy them.

Thank you once again, lovely people. Thank you for reading, for your lovely messages, for answering newsletter and social media questions, for suggesting titles and chapter names, and for being on this strange writing journey with me. Thank you for loving the possibilities of magic on the edges of our profoundly odd world.

Thank you for being you.

Now come on in and meet the stories. It's perfectly safe, I promise. They're almost all house-trained, and they almost never bite.

Not hard, anyway ...

Kim x

Want to be in touch? Find me via my website at www.kmwatt.com, or jump to the social media links below.

facebook.com/KimMWatt
x.com/kimmwatt
instagram.com/kimmwatt

The Chicken & the Universe

The writer leans back in her chair and takes a sip of tea. "Of course, there is an endless well of possible ideas. So much to choose from, but one must consider the freight of meaning and message behind the stories. The symbolism. The weight of metaphor."

The listener nods gravely. "So what do they ***mean****, these stories?"*

The writer smiles. "What do ***you*** *think they mean?"*

So ... That writer is not me, evidently. But here's a story about a chicken, because someone said to me that chickens are cool, and we should have more stories about chickens.

That's good enough for me.

THE SUNSET HAD BEEN LOW AND RED, STAINING the stretched black clouds that littered the horizon the colour of cinders, and turning the leafless trees on the fells into blasted, skeletal remains. In the brooding darkness that followed, the fire on the peak was the only light to be seen, flimsy as it was. The wind whined and spat around it, stealing embers and flinging them aloft. Somewhere in the distance a dog howled, but up here was only bare rock and frozen earth, dimly lit by the fire and surrounded by a grinding, angry dark that seemed to resent being held at bay.

"Here, move the tablecloth," someone said. "It's going to catch light."

"It's not a tablecloth," another man said, sounding irritated. "It's the cloth for the altar."

"Well, it were a tablecloth when I bought it. And it's going to be a fire hazard in a minute."

There was some grumbling, then someone emerged from the deep shadows around the fire and crouched to gather up the altar cloth (which still had a Tesco Home sticker on it), a bag of black candles, and a cardboard box that clucked in alarm as he lifted it. He tripped on the hem of his dark robe as he turned to move away from the fire, and almost dropped the box.

"Careful!" the man who'd been worried about the tablecloth said. "She's a good layer, that chicken. Don't want to lose her."

Still clutching the box, Scott glared at his companion, a big man with thinning hair wearing a large plaid dressing gown over a worn winter fleece.

"Why on earth did you bring a chicken you don't want to lose?" he demanded.

"She was easy to catch," the big man said, and took a mouthful from a can of lager. "Not that she probably will be again after this."

"Well, no. She's – *it's* a sacrifice, Glen. You won't need to catch it after this, because its soul will have been offered to the Eldritch Ones."

Glen frowned. "You didn't say anything about a sacrifice."

"I told you we needed to make an offering."

"Yeah, but I thought we'd just sort of offer her up, and they'd say, well, thanks, but we don't really want a chicken. No one ever really says yes to that sort of thing, do they?"

Scott put the box down safely out of reach of the fire and pinched the bridge of his nose. What had he been thinking, getting Glen involved in this? The man was wearing a dressing gown, for the Old Ones' sakes. He tugged on the sleeves of his own, rather more appropriate black robe and took some comfort in the heavy material. With any luck the Eldritch Ones would just eat Glen and his damn chicken at the same time.

"Glen—" he began.

"Have a lager. You're very stressed." The big man was holding a can out to him, smiling encouragingly. "Look, it's a beautiful night and you're all wound up. We can sort this chicken thing out later."

Scott took the beer with a sigh. He may as well. It was only six o'clock. He was going to have to put up with this sort of male bonding ridiculousness until midnight.

SCOTT WATCHED as Glen threw another log onto the fire, sending sparks belching up into the darkness. The stars were out, cold little pinpricks above them, but there was no moon. Not tonight. It was the perfect night to bridge the gaps between dimensions, to draw unseen terrors into being and send the world reeling into madness. He sipped his beer and smiled contentedly. The only downside was having to put up with Glen, but he had needed some extra muscle for carting the wood for the fire, as well as a Land Rover to get them here, and also the potential for a human sacrifice handy in case the chicken didn't do the trick.

He'd been planning this for a long time. A *long* time. His grandfather's old books had held all sorts of hints and conjectures, and it had taken Scott most of his teenage years to really understand what the old man had been hinting at. Power. Eternal life. Riches. Adoration. But most of all, yes – *power*. He'd spent the last two decades deepening his research, even earning a PhD in obscure religions and philosophies. It was amazing the material libraries and museums gave you access to as soon as you mentioned writing dissertations.

And now ... here. Here, in the heavy night of the winter solstice, on one of those terrifying nodes of land where nothing wanted to grow, that even the birds avoided, here with the fire burning and the darkness pressing down around them, and he could almost touch the thin edges of the cosmos, almost taste the glory of—

"You want a sandwich?" Glen asked. "I've got roast beef and horseradish or cheese and pickle. I couldn't remember if you were vegetarian or not."

Scott almost crushed the half-full can of lager, then

forced his hand to relax, not without difficulty. "You realise this isn't a picnic?" he snapped.

Glen regarded the sandwiches, one in each huge hand. Scott could see thick slabs of white bread through the cling-film, and his stomach grumbled unhelpfully. "I don't see how you can do your ritual thingy on an empty stomach," Glen said. "I mean, it must be tough work, summoning ancient gods and so on."

Scott peered at him in the uncertain light, not quite sure if his cousin was joking or not. He was such an uneducated lump that it was hard to tell sometimes. Still, at least he hadn't objected to Scott's 'experiment into the beliefs and rituals of certain early cultures that inhabited the area'.

"Cheese and pickle," he said. "Too much red meat is bad for you."

Glen handed him the sandwich, and sat down cross-legged on the rough ground. "Maybe. Probably more so for you office types. The rest of us burn it off."

Scott opened his mouth to point out that it was less about metabolism and more about arteries and cholesterol, then took a bite of sandwich instead. There was no point arguing with someone like Glen. He'd be irrelevant before long anyway.

Midnight took a long time to arrive. Glen marched around their perch high atop the moors, dressing gown flapping about his legs in the wind, pointing out favourite constellations and talking about some irrelevant local history, while producing a seemingly never-ending variety of snacks from the cooler in the back of the Land Rover. He even started singing at some point, and Scott seriously considered making some sort of pre-sacrifice of him, just to shut him up.

But finally the alarm on Scott's phone went off, and he scrambled from the front of the 4×4, where he'd been sheltering both from the cold and Glen. Thirteen black candles already circled the fire, nestled into tall glass sleeves to protect them from the wind (Glen had called them 'very designer', but Scott figured the Eldritch Ones wouldn't mind too much), and he crouched to light the first of them. He was surprised to find his hand shaking, and it took three attempts with the long kitchen lighter before the wick caught. Blood was roaring in his ears, and he started to mumble the words of the chant under his breath. They worked like a mantra, the harsh syllables focusing his mind, his tongue struggling with the familiar yet clumsy shape of them.

"Bring the chicken," he commanded Glen, drawing an ancient stone knife etched with ugly engravings from under his robe.

Glen looked unimpressed. "I thought we were offering her to them? What's the knife for?"

"I told you it was a sacrifice. What did you think – I was going to put a bow and a gift tag on it?"

"She's not an it. Her name's Elsa."

"Elsa?" Scott managed to ease his grip on the knife's cloth-wrapped handle. He didn't want to damage it. If this didn't work, he was going to have to smuggle it back into the museum in Alaska. But it *would* work, if his cousin would just stop being such a pain and give him the damn chicken.

"The girls named her." Glen picked up the box and cradled it protectively.

"I'll replace her. It." Scott beckoned impatiently, and his phone beeped. Five minutes.

"You can't just *replace* her. It wouldn't be her!"

"It's a chicken!"

"It's *Elsa!*"

The men glared at each other across the ring of firelight, the candles guttering in the wind and smelling faintly of liquorice.

"Give me the chicken," Scott said, in the manner of someone who knows he will be commanding dark forces within the hour.

"No," Glen said, in the manner of someone who loves his chicken.

"Glen. I need the chicken."

"No." Glen took a step back. "I did not agree to you slaughtering Elsa."

"Stop calling it Elsa! You're making it worse!"

"Stop calling her an it! And put the knife down. You always were a weird little sod."

"I'm not *weird.* And at least I'm not some uneducated *farmer!*"

"You're trying to kill my chicken. You're weird."

"I am not weird!" Scott forgot all about preserving the ancient knife and ran at Glen with it raised over his head, shrieking the guttural words of the summoning spell as he went. The night shivered and pulsed. Glen, half-turned to run for the Land Rover, stopped mid-stride and stared in

horror as colours writhed across the sky. They were greens and purples and reds, but not like any the men had seen before. They were the colours of putrefaction, of old bruises and rotting wounds, but worse, much, much worse, and they moved with unseen life, as if something terrible pushed against the sky from beyond.

"Yes!" Scott screamed. "Yes, yes, yes! Come to me, ancient ones! Come to me!"

"You freaky little—" Glen threw himself out of the smaller man's way, losing his grip on the box as he stumbled over the rough ground. He fell to one knee, catching himself on his hands, and the box tumbled end over end twice before the seams split. A pretty but bedraggled bantam hen squeezed herself out and bolted, swerving drunkenly from side to side as she ran. "No, *Elsa!*"

"Shtlothgh! Agnoztheng! Grgneth bethngals!" Scott stood over his cousin with his feet planted wide, his head flung back. Blood was roaring behind his eyes like the beginning of a migraine, and the colours swimming across the sky felt like they were drowning him. "*Shtlothgh amngeron bectith!* Awake! Arise! Come to me!" He knew the last words weren't entirely necessary, but they sounded good. Wait until Glen saw what came down out of that terrible night to serve Scott. Let him see what the *weird* one could do. Let him see *power*. "Come, take this sacrifice I lay before you! Come, for he is yours!" Scott waved the knife meaningfully at Glen, and the bigger man looked at him in astonishment, then scrambled to his feet.

"Buggar off, you little monster. I try to help you out, show some interest, like, and now you think you're going to sacrifice me? Bollocks to that." Glen took a wary step toward the Land Rover, not taking his eyes off his cousin.

"Don't move," Scott hissed. "They're coming. Can't you feel them coming?"

The fire gave a great, belching roar, lifting high toward the hideous sky, then flattening out across the ground as if under an immense downdraft, burning green at the edges.

"All I feel is the great need to get away from you," Glen said, and scuttled off sideways, trying to keep an eye on Scott and not trip over at the same time.

"Shtlothgh! Agnoztheng!" Scott sprinted after Glen, the sickly light running off the knife and splintering at strange angles, describing arcs and ugly, meaningful shapes as it fell. The sky pressed low, like the belly of some pregnant beast, and the movement within it was hungry and violent. The wind was building, cold and furious, tearing at the heather that ringed the peak and raking angry fingernails over the men's clothing. Glen broke into a run that would have impressed his old rugby coach, who had always said he was never built for speed, and the world shivered and bled and groaned.

It was the robe that did it. The beautiful, expensive, special-order-from-America robe. The long, majestic robe that was really made for someone rather taller and broader than Scott (large had probably been the wrong choice). He stepped on the edge of it and pitched forward with a yelp of fright, and Glen spun around in time to see his strange cousin go face-first into a cairn that collapsed obligingly.

The sky shook with fury, rent with ugly splits that bulged open onto some eternal, unquiet darkness, then re-closed, as if a colossal beast were struggling to tear its way out but couldn't quite get a grip on the world. Something howled at the edge of hearing, something that wasn't a dog. It was a howl of terrible, furious pain and endless hunger, and Glen raised his hands instinctively to fend off something unseen.

Then it was gone, the echoes still rippling around the rocks and scrub of the empty fells. The sky healed, folded, became smooth, and faded from green to purple to the plain velvety black of deep winter night. The stars ventured cautiously out again, and the fire crept back to its proper place as the wind faded away.

"My ndose!" Scott wailed, pushing himself onto his elbows.

"Ow," Glen said, not entirely sympathetically. There was blood dribbling generously from Scott's face, and he appeared to have a sprig of heather embedded in one cheek.

"Ndamn you!" Scott said, struggling to his knees. "You bruined it!"

"Hey, you just tried to kill my chicken, and I'm pretty sure me as well. I'm not sorry."

They glared at each other, then Scott looked down at the knife, still clutched in one hand. The blade was snapped off where it had been driven into the ground. "Ndammit."

"What were you even trying to do? What was that?"

"De Eldritch Ondes," Scott said, pinching his nose to try and stop the bleeding. "Dey would have gibend me grabe power."

Glen regarded the smaller man, his robe pulled off one

shoulder to reveal a skinny chest and a blood-spotted thermal undershirt. "I see."

"I would habe ruled de world." Scott looked at the knife sadly. "All ruined becaude of your stupid chicken."

"Whatever." Glen skirted his cousin. "I'm going to put the fire out. Then I'm going home."

THERE WERE ice packs in the cooler, and Glen took one to Scott, still seated morosely in the ruins of the cairn. "They'll help the swelling."

"Danks."

"You don't deserve it."

Scott watched Glen turn the Land Rover headlights on the dying fire, the big man swigging from a hip flask as he collected the tablecloth and the candles. It was true, he *didn't* deserve it. He'd been so close! That pregnant, bulging sky, the screaming wind – it had been going to work, but all because of a stupid chicken ... He closed his eyes and put the ice pack over them. He shouldn't have involved Glen. That was clear. Next time he'd just hire a 4×4 and buy a goat or something. If there was a next time. The conditions wouldn't be right again for another twelve years, and he'd have to find another meteorite knife in the meantime. That wasn't going to be easy. The museums were starting to cotton on to the fact that things went missing when he was around, although they couldn't prove anything. Plus he was getting older – what good was eternal life if you had bad knees and got up twice in the night to pee?

"Scott?"

Glen's voice sounded strange, and Scott supposed it was stress. Probably had no idea how to deal with what he'd just seen. Probably on the verge of a breakdown. Feeling somewhat superior, he took the ice pack off. "Yes?"

"Come look at this."

Groaning, Scott pulled himself out of the wreckage of the cairn and tottered over to his cousin, who was crouched next to the remains of the fire with a torch in one hand. "What?"

Glen pointed with the torch, wordlessly, and Scott followed his gaze. For a moment he couldn't see what Glen meant – it just looked like a little scrap of shadow, maybe a small piece of cloth torn from his robe. Then it moved, and as it moved it swam with ugly, ancient colours, with the flesh and texture of different dimensions, and Scott heard an echo of senseless howling in his ears.

"What the hell is that?" Glen asked.

"I— I'm not sure." The creature, the terrible scrap of horror, was still moving. Moving toward them, scuttling over the ground with many legs, or none – it was impossible to see. There might have been tentacles, or tendrils, teeth or claws or horns, but the mind turned firmly away from identifying them. The mind, in fact, refused entirely to accept what it was seeing, and the thing crept closer, carrying with it a stench that stained the soul more than the senses.

"Is that what you were summoning? Your shag-zag thingy?"

"I— Well, I don't know. No one's ever described one before." The creature made a sudden dart toward the men, and they both straightened up and stepped hurriedly back.

"Well, command it or something."

"I don't think that's an Eldritch One."

"If no one's ever described it, how do you know?"

"Well—" The thing made a rush for Scott's foot, moving with a horrifying stop-action stutter, and he shrieked, falling backward over their pile of firewood and scrabbling away on his back like a crab.

"Tell it to stop!" Glen shouted, keeping the torch on the creature. "Command it, go on!"

"Stop!" Scott screamed. "Stop, stop, I command you, as master and ... and— *nooo!*" Because the thing went *through* the wood as if it had no concept of how physics worked in this dimension, heading single-mindedly toward the man who had called it so clumsily into being. Scott could hear that howling, lonely and gleeful and greedy and utterly, utterly soaked in madness, building as the thing got closer, and he was aware he was still screaming, but he couldn't stop. His vision was swimming with terrible colours, and the night was colder than anything he had ever experienced, ever imagined, and oh, he'd made a mistake, he'd made such a mistake. This was why no one talked about his grandfather, this was why he'd just been forgotten, this was why the books had been put out to be burned before he'd saved them in his teenaged foolishness, and now what had he done? He would be lost, *lost*—

Something small and round and brown dashed over his belly, and suddenly the howling was gone, cut off as completely as a power cut. He could hear nothing but his own screaming, and the night was dark and clear and star-pocked above him. He blinked, gulped, and gave another hesitant little half-scream, but his heart wasn't in it. Two wide yellow eyes peered into his curiously, and the chicken swallowed hard a couple of times, then jumped off his belly and pattered toward Glen, who was clutching the torch in one hand and a large rock in the other.

She pecked his boot and looked up at him expectantly.

"Good girl," Glen said, his voice uneven, then put the rock down and tucked the chicken under one arm. "Well done."

She burped, swallowed again, and clucked a few times.

There was silence on the fells for a moment, then Glen said, "If I have to take her to the vet, you're explaining it."

Scott didn't argue, just stared at the vast and suddenly unfriendly universe, and thought it was time for a new career. Maybe something to do with chickens.

Dragons & Knights

My dragons tend to be small and modern, and to have endless appetites for tea, cake, and crime-solving.
But these are not the only dragons, even though they are very representative of dragons today – small, and secretive, and as wary of humans as they are full of hope for them. And they are right to be wary. The insatiable human appetite for land and space and dominance pushed dragons to the very edges of the world, and the bigger kinds didn't survive it. They were too big to hide, too hungry to exist on rabbits and fish and the occasional purloined sheep. They were labelled pests and threats, and of course the incalculable value of dragon scale had no bearing on this. Of course not.
So while some dragons adapted and persisted, others did not.
And the world is poorer for it.
Once, though, the world was alive with dragonkind.
Once upon a time ...

The dragon nestled among the rocks on the mountain peak, her heavy paws resting on rock chipped and cracked by the weight of long generations of clawed feet, her flanks pressed against boulders worn smooth and concave by the passage of countless centuries of scaled bodies. She watched the valley below with eyes that reflected the colours of the sunrise, warm orange shot through with burned pinks. There had been smoke in the forest at the end of the valley during the night, rising from the point where the trees started to thin and give slowly to the long grass of the valley floor. If she knew humans – and she did, because every good guardian must know the risks to their holdfast – they'd already be up, moving with first light. Forests are damp and cold places when you're trying to keep your fire low and smokeless. No one would have slept much. They'd reach the lake at the base of the cliffs by midday. She waited.

The humans came out of the shelter of the trees just as the sun was creeping across their tops and raising steam from the damp leaves. They marched with purpose – no straggling band of outlaws, these. Four men on horseback led the way, and more horses walked behind them, laden with supplies. The guardian licked her chops. To either side of the supply horses, as well as behind, marched men on foot, their armour dull in the morning shadows. There were maybe twenty in all (numbers were unimportant to dragons – there were either enough or not enough), and they were all armed. She could see longbows and spears as well as swords, and two men carried staffs from which the flags of the knights' houses hung limply. She knew the colours, though. She'd had dealings with them before. She got up and stretched like a cat, all arched back and extended claws, then slipped off the edge of the cliff, taking on its dull greys and moving with slow grace toward the caverns. It was time to raise the dragons.

"Here we go, lads," Sir Roger said, bringing his horse to a halt in the shelter of the last tree. Ahead of them swept a sea of long green grass, running smooth and uninterrupted all the way to the placid blue of the lake at the foot of the mountain. The crisp light spilled across the steep cliffs, and they were rendered in shades of pale grey and nearly white, pocked with deep shadows which were the entrances of dragon holes. Those cliffs were insurmountable, and the peak reached high and jagged to the thin blue sky. It was entirely the sort of place one might expect dragons, and they'd passed the last sign of human habitation three days back. Up here was wild country and wild beasts, not even a shepherd's track to guide their way. Just the mountain, growing bigger and more ominous with every step forward. He knew some of the younger men, who had never faced a dragon before, were nervous. Scared, even. Hell, he was nervous himself, and not afraid to admit it, even though he'd bested dragons not once but three times before. He had every intention of making this the fourth.

"Now," he said, stroking his grey beard as if soothing a pet. "They are not to be underestimated, these dragons. They are old, and crafty. But neither should we fear them, as some supernatural creatures beyond our ken. No, we must treat them with respect and honour, as worthy adversaries, and prove to them that we are no less!"

The youngest knight yawned, and his horse did a bored little sideways shuffle. The other two knights shared an amused smirk, and Sir Roger glowered at them.

"Do not take this lightly, sirs! We ascend now into the realm of the beasts!" He flung his arm out to point in the direction of the mountain, although the moment was ruined somewhat by his gauntlet flying off his hand and into the long grass. His squire rushed forward to find it, and his horse shifted her hindquarters and farted. He sighed. No one had any sense of occasion these days. Why, when he was a young knight—

"Shall we be off then, Sir Roger?" Sir Tom said. He was a big man with long legs and a large belly – curiously like a pumpkin on stilts, to Sir Roger's mind.

"Fine, fine. Let's just go, then." Sir Roger snatched the gauntlet from his squire and nudged his horse forward. They'd see. Just wait until they were face to face with a real, fire-breathing dragon. Then they'd see.

HIGH LORD FLORENCE perched at the mouth of the cavern, her great wings flexing slowly above her. She hadn't bothered to camouflage herself against the rocks, but wore her true colours of deep, rich reds as she watched the party advancing across the valley floor.

"A big group," she observed to Stella, who had been the first to spot them.

"Unusually so," the smaller dragon agreed. "Not a sole challenger this time, then."

"Oh, there never is, even when they say there is," the High Lord said (Lord was a non-gendered term to dragons. In fact, the whole gendered thing was more of a human issue. Dragons didn't consider it much. Any dragon could lay eggs, if they so wished, and names were chosen based on what suited their little faces when they hatched. Or whatever the first thing they bit was, hence a surprising number of dragons called "Toe", and "Snout"). "But honestly, they're such little things, and completely scale-less. No wonder they need to help each other out."

Stella snorted, and scratched behind her ear with one heavy back claw. "Shall we all go down, then? Show of numbers and all that?"

High Lord Florence considered it. They weren't a big clan, and being rather large dragons they tended to keep to their own little family groups much of the time, unless a meeting was called. At the moment there were seven of them living in the old mountain, the seat of the dragon Lords. "May as well," she said. "It's a nice day for it."

The party of knights and fighting men had almost reached the edge of the lake (the waters looking desperately cool and inviting, because it was proving to be an unseasonably warm day, and armour is not known for its suitability to a hot climate), when the first of the dragons took to the sky. The men had been able to see them for a while, first as splashes of colour against the pale cliffs, then as unclear silhouettes. Only now did they truly appreciate the vast size of the beasts, as deep red wings snapped open against the vault of blue sky and the dragon rose into the air, tail curling gracefully behind her, four legs tucked up neatly against her belly. A second dragon followed, all pale greens and blues, harder to see against the sky. This one was smaller, but even at this distance they could tell she'd dwarf the tallest horse they had. Another took flight, purple this time, and another, and another, until there were seven dragons circling the peak, dropping above and below each other in a graceful dance that seemed to be a display as much for them as it was for the knights.

One of the men crossed himself and began to pray loudly, and Sir Roger glared at him. "Well, that's not going to help, is it?" he snapped. "Do your job and hold your tongue, and we'll emerge victorious."

Sir Pete, the youngest knight, unused to Sir Roger's rather less than devout ways, opened his mouth to object and Sir Tom waved him to silence. "No room for that here," he said. "We've got dragons to deal with." And he slid off his horse and walked the remaining distance to the edge of the lake, unsheathing his sword as he went.

Sir Roger followed him, giving his reins to the praying man and telling him to make himself useful, and the two men stood staring up at the dragons, still circling their peak with unhurried wing beats. Sir Roger rather fancied he could hear them from where they stood, heavy and leathery and dangerous.

"They're expecting us."

"Of course they are," Sir Aldemar the Great, the fourth knight of their expedition, said. "They'll have seen us days ago, probably. They don't just hang around the mountain doing nothing, you know."

The other knights agreed, and Sir Roger said, "Well. No time to waste. Let's get set up."

High Lord Florence landed on the boulder that crowned the mountain (put there for that very purpose), turned slightly to make sure her profile was good, flexed her wings and let out a roar and a gust of flame. She was gratified to hear some faint shouts from the camp at the edge of the lake, and a splash as someone fell in the water.

"Oh, very good," Percival said approvingly. "Look, their tent fell down, too."

"Oh, that's a shame. It's taking them long enough as it is."

"I know. My wings are getting tired." Percival yawned, exposing worn old teeth. "I shall fall asleep before all the fun starts at this rate."

"We can't have that." High Lord Florence took off again, catching the air gracefully. "You sit and do some posing. It's good to have variety."

Percival clambered onto the rock and threw himself into the posturing with gusto.

"But it roared!" the praying man wailed. "The beasts will devour us all!"

"Who brought him along?" Sir Roger demanded. Bad

enough that he was babysitting Sir Pete, but this one was making such a fuss. And when he'd dropped the tent pole he'd broken one of Sir Roger's favourite drinking horns, too.

"Sorry, my bad," Sir Tom said. "My regular cook got bitten by my dinner, and he can't walk too well yet."

"The dinner or your cook?" Sir Roger asked.

"Um. Neither."

"That man is right, though," Sir Pete said, hands on his hips and his breastplate blinding in the sunlight. "Those monstrous things are just waiting to pounce, but you're telling the men to set up shelter rather than defences!"

Sir Roger and Sir Tom exchanged glances. Sir Aldemar looked up from his sketching and scoffed loudly, then went back to drawing the dragons circling the peak. They were even bigger and fierier on paper.

Sir Roger poked Sir Tom in the chest. "Your nephew. Your problem."

"A curse on family and a pox on bitey dinners," Sir Tom grumbled, and pointed at his nephew. "Take whiny cook there and your men. Retreat to the edge of the forest and set up camp. Do not on any account return."

"What? No! I have come to fight dragons! And besides" —the young knight gave the two old men, and the skeletally skinny, even older Sir Aldemar the Great a dubious look— "you might need my help." He flexed his muscles proudly to prove it, although the over-shined armour just made him look as though he were shrugging brightly.

"I hope you're not arguing with me," Sir Tom said, scowling. "Don't make me go home and tell your mother you were arguing with me."

"You can't make me leave just when it's going to get interesting!" Sir Pete wailed.

"By the Old Ones, just do it, would you?" Sir Tom glared at the young man until he turned and stomped away, muttering under his breath and swearing roundly at the men as they scrambled to catch up with him.

"Well done, Petey," Sir Roger called after him. "We'll need a nice warm meal once we're finished here."

"Oh, don't rub the boy's nose in it," Sir Tom said, but he was grinning.

"Well, if all the drama is over," Sir Aldemar the Great said, without looking up from his sketching, "Are we going to get on with things or what?"

The dragons watched with interest as a small contingent led by a knight in very shiny armour marched back the way they had come, taking one of the horses with them.

"That's interesting," High Lord Florence said.

"He must be new," Percival observed.

"One less to deal with."

"True, but the horse ..." Stella licked drool from her chops.

"There'll be plenty to go around," the High Lord assured her.

They watched until the small party was a comfortable distance away, then turned their attention back to the men on the shore. Three tents had bloomed like fat white toadstools along the edge of the lake, and the two old knights in their tarnished armour stood outside them, looking up at the mountain. The third knight was still seated, legs straight out on the ground in front of him, scribbling away.

"I'll take that one," Percival said. "He looks about my age, in human years. Should have some cunning about him."

"Fair enough," High Lord Florence said, and looked at the other dragons, ranged to either side her on the mountain top, all watching the humans avidly (the flying in circles had become a little boring). "Dragons. Be smart, be careful, be *dragon*. Onward!" And she threw herself off the cliff edge, plunging down to the water like a high diver. Her wings snapped out as the lake raced to meet her, and she arrowed across her reflection toward the men on the shore, her talons low enough to catch the surface and splinter it into spray, her jaws wide with fire and delight, hearing the wings of her dragons strong and sure behind her.

"HERE THEY COME!" Sir Roger shouted, and even Sir Aldemar the Great scrambled to his feet, then stood swaying from getting up too quickly. "Stations!"

The men who were left rushed to their places, barely speaking to each other. They were no random soldiers, but hand-picked and faithful comrades of the old knights. They'd seen these confrontations before, knew what they needed to do and when they needed to do it. They didn't need to be told how to face dragons.

"Be brave, my friends!" Sir Roger bellowed as the red dragon came roaring across the lake, vast wings skimming the surface and stirring it into turbulence as she rode a gust of flame toward them. "Stand strong!"

"Astonishing," Sir Aldemar mumbled. "I must remember that shade of red." And he drew his sword, standing his ground to the right of Sir Roger and Sir Tom, the men and tents behind them, each of them with plenty of room to move.

The dragon snapped upward as she reached the beach, bringing her taloned back legs down to touch the sand, wings shivering behind her as the other dragons landed, three to each side, filling the beach with colour and power and beauty. The red dragon was twice as tall as Sir Roger when she sat back on her haunches, and her incisors were as long as his finger. She lifted her head and roared, and the sound shivered the sand of the beach and the earth under his boots. She lowered her head to inspect him with eyes that were deeper than the sea, and drew her lips back from those terrifying teeth.

"Sir Roger," she said.

"High Lord Florence. Lovely to see you again."

"The pleasure is always mine." She inspected the table in front of him. "Oh, you made the pieces bigger! Thank you so much – Percival has some difficulty with the tiny ones. Arthritis, you know."

"I'm just fine," Percival rumbled, climbing up the beach and sitting himself on the opposite side of Sir Aldemar the Great's chess board. "It's just tricky to tell the difference between the queen and the bishop when they're so damn tiny."

"High Lord Florence, the cook has come up with something new," Sir Roger said. "He calls it a ... scun."

"Scone," one of the men called from the line in front of the tents.

"Ah. *Scone*. Would you care to try one?" He waved at his squire, who rushed forward and offered the dragon a large basket filled with current-studded, golden buns as big as a man's hand. "The tea's just brewing."

"Oh, how wonderful!" She selected one and nibbled on the corner gently, eyes half-closed. "Well, that's just perfect. So tasty."

"Here you are. Before I forget." Stella set a basket next to one of the tents. Inside, dragon scales – harder than metal, lighter than a blade of grass, beautiful and impossible and flushed with magic – glittered and shifted, sliding over each other with musical whispers. "There's also some eggshell in there. Looks a lot like dragon skull, and just as hard."

"Eggshell?" Sir Tom said. "Are congratulations in order?"

Stella flushed an attractive purple, and the men cheered.

"Well, now the pleasantries are over," Sir Aldemar the Great leaned over and tapped the chessboard. "Your move. I've been looking forward to this – I know you'll be a worthy opponent."

"Victory shall be mine," Percival announced, and moved his pawn.

"I will ride roughshod over the bones of your minions," Lord Aldemar replied absently, considering his move.

High Lord Florence looked at Sir Roger. "Should we worry about the men you sent away?"

"Oh, no. Not at all. I've got someone on lookout. We'll make a lot of noise if he comes back – you know the sort of thing. Bang some shields and shout and jump around a bit. Maybe one of your young ones can singe Pete's toes and drop him in a tree or something."

"Always happy to help." The High Lord took a sip of tea, then rested her chin on her paw and studied the board carefully. They were at a draw after the last expedition, and she fully intended to be the one to break it.

Glenda & the Horsemen of the Apocalypse

I have, over the years, tried many bits of writerly advice. Some have worked, others have not. One which I always rather liked was to keep a notebook by the bed, so that one could wake up with an idea in the middle of night and scribble it down immediately, before it was lost. That seemed eminently practical, and I did do it for years.

I didn't often write in the notebook, though, and when I did it often wasn't legible.

And I think the only thing that ever came from it was the title of this story, which I found mightily confusing the next morning, but also kind of irresistible ...

Glenda checked her hair in the hallway mirror, adjusted the collar of her blouse, then opened the door with a gently quizzical smile on her face. It was three p.m. and she wasn't expecting anyone, which meant it was probably someone collecting money for something, or else some of those nice religious folk. Whoever it was, she always listened politely, and if it was a reasonable time for a cup of tea and a little cake (like now), she'd invite them in, because it must be dreadfully hard to go around knocking on doors and being turned down. People could be awfully rude. She'd once seen Mr Carter, who lived across the road and down two doors, brandishing his walking stick and using some very unpleasant language while he chased some poor young man halfway down the street. Ridiculous. Of course, some of these door-to-door people could be pushy, but it didn't mean you had to buy what they were selling, or be nasty about it. A nice firm hand was all it took.

The man on the doorstep had stepped back while he waited, his hands in the pockets of his jeans and his face lifted to the early spring sky. His shoulders were broad and muscular, and his T-shirt fitted them in an only-just way. Not a religious type, then, she imagined. They didn't tend to wear T-shirts in quite such a showy manner. Or wear T-shirts at all, for that matter.

"Can I help you?" Glenda asked brightly.

A white-toothed smile broke across the man's face, then faltered as he examined her. Glenda didn't much care for the way he was looking at her. It was *appraising*, and she lifted her chin slightly.

"Do you need help, young man?" He might be terribly good-looking, but that look was only barely on the right side of rude, and she wasn't having any nonsense. Not on her doorstep.

"Mrs Glenda Holt?" he asked, his voice deep and smooth.

"Yes, that's me." She gave him her own appraising look.

He wasn't just young and rather pleasing to look at – he positively glowed with robust health and good humour. She half-expected bluebirds to start flitting around his head.

"*Huh*. You're not quite what I expected."

She frowned. "What on earth are you talking about?"

"I just … I suppose I expected someone … well." He shrugged and lavished a smile on her. It was the sort of smile she imagined made quite a lot of young girls go weak at the knees. And boys, for that matter. Although she was rather too old for that sort of thing.

"If you were expecting Glenda Holt, you've found her. Now how can I help you?"

The young man ran a hand through an overabundance of blond locks, his smile fading. "Are you the *only* Glenda Holt?"

"Certainly the only one who lives here. Now are you going to tell me what this is about, young man? Because I was just about to sit down with a cuppa."

"Oh, that'd be nice." The smile was back.

"That wasn't an invitation. You haven't even told me what you want." Her patience was starting to wear thin.

He looked puzzled. "Well, we're meeting here."

"Who are?" This was proving much more frustrating than even the trickier religious sorts.

"All of us." He spoke slowly, as if she were being a little slow, the way so many young people did with their elders, and Glenda planted her feet more firmly on her old mat and glowered at him.

"See here, young man—"

"Oh, you're here already," a new voice called from the gate, interrupting her. They both turned to look at a portly man bustling up the garden path, his chest and belly leading. He was clad in a green three-piece suit that didn't fit quite as well as it could, and his scalp gleamed through his combover. "Trust you to be early, Pest."

"Just because you can never work to a schedule," the young man replied. "Anyway, it appears D hasn't even stopped by yet. Glenda doesn't know about the meeting."

"That'll be Mrs Holt to you," Glenda said, and glared at the new arrival. "And who might you be?"

"*Hmm.* Interesting." The green-clad man gave Glenda the same evaluating look the younger man had, and her frown deepened.

"Just because I'm an old lady, don't think I'm falling for your scams," she said. "Either you tell me exactly what you're both doing here, or you can get on your way before I call the police."

"No scams, madam!" Green Suit looked horrified, one hand pressed to his chest. He seemed disproportionately short standing next to the man he'd called Pest, but he was no less broad. "I am an associate of Pest here, and our mutual colleague was meant to set up a meeting with you. I'm not at all sure what's kept him."

"Well, that's not my problem. And unless you have some official papers from the council or something, you can get out of here." She stepped back inside and closed the door firmly as the two men exchanged confused glances. She turned the deadbolt, then went to lock the back door. Just in case.

She was just sitting down to watch Bondi Vet when the doorbell rang again. She frowned. It was five p.m. Some people had their dinners at five p.m. (although not her. She waited until half past six. Five p.m. felt, well, *old*). Five p.m. was not the sort of time to be ringing people's doorbells willy-nilly. She got up and went into the hall, bristling with indignation.

When she opened the door, Pest and his friend were both standing a respectful distance away from the step. She frowned at them. "What?"

"Has our colleague been by yet?"

"Don't you think you would have known if he had, considering you're still on my doorstep? Have you been here this whole time?"

"Well—"

"Get out of my garden, both of you. I *will* call the police."

"Madam—"

Glenda grabbed the late Mr Holt's cricket bat from the coat rack behind the door and shouldered it, stepping out into the scented evening. "Don't make me say it again."

"Understood." Green Suit backed away, hands raised apologetically, and Pest followed with an amused little half-smile on his full lips. Glenda watched them until they were out of the gate and walking away, then went back inside and poured herself a small whisky. Her hands were shaking.

She didn't expect to sleep very well, but the whisky had other ideas, particularly when she had a second one after dinner. There had been no more doorbells, and when she peered out of the window before closing the curtains there was no one outside, not even any unfamiliar cars on the street. Maybe she'd scared them off, although she had a feeling that wasn't the case. They hadn't seemed the sort to be scared off easily. Never mind. If they came back tomorrow she'd meet them with phone in hand and the police already dialled.

She woke with first light, padding softly through the familiar rituals of waking – opening curtains and brushing teeth and brewing tea and turning the radio on for the news, although she tried not to listen too closely these days. There was never anything good on it. Or if there was, it was a fireman rescuing a duckling to set against floods and corruption and conflict. Not much balance.

Her doorstep was empty when she ventured out to the shop after breakfast. She didn't need much, but she liked to walk to the local shop every day. Twenty minutes each way, and it cleared her head nicely. Which was just what she needed after yesterday.

SHE WAS HOME AGAIN, and deciding between weeding the back garden or baking a cake for bridge club tomorrow night when the doorbell rang. She frowned, shoulders tensing. Surely it wouldn't be them again. She'd been very clear. *Very* clear indeed. But the amount of people who just didn't take you seriously when you were a woman, let alone a woman of a certain age . . . She straightened her back, put her phone in her pocket, and strode to the front door. She was done being polite.

She jerked the door open, a scowl on her face, cricket bat already shouldered, and the man on the doorstep jumped back with a yelp.

“Oh! Frank! I’m sorry.” She put the bat down hurriedly, flushing.

“It’s okay, Glenda. No harm done. Is everything alright?”

“Yes, sorry. I thought you were someone else.”

“I see.” He gave her a puzzled look. “Well, I was just passing, and thought I’d stop by. Do you need a lift to bridge tomorrow?”

“No, thank you, Frank. You know I like to have my own transport.”

“Well, if you’re sure.”

“I’m sure.” She waited while he looked at her hopefully, then eventually accepted that he wasn’t going to be asked in. Just like last week. And the week before.

“Well, I’ll be off, then. See you tomorrow?”

“Yes, see you then.” She closed the door as he walked away, shaking her head. He was terribly slow on the uptake. Of course, she probably shouldn’t have gone to dinner with him that once. But it had been ten years ago. One would think the message might have got through by now.

The doorbell rang when she was halfway back to the kitchen and she turned around with a sigh. What now? *Oh, I just happened to have a spare ticket to this show that you might like?* Or maybe, *I’ve got a voucher to this new restaurant, shall we try it?* If such persistence had been deployed in a rather more suitable manner it’d be quite admirable.

She opened the door, already starting to say, "Frank, look," and stopped short as the man on the path looked up at her. He was tall and slim, his face all grave angles and smooth dark skin.

"Mrs Holt," he said.

"Yes?" He didn't look like he was collecting for anything, or peddling religion. He looked ... she wasn't sure. But not like anyone who would be going door to door. Not for anything.

"I believe my colleagues visited you yesterday." He made a graceful gesture behind him, and Glenda saw the two men loitering at the gate. Green Suit looked uncomfortable in the mild sun, but Pest stood with his arms crossed over his broad chest and his hair picked out in gold, smiling at her.

She frowned. "Look, I don't know what you're playing at, but—"

"Mrs Holt, I do apologise for them. They were impatient. I have serious matters to discuss with you, however."

"Well, discuss away, then."

"Perhaps inside would be better?"

"Why on earth would I let any of you into my house?"

He smiled. "You could keep hold of the cricket bat, if you wish."

She glanced down at it, and scowled. "Even so."

"Aren't you curious?" He tilted his head as he spoke, still smiling, and she watched the way the sun caught the angles of his face. There were far too many of them – he was in need of a good meal, by the looks of him. And she wanted to say, *not curious enough to let three **very** strange men into my house,* but it would have been a lie. And something about the man on her doorstep said he wasn't a person anyone lied to.

She sighed, and tapped the bat on the floor lightly. "Alright. But there's nothing to steal in here, and I'm not signing up for anything."

"Of course not."

"And I don't need saving. I'm quite capable of saving myself."

"Indubitably."

She watched him for a moment longer, trying to decide if he was being patronising or just extraordinarily guileless. He certainly wasn't smirking.

"Fine," she said. "Come in. But I'm not making any fancy coffees. Tea or instant."

"Tea will be wonderful."

Glenda led them through to the sun-filled kitchen, wondering what she was thinking of. But it was certainly the most interesting thing that had happened since she'd adopted her cat Scoundrel and he'd bitten the postman on his first day.

She served tea in her not-for-best, mismatched mugs and opened a packet of Jammie Dodgers.

"If I'd known you were coming, I would have baked something."

"This is perfect," the tall man said, picking a biscuit up and examining it. "Very pretty."

"Pretty? Well, I suppose." She sat down and frowned at the three men crowded around her little kitchen table.

"What can I help you with?" She felt calmer in here, more in charge. Although she had brought the cricket bat in with her, just in case.

The tall man rolled the biscuit in long, dark-skinned fingers, inspecting it as if he'd never seen one before. "What is it?"

"What *is* it? It's a Jammie Dodger."

"D, you've had them before." Green Suit grabbed two, then saw Glenda's face and put one back guiltily.

"I have not had one before. How does one *have* them?"

"It's a biscuit," Glenda said, bewildered.

"Ah. I see. I have heard of these." The tall man held the biscuit out at arm's length, squinted at it, then licked it. His tongue was blue. A bright, lizard-like blue. "*Hmm.* Very nice." He licked the biscuit again, and Glenda stared at his companions.

"Is he alright?"

"D doesn't get out much," Green Suit said.

"I'm out all the time," D protested, still licking the biscuit. His tongue really was extraordinarily blue, and she wondered if it was a disorder of some sort.

"Not the sort of out that has biscuits," Green Suit replied.

"Oh, a kitty," Pest said suddenly, and made a smooching noise. "Here, puss puss."

Scoundrel had slouched into the room. He gave Pest a baleful look.

"Don't touch the cat, Pest," D said sharply.

"Aw. I like cats."

"He bites," Glenda said, dunking her biscuit in her tea.

D copied her, watched her bite the soggy bit, then did the same, scattering damp crumbs on the table. "Oh, dear."

"Can't take you anywhere," Green Suit said, rolling his eyes expressively at Glenda.

Scoundrel hissed, and Pest said, "*Ow*."

"I told you not to touch the cat," D said. "We're guests."

"I didn't touch him! He just walked up and *bit* me!"

"Likely story," Green Suit said.

"He did!"

"He does do that sometimes," Glenda admitted.

"Is he up to date on his vaccinations?" Pest asked, rubbing his ankle.

"He's not going to give you *rabies*," Glenda snapped.

"Oh, I've already got that," Pest said comfortably. "I'm more worried about what I might give him."

Glenda stared at them, at Pest with his perfect skin and sparkling eyes, and Green Suit surreptitiously stashing two Jammie Dodgers in his breast pocket, and D absently stirring his tea with one long finger. She pushed her chair back from the table, folded her arms across her chest and planted her sensible shoes firmly on the floor. "Right. Start talking. And make it good, otherwise you'll find Scoundrel isn't the only one that bites."

Green Suit gulped at his cup noisily, and Pest suddenly became very interested in the hem of his T-shirt.

D took a sip of tea and said, "Very nice, this."

"It's just plain old Yorkshire tea and Jammie Dodger biscuits, not high tea at the Ritz Carlton. What are you three playing at?"

D interlaced his fingers carefully, and lifted his dark eyes to hers. "We have a vacancy."

"A vacancy?"

"Yes. A position needing to be filled."

"Well, I don't know what you're doing here, then. I'm retired."

"This is not the sort of position that is limited by age. Luckily."

His companions chuckled, and Glenda frowned. "What're you talking about? Kids, all of you."

"Appearances can be deceiving."

"Well, I'm still not looking for a job."

"You're our ideal candidate."

"Me?"

"Yeah, about that, D—" Green Suit started.

"It's her."

"Well, maybe, but—"

D turned and scowled at Green Suit. "It's *her.*"

"If you're quite done arguing among yourselves," Glenda said sharply, "Why on earth would you think I'd be your ideal candidate? What do you even *do?*"

"We bring on the Apocalypse," D said, and smiled.

THERE WAS QUITE a bit of confusion after that. Glenda ordered them out of the house and started waving the cricket bat around when they didn't get up quickly enough. Green Suit got overexcited and broke the table in two when he put his mug down. D saved his tea and a biscuit as the table collapsed in front of him, and Pest pushed his chair back, laughing like a five-year-old while Scoundrel scratched himself furiously on the windowsill. Jammie Dodgers were scattered all over the floor, swimming in a mess of spilt tea and the remains of a broken vase of flowers, and when Glenda took a swipe at D with the bat she slipped on a daffodil and went down hard enough to jolt her spine and bite her tongue. She sat there, amid the debris of her rather old and lovely table, and said plaintively, "I only let you in to be polite."

"I'm very sorry about this," D said, setting his cup on the kitchen worktop and helping her up. "Shall I make more Jammie Dodgers?"

"They come from the shop." His hands were desperately cold, and she wondered if his skinny jeans weren't a bit too skinny, his cheekbones just a little too high under his smooth skin.

"Tea?" he suggested.

"Do you know how to make it?"

"I observed you. It didn't seem complicated."

"It's not hard to make tea, but it *is* hard to make good tea." She pointed at Pest, who was still giggling. "You – clean up this mess."

"Yes, ma'am." He jumped to his feet and started picking up shards of vase. "Also, I'm very sorry, but I think I gave your cat fleas."

"Fantastic."

Making tea calmed her. There was still a tremor in her hands, but that was hardly surprising. She'd just tried to take someone's head off with a cricket bat. And she had three men in her kitchen who didn't have a shred of sense among them. Not that many did, but this seemed excessive.

"We can sit in the living room," she said. "Since I no longer have a table."

"Terribly sorry about that," Green Suit said. "I forget my own strength." He puffed his chest out proudly even as he tried to look contrite, and Glenda caught Pest rolling his eyes as he bundled up the daffodils. Her lips quirked into a smile that she forced firmly down again. Well, it *was* interesting.

She led the way into the living room and opened the windows a crack, letting in the smell of cut grass and damp earth.

"So," she said. "You bring on the Apocalypse. Is this your religion, or something?" *I gave your cat fleas. I forget my own strength.* She pushed the thought away.

"No," D said. He'd sat down in the middle of the sofa, the other two wedged in uncomfortably to either side of him, leaving the armchair free for her. She didn't sit. "People *use* us in their religions, but we're older than such things. Outside such constraints, if you will."

"I see." Glenda sipped her tea. "So if you're not priests ...?"

"We're the horsemen of the Apocalypse," D said.

"I see," she said again. "Shouldn't there be four of you?"

"As I said, we have a vacancy."

Her hand surprised her by trembling a little, and she covered it up by putting her mug down and taking the chocolate box from under the coffee table. She offered it to the men, and D took one, slapping Pest's hand away.

"Hey!"

"Don't touch." D gave the younger man a chocolate, then took one for himself.

"Bet it's the cherry one," Pest muttered. "I hate the cherry ones."

"Be quiet."

Glenda chose a caramel for herself and sat down, nibbling on it thoughtfully. "Death, Pestilence, War and Famine, right?"

"They are the most common names for us, yes."

"I'm Pestilence," Pest said cheerfully. "I really am sorry about your cat's fleas."

"And you?" Glenda nodded at Green Suit.

"War," he said, looking aggrieved. "Surely you saw my strength—"

"Be quiet," D said again.

"Which makes you Death, doesn't it?"

"I am."

"Well, I hope you don't mind my saying, but you all seem terribly ordinary."

"We're all very ordinary things," Death said. "We're everywhere, after all."

"So what happened to Famine?"

"Well, he sort of ... decided to explore other career options," Death admitted.

"He quit?"

"Yes, he said there was nothing for him to do. Humans are doing far too good a job of starving themselves and each other."

"But ... if people are still starving – and I know they are - surely that's his work. And it's happening everywhere."

"He didn't need to create famines, though. There's no call for them anymore. Pest here can still go around stirring up new diseases and reawakening old ones. War whispers in lots of ears."

"I don't whisper."

"Evidently," Glenda said. "But you can use your inside voice for the moment."

War looked embarrassed, and eyed the chocolate tin.

"I will never be out of work," Death continued. "But Famine ... the world's starving itself. Humans on strange diets, or over-farming land, or changing the climate, or just not helping each other ..." He shrugged. "He was out of a job."

"Well, you've got the wrong woman," Glenda snapped. "I would never starve anyone. Quite the opposite. I do everything I can to make sure people eat. I work at the food bank and Meals on Wheels. I donate to food drives and aid agencies. I take food to anyone I know who's having a hard time. I—"

"You make sure your grandchildren eat till bursting," Death said, a smile blossoming across his face. "Yes. You're perfect."

"How am I perfect? I *am not* Famine!"

"No. You're the opposite. The new horseman. You're Plenty."

Glenda stared at him, black spots starting to swim in her vision. When Pestilence jumped up and grabbed her arms she didn't even protest, despite the heat in his hands that made her skin crawl. She could dimly hear him saying something about putting her head between her knees, and she closed a hand around her knitting needles, wondering if she'd have more luck with them than she'd had with the cricket bat.

"But I can't be," she managed, her heart surging in her ears. "I can't ..."

"I'm sure, Glenda. Death is always sure."

"He is," War agreed. "It's very irritating."

"That's unnecessary," Death said.

"It *is* annoying," Pestilence said. "Really. You should give it a break some time."

Death grunted, and looked at Glenda. She tightened her hand on her knitting needles. "But I'd have to leave," she said. "My kids ... my grandkids ..."

"You've already left," Death said gently.

"What do you mean? Of course I haven't!"

"Why do you think my colleagues had to wait for me to arrive?"

She glared at him. "Rubbish! I'm not *dead!*"

"You are, actually," Pest said. "Heart disease. Sorry. You keeled over when your boyfriend left."

"He is *not* my boyfriend."

"Well. You did."

Glenda got up unsteadily, slapping Pest's hands away. She tottered into the hall. There was somebody lying there, just behind the door, her face pressed into the ground and one hand under her body. She had bobbed grey hair, like Glenda's, and wore a pretty pale blue cardigan over grey slacks and a white blouse. Glenda looked down at herself where she stood, plucked at her cardigan, then turned back to Death, watching her from the living room.

"I didn't say goodbye," she whispered. "Not to anyone."

"I don't choose the way," Death said. "I only witness the passing."

"But I don't *want* to be a horseman. I don't want to hurt anyone."

"Think of them as temptations," War said, his voice surprisingly soft. "No one has to pick up the chocolates, any more than they have to pick up the gun." He was cradling the chocolate box as he spoke, and she frowned at him. He put it back hurriedly.

"What if I say no?" she asked Death.

"Then you pass on." He shrugged. "In time, I'll find someone else."

"And what happens then? When I pass on?"

"No one knows."

Glenda hugged her arms around herself, glancing back at the body in the hall. When had her hair got so thin on top? When had she got so *old?* "And if there's no Plenty?"

"People continue to starve, Famine or no Famine."

"So I'd stop people starving?"

"Yes. What they do after that is up to them. It's always up to them."

She considered for a moment. "I don't even know how to ride a horse."

Death smiled. "Well, they're not real horses. They're somewhat metaphorical."

"I've still got my old Vespa. Can I ride that instead? I haven't had it out in years."

"Well, like I say, the horses are metaphorical—"

"So I can have a metaphorical Vespa?"

Pestilence started laughing. "Dude, *yes.* I want a metaphorical Vespa too."

"You can't have one. But Glenda can. Why not." Death swept her a sudden, stately bow, and said, "Welcome to the Apocalypse, Plenty."

"Thank you," Glenda said, and straightened her cardigan. "Should I make us a pack-up before we leave?"

Anatidaephobia

Some stories start with an idea, a situation, a what-if. Some start with a character too striking not to write down. Still others start with a single line. In this case, with the line, "We really thought we knew how the world would end."
What happened after that ... Well, stories have their own lives. And I should really remember not to feed them after midnight.

We thought it would happen in a rush, in a grand, crashing terror of spaceships and explosions, or plagues and rotting flesh, aliens and zombies and all of us turned against each other in an instant as the flimsy layers of civilisation were torn away like so much shed skin. We were prepared for that, in a weird sort of way, with all our books and movies and TV shows and video games. We really thought we'd know the end of the world when we saw it, because we'd rehearsed it so many times.

Do I have to tell you we were wrong?

No, I reckon you already know that, because you're here. You've been watching it, same as me. Or maybe you don't think it's the end. Maybe you think this is the new normal, some abominable evolution, and I'm just one of those whining children who clutch the past like a favourite toy. We'll see.

But watch out for the damn ducks.

WHEN I WAS in my late twenties, I guess, or round there, rubber ducks were all the rage. Everyone had flotillas of the damn things lined up in their bathrooms. People had bride and groom (or groom and groom, or bride and bride, whatever) ducks on their wedding cakes. There were devil ducks, and biker ducks, and ballerina ducks, and chef ducks, and you could buy them at supermarkets and garages and bookshops and bloody duck specialty shops. There were teeny little choking hazard–sized ducks, and absolutely enormous ship-sized ducks, in every colour you could think of, although yellow was still the classic. Bright, gaudy yellow, the colour of an egg yolk. They were our generation's ironic wink to the bathtub toys of our childhood, couched in such a way that we could legitimately keep them in our baths still and not feel we were weird little child-adults, fetishising our infancy. And I suppose – if you don't know better – that they're cute, so, you know, why not.

Is this water for me? Thank you. It makes my vision go a bit funny, even thinking about them all. *So many.* But it's safe in here, isn't it? *You* haven't got any – nothing on your desk, or any ducky wall art, thank Christ.

Did you know the bloody things even got inducted into the Toy Hall of Fame? Yeah, that's a real place. The things were bigger than Cabbage Patch Kids, or My Little Ponies, or any of that stuff. They reached every margin of society, every remote and blissfully duck-free part of the globe. Even the scientific community were talking about them – a bunch of them were in some containers that got swept off a cargo ship (along with blue rubber turtles, green rubber frogs, and red rubber beavers, but you never hear about those. Only the godforsaken yellow rubber ducks). Next thing, scientists were going on about all the information these drifting lumps of rubber were giving them about ocean currents and the like. I mean, don't they have instruments for that sort of thing? I don't know. I'm not a sea scientist. Oceanographer. But it just made them more popular. They were everywhere. They *are* everywhere.

Big change starts with small things. We all know that. A journey of a thousand miles starts with a single step, blah blah blah. Revolutions turn on a pinhead, and wars start with the drop of a glove. *We know*. But when you're in the middle of it all, small things are just, well, small things. Business as usual. Everyday injustices that make you shake your head, and smile extra-wide at whoever's "other" today, and drop a few coins in a homeless person's mug, feeling both guilty and virtuous.

And then the small things become big things, but

there's still nothing you can do. You can't change laws. You can't change policies. Sure, you can vote, but what's the point? It's a drop in the bucket. You can protest, but who's listening, really? Only the already converted. So on you go, life uninterrupted, and new politicians get in, playing the same cruel games under new and shiny names, and little quarters are given so they can take bigger halves. It's just *life.* You and me, we could never change that.

Well, maybe *you* could. You've got a degree and an expensive suit and a big office. I'm wearing the same jeans I have for the last week. Anyway. We weren't talking about that. You asked me how it started.

I CAN'T BE ENTIRELY sure, of course. But I first noticed it – noticed *them* – that winter. There are always a few places being *quirky*, eschewing traditional Christmas decor for whatever's de rigueur this year. Monotone trees, feathers, wood, whatever. At some stage it was black trees, which I didn't mind. They offset all the saccharine tweeness everywhere else. But, as always, it got overdone, and suddenly it was just tasteless.

Anyway, there had been duck decor before. Like I say, it crept up on us. I'd already seen plenty of places with ducks in Santa hats and duck ornaments and bloody ducks on top of Christmas trees. But that winter there were more. So many more. Even places that normally went for more traditional stuff – my office, for example. There was a woman in the cubicle next to me, Holly, and she always put little decorations out. Easter, Valentine's, whatever.

And she embraced the ducks completely, because of course she did.

She had zombie ducks that Halloween, and I tell you, they scared the crap out of me. She had one on the divider, looking down at me with these awful, bloodshot eyes, and sometimes I'd think it *moved,* and then I'd tell myself it was just the divider – they may as well've been made of cardboard – but I didn't believe it. Not with the way it looked at me. I asked her to put it on her desk, but she already had too many on there, and ... I dunno. I didn't want to admit I was afraid of it, I guess. So I put up with it, until the day it *fell* on me, and I screamed, I admit it, I screamed and threw it at her and told her to take her damn ducks and, and ... well, you can imagine what I said. It earned me a visit to HR. She was pretty snotty with me after that, and when she took the Halloween ducks down, she put the Christmas ones *up*.

I'm not proud of what I did. They were her ducks, and I should've just let them be. But *she* shouldn't have lined them all up like that, *looking* at me, when she knew I hated them. She shouldn't. I even told HR that I had anatidaephobia, but they said it was made up, that it wasn't a real phobia at all, and I had to replace all the bloody Santa and reindeer and horrible little elf ducks. All of them. And she immediately lined them all up on top of the divider again, so every time I looked up there were these dead eyes, all staring back at me. As if they knew what I'd done to their predecessors. I kind of wish I hadn't taken them home to do it. The whole apartment smelled of burning rubber until February.

So there were Holly's bloody ducks at work, and more

of them in the lobby come December, because some bright spark had decided to dress the tree with them, and every tree I passed elsewhere seemed to have at least a few of them, and no one I spoke to even seemed to have *noticed.* It's like I said – change comes too small to see. But I saw. Oh, God, I saw. The world went yellow and orange. Everywhere ducks – yellow ducks and blue ducks and red ducks but mostly just yellow ducks and orange beaks, yellow and orange, yellow and orange. We expected Armageddon and we got, what? Duckopalypse?

BUT AT LEAST I could go home, and draw the curtains, and turn off the TV, and read books that featured absolutely no rubber ducks of any sort. Which did rule out a lot of new releases, but there are always plenty of old, blissfully duck-free books around. I stopped going out with friends after our favourite pub not only decorated with rubber ducks, they started floating them in the pints. In the pints! I had a G&T instead, and there were little rubber duck ice cubes in it. I couldn't drink it. They were looking at me. They're always looking at me.

I started to call in sick to work after the company changed all the screensavers to rubber ducks floating across the background. It would start with one or two, as soon as you'd looked away from the screen for more than a moment, then more would come, and more, until there were dozens of them pouring across, a horror show of grinning beaks and staring eyes. This was after Christmas, when I thought I'd got through the worst, and all the decorations would be put away, and the ducks would fade like those annoying bloody Christmas Elf on a Shelf things. But it just got worse. People were wearing duck earrings, duck jumpers, duck bracelets. They'd become the latest fashion statement. I couldn't go on Facebook anymore, because instead of kitten videos, or people doing ridiculously silly and painful things, there was nothing but duck videos.

And I mean *nothing*. Not from anywhere in the world. No political discourse, no outraged posts about vaccines or GMOs or chemtrails or whatever the hell – just ducks. Ducks in coats, and ducks in hats, and kids pushing ducks in strollers. Hell, I think I even saw a photo of an actual duck pushing a rubber duck in a stroller. There were programmes on TV about the "latest phenomenon sweeping the globe", and every ad had a duck in it somewhere, like not to have one was something akin to forgetting to bow to the queen.

And no one questioned it. No one said, hey, why aren't we talking about the *problem* with all these ducks? Why aren't we looking at what they're distracting us from? Why aren't we hearing about war, and famine, and death, and disease anymore? What happened to the four horsemen stalking the land? Where the hell did all these ducks come from instead? Or maybe people were questioning it, but they were probably all like me – too scared to go out and talk to people because every space was full of ducks, and too scared to go online to find anyone to talk to because going online meant navigating more damn ducks. I don't know.

I STOPPED GOING to work entirely the weekend after they wallpapered the building with rubber duck paper. To boost morale, apparently. I walked into the lobby, turned around and walked out again. Called from home, said a death in the family meant I wouldn't be coming in for a while. My supervisor said she was very sorry, and sent around a delivery from the florist – a bouquet of rubber ducks. I told the delivery guy they were from my cheating boyfriend, and told him to give them to the first person he saw outside. No way they were coming in. No way. My home is my haven.

Was my haven.

Up till then, I'd sort of persuaded myself it was just one of those things, like Grumpy Cat, or Doge – everywhere for a while, then the craze would die down and something else would replace it. Okay, it was a lot more extreme, what with the news networks having ducks all over the studio, and the newscasters sitting down among drifts of them, or on rubber duck chairs, and news stories about them swamping everything else. Scientists were studying them. Schools were spending half their budget on them, claiming they were educational tools. Writers were writing about them. Artists were painting them, or sculpting them, or sculpting *with* them. No one was talking about refugees, or the NHS, or even the value of the pound, which just goes to show how serious it was. When capitalism loses its rabid focus, you know we're screwed. Bright-eyed people on city streets sang the praises of the rubber ducks, and food banks gave them away by the bucketload. Governments were even using them to broker peace deals in the Middle East, apparently. There were pictures of stern men in traditional dress, and soldiers with assault rifles held to attention, surrounded by waves of rubber ducks. You could see the men's eyes straying to them, distracted from the visiting dignitaries in their suits and red faces and sly smiles. But still – it *could* have been a craze, right? It could have been just that.

Until the morning I opened the curtains – the curtains on my third-floor apartment window – and found my window box full of them, little yellow bodies rimed with frost, flat eyes staring in at me. I screamed, and jerked the curtains shut, and swore I hadn't seen them, but when I checked they were still there. They were at all the windows.

I got rid of them, of course. I wasn't about to touch them, or bring them inside, but I got a broom and knocked them off, and just hoped they didn't hit anyone below. I couldn't imagine who had put them there. They'd have needed a fireman's ladder. It was a crappy joke, if that's what it was. Not that it could be anything else, of course. Or so I convinced myself as I heated the last of my baked beans for breakfast. I had to go out, to brave the duck-infested town and shops. I hated even the thought of it, but the cupboards were literally bare. It was shop or starve.

When I got back, there were no ducks on the windowsill.

They were on my kitchen worktops, on my little fold-up table, clustered together on the sofa and peering out from behind the bookshelves. My first thought was to run, but where to? There were even more ducks outside now. Someone had been painting them on the pavements, and the bollards had been replaced by them, and the shop windows were full of them, and even the damn cheese blocks were in duck shape. You'd think I'd become numb to it, but every new flash of orange beak was an assault on the senses. I called a locksmith to come and change the lock, then pulled on some rubber gloves and began to clear the room. It took six big bin bags before they were all out in the dumpster behind the house. The locksmith said it was romantic. I said it was psychotic, and he just gave me a confused look and handed me my new key.

Netflix was nothing but duck movies and duck documentaries, so I dug out some ancient DVDs and found my old player under my bed. I pulled the curtains and watched a mercifully duck-less edition of *Labyrinth*, a tea clutched to my chest while I craved a chocolate hobnob. But the shop only had duck-themed packets, so I hadn't got any. I fell asleep on the sofa, waking to a cramped back and a sea of ducks that swept across every surface of the apartment, every shelf, every chair, in boxes and in the sink and piled high in the toilet bowl. I couldn't even see my stained old rug underneath them. All looking at me out of bulging pale eyes. All smiling their orange smiles as if to say, *see? Isn't this* ***fun?***

SO HERE I AM. I honestly thought about burning the whole damn apartment block down, but I didn't fancy getting arrested, and I'm still hoping that order will reassert itself, that everyone'll go back to cat videos and dissatisfaction and barely controlled anger. I'm still not entirely certain I'm not hallucinating it, that it isn't anatidaephobia run wild, so I'm not just afraid that a duck is watching me, but I'm *seeing* them watching me, too. But, then again, no one's saying they're not there. Unless I'm hallucinating that, too.

What do you think, Doctor?

She nods, steeples her fingers. Her office is bland, duck-free – I'd checked. It was a voluntary commitment, and no way was I crossing the threshold if they'd decided the most soothing decor was rubber duck yellow, accentuated with rubber duck lamps. But no – everything is beige and pastel, innocuous water colours and faded floral cushions. It makes me feel safe. Telling her these things makes me feel safe. And now I want her to tell me I'm not crazy, because then I can figure out what to do next.

She smiles at me, a measured smile that is both warm and professional. Trustworthy. She knows. She understands. She'll give me some meds, or prescribe me some therapy, she'll help *me* understand. I'm safe. There are no ducks that can reach me in here, that smile says. This is a safe haven. *This* is where I need to be. Everything is going to be alright. I smile back, feeling protected and comforted, a child tucked in with a favourite toy.

"Quack," she says, and throws me a rubber duck.

Understanding Fences

I would like to say this story is born of some lofty philosophy or close-held belief.
But it's not, of course.
It's just what comes from walking on the edges of town as the dusk comes in, with the houses huddled behind their hedges and spilling light from inward-turned windows, and seeing a cat watching me pass with utter, utter indifference.
Such things are stories built on.

The creature who looked like a man stalked through the long grass beyond the houses as the dusk drew deep and burnt orange around him. It outlined his long limbs in gold, and turned his dark hair into something alive with strange colour and movement. Although maybe it was like that anyway.

"You again," the cat said from her perch on a fencepost. It was a lost post, belonging to a fence that had been there once and vanished, or that had been intended to be there, but had never arrived. It was also a good post for keeping paws out of the long grass, which was beginning to gather dew.

"Me again," the man-shaped thing agreed. He kept walking, his gaze on the houses. They were separated from him by the strip of untended grass, as well as a tall fence designed to keep people in. Or out. The creature had a shaky grasp of fences. It seemed humans designated meaning to them almost arbitrarily. One fence would be for privacy, another for security, and yet another was merely decorative. People could be fenced in, which was bad, or sitting on the fence, which was also bad – as well as potentially uncomfortable, in his view. Depending on the fence, of course. So it seemed to him that the only good option must be to be *outside* the fence, yet humans put their houses *inside* them. He had long ago concluded that humans and fences were not for the likes of him to understand. Not fully, anyway.

"Do you understand fences?" he asked the cat, who had jumped from her post and was following him, her whiskers twitching at the evening chatter of the birds.

"What?"

"Fences. I don't understand them."

"I mostly disregard them," she said. "Except for the one at seventeen. That one keeps two yappy little terriers in. I like that fence."

"But does it keep them in, or does it keep you out?"

She tilted her head, examining him with pale green eyes. "Nothing keeps a cat out. I merely choose not to go in."

"So the dogs keep you out."

Her tail twitched. "I could go in if I wanted. I do sometimes, when they're inside."

"Yes, then," he said, and adjusted his coat. It was a long thing that flowed at the bottom, swirling in unseen breezes and constantly shifting with the movement of its contents.

"You can't bring those here," the cat said, eyeing his coat.

"They are everywhere," he replied, reaching into the folds of the cloth. He withdrew something small and ill-defined, a scoop of darkness that puddled over his hand a little sadly.

"I don't want them," the cat said.

"You don't get to choose all things."

The cat looked put out, as if no one had informed her of that before, and the creature blew softly on his little handful of shadow as the night drew tighter around them. The thing humped itself up, then abruptly flowed off his palm, arrowing toward the houses in some way that wasn't quite flying. It was more as if the darkness blended with the air, making itself a part of the fabric of this reality.

"Stop that," the cat snapped, watching the thing go.

The creature looked at her. "It is what I do."

"Don't you think people have enough to deal with? They don't need your poison too."

"It's not poison." More blobs of shadow were flowing from his coat, reflecting the deep blue shadows of the evening, the fading sun veining them with gold. There was an uncomfortable beauty to them, a glory to their threat. The cat batted at one as it came too close to her, her claws passing through it as if it were no more than mist. It reformed and fled for the houses, leaving an anxious little chuckle behind.

"Stop it," she snarled at him. "There don't have to be so *many*, at least."

"There are always more than we realise. More than we remember." His coat was disintegrating around him, dissolving into little shadow beasts that floated over the fence, or scurried under it, suggesting legs or wings or teeth or claws as they went, rushing toward the windows that spilled gold light over the gardens.

"No one's built to cope with so many. Especially not humans."

"Yet they do."

"Not well, though," the cat said. "And you don't have to live with them while they try."

"Yes, that must be odd. They are interesting things, aren't they? Do you understand them?"

"They don't even understand themselves."

"But that is much harder than understanding others," the creature that looked like a man said. "Understanding oneself is a complex task."

"Maybe for you. Cats understand themselves perfectly."

"Do you?" the creature asked. "How nice for you to be so simple."

The cat growled, and the creature smiled, showing neat white teeth. With his coat gone, he wore a T-shirt in the gloom. *Social Distancing Since Forever,* it said, and there was a shaggy, vaguely humanoid shape on it, peering out from behind a tree.

"Are you finished here?" the cat asked. "I'm going to

have to go and keep an eye on things, since you can't keep your little monsters to yourself."

"Some things are never finished," the creature said, and when the cat glared at him, he shrugged. "What difference does it make to you? They are not for you."

"They affect me anyway," the cat said, and flicked dew distastefully off one paw.

"Right now, I have no more to give," the creature said, spreading long-fingered hands.

"Don't pretend they're gifts."

"Aren't they?"

The cat looked like she'd quite like to bite the creature, but some desires are unwise, and a smart cat knows what risks are worth taking. So she merely bared her teeth and followed the path the shadows had taken, slipping through the metal bars of one of the fences and vanishing into the hedge beyond. The creature that looked like a man heard a sudden chorus of hysterical barking from the next house along, and a human shouted, "God*damn* it, *shut up!*"

The dogs ignored the human and did what dogs do, and the cat taunted them by her very presence, which is what cats do. The creature supposed she did understand her own nature, in some ways, but he doubted she understood all of it. The nature of all thinking things is at least as complex as the nature of fences.

He kept walking along the edge of the fence, one hand out to brush the leaves on the bushes that lined the grassy path. They curled and shivered with new spring growth in his wake, dreaming of sunshine.

MONTHS LATER, as frosts whispered in quiet places and leaves curled with captured fire, the creature that looked like a man sat on a smooth wooden bench across a small road from the row of near-identical houses, one leg crossed neatly over the other and his hands clasped in his lap. The bench had a plaque on it which read, *Mrs Ivy Hamble,* and the creature was wondering if that was a name the humans had given to the bench. And if so, was it a married bench? His understanding was that *Mrs* was a title bestowed on married women – men did not change their titles whether they were married or not, which struck him as confusing. Did that make men less married than women? Or merely less changed by it? And how had a bench come to be married? He had heard that humans objected to *other* humans marrying one another, so he couldn't see how a bench had managed it.

"Are you married?" he asked the bench, but the bench didn't answer.

"Are you chatting up that bench?" the cat asked, padding across the smooth tarmac of the road to join him. She jumped up next to him, the glow of the streetlights rendering her tabby fur in the dramatic hues of a tiger.

The creature pointed at the plaque. "It says it's married."

The cat looked at the plaque, then at him. "Dude," she said, and offered nothing else. He assumed that meant she didn't know either.

They sat for a while in companionable silence. Winter was gathering autumn close, cradling her as the last of the leaves faded, and bringing her own icy silences to the deep stretches of the night. Most of the houses were dark, only the glimmer of nightlights showing behind curtains, and the occasional cold glow of a TV screen keeping the sleepless company.

Then the cat said, "You've not brought more, have you?"

The creature raised his empty hands to show her. His T-shirt today read, *Believe In Yourself,* and had a long neck rising from a still lake on it.

The cat shifted her weight, puffing her fur out against the chill. "Good. Honestly, that was a hell of a mess. The anxiety. The second-guessing. The sleepless nights. I can only take so much of being clutched like a kid's blankie, you know."

"Blankie?"

"Security blanket. You know, kids use them to keep monsters away."

The creature nodded as if he did know, wondering what power must be infused in these blankets. Belief, he supposed. "Do they make them themselves?"

"What?"

"Blankies."

"I don't know. Sometimes? I think they mostly buy them, though. Unless someone's really into knitting or whatever."

Knitted monster repellents. Humans really were extraordinary.

"And I had to wear a bonnet," the cat said.

That pulled him out of his consideration of blankies. "What?"

"He made me wear a bonnet."

The creature gave the cat a troubled look. "For the

sun?"

"No, you turnip. Because he was designing Halloween costumes for cats, and somehow he felt a Little Red Riding Hood bonnet was a good idea. I had to *model.*"

The creature nodded. "This was his idea?"

"Yes! And the spider outfit was fine, and I quite liked the abominable snowman one – lots of snuggly padding – but the bonnet was too much."

"Did you bite him?"

"Of course."

The creature clicked his tongue.

"A *bonnet.*"

"Still, this doesn't seem so bad."

"Oh, I'm just getting started. The garage is now a workshop, where he builds cat forts, and I have to sit in them so he can photograph them. He has castles in there, and spaceships, and race cars, and a whale, for some reason." The cat wrinkled her nose. "I don't understand the whale."

"I don't understand how the castle fits in the garage. Or the spaceship."

"Well, they're not *full-size*— never mind. Anyway, there's sawdust and bits of fabric and drawings and stuff everywhere, and he's chucked his job in. Meanwhile she's still working, but she's also decided to become a vegan sustainable living blogger."

"This is her idea?"

"Yes. Only she works in some city thing that directly contradicts the whole lifestyle she's going for, so now she cries every morning before breakfast, after she's been up since four a.m. pickling sprouts, or something."

The creature was trying to catch up. "Working in a city

contradicts being a vegan?"

"No, her job does."

"Is she a butcher?"

"What? No."

"Or does she make cheese, perhaps?"

The cat growled. "No, look, I think it contradicts the sustainable thing, mostly."

"Her job is unsustainable?"

The cat bared her teeth at him. "This conversation is unsustainable."

The creature nodded. "I agree."

They both fell silent for a moment, watching the sleeping houses. A light went on in a small window – a bathroom, maybe – and somewhere in the distance a car passed, the very sound exhausted.

Finally the creature said, "They both have their ideas, though."

"Yes, damn you. And they're both convinced that it'll work, and they spend whatever scraps of free time they have planning how to move to some tiny home in the country, with a big workshop for him to build more cat forts and sew more bloody cat bonnets, and they don't go out, and they spend their *lives* working on their damn ideas." The cat's tail was twitching.

The creature nodded. "This is as it should be."

"No," the cat said. "*As it should be* is them *both* going to work and leaving me alone, and no one crying into my fur because the wings on my costume fell off – which I had nothing to do with, by the way. The structural integrity of that costume was not good – or because the door to the Rapunzel tower is too small, or because someone left a

nasty comment on the blog. *As it should be* is them in front of the TV every night, not working in separate rooms. *As it should be* is me getting proper cat food, out of a packet, and none of this homemade rubbish. I had chicken necks last night. *Chicken necks!*" Her tail had gone from twitching to thrashing.

"But humans need ideas," the creature said. "They need ideas to build dreams on. And all humans need dreams. I know this."

"*How?* You don't even know what a memorial bench is!"

The creature shrugged. "Because some things are shared by all thinking creatures."

The cat almost spat at him. "You've made them miserable. You *always* make people miserable. You and your little dream monsters, coming in and biting people and spreading *ideas.* Why can't you just leave things alone?"

"Because people forget to have ideas. They get all caught up in *doing*, and forget that *being* human means having ideas. It means having dreams, even if they're hard ones, or impossible ones. Even if trying to reach them makes them miserable in some ways. Because there is joy in dreams, joy that will outweigh the misery, and they can't have dreams without ideas."

The cat looked as if she were considering biting him once again, and also possibly feeling that the satisfaction of it might outweigh the consequences. "But why *these* dreams?" she asked finally. "Why not some nice easy dreams, like, I don't know ... building a gazebo in the backyard?"

A gazebo. The creature rolled the word over in his mind. Such lovely things, words. But aloud he just said, "I don't give them the dreams. My little monsters merely open them up to the possibility of them."

"Like a wound's open to infection?" the cat asked, arching her whiskers.

"Like a flower's open to pollination," he replied, then shrugged. "But yes, that too."

The cat got up and shook herself off. "Well, keep the damn things to yourself for a bit. I've got enough to deal with. The humans with those bloody terriers have a doggy day care now. A *doggy day care.* There's about ten of the damn things there every day. Do you know how much they stink? And *bark?*"

The creature smiled at her. "So many dogs to tease. That's nice."

She growled at him, but she also arched her head into the touch of his hand as he scratched her between the ears. "I'm off. The four a.m. crying while writing will commence at any moment."

"I thought it was sprout pickling."

"It varies. Sometimes it's soap-making, or fermenting things, or designing graphics. But there's always crying."

The creature nodded gravely. "I believe it's good for the soul. Or eyes. Maybe both."

"All I know is it's bad for my coat," the cat said, and jumped to the ground, stalking across the tarmac to the house in front of them, where a light had gone on downstairs.

The creature that looked like a man watched her go, feeling the ebb and flow of thoughts and hopes and fears around him, some conscious, many not. Dreams were hard, he thought. Hard to grasp, and hard to hold onto once one someone had them, but impossible to live without. They were hope made personal, belief made palpable. They weren't pretty things, though. They were demanding and hungry and brutal and all-consuming, which was why it was so much easier to ignore them, or to put them aside for another time.

But once the idea was in there, they were also impossible to ignore.

He held up a little shadow beast that had collected on his palm, and peered at it. It puddled there, amorphous and dangerous, and after a moment he blew it softly into the air. It drifted for a moment, then shot off in search of prey. They didn't always survive. Sometimes the bite wasn't deep enough, and the ideas couldn't take root. Or the humans were too entrenched in *doing* to do more than dismiss them, or, tragically, sometimes they held the dreams so close that they suffocated them, never allowing them water or light to grow.

Because dreams, like ideas, are dangerous.

And letting them grow takes courage.

The creature got up, dusted his hands off, and looked at the bench. "Nice to meet you, Mrs Ivy Hamble," he said to it, then strolled away down the path, the streetlights burnishing the ends of his hair. Behind him, ideas searched for fertile ground, and dreams swelled around them like blossoms, and lights went on in silent houses as people sat up in the dark and thought, *Yes. Yes, it'll be hard, but it'll be worth it.*

As dreams always are.

And there's nothing even the cats can do to make their humans be sensible about it.

Curse of the Sock Monster

I have actually searched back through my notes to see where this story came from, but the truth, as with many of my stories, is that I have no real idea. Sometimes stories just happen, and I write them down, because that's what you do with stories. Otherwise they moan and scratch in the night, and you can't sleep for the gnawing on the doorframe. And, I mean, ***something's*** *stealing the socks, right?*

"But how can you have no socks?"

"It's the sock monster, Dad."

I dug through Sam's drawer again. It wasn't that there were *no* socks, it was that not many of them seemed to match, and the ones that did had holes in them. Big holes. Sliding on the rug in your stocking feet holes. I gave him my sternest look. "What've you been doing with all the socks?"

"It's not me. It's the sock monster."

I sighed. "Well, you're just going to have to wear

different socks." I balled up a ruined pair and tossed them across the room. Thomas the Tank Engine stared at me out of one mournful eye, a hole swallowing the other. "How about ... one Ironman, one Hulk?"

Sam shrugged and held his hand out. "I don't care."

"Good for you." I gave him the socks and went to make sure the sock monster hadn't been at the porridge.

THE DAYS always go so quick. I ran out of the door that afternoon, cursing myself for forgetting that we needed to go shopping, which meant I had to drive. It always takes longer to drive to school – all the parents out in their hulking SUVs and people carriers, double-parking and waving and air kissing. My poor old car clattered and belched exhaust fumes and stalled at the lights, and when I finally pulled into the pickup area there was a grim-looking woman standing next to Sam, holding his arm at a too-high angle, like a teddy bear being hauled about by a careless toddler. I swung out of the car, waving. Sam waved back enthusiastically – I guess I've still got a couple of years left before he's impossibly embarrassed by me.

"Sam! Sorry I'm late – traffic. Let's go!"

"Mr Moore, a word?"

I tried on a flirty sort of smile. "I can't leave the car here—"

"It won't take a moment." Her face had the same sharp angles as her shoulders, hair terrified into submission.

I sighed and closed the car door. "What can I do for

you, Mrs Jones?" Who's called Jones? I mean, really? It's like Mr Smith.

"We had sport today—"

"Oh, no— oh. No, I packed your gear, didn't I, Sam?"

He opened his mouth to reply, but the teacher talked straight over him. Nice. "His socks, Mr Moore. His socks were in a deplorable condition."

That seemed like a bit of a harsh indictment of an innocent pair of socks to me, but judging by Mrs Jones' immaculate blouse after a day surrounded by seven-year-olds, anything less than starched and bleached probably wasn't up to standard. "I don't understand," I said aloud. "His PE gear's washed after every class."

"They were clean." She glared at me, as if I'd somehow disappointed her, and I fought the urge to put my hands behind my back and bow my head, the naughty kid being told off after class.

"Then I'm afraid I still don't understand."

She whipped a hand from behind her back and brandished a small white sock at me, damning evidence of my failure. "Look at this, Mr Moore. Do you understand *now?*"

I stared at the sock, which had most certainly been in one piece when I tucked it into its twin and zipped it into Sam's backpack last night. The toe swung forlornly, just a few threads attaching it to the foot, as if someone had tried to turn it into a very small legwarmer.

"Mr Moore? Do you see that this is unacceptable?"

I snatched the sock off her and shoved it in my pocket, my chest tight and my cheeks painfully hot. How dare she? Out here, in front of everyone, waving a perfectly clean sock at me like a murder weapon, like indelible proof of my *lack.*

"I'm very sorry, Mrs Jones," I said, my voice as level as I could make it. "I don't understand how this happened."

"It's not me you need to apologise to," she said, and pushed Sam in front of her. His face twisted with irritation, and I crouched in front of him.

"Sorry, kiddo."

"It's not your fault," he said. "It's the sock monster. *She*"—and he jerked his head with great disdain toward Mrs Jones—"*She* doesn't believe me, though. She says it's carelessness."

I looked up at the teacher, trying to keep my expression friendly. "Carelessness?"

"The evidence speaks for itself." Her mouth was a tight wound in her face. "I feel you may be overstretching, keeping him at this school."

I bared my teeth in something I hoped passed as a smile. "I appreciate the feedback, Mrs Jones. Have a lovely afternoon." And I took my son's small hand in mine and went back to my rust-stained, dented car, my head as high as I could carry it. There wasn't much else I could do.

WE HAD mac and cheese for dinner, sitting at the little kitchen bar while Sam told a convoluted tale involving various classmates, and I wondered glumly how long I actually could keep him in the school. It wasn't easy on freelance wages. But going full-time, even if I could find a position, meant after-school care, and I didn't want to do that. By my figuring I'd have to land a bloody good job to make it worthwhile, anyway.

"You're not listening," Sam accused me.

"I ... no. I'm sorry. I wasn't."

"Are you worried about the sock monster?"

"Should I be worried about the sock monster?"

"What if she eats all the new socks?"

"The sock monster's a she?"

Sam gave me the exasperated look only seven-year-olds seem to have really mastered. "Why not?"

"Well, very true. I imagine being a sock monster is an equal opportunity position."

He snorted – probably more at my cluelessness than at my pathetic joke – and slid off his stool, carrying his bowl carefully to the sink. "I don't think we should have put the new socks in the drawer."

I watched him rinse his bowl and put it in the dishwasher, still well-crusted with cheese. "I'm sure the sock monster only likes old socks."

He frowned. "But new socks are nicer."

"Maybe to us, but sock monsters probably have different tastes."

He gave a very adult sigh. "I hope you're right. I don't want to have to go through the sock thing with Mrs Jones again."

"Sam, I won't be angry. Just tell me the truth."

"It wasn't me! I *told* you we shouldn't have put the new socks in there!"

He was close to tears, and I wasn't far off either. I'd picked up a pair of brand new socks, still chatting happily, and unrolled them to find one had a hole in the heel, the other a great tear under the foot. The next pair had holes in the toes, the third tiny rips like they'd been run over a grater, and all of them, *all* of them were unusable. And we'd just bought them yesterday. I pinched the bridge of my nose, imagining Mrs Jones grinning humourlessly over this latest evidence of my poor parenting skills.

"Sam, there's no lies in this house. You know that, right?"

"I'm not lying!" He screamed it at me, tears spilling onto his pink cheeks. I shook the socks at him, hating myself for it.

"Then what's this? What did you use? Scissors? Why? *Why*, Sam?"

"I didn't do anything! It was the monster! It was!"

I stared at him as his words dissolved into a wail, and realised that he believed it. He really believed it. I dropped the socks and scooped him off the bed, skinny arms and legs everywhere, hugging him to my chest. "I'm sorry," I said, kissing his forehead as he tried to push me away. "I'm really sorry. I should have believed you. It's okay. It's okay." I sank into his solar system sheets and rocked him, surrounded by distant stars, fear, and confusion.

I CALLED the school and told them Sam was sick, then took him to the local surgery. The GP checked him over cursorily – taking his temperature and peering into his eyes with her little eye thing, then finally listening to his chest before she smiled at him and said he could wait outside. He looked at me questioningly, and I nodded, waiting until the door snicked shut before I looked at the doctor.

"Well?"

She sighed and went behind her desk to sit down, distancing herself from me. "There's nothing wrong with him."

"Okay, but this behaviour—"

"Chopping up socks?"

"He's blaming it on monsters. Lying."

She gave me the knowing smile of a parent who's been there, seen that. "Hardly unusual. You might want to look at how much time you're spending with him, though. In my experience, this sort of thing tends to just be attention seeking."

I leaned back in my chair and watched her clicking the keys with her short, sensible nails. It all sounds so simple when it's not your kid. When it's not your life.

Friday night is fish'n'chip night, and we ate in front of the telly, making chip butties out of white bread and lashings of ketchup. Sam giggled his way through the whole meal, perfectly happy to have an unexpectedly long weekend. I wasn't as happy – I'd managed to persuade the GP to give me a note, but it'd be another black mark. The dear Mrs Jones had sent me a clipped, formal email that all but came straight out and said I'd kept Sam home because I couldn't care for him properly. She very sweetly reiterated the school's uniform and attendance policies, and suggested that maybe I needed to think about other options if I couldn't stick to them. I wrote a very angry reply that included my own suggestions about what she could do with her advice, then deleted it. It made me feel better, though.

Now I picked up our greasy plates and pointed Sam at the stairs. "Go wash up. Don't touch anything on the way, alright?"

"Alright!" He bounced off the sofa and pounded upstairs, sounding like a small, pyjama-clad elephant.

I was stacking the dishwasher when his voice floated down to me. "Dad?"

"Yeah?"

"I think the monster's been." His voice was wobbly, frightened, and I dumped the plates unceremoniously, taking the stairs two at a time. He was standing in the doorway of his room, soap suds still smeared on his knuckles, shoulders hunched toward his ears. He looked up at me fearfully. "I didn't do it," he whispered. "I *didn't*."

I stared past him, into his room. It had been tidy when I'd come to pull the curtains, toys stacked in their corner, books away on their shelves. Now socks were strewn across the floor, scraps of torn fabric littering the carpet like the scales of some strange, decimated fish. The windows were closed. The doors were locked.

I put a hand on top of Sam's head. "Stay here." I hoped I sounded more confident than I felt. I edged into the room cautiously, checking behind the curtains, rattling the windows on their latches. Nothing. I opened the cupboard, then crouched at a safe distance to check under the bed. There was nothing but an alarming amount of dust bunnies and an old book. But he hadn't had time to do it himself. Had he? Maybe when I was writing my fuming email? Had he done it then, hidden the evidence, and just thrown them out of the drawer now? That must be it. It had to be. I ran my hands back over my hair, looking at the eviscerated socks. There went another ten pounds, and it meant we'd have to go shopping again tomorrow. I closed my eyes, took a shaky breath, and said, "It's okay. I think the monster's gone."

Sam ran to me, wrapping his arms around my waist. "Why?" he demanded, and I could see tears on his cheeks. "Why's she doing this?"

"I don't know," I told him honestly, and crouched so I could hug him. "But it's okay. It's going to be okay." He started to cry while I rubbed his back, feeling the skinny knobbles of his spine under my hand, and hoped I wasn't lying.

There's this romantic notion of what it's like to share a bed with your kid, but it never works that way in my experience, especially when you're both trying to fit into one kiddie-size bed. Which is why I was awake when I heard it. Sam was snoring, and had just hit me in the face with an out-flung arm, so I was lying there staring at the ceiling with a smarting eye when I heard *chewing*.

My breathing stopped, just *stopped*, as if I'd forgotten how to do it, and I heard the scrape of a drawer being pulled a little further open, a gulping swallow, then more chewing. I slid my hand toward the edge of the bed as carefully as I could, resisting the urge to sit up and shout. The chewing stopped and I froze, taking deep, slow breaths, a dreamer in the depths of sleep. After a moment there was the scrape of something hard – nails? – and the sound of tearing fabric, then the chewing started again. I resumed my slow-motion reach for the light, too wary of disturbing the intruder to turn and look at him. What kind of freak was this, anyway? He'd been sneaking into my son's room, going through his drawers? I'd tear his head off.

My hand had made it to the switch on the light cord. This was it. I'd only get one chance – light on and jump, and don't think about whether he was armed or not. Some weirdo climbing into kids' bedrooms to chew on socks, probably not. I'm not the biggest guy, but I was pretty sure my fury right then was going to be enough. I hit the light and jumped.

The dog-sized thing standing on its back legs, rooting through the sock drawer, turned horrified yellow eyes on me, enormous pupils contracting as the light hit it. It screamed, I screamed, and Sam sat up on the bed and joined in. My jump was off, because I'd assumed I was about to tackle a full-sized human, so I bounced off the chest of drawers as the creature dropped to all fours. I almost landed right on top of it, and it tried to bound away from me. I flung myself at it, still half-convinced that it was some kid in a costume, and it screamed again, swiping at me with nasty-looking claws that barely missed my nose. I had my hands on it now, scrabbling to get a grip on the thing. It moved like a cat, all muscular wriggling and slick fur, thrashing around with those horrible talons while I bellowed abuse and Sam kept screaming, and it hissed and spat and swore right back at me.

And then, somehow, I had its throat in one hand, my

fingers almost meeting at the back of its neck, my other hand trapping its powerful back legs down so it couldn't disembowel me, its front paws scrabbling at my arms, shredding my T-shirt and tearing the skin.

"Stop it!" I shouted. "Stop it right now, or I swear to God I'll snap your neck!"

It stopped, eyes narrowing, and I could see the rapid rise and fall of its chest, hear its panting breath. It smelled faintly of fabric softener and dust.

"Dad! Dad-*dee!*" Sam was shrieking, and both the monster and I looked up at the bed. He had a pillow in his hands and looked like he wasn't sure who to throw it at.

"It's okay, Sam. It's okay. You go downstairs."

"No!" He screamed the word at me – at both of us. "The monster'll take you away and then I won't have *anyone!*"

"Oh, Sammy—" I wanted to scoop him up off the bed, to assure him I wasn't going anywhere, but I couldn't let go of the creature. "Okay. You sit right there, alright? No closer."

He sobbed something incoherent, but stayed where he was, and I looked back at the monster. It glared at me.

"Have you been stealing Sam's socks?" I asked. It blinked at me, then pointed at its neck. I could feel its throat move under my hand, and I eased my grip carefully. It swallowed, eyes squinting in pain, and I tried to convince myself that I didn't feel guilty. "Don't try anything," I warned it.

It rolled its eyes. "Considering you still have a death grip on me, what am I supposed to try?" Its voice was unexpectedly musical and quite certainly female. The sock monster was indeed a she.

"I dunno," I said. "Monster stuff. Magic, whatever."

"Monsters aren't magical." She touched my hand, the pads of her paws smooth. Her claws had retracted. "Please. That's really hurting."

I tightened my grip. "You would say that. What, I let you go and you attack us?"

She gagged, eyes squinting in discomfort, and Sam gave an unhappy little wail. I eased the weight of my hand. They were both looking at me reproachfully, and I flushed. "You might have!"

"If I wanted to do that," the monster whispered, "I've had plenty of chances. And *you're* the one who jumped *me!*"

I stayed where I was for a moment, then groaned and sat back, letting her go. "Don't try to run," I warned her.

She nodded, pushing herself up onto one elbow. "Not much point. You've seen me now." Her voice was raspy, and I gave up pretending I didn't feel bad. In truth, I felt ridiculously guilty.

"Here," Sam said, and offered her the glass of water from his bedside table. She took it gratefully in both hands, long hair swinging like a fringe from her arms as she drank.

"Thank you," she said when she'd finished. "That's better. So – what's it going to be?"

"What's ... what d'you mean? Why are you eating our socks?"

She stared at me. "*That?* You attacked me for *that?*"

"Well, you were sneaking around our house," I pointed out, ignoring the prickly, guilty heat on my shoulders.

"I'm a monster. It's kind of in the job description."

"You have a *job description?*" I was starting to feel very strongly that the mushy peas had been off, and this was all some weird hallucination.

"Yeah. We start with sock or pen stealing, then graduate through under-bed haunting, closets, and finally attics and basements. Indoor monsters, that is."

"Indoor monsters."

"Well, yeah. Bridge monsters are too clumsy for the fine work, water monsters can't, obviously—" She stopped as I held up a hand. "What, you didn't know?"

"Monsters don't exist," I told the monster sitting on the bedroom floor, and she rolled her eyes like she'd been spending a lot of time in teenagers' bedrooms.

"Yeah, clearly." She sat up, claws popping out and making me draw back in alarm. She gave me a peevish look and started grooming the tangles out of her thick coat. "So you obviously don't know what happens when you catch a monster, then."

Well, what the hell. "What happens when you catch a monster?"

"You get to wish the monster onto someone else," she said patiently, worrying at a particularly stubborn knot. "Honestly, humans. How do you get through life without falling into troll-holes, or tripping over pixie mounds?"

I squeezed the bridge of my nose. Monsters and pixies and trolls, oh my. "What if we just want you to go away?"

"Doesn't work that way. I was assigned to this house. I can only leave if you wish me on someone else's."

"Is there ... is there a monster under my bed, too?" Sam whispered.

She gave him a wide smile, surprisingly sweet for the

teeth it revealed. "No, kiddo. And – don't let on you know – even if there was, you don't have to be scared of them. They only eat dust bunnies and burglars."

"Burglars?" he repeated, awestruck.

"Absolutely." She winked at me, and I felt my lips drawing into an answering grin. God, I needed to get some friends. I was bonding with a sock monster.

"So, we just have to give you an address?" I asked.

"Not even that. A name will do."

My grin widened. It couldn't hurt. Hallucination or not, it couldn't hurt. "I can work with that."

AND NOW YOU'RE expecting me to say, *and that was the last we saw of the sock monster*.

Only it wasn't.

I know you've guessed who we sent her to. It was an obvious choice. But what I hadn't actually realised, through my own fear and anxiety and put-upon-ness, was that Mrs Jones was less hard and more *brittle.* Fragile. By the end of term she'd had to be removed from the classroom, because she was making all her students take their shoes off so she could examine their socks for holes, and burst into hysterical tears when she was the only one in the room with laddered tights. There was indefinite leave and hospitalisation for exhaustion, counselling for the kids (although, as Sam pointed out, they'd all just found it hilarious. They needed counselling for the pre-sock monster Mrs Jones), and a round, bubbly substitute was brought in, opposite in every way it was possible to be.

Her name – I swear I'm not making this up – was Mrs Smith.

We visited Mrs Jones in the hospital a few times, both of us feeling guilty about the sock monster thing. I hadn't thought she'd take it so badly. She was very sweet to us, her hair a loose halo on her shoulders, voice softened by medication. She said she didn't get many visitors. I offered to water her plants, and she was so grateful that I felt guilty all over again.

The sock monster was investigating the remnants of Mrs Jones' stockings, one pair looped casually over her horns, when I flicked the light on. She hissed, spinning around, then stopped as she saw me propped up on the bed.

"You," she said, sounding more resigned than angry. "What, you going to send me to drive some other poor soul to distraction?"

"No," I said. "I want you to come back."

She looked puzzled. "Why?"

"Because when she comes home, you can't be here. And I can't wish you on anyone else. It's not right."

She thought about it for a moment. "Well, there's no law saying you can't wish me back on yourself. I just don't think anyone's ever done it before."

"There's a first for everything. Do I need to actually catch you?"

"Oh, no. Please don't." She looked distressed, and I sighed. Man of the year, me. Even scaring monsters.

I got up and said, "See you there, then?"

"Sure." She was already sliding under the bed. I tipped a salute to a portrait of the late Mr Jones and left.

So right now, the sock monster (her name is Delila), is watching TV with Sam. She graduated to dust bunnies quite quickly, which makes life easier – I've got plenty of those, and keeping the whole house in socks was getting quite expensive. As soon as I've finished this, I'll shepherd them upstairs, and we'll read a bedtime story. Delila loves them even more than Sam does. They'll snuggle in, one on each side of me, the monster and the boy, and by the time I'm finished at least one of them will be asleep. Unless the stories get the monsters wrong, of course. Then Delila will sit up and snatch the book off me, and huff, *humans*. And she'll tell her own stories, ones full of myth and magic and strange, wild, monstrous beauty. So much beauty that sometimes I get my stories wrong deliberately.

And, later, I'll come back down here and write out her tales about the things we don't see and don't know, and don't even believe half the time. Stories that bridge the gap between the real and the unreal – or what we believe to be unreal.

Stories like the one I'm telling you now.

Coffee, Cake, & Ghoulets

I would really like to claim that this story was well planned, and that I spent an enormous amount of time considering the implications of a reaper with a cake fixation and a soft spot for kittens and doilies.

In truth, the only thing I can point to is that I once went to a café in Australia that had coffin-shaped coffee tables. They were very cool, if most un-Gertrude-like.

And, some years later, I wrote this story.

"Stop it," the reaper said.

The ghoulet rolled onto its back, displaying a pale moon of a belly, and the reaper sighed. She leaned over and scratched bony fingers through the creature's fine hair.

"We have to go," she told it. "You can't be out here, you know."

The ghoulet flopped upright, knobbly knees up around its ears, and peered about the graveyard. Moonlight silvered the trees and turned the wilting flowers into pastel water-colours, motionless and silent. He looked up at the reaper questioningly.

"I know there's no one here *now,* but that doesn't mean the night watchman won't come by to check on things."

The ghoulet grinned, exposing rows of sharp, erratically aligned teeth.

"No," the reaper said firmly. Her name was – or had been, she didn't have an awful lot of use for it these days – Gertrude, and she was tired. She wished she could still drink tea. This was turning into the sort of night where a more technically alive person would drink tea. Possibly spiked tea. "Come on. Into the, um, nice box thing." She pointed at a large object draped in dark cloth, sitting askew on the edge of a grave.

The ghoulet looked at the object, then back at Gertrude. He gave a little coughing cry that sounded something like a cat hacking up a hairball, then dropped to all fours and took off across the graveyard. His fat belly brushed the short-cropped grass as he ran, flabby limbs unpleasantly spider-like in the night.

Gertrude pinched the scant skin of her forehead. "Well, damn," she said, and sighed again. At least she didn't get migraines anymore. Because this would *definitely* be giving her a migraine. She hitched her robes up with both hands and set off at a sprint after the ghoulet, dodging between the graves with bony, sure-footed grace.

Her mobile was ringing by the time she got back to the cloth-draped cage and bundled the ghoulet unceremoniously inside, where he sat grunting and coughing grumpily with his siblings. She fished the phone out of the folds of her robes and stabbed the screen with unnecessary force. A crack splintered across the flat glass, and she used some language she'd never had much use for in pre-reaper days.

"Hello?" she demanded. She'd cracked her shin on a gravestone in the tussle with the ghoulet, which had done nothing to improve matters. And this was going to be another call from Departed Human Logistics (DHL), wasn't it – they'd have missed a soul and she'd have to go and reap it manually. Just what she needed, with a cage full of whining baby ghouls and the night almost gone.

"Reaper Leeds?" The voice had the flat, toneless note of bored assistants everywhere. "Please hold for GR Yorkshire." A soundtrack of looping water droplets and sighing angels replaced the voice before Gertrude could respond. Not that she had any choice. She tugged the cloth back over the cage, quieting the ghoulets, and waited.

"Reaper Leeds." GR Yorkshire's voice flooded the phone, warm and ringing with baritone confidence. "How's that ghoulet problem coming?"

"I'm on top of it, sir. Just caught a litter in Killingbeck graveyard."

"Any sign of the ghouls themselves?"

"No, sir."

"*Hmm.*" The word was a rumble, a deep underground earth-moving sound. "That's unfortunate."

"Sir, I'm not equipped to—"

"Oh, I know, Reaper Leeds. I know." There was a sigh in his voice, and Gertrude felt absurdly disappointed in herself, as if it were somehow her own oversight that she wasn't a creature control reaper. "But you are looking for signs? Overturned graves, broken headstones, the usual drill?"

"Yes, sir."

"Well. I think they're over the border in Lancashire, myself, and just coming across to lay their bloody eggs. Or someone's *bringing* the damn things over. But it's not like Grim UK are listening to me. Oh no, they just say the days of such skirmishes are over, and I'm holding onto the past, not *moving with the times*. Am I not talking to you on a mobile telephone, Reaper Leeds?"

"Umm, yes, sir."

"Exactly. Behind the times. Ha!"

Gertrude held the phone away from her ear at a burst of furious static, then put it back. "Yes. What can I do for you, sir?" she asked, before he could start listing any more grievances against Lancashire.

"Eh?"

"Is there something you need?" GR Yorkshire wasn't exactly in the habit of calling his reapers up for a chat. Well, not her, anyway. Maybe he had a regular poker night with other reapers, and she just didn't know about it. Even for a reaper, she wasn't particularly social.

"Why? Are you in a rush? Am I *inconveniencing* you by calling you on your mobile telephone?"

"No sir, of course not. But I do have a cage of ghoulets to deliver to the unnaturals rescue centre, and I don't want to run up against a night watchman or anything."

Although, never mind what she'd said to the ghoulet – judging by the state of the place they couldn't even afford a groundsman, let alone a night watchman.

"Huh. Well. Yes. We can't be having any unnecessary civilian incidents. Ah, you're going to have to take the ghoulets home with you."

"I'm sorry?"

"No need to be sorry, not your fault."

"No, sir—" Gertrude squeezed the bridge of her nose, trying to ignore the growls coming from the cage. "I think I misunderstood. Did you say you wanted me to take the ghoulets *home?* With *me?*"

"Yes, exactly. Well done, Reaper Leeds."

"But sir—"

"Secretary Reaper will sort out some compensation. The damn Witch Council say they can't take any more ghoulets at the moment. Should've known, bloody witches. One minute they're going all gooey over them, the next they've grown bored of the whole thing and are saying we can't make them take any more. If this was the old days—" He stopped, and Gertrude heard him take a deep breath. When he spoke again, the peevishness was gone, replaced by the familiar, muscular tones, thrumming in her ear. "Anyhow. I know I can rely on you, can't I ..." There was the sound of rustling paper, then he added, with a note of triumph, "Gertrude?"

She looked at the cage. A corner of the cloth had been tugged through the bars, and she could hear chewing and slobbering coming from inside. She pinched the bridge of her nose. "Yes, sir."

"Well done, well done, Reaper Leeds. Ah ... yes." There

was a pause, and she could hear the clatter of his bony fingertips on a table. "Well. I'll hand you back to Secretary Reaper." There was a crash, a piercing digital beep that made Gertrude jerk the phone away from her ear again, and then the sound of GR Yorkshire shouting something at his assistant.

"Reaper Leeds?" the bored voice was back, although it sounded a little more anxious now.

"Still here."

"Good. Additional funds will be credited to your account to allow for potential property damage by the ghoulets, and to cover the extra work of procuring sustenance for them. You—"

"Procuring sustenance?"

"Feeding them. You—"

"I know what it *means.* But you expect me to feed them in my *apartment?*"

"Or wherever you choose to house them. Funds will be made available if you wish to rent, for example, a storage unit or small crypt."

"I'm almost certain you can't rent a crypt on a monthly basis, and I don't think a storage unit is a great place for hungry ghoulets, do you, Ethel?"

"That is, of course, entirely your choice—"

"*Ethel.* Please."

There was a pause, the sound of a door closing, then the secretary said in a low voice, "What do you want me to do, Gertrude? These ghoulets are showing up *everywhere*, and the witches won't take them. They say they've already got too many, and they're just too difficult. None of the other divisions want anything to do with them."

"I understand that, I do, but this is really not my job."

"I know. But we can't just leave baby ghouls running wild across Yorkshire, can we?"

"Well, no, but I live in an *apartment!* What do I do with them?"

"Fill the bath with grave dirt so they've got somewhere to sleep, feed them some chicken, and teach them to be good little ghouls. That's it."

"That's it, is it? No ghoulish nursery rhymes at bedtime, or graveside etiquette lessons?"

There was a pause. "I don't think that'll be necessary," the secretary said, sounding uncertain. "Unless, of course, you want to."

"No, I don't *want*— never mind." The secretary was the closest Gertrude had to a friend these days, but Ethel had been a reaper for a long time. A *long* time. There wasn't exactly a lot of movement in the reaper job market. Although, it was also possible she'd always been this serious. Gertrude sighed. "Just put the money in my account. And this is temporary, alright? I'm not raising ghoulets to ghoulhood." Not least because chicken wouldn't keep them happy for long.

"Absolutely. We're working on a solution." The secretary sounded much more confident, but it didn't exactly impress Gertrude. She thought it was probably less confidence in a solution than confidence that she had something scripted to say.

IT TOOK Gertrude four trips up the three flights of stairs to her apartment, dragging two precariously full bin bags of grave dirt on each trip, before the bath was full. And she was fairly sure the woman in 2B had heard her. She could feel herself being watched, or as much as she could be with the lights off in the windowless stairwell. But there was no point in worrying about it. She had more pressing things to deal with.

She folded the bin bags neatly and put them back under the sink, then went to peek into the bathroom. The ghoulets had fallen on the sack of fried chicken eagerly enough, although they seemed a bit unimpressed by the secret spices. One had thrown up violently on her good hand towel, but with that out of the way they'd returned to the chicken, crunching through bones and splattering shreds of skin across the walls and floorboards. She was going to have to re-paint before she moved, that was clear.

Now the bathroom was quiet, the muted light from the street slipping through the uncurtained window to light snoring mounds in the tub of dirt. There was an unpleasant-looking puddle next to the potted fern, and Gertrude made a mental note to buy puppy training pads. The secretary was going to have to be generous with the compensation.

She eased the door shut and wedged a chair under the handle, the back across the frame so it couldn't be pulled open from the inside, then went to put the oven on. She'd make a Victoria's sponge. There wasn't much in life – or afterlife – that a little baking couldn't make better.

Someone was knocking at the door. Gertrude sighed, closing her book with a finger marking her place. It'd be 2B. Sure enough, a quiet voice drifted under the door.

"Hello? I ... thank you for the cake. It was lovely."

Gertrude scratched her ear. She always left some cake outside 2B, in a small pink tin decorated with kittens. She liked kittens. They didn't like her so much – animals were never too keen on the whole not-technically-alive thing.

"I brought you some coconut biscuits. They're from work. Sorry, I know that's cheating, but, well ... it's better than me trying to make you something." The woman outside the door gave an uncertain sort of laugh that faded to a sigh. "Anyway. Thank you."

Gertrude waited until she heard the woman's footsteps fading back down the stairs before she got up and retrieved the tin from the mat outside. She'd given cake to all her neighbours when she first moved in, but hadn't got so much as the empty tin back from anyone except 2B. She seemed nice. A little broken, perhaps, but wasn't everyone? She sniffed the coconut biscuits and put them in the box with the rest of the Victoria's sponge. She'd give it away when she went out tonight.

She picked up her book and settled back into her favourite chair, plumping the throw cushions and draping a fluffy pink blanket across her lap. She had a couple of hours yet before she'd go out. The sun didn't exactly make her cower and hide, but it did hurt her eyes these days, and her skin burned horribly. So she read in the day, or baked, or simply sat watching the shadows shorten and lengthen across the floor of the apartment, her thoughts running in the strange dim fields that were as close as she got to sleep.

THE GHOULETS WERE RAMPAGING around the apartment when she let herself in. The chair had held, but they'd chewed a hole in the bottom of the door. The pantry was open, bags of flour (plain, pastry, self-raising, bread) disembowelled and scattering explosive halos across the kitchen floor. Golden syrup and honey spilled from shelf to shelf in slow motion cascades, and packets of chocolate chips, dried fruit and marzipan were strewn haphazardly across the living room and down the hall to her bedroom door. Powdery footprints tracked across the rugs and decorated the sofa, and there was a baking goods-encrusted ghoulet sitting on the coffee table, trying unsuccessfully to lick his belly clean. Gertrude stood in the doorway, watching them in dismay, then hurriedly slammed the door shut as three of the creatures made a dash toward her, long-limbed monsters trailing flour and cocoa powder behind them.

"No," she said. "No, no, *no! Bad* ghoulets. *Bad!*" The one on the table spat a mouthful of floury fur at her, and another squeezed between her legs to start scratching the door energetically. She opened her Tesco's bag and pulled out a raw chicken. "Dinner. Now." She marched into the spare room with the chicken held aloft, and threw it into the bottom of the cage. The ghoulets crowded around her legs, drooling and distrustful. "Get in there. You obviously can't be trusted, so into the cage it is. Go on!" She grabbed two of the ghoulets by the scruffs of their necks and hefted them after the chicken, their skinny legs pedalling wildly. They pounced on the carcass without a backward glance, tearing at the flesh with bony fingers and snapping teeth, and their siblings charged in to join them. Gertrude dropped two more chickens in then locked the cage and stepped back. The ghoulets didn't even look up. She went back into her devastated living room and looked around wearily. This was going to take the rest of the night to sort out. And then there was the bathroom. She pinched the bridge of her nose and went to get a bucket.

The phone rang just as Gertrude was scraping the last of the golden syrup out of the joints in the shelving. She eyed it balefully, then stripped off one flower print glove and checked the display. It was the secretary – she'd have preferred DHL, to be honest.

"Hello?"

"Reaper Leeds?"

"Yes, Ethel."

There was an uncertain pause on the other end of the line, and Gertrude could hear the nervous tap of the secretary's fingertips on her desk. "Ah ... we have a report of ghoulets in Harehills Cemetery."

Gertrude looked at the bin bag full of flour and beyond-saving cushions. She was going to have to throw her rug away, too. She loved her rug. She'd bought it from a very nervous travelling salesman, back when there were such things. "Is the unnaturals centre taking them in yet?"

"*Mmm*. No. Not as yet."

"I already have eight ghoulets in my apartment, Ethel.

I'm not even allowed a *hamster* in my apartment. The landlord was quite clear."

"Well, more funds will, of course—"

"They chewed their way out of the bathroom and broke into the pantry. They destroyed most of my baking supplies. And they threw up on my sofa. Twice."

"Yes, I understand the difficulties—"

"I don't think you do. How am I even meant to catch more ghoulets, when I have to keep the ones I've got locked in the cage? And it's no life for them."

"It's a temporary solution—"

"One moment." Gertrude's phone was beeping with an incoming text, and she checked it quickly. DHL. Brilliant. Now she had lost souls to deal with too. She sighed deeply enough to compete with GR Yorkshire's on-hold music and said, "Ethel?"

"It's really better to use our titles, Reaper Leeds."

"If I'm going to be a ghoulet nanny, I expect a little more personal treatment than usual," she said, startling herself. She usually didn't mind the cool efficiency of the after-death services. They were clean, simple. One always knew where one stood. But this ... she looked around, tucking the phone against her shoulder as she peeled her other glove off and threw them both into the bin bag. They were as irredeemable as her rug. There was golden syrup and flour caked in the feather trim around the wrists. "I will go and get the other ghoulets. But this really can't continue."

"We are doing our best, Reaper Leeds."

She supposed they were, at that. It wasn't like they'd be happy about increasing her funding just because of ghoulets.

She hung up and checked the text. DHL hadn't been able to reap a soul in Hunslet, which was in almost exactly the opposite direction to Harehills. She sighed again. This was the problem with automated systems. Once, reapers had done all the reaping, and souls were rarely missed. Now there was barely a night where she didn't have a call out. DHL just didn't allow for some souls being a little confused, or reluctant, or simply scared. For souls being human, or at least very recently so. And she never felt it was right, somehow, people being reaped by remote servers.

But that was progress for you.

It was almost three a.m. when Gertrude came back in, dragging a large bin bag full of chicken carcasses in one hand and an enormous storage crate in the other, the top firmly bungeed down. There was a lot of scraping and muttering coming from inside the crate as she bounced it up the stairs, but she really didn't care. So far the slick plastic had resisted their attacks, and that was all that mattered right now.

She was on the first landing when she heard the door to the street bang open below. She froze as the lights came on, pale and sickly but more than bright enough to see that the bag of chickens was bleeding onto the tatty wooden flooring. Maybe it was someone from one of the downstairs flats? But no, she wasn't that lucky. She could hear footsteps coming up, not entirely steady, and she hurried toward the last set of stairs, the ones that led up to her own apartment, already knowing she wasn't going to make it. She could carry an awful lot, but that didn't mean she could carry it quickly.

The steps behind her had stopped, and she knew whoever it was could see her. She didn't turn around, just dragged the crate up one more stair.

"Do ... do you need some help?"

Gertrude peeked over her shoulder, the hood of her robe hiding her face. It was her. 2B. She was standing with one hand on the wall, a handbag dangling in the other. She wasn't exactly smiling, but she didn't look panicked, either. "Ah, no. Thank you."

The woman looked at the puddle of chicken blood on the landing, then at Gertrude's hunched form. "The ... your cakes. I really love them."

Gertrude straightened, her grip on the crate easing. "Really?"

"Yeah. They're amazing. Better than anything we sell at the cafe." The woman took a step forward. "Are you sure you don't need any help?"

Before Gertrude could answer, one of the ghoulets launched an attack on the roof of the crate, making it jump and almost slip out of her grip. She grabbed it with both hands, dropping the bag, which promptly fell sideways and disgorged badly wrapped chicken carcasses. They thumped fleshily down the stairs, noisy in the silent stairwell. She closed her eyes, hoping 2B wouldn't notice the scuffling coming from the crate.

The woman looked at a chicken that had come to rest by her feet, then crouched to pick it up. "Either I'm more drunk than I thought," she said, "or you've had a few, too. Who bulk-buys whole chickens at three in the morning?"

"They were on special," Gertrude said, which was actually true. "They put all sorts of things on special in the middle of the night."

"I guess they do," the woman said, and picked up another chicken. "I'm Emma. Pass me that bag."

And Gertrude did.

Of all the strange things that had happened since Gertrude became a reaper, she was fairly sure that none of them were as strange as brewing tea for Emma at half past three in the morning, the chickens stuffed into her fridge and the crate of ghoulets deposited in the spare room.

Judging from the mystified expression on Emma's face as she stared around the pink, ruffled living room, she was finding it a little strange, too. But she drank a cup of tea and ate four chocolate chip cookies, while Gertrude brought a rose-decked cup up to her lips and took it away again, untouched.

"So do you sell your cakes?" Emma asked, poking one of the surviving doilies on the coffee table with a slightly unsteady finger.

"No, not really. I just make them for me."

Emma abandoned the doily and looked pointedly at the untouched cookie on Gertrude's plate. "I can see that."

"Oh, well. I can't eat them all myself." Gertrude could feel her ears getting warm, and wondered, with something like astonishment, if she could actually still blush.

"You should sell them," Emma said. "I'm serious. Open your own place."

"Well, I'm not good in the days. I'm highly photosensitive. But that's really nice of you."

"It's not nice. It's true. You're lucky to be so good at something." Emma looked down as she spoke, her shoulders hunching forward over her tea. "I'm not much good at anything."

"I'm sure that's not right."

"It is, though." She shrugged and took another sip of tea. "I've never done anything, or been anything. Now I work in a coffee shop with kids half my age." Her voice was flat, accepting, but the skin of her face was drawn taut with the hurt of it.

Gertrude looked down at the table, scarred by the ghoulets' claws, and said, "No one has ever given me anything back for my cakes. Most people don't even bother to say thank you. And no one's ever knocked on my door before. Not once."

Emma was silent for a moment, then she laughed. There was a sour sort of sadness running under it, but it was genuine. "What a pair," she said. "What a perfect pair."

IT WAS early evening a week later, and Gertrude was chasing a ghoulet around the living room with a tea towel. The creature had got chicken skin stuck in its teeth three days ago, and it was starting to stink. Well, stink *more*. There was still no more word from the secretary, although Gertrude had to admit that Reaper Central had been generous with the funding. They had to be, really, considering that she now had twenty-three ghoulets living between the bathroom and the spare room. She'd solved the breaking out problem by lining the bottom half of the doors and walls with sheets of metal, and both rooms were knee-deep in graveyard dirt. If this was going to carry on, she really needed to move somewhere bigger, but it was hard enough moving on her own at the best of times. Moving twenty-three ghoulets and who knew how many cubic metres of graveyard dirt unnoticed was going to be tricky.

A door slammed downstairs, and she paused in her pursuit, frowning. She thought she'd heard something else. A cry? The ghoulet scrambled up her bookshelves and grabbed a winking porcelain cat, hefting it gleefully. She touched a bony finger to her lips, and the ghoulet stared at her, confused. A thud, faint through the door, the sound of someone falling on the stairs or crashing into a wall. She stepped to the door, slipping the latch and easing it open to let in the muddy scents of damp and dust and boredom. She really should move. She could afford somewhere nicer on ghoulet nanny wages.

There was a cry, bitten off, and she pulled the door wide at the sudden thunder of running feet, flight and pursuit. She hurried to the top of the stairs as Emma lurched onto the landing below with blood on her cheek. She lunged for her apartment door, but someone out of sight around the turn of the stairs grabbed her, jerking her backward and almost out of sight. Gertrude stared at the woman's fingers clawing at the stained boards, and heard a man snarl something ugly and violent behind her. The fingers vanished, and Gertrude followed, feet bare and silent and fast.

From the landing she could see Emma. She was halfway

down the stairs, pinned to the wall and clawing at the man's hand on her throat. Her eyes darted to Gertrude, and she shook her head minutely, the message clear. *Don't. He'll kill you too.*

Gertrude nodded understanding, then spun her scythe with an oddly brutal elegance. It whispered through the air, sharp enough to sever a soul from the world, and she brought the blade to a halt resting against the man's throat. He froze.

"Put her down," she said pleasantly.

The man released Emma and she skittered away, wide eyes fixed on Gertrude.

"Turn around." Gertrude didn't move the scythe, so he turned in the hook of it, his face twisted with fury.

"You—" he began, and she tutted.

"I have no interest in what you have to say. You can go quietly, or I can reap you. Your choice."

The man hissed something wordless, and she let the scythe drift across the skin at the back of his neck, raining severed hair across his collar, blood beading on the skin.

"No," she said, her voice mild.

After a moment he said carefully, "I'll go."

"There we are, then." She dropped the scythe away and stood watching him, her face hidden in the depths of her hood. "Run along."

He took a wary step across the landing, then turned back to spit at Emma. She flinched as if he'd thrown a punch, and he glared at her, then started down the stairs. Gertrude watched him go, thinking that he'd be back. He was the sort of person who would convince himself she hadn't scared him, that he'd just let her *think* she had, that he'd left of his own free will to wait for a better time. She sighed. She couldn't kill him. Reapers don't kill people. They merely hold the door.

So she just held a hand out to Emma and helped her to her feet.

"Are you alright?"

"What … is that?" Emma asked, and for a moment Gertrude thought she meant the scythe, which seemed fairly self-explanatory. Then she heard a joyous, hairball-hacking cough, and she spun around to see the ghoulets pouring down the stairs and across the landing, teeth bared and legs flailing wildly. One lost her balance and tumbled into her siblings, setting up an avalanche of ungainly limbs and snapping mouths and hungry bellies.

"Oh dear," Gertrude said, without any great concern, as the man on the stairs below them shrieked. "*Bad* ghoulets."

Hungry ghoulets are terribly efficient, and the man didn't manage more than the one scream. Clearing up the blood splatters took longer, but it was done before dawn, and Gertrude personally thought the most suspicious thing was how clean the hallway actually was now. She made Emma another hot lemon and honey, and watched her top it with a generous glug of brandy that she'd brought up from her own apartment. The sated ghoulets were sleeping in a pile-up of pale fur and bulging bellies in the middle of the floor.

"So you're stuck with them until they grow up."

"Yes."

"And become ghouls."

"Yes."

Emma pressed the ice pack against her cheek again. "And you still have to go out and reap souls."

"If the system fails, yes." Gertrude had pushed her hood back – it seemed a bit pointless keeping it up now – and her hair hung flat and pale against her hollow cheeks.

"This is so ... *goth*," Emma said.

"What?"

"Just – scythes, and ghouls, and grave dirt in the tub."

"Well, I can't help that," Gertrude said. "We've been doing it longer than them, anyway."

Emma put the ice pack down and stared at the lemon drizzle cake, pale golden and soft as clouds. "And you're getting compensation because no one knows how long till the ghoul situation gets sorted out."

"Yes. Did you get hit quite hard on the head? Only you keep repeating things."

"Quite hard, yes. But I also have an idea."

"An idea?" Gertrude said doubtfully.

"Yes. Listen."

Gertrude listened.

"REAPER LEEDS? Please hold for GR Yorkshire."

Gertrude stared at the secretary. "Ethel, you're right in front of me. *He's* right in front of me."

"Oh. Yes. Right. I'm not very good in person."

Gertrude patted the secretary's shoulder, feeling bones

shift beneath her robe. "Never mind. Come in. Come in, sir."

"Reaper Leeds – wonderful to see you again!"

"Yes, sir." Wonderful. It had been a few hundred years since the one and only time they'd met in person, and it had been strictly business. Only Grim Reapers can reap those who become reapers. She had been given a choice, of course, but when it came down to reaping or being reaped – well. Not many reapers said no.

"So, explain this place to me again," GR Yorkshire said.

They'd come in the back door, and Gertrude led them past the office and the storeroom to one side, her tidy kitchen and the stairs up to the apartment on the other. It was small, but that was okay. It didn't need to be big.

"It's a cafe," she said.

"A ghoulet cafe."

"*The* ghoulet cafe." She couldn't help feeling a thrill of pride as she said it. "*Dead Good Cafe*. Coffee, cake, and ghoulets."

GR Yorkshire frowned and stopped in the doorway as the cafe opened up before him. The windows were draped with heavy layers of curtains in shades of purple and grey, and the walls were rendered in rough stone. The chairs and sofas were low and soft, and more heavy curtains and decorative hangings turned clusters of tables into semi-private alcoves. Red and orange lamps lit the room in a dim glow, candles burning on the tables. Music pulsed and groaned around them, and most of the customers had a clear preference for black clothes and piercings. Ghoulets snored among the stacked cushions, or accepted snacks from the clientele, and a few were having a wrestling match in a clear patch of floor.

He stopped short. "You have ghoulets and humans in here together."

"Yes, sir. Hiding in plain sight, sir."

"But—"

"Cat cafes are very popular these days, sir. No one sees the ghoulets for what they are."

"But—"

"And you did want a solution to the ghoulet problem, sir."

"Yes, but—"

"Imagine if GR Lancashire saw this," the secretary said in a wondering voice. "Making an *asset* out of ghoulets!"

Gertrude grinned. "My thoughts exactly, Secretary Reaper."

"Well, yes, but—"

A woman in a brightly coloured sundress hurried to meet them. She should have looked out of place in the gloom, but she had bones sticking out of the pocket of her apron and a tray of coffee mugs in one hand. "Hello! Mister Grim Reaper, sir. I'm Emma."

"Emma?" GR Yorkshire said weakly, as she shook his hand enthusiastically.

"My human business partner, sir," Gertrude said. "And friend."

"But—"

"Never mind Lancashire – *Grim UK* will be so impressed," the secretary said. "Talk about moving with the times! Gertrude – I mean, Reaper Leeds, this is setting the standard!"

"Why, thank you. What do you think, sir?"

GR Yorkshire heaved a sigh that blew out two candles and made a couple sitting at a table nearby shiver in alarm. "I wish I could still drink whisky," he said, a little sadly, and Gertrude patted his arm.

"I'll get you a glass, sir. The smell's still the same."

She led him across the Turkish rugs and showed him to a coffin-shaped table. He sat down, watching the couple drinking cocktails from skulls.

"How come they don't leak?" he asked.

Gertrude followed his gaze, but Emma answered before she could.

"Oh, they're fake, sir," she said. "If enough things are fake, no one notices the things that are real." She plucked a bone from between the sofa cushions and flicked it to a ghoulet, who caught it and crunched it down eagerly.

"Oh." GR Yorkshire said. "Well. Always good to have some human insight, I guess." He watched a woman with a top hat crowning her extravagantly green hair stoop to rub a ghoulet's belly. It wriggled and grunted in delight, and he shook his head. "Gods know, I don't understand them."

"We don't understand ourselves," Emma said. "But everyone knows you can't ever go wrong with good cake." And she smiled up at Gertrude, who smiled her bony smile back.

That, at least, was a truth that held for both the living and the not-technically-so, and everyone in between.

You Can Get Anything at the Market

Sometimes I have reasons for stories.
Sometimes I don't.
This is definitely a don't.
Although I do believe in politeness even with cold callers – unless they're trying to scam people. In which case I say all sorts of nasty tricks are permissible.

"Speak English," Gareth demanded, his knuckles white on the phone as he held it out in front of him.

"Sorry, sir," the person on the other end said, a little fuzzy through the speakerphone function. "I will speak more clearly. My records indicate you were involved in a vehicle accident that wasn't your fault—"

"Can't understand a word you're saying," Gareth said, with some satisfaction. "Where're you calling from? Bangladesh?"

"Glasgow. Were you involved in such an accident?"

"*Glasgow?* Likely story. If you want to talk to me, you'll have to find someone who can speak English. Where's your manager?"

"If you'll just let me adjust my headset, sir, I can—"

"No, forget it. If you want to talk to me, get someone English to call me next time." And he hit disconnect, then turned around to grin at his wife. "That'll teach them."

"I'm sure it will, dear," she said, tugging a little more wool free of the skein.

"If you're trying to scam someone, you should at least have the decency to do it in your own country."

"I'm sure you're right, dear." She personally thought the caller *had* sounded Scottish. But she supposed that was still another country, if not the sort Gareth meant.

"The cheek of it! And as if I've had a car accident. *As if.*" He considered it for a moment. "You haven't, have you, Lou?"

"No, dear," she said, holding her knitting up and frowning at it. She'd missed a stitch somewhere, and now everything was going a little wonky.

"It's bad enough that I can't even call the bank without being put through to Bombay or somewhere."

Louise wondered if that meant he preferred the scammers to the bank. He certainly seemed to relish telling them all how wrong they were. "I think it's Mumbai now," she said, mostly to her knitting.

"Can't they find people in this country to do the job?"

Louise didn't answer. It wasn't really a question, after all.

The phone was ringing. Ringing, ringing, ringing, insistent and shrill. Louise sat up in bed and looked at her own phone, dark beside the bed, then poked Gareth.

"Gareth. *Gareth*. Is that your phone?"

He grunted and rolled over, slapping at the bedside lamp. It flooded the room with soft light, making Louise squint, and he pawed his phone off the bedside table. "It's not me. It must be the landline."

Louise touched her mouth with one hand, her stomach suddenly tight. A call at this hour could never be good news. She swung her legs out of bed and pattered out into the upstairs hall, hurrying down the stairs so fast that she almost slipped in her bare feet. She grabbed the handrail to steady herself, her heart going too fast. It wouldn't help anyone if she fell.

The phone was still ringing when she rushed into the kitchen, cursing herself for getting rid of the extra phone upstairs. But no one ever used the landline anymore. It was all mobiles. She grabbed the phone out of its cradle and pressed it to her ear just as there was the *clunk* of disconnection.

"Oh, no," she whispered, and stared at her reflection in the window over the sink, a slim woman verging into skinny as the years ate at her edges, her hair flat from sleep. How did one find the number from a missed call? There was something you dialled. Three? No, there were more digits, but between her sleep-befuddled mind and a rising panic that Something Bad had happened, she couldn't think of it.

She pressed the cordless phone to her chest and hurried upstairs.

The light was out in the bedroom, and she had to grope her way to the bed. “Gareth,” she hissed. “Gareth?”

“What?” he demanded, his voice thick with sleep.

“I missed the call. What’s the number to call back?”

“Leave it, Lou. It’ll just be some scam call again.”

“At this hour?”

“Yes. Go to sleep.”

Louise considered it. Maybe he was right. She *wanted* him to be right. And if was urgent, they’d call back, wouldn’t they?

She set the phone on the bedside table and slipped back into bed, pulling the covers up to her chin. She lay there staring at the ceiling, the old beams barely visible in the dark. Staring, and waiting.

SHE WAS FAIRLY sure she’d only just fallen asleep when the phone rang again, but there was enough early light seeping around the windows to lend the room soft outlines. She sat bolt upright, pawing for the handset, while it *brinnng-brinnng*-ed around the room wildly. She didn’t recognise the ringtone. It must’ve reset itself to something that sounded strangely like the rotary phones she remembered from her youth.

She was fumbling to answer it when Gareth snatched it off her and hit answer, then immediately put it on speaker. She stared at him as he bellowed, “Hello?”

There was no response, and he glared at the phone as if he could stare down the person on the other end.

"Hello? Who is this?"

Still nothing.

"Answer me!" he shouted, loudly enough that the cat, who'd come to the door to see what the commotion was, put her ears back and stalked away again.

"I'm reporting this number," Gareth announced, and hung up, then handed the phone back to Louise. "See? Scam calls. You've got to be firm with them."

"I suppose so," she said, and put the phone back on her bedside table, wiping her hands on the duvet cover as Gareth lay back down and promptly started snoring. She listened to him for a bit then went to make a cup of tea and feed the cat. Her hands still felt oddly greasy.

Brinnng-brinnng. Brinnng-brinnng.

Louise froze, a biscuit halfway to her mouth.

Brinnng-brinnng.

It was coming from upstairs. She'd left the phone on the bedside table.

Brinnng-brinnng.

A thud, probably Gareth's feet on the floor.

Bri—

"Hello?" His voice reverberated through the floor. "Who is this? How dare you harass us? I'll have you up for stalking!"

There was a brief silence – too brief for anyone to

answer, so he was probably just waiting to see if anyone would.

"I'm recording this! I'm giving it to the police, or ... or Interpol! They'll dig you out of your little hellhole in Delhi or wherever you are!"

There was another pause, then the thuds that indicated Gareth was on his way to the bathroom, and Louise ate her biscuit quickly, brushing the crumbs off the kitchen bar and making sure she'd put the biscuit tin away before she put the kettle back on.

He emerged in the kitchen still flushed with indignation, the phone grasped in one big hand. "Did you hear that, Lou? They called again!"

"Oh dear," she said, sliding a mug of tea in front of him.

"And they didn't even *say* anything. They just sat there *breathing*."

"Oh." She wrinkled her nose.

"I'm going to report them. I'll get them arrested. Or fired, at least."

"Is that really ..." She trailed off as he glared at her over his mug. "I mean, they're just doing their job, aren't they?"

"Calling people in the middle of the night?"

"Well, no. But it might have been a mistake, mightn't it?"

"Just like it's a *mistake* that they call us right as we sit down to dinner every night? Just like it's a *mistake* that none of them can even speak English properly, and it gets people all confused?"

"No, dear," she said, swallowing her sigh. She didn't think *confused* was at all the right term for what Gareth was, but there was no use arguing. There never was. Not for the first time, she wished he had been one of those people who just never retired, but worked right up till the end. Life would be a lot more peaceful. And then, with a stab of guilt, she said, "Would you like a poached egg?"

Gareth was poking at the phone, frowning. *"Hmm?"*

"A poached egg, dear."

He turned the frown on her as he put the phone to his ear. "It's not the weekend."

"Yes. Of course." She looked around the kitchen, and decided she'd have to go shopping today. Possibly for a while.

"Lou, what's this number?" Gareth asked, holding out a piece of paper he'd just scrawled something on.

She squinted at it, then put her glasses on so she could see better. "It's our number, dear."

His frown deepened. "It can't be. I called 1471, and they're meant to give you the last number that dialled in if it's not withheld."

"Maybe your own number comes up if the actual one's withheld."

"Don't be ridiculous. Why would it do that?"

She spread her hands in defeat. "I'm going to take a shower."

"What about the egg?"

"It's not the weekend," she said, and headed for the stairs before he could say anything else. She was tired, and not just from the broken sleep. She needed a day out.

The phone was ringing again by the time she got upstairs, but she just turned the shower on to drown it.

"STOP CALLING!" Gareth was shouting down the phone as she came back downstairs, already with her jacket on. He jabbed the disconnect button and set the handset back down on the bar. His sparse hair was a little wild at the back, as if he'd been rubbing his hands through it.

"Still?" she asked, taking her bag from behind the door.

"Yes! And still no one *says* anything!" He blinked at her. "Where are you going?"

"Town."

He looked at the clock on the microwave. "But it's only eight thirty."

"The market's on today. It's best to be early, otherwise it's all picked over."

"Oh." He watched her take her keys from the hook on the wall, then said, "Will you be back for lunch?"

"Maybe. I usually meet Fi for lunch on Wednesday, though."

"Oh," he said again, then straightened his shoulders. "Well, I'll get this sorted out while you're gone. Don't you worry."

"I won't, dear," she said, and kissed him on the cheek on the way to the door. The phone was ringing as she closed it behind her, and for a moment she considered telling him just to unplug it from the wall, but he'd only say they shouldn't have to. Which was true enough, but not the real reason. She beeped the car open and wondered if he'd consider taking up golf, or model trains or something.

Although she supposed there was less opportunity for shouting with those.

Her phone rang while she was eyeing up the aubergines, wondering if she could chop them small enough that Gareth wouldn't be able to tell they were in a shepherd's pie. And also weighing that against the fact that she was quite sure that there would be road miles on them, if not air miles, which seemed to negate the purpose of buying at the market. She fished the phone out of her bag, swallowed a sigh, and stepped away from the stall to answer.

"Yes, dear."

"Have you had any calls on your mobile?" he demanded.

"This is the first one."

"They've started calling my mobile!"

"Oh dear."

"And they're still not *saying* anything!"

"So how do you know it's the same ones?"

"Who else would it be?"

Louise rubbed the soft skin between her eyes. "Quite. Maybe you should unplug the home phone and leave your mobile off for a while. I'm sure they'll get bored soon."

"They're *my* phones! I want to use them!"

"Alright, dear. I'm in the middle of paying. I have to go."

"Why did you answer in the middle of paying? That's very rude, you know."

"I thought it might be urgent," she said, and hung up, looking around the clutter of little stalls in the marketplace. She'd suddenly lost all desire to keep shopping. She slipped the phone back into her bag and headed for her favourite coffeeshop instead, hoping they had carrot cake today. She'd feel better after some carrot cake.

THE PHONE RANG AGAIN as she was lifting the first bite of cake to her mouth, and she looked at the display for a moment, then ignored it, savouring the hit of rich, faintly tart icing against the warm spices of the cake itself. She closed her eyes, barely managing not to *mmm* out loud, then sighed as the phone rang again. She picked it up and answered.

"Yes, dear."

"They finally spoke!"

"Did they?"

"Yes! Definitely foreign. Not Indian, though. Maybe Romanian, or somewhere over there."

"Not Scottish?"

"Scottish? Don't be silly. They're always foreign."

"Of course." She took another forkful of cake. "What did they say?"

"That was the weird bit. They just kept repeating what I said."

"That *is* weird."

"They're mocking me. Trying to get to me. But I've figured out how to record them. I—" He was cut off by the *brinnng-brinnng* of the landline, raucous even over the phone, and Louise shivered. It was hungry sound, insistent and demanding. "I'll call you back," Gareth said, and the line went dead.

Louise set her fork down and picked up her mug, frowning faintly. He wouldn't call the police yet, she was sure. He was too excited about it all, and if he was trying to record them, he'd definitely do that before reporting the calls to anyone. There was time. She glanced at her watch and decided she wouldn't call Fi about lunch. She'd go to the supermarket and get some nice lamb for dinner, then go home and see what was happening. Gareth could manage until then.

Gareth called again while she was in the supermarket, standing in front of the baked beans and trying to remember if she had any left in the pantry.

"Yes, dear," she said.

"They're talking to me!"

"Weren't they doing that before?"

"No, I told you – they just kept repeating what I said."

"Oh. I see. So what are they saying? Have you asked them why they keep calling?"

"Yes. But they just keep telling me to speak English!"

Lou pressed her fingertips to the corner of her mouth to contain a smile. "Do they?"

"Yes! It's so rude. And—" *Brinnng-brinnng.* "*Dammit!* They're calling again! They just won't stop!"

"You could unplug the phone, dear."

"But they're calling my mobile, too," he said, raising his voice over the sound of the ringing phone, which was threatening to overwhelm the speaker. "They're calling it now!"

"Oh dear."

"I have to—" He broke off, and she heard the ringing stop, then Gareth shouting, "Hello? *Hello?*" before the phone went dead.

She put her mobile back in her bag and picked up a can of beans, then shrugged and bought a four-pack. One could never have too many baked beans.

She made it almost to the checkouts before her phone went again, and she answered it with a sigh.

"Yes, dear?"

"Lou?" There was an unfamiliar quietness to his tones, and he sounded very far away, as if he were standing too far from the phone. She wished he wouldn't use speaker all the time. She hated hearing her own echo.

"Are you alright, dear?"

"They won't stop calling," he said, and there was an odd hollowness to his voice.

She frowned. "Are you in the bathroom?"

"Yes. It's too loud downstairs. The phone just keeps ringing."

"Well, *unplug it.*"

"I did," he said, and she examined a display of new season tulips.

"You can't have. It can't ring if it's unplugged."

"But it *is.*" And now she recognised the quiet in his voice. It was an almost-tears quiet, and she hadn't heard it since that awful phone call a year or so ago, the one about his brother.

"Gareth?" she said gently. "Why don't you go out into the garden? I'll be home soon. I'm almost done shopping."

"But they won't stop *calling.* And they keep saying I've been in an accident, or that I need insurance for my white goods, or that HMRC has opened a tax case against me, or that someone has my NHS number."

"The lawn could really do with a trim, dear. Leave your mobile inside."

"But why won't they *stop?*"

"I'm sure I don't know. But could you give the hedge a bit of a clip, too? It's already getting away on us, and it's only April."

"The hedge?" he asked, and dimly, she could hear the phone ringing in the background.

"Yes, dear."

"Okay." She could hear him gathering himself, and a moment later his voice came back stronger. "Yes. Can't have it getting out of hand like that Howard's down the road. Have you seen it?"

"It's most unruly," Louise said.

"It's a disgrace!"

"Quite," she said, and waited until he'd hung up before she picked up a bunch of the tulips and headed for the checkouts. She quite liked tulips. They were a rather peaceful sort of flower.

Both phones were ringing when she carried the shopping bags into the house and closed the door behind her. The cacophony of it rattled around the kitchen, screeching and insistent, and through the big glass panels of the conservatory she could see Gareth marching up and down with the mower, ear protectors clamped over his ears. She set the bags down next to the fridge and picked up the house phone.

"Stop," she said, and the mobile fell silent immediately,

the abrupt quiet rushing around her and making her ears ring.

There was no response for a moment, then a small voice said, a little gleefully, "I can't understand you at all."

"This is done," she said firmly, and there was pause, during which she could hear a faint whistling sound, like wind in high, far places. She looked at the phone base, which was unplugged from both the power and the phone line itself, then poked Gareth's mobile. It was off, the battery lying next to it on the breakfast bar.

"You have tax?" the small voice offered. "We can help protect your ... car accident from the NHS."

"Now you're not even making sense," she said, and took a small tin from behind the flour, where Gareth would never go. She opened it, revealing a half-smoked packet of cigarettes and a lighter (which she hadn't had out since Christmas a year ago, but it comforted her to know they were there, stale as they were), a couple of fancy chocolate truffles, and a small brown envelope with rough edges. She took it and the lighter to the sink, cradling the phone between her shoulder and her ear.

"We trade in discomfort," the voice said, suddenly so close and clear that she jumped. It was smooth and unaccented, and something in it raised the hair at the back of her neck. It was a whisper in the ear in the night. "We trade in *uncertainty*."

"And you've done very well," she said.

"We sell hurt and buy pain."

"You must do a roaring trade," she said, flicking the lighter a couple of times unsuccessfully, then shaking it. There was still gas in it. She could see it.

"We can be transferred. Reused. Offered again."

"Thank you, but no," she said, finally getting the lighter going.

"We are tireless. We are *hungry*."

She shivered, and put the envelope to the flame. "How unpleasant for you."

"We—" The voice broke off, then said, the words soft and seductive. "We can finish the job."

The corners of the envelope had caught, curling and charring and giving off a sickly green flame. Louise dropped it into the sink. "No thank you," she said.

"But he is not broken. Not yet."

"I never wanted that," she replied, and hung up just as the voice started screaming. It still rang on the edges of her hearing, though, lingering until the envelope had crumpled to ash, which she washed down the sink. "I never wanted anything *broken*," she told the empty kitchen. "Just different."

"Lou?" Gareth called from the back door, and she peered into the utility to look at him. He was standing on the outside mat in grass-encrusted wellies, his ear protectors still on. "Are you okay? Has it stopped?"

She gestured to him to take the ear protectors off. "They're not ringing now, dear. I'm sure they've just got bored."

He pulled the ear protectors off but clutched them in both hands, as if ready to put them back on any moment. "I hope you're right."

"I'm quite sure I am, dear." She turned to go back into the kitchen, and stopped as he spoke again.

"I don't suppose ... could you make me a cup of tea, please?"

She looked at him for a moment, then smiled. "Of course. Would you like a biscuit, too? I got some nice ones at the market."

"Oh, yes please." He gave her a very small smile, then said, "You can get anything at that market, can't you?"

She glanced at the sink. "You wouldn't even believe it."

And then she went to make the tea and open the biscuits, and eventually to plug the phone back in, wondering how long it would last this time. Before the rage and frustration all bubbled up again, with a new target or the same old ones, and she had to go back to the market, and to the little stall that was only ever there when she needed it to be, or that she could only *see* when she needed to. The little stall that sold strange things in small envelopes, things that had to be scattered in the tea to bind the charm, and burned to release it.

Charms that promised to change things, although they themselves were different every time. Different, and *sneaky*. She didn't trust them. The nightmares and insomnia after she'd grown tired of him blustering about immigrants had lasted far longer than the charm had. The bank error that had lost all their money (and almost the house), after his complaints about the homeless and disenfranchised, had been slow to be corrected. And now that tearful note to his voice after the phone calls. His hesitancy now.

No, she didn't trust the charms, and she didn't like them. But now she'd found them, she didn't know how to stop, either. Because they worked. And she didn't know how else she could cope with him, other than to leave. And she didn't want to do that, for reasons she wasn't even entirely sure about herself.

Or maybe she was, she thought, as Gareth traipsed inside in his socks and sat staring at his dismantled phone. Maybe she was too old to leave, not for her, but for him.

Which was no real reason, but it was her choice.

Just as it was her choice to break the charm before it went too far. Which she could always do, couldn't she? She always had, anyway.

We can break him.

She shivered in an odd mix of horror and delight, and put a plate of biscuits in front of him.

"Howard's hedge is looking worse than ever," he announced, with some satisfaction. "I'm going to have to have words."

"Must you?" she asked, pouring out the tea.

"Someone has to."

She glanced at her bag, where a new envelope nestled inside one of the inner pockets. She didn't need it yet, but she would.

Learning was a lifelong endeavour, after all.

The Pie of Hate

*I'm not really a story prompt person. For some reason they always feel a little constrictive, like someone shoving an idea in front of you and yelling, "Write this **now!**"*
*And pretty much the best way to ensure I **won't** do something is to tell me I must do it immediately. In a creative sense, I mean. Obviously if you tell me I must vacate the area immediately because there's a sea serpent on the loose, I'll get my shoes on and retreat to a good vantage point from which to watch sea serpent shenanigans.*
But every now and then Twitter and its many story prompt bots throw up something that catches my imagination. In this case:
Somewhere, a sous-chef bakes a pie of hate.
Almost as good as sea serpents, that.

"And I need it by three p.m."

Of course you do, Simone thought, and spotted the dog

nosing around the sack of potatoes the kitchen porter was peeling. Today's outfit involved a lot of pink feathers and rhinestones. The dog seemed to feel her scrutiny and looked up, baring its teeth, then lifted a leg to wee against the sack. Simone swatted a potato off the bench, landing it close enough to the dog to make it jump away, yipping anxiously and widdling on the floor as it went.

."Careful!" Mrs A snapped. "You almost dropped that on Fabien!"

Oh, if only. The dog was trying to bite the porter's leg now. It shouldn't even be in here. If they got inspected— her train of thought was broken by Mrs A snapping her fingers close enough to Simone's nose that she felt the wind of the movement.

"Are you even *listening?* My God – just the best and the brightest in here, aren't you?"

Simone wiped sweat from her face with her forearm. "Mrs A, I can make you a pie, but we're getting ready for lunch right now. Having it done for three's going to be difficult."

"I didn't ask your opinion on it. I told you what I wanted. If you're not capable, I'm sure we can hire someone who is."

For a brief, satisfying moment, Simone considered just saying, *okay,* switching her burners off, and walking out. But she'd come here for the experience of working under a head chef whose talent was only surpassed by his ability to be absent the majority of the time, and she wasn't going to let a pie spoil things. She stretched her face into something that felt like a smile. "I will make sure you have a pie by three p.m."

"I want *you* to make it. Everyone knows you make the best pastry."

Simone bit back a sigh. This was *not* on the job description. She had the whole damn kitchen to run, a busy Saturday lunch and dinner ahead, and when the head chef did finally turn up he'd spend most of his time swanning around tasting things and doing his best Gordon Ramsey impression without ever actually getting his hands dirty. She wasn't sure she'd actually learned anything from him yet, other than the (admittedly excellent) dishes he came up with – although she wasn't sure when he created them, as she'd never seen him touch a pan in the kitchen. Mostly he spent his time posing for photos with the diners and charming Mrs A, which included indulging her bonkers requests. Last week Simone had been tasked with putting together a five-course menu for a bloody doggy dinner party at the same time as getting Sunday lunch out.

Thank God for Zack. The sous-chef had not only managed to get all his people desserts done, but he'd also made something bizarrely beautiful and dog-friendly for their canine guests, too. She wondered if he was ahead enough to take on some of her prep again. Because he was an amazing pastry chef, but she still made better pastry than him. She made better pastry than any chef she'd ever encountered, which was just a simple fact. One of the top pastry chefs in London had told her she had magic fingers when she'd worked with him briefly. He'd then tried to demonstrate his own magic fingers, and she'd emptied a bowl of lemon tart filling over his head before walking out. Really, considering some of the places she'd worked, doggy dinner parties weren't that bad.

"Alright," she said now. "Any specific meat, or just meat?"

Mrs A unfolded a flyer and peered at it. "It doesn't say. Just *savoury pie competition.*"

Simone wasn't surprised that Mrs A wanted a pie that she could pass off as her own, but she was at least a little surprised that the hall's owner wanted to enter a Women's Institute competition. This must be her next big thing – Mrs A, the domestic goddess, impressing all the local village ladies. Not that anyone would believe for a minute that she'd actually made the pie herself, but that was beside the point. She could go and bestow the largess of her presence on the village fête that was already underway in the grounds. Simone had no objections to Mrs A being out of the restaurant for the day. But she could have given them a little warning. Aloud, she just said, "I'll see what we've got that looks the best."

"Good." Mrs A spun on her heel. "Fabien? *Fa*bien!" She walked off, screeching for the dog. Simone pinched the bridge of her nose, wondering if it was too early for a drink.

LUNCH HAD BEGUN. The kitchen roared with clattering plates and hissing pans, with swearing and laughter and the growl of extractors. It looked like chaos from the outside, gas burners roaring and chefs swinging past each other in some precarious choreography, someone shouting for service, someone singing off-key, someone else roaring for another pan, dammit, who took his bloody pan? To Simone, it was both familiar and hectically beautiful, and she glanced at the clock on the wall reluctantly as she dropped salmon in a pan to sear and pivoted back to plate up the potatoes.

"Zack!" she called. "Cover me? I need to get this damn pie done."

"Of course, *chérie!*" he said, flinging oil into a pan with an exaggerated flourish. He liked to affect some sort of weird French accent, but Simone thought he was actually from Birmingham. The accent slipped quite badly after a few beers. "Tell me how you want me."

"Oh, hilarious." She slapped his bum with her spatula as she passed him. "Don't let the heat ruin your hair."

She was working butter into pastry flour, her eyes on the front line, shouting to the porter to bring another tray of garnish through, or to clean that spill before someone slipped, and wondering if the head chef planned to show, when the dog came into the kitchen with his ridiculous strut.

"*Goddammit!* Get that bloody dog out of here!" she bellowed, hands thick with dough. *"Freddy!"*

The porter spun toward her shout, his eyes wide with alarm, and the plates stacked in his arms toppled out of his grip with the slow-motion inevitability of a slinky let loose on the stairs. *"Nooo—!"*

"Freddy, dammit!"

The dog yipped, the sound almost lost in the calamitous explosion of plates shattering on tile, and bolted down the front line, tail tucked between his skinny legs. Zack yelped, aimed a foot at the dog, slipped on a half-squashed chip and lurched into the stove, catching the handle of pot and launching *jus* across the pass. A waitress squeaked and ducked, barely avoiding the sauce. Albert dropped his pan and lunged after the dog, who was cowering in the corner by the fridges, shaking so hard his rhinestones were clattering. He saw Albert coming, gave a miserable howl, and bolted again, leaving Albert sprawling to his knees behind him. Freddy dropped into a crouch, arms out like a goalie while the older man cursed creatively from the floor and Zack tried to calm the waitress. It was only her first week, and she had already regarded the chefs with something close to terror before having *jus* flung at her.

"Get. That. Dog!" Simone didn't often shout, but she was almost screaming now. Fabien feinted left. Freddy flung himself forward, his grunt turning to a yelp of pain as he belly-flopped amid the shattered plates. Albert tried another grab, slipped on a shard of soup bowl, and landed on his back as Zack came bounding through the carnage, whipping a tea towel like a lasso. Simone wasn't at all sure what he thought that was going to accomplish, and as Fabien sprinted for the back door she jumped from behind her counter and scooped him off the ground in a shower of half-made pastry. He wriggled and snapped, whimpering in fright, and she trapped him against her chest. "Stop it, you little git, or I'll shove you in the freezer," she told him. He stopped wriggling and stared at her in round-eyed fright. Although he usually looked like that.

Someone said hesitantly from the pass, "Check on?"

No one moved. Albert sat up, rubbing the back of his head. He'd hit it on the fridge. Freddy picked a splinter from his palm. Zack offered Albert his hand. Simone shook her head at them all.

"Check on!" she shouted. "Move, move!"

There was a sudden scramble of activity, and she glared at the dog. "This is all your fault." He wagged his tail hesitantly, and started licking buttery flour off her hands. "Stop that!" He stopped, and she became aware that there was … a smell. She closed her eyes. Oh, no. No. Horrible bloody animal. Horrible bloody *scared* animal. "Freddy," she said, "Has … is there …" she trailed off, and the young porter looked at her quizzically, broom in hand. Then he looked at her apron, and his eyes widened.

"Oh. Oh, Si, the … he … the dog …"

"I thought so." She tightened her grip on the creature and headed for the pantry. "I'm going to go and change. And put this bloody creature out of the way somewhere."

By the time she got back into the kitchen, smelling marginally less of dog by-products, the head chef was standing over her pastry bowl, frowning at it like it was personally insulting him. He looked up as she approached the bench.

"Coffee break, Simone?"

"No, chef."

"Calling home to Mum?"

"No, chef." She kept her face still, biting down on the words she wanted to say. No point getting fired before she quit.

"Not that busy, are we? Two chefs fine to run the whole service?"

Well, they kind of have to, since I'm not allowed to say no to making a bloody pie for Mrs A. "No, chef."

"Huh. Better get back to it then, hadn't you?" He swept out of the kitchen, whites immaculate, and Zack made an extravagantly rude gesture at his retreating back. Simone grinned.

"You guys alright? Need anything?"

"We're on it," Zack said. "Get your pretty little tart made, you tart."

Albert grunted something that might have been amusement or might have been more swearing, and Simone went back to her pastry, stopping to check Freddy. He'd managed to convince the pretty new waitress to patch up his hands, and was singing something tuneless to himself as he went back to the sink. All back to situation normal, then.

"HAS ANYONE SEEN FABIEN?" Mrs A demanded. She stood with her hands on her hips, blocking the pass and scowling at Albert, who scowled back and grumbled something under his breath.

"Mrs A?" Simone said, leaving the pan of braising meat and ushering the woman out of the way. "Is everything alright?"

"Fabien was meant to be with my useless assistant," the woman said, and Simone felt a pang of sympathy for the assistant. "But the silly boy went and let him out of the office. I thought he might have come down here."

"*Mmm*, no," Simone said. "Probably a bit busy for Fabien down here, anyway."

"He does like it, though. I imagine he's looking for scraps. You don't feed him, do you? He has a strictly monitored macrobiotic diet."

"No, we don't. But we'll keep an eye out for him."

"Well. Do that. And how about that pie?"

"Just doing the meat now, Mrs A. It'll be finished in time."

"I should think so, too." She crossed to the stove, almost sending Zack crashing into the counter as he tried to avoid her, hot pan raised at eye level and spitting on his hands. "Watch where you're going," she snapped at him, and leaned over Simone's pan, sniffing the rich dank aroma of the cooking meat. Zack swore soundlessly at her back and shot a furious look at Simone. She gave him a *what can I do* shrug.

"Well. It smells acceptable," Mrs A said, and straightened up, smoothing the flat front of her dress. "Just make sure it's done in time."

"Will do," Simone said, and watched the woman walk past the stoves and out of the door into the dining room.

"So what're you playing at?" Zack demanded. Lunch was over, clean down and dinner prep under way, the pie collected and borne off, exquisitely golden and still softly steaming, to be judged. "Where's the mutt?"

"Out of the way," Simone said, and checked the prep list. "Have you got the chocolate fondants done?"

"*Oui, chérie* – out of the way how?"

"Just out of the way so he doesn't come crashing through in the middle of damn service again, okay? What are you, the dog police?"

"No, but I don't want *her* in here in the middle of service again, either."

Simone patted his cheek. "It'll be okay, poppet. Now get your faux-French bottom into pastry and do the meringues."

"That's harassment, that is." But he went to get the eggs from the pantry anyway, and she hoped she'd pushed the dog's sparkly pink costume deep enough into the rubbish. She didn't want that being spotted.

THE FINAL JUDGING of the savoury pies was done by the Women's Institute chair and a local (and painfully minor) celebrity. He'd enjoyed the gin tasting quite a lot, and was trying to impress some of the younger W.I. members with his recollections of being disqualified in the first round of *Stars In Their Eyes*. He'd performed a Sonny and Cher number, but his Cher had dropped out, so he'd elected to perform both parts, donning and removing a wig frantically through the whole thing. It was, one of the women muttered to another as they watched him butcher a bacon and egg pie, a shame that they'd bothered with the whole celebrity thing. They'd have been better off getting the local pub's Newfoundland to judge. He'd been in the newspaper too. Her friend smothered a chuckle and told her to behave herself. She was just looking for an excuse for when her spinach and feta pie didn't win.

Dierdre, the Women's Institute chair, stopped in front of Mrs A and examined her pie with a critical but appreciative eye. Even cooled, the crust had a luscious golden sheen to it, and she could smell the rich scent of the meat wafting from the top. The minor celebrity joined her, grinning at Mrs A a little owlishly, and the landowner graced him with a smile. She extended one slim hand and leaned forward enough to allow him a good look at her generous cleavage.

"Mrs A," she said.

"Divine," the minor celebrity breathed, and Dierdre rolled her eyes. She had thought she was too old for eye rolling, but it turned out there was plenty that called for it at this particular fête. This pie, for one.

"Made it yourself, did you, Mrs A?" she asked, making a note on her clipboard.

"Of course, Deidre," Mrs A said stiffly. "What a question!"

Deidre examined the commercial-sized tin, and said, "What is it?"

"A ... a pie. A savoury pie."

A ripple of laughter ran across the observers, and Mrs A flushed. Deidre sighed. "What *type* of savoury pie, Mrs A?"

"Oh. Oh, of course. I ... ah ... Well. I seem to have forgotten." The laughter was louder this time.

"You seem to have forgotten?" Deidre said, and the minor celebrity talked over her.

"It looks perfectly wonderful, Mrs A. I'm not surprised you forgot – long old day, eh?" He grabbed the knife from the board and stabbed at the pie, the crust flaking and splitting generously. Mrs A gave Deidre a self-satisfied sort of smile, then turned back to the minor celebrity.

"Can I help you with that?" she breathed.

"Well, actually," he said, jiggling the knife and frowning. "I'm not sure. Are there bones in here?"

"Bones? Of course not. Don't be ridiculous."

"It's just that the knife seems to be stuck." He tugged it out, the crust pulling with it a little, then settling back.

Deidre took the knife off him. "Let me see." She jabbed it into the pie, and it sliced through the crust effortlessly. "I don't see— oh. Wait." The knife had caught on something hard, and she twisted it irritably. "Mrs A, *have* you left bones in here?"

"Oh. Well. Now you mention it, I was using this very *experimental* recipe book by a rather wonderful American chef. You won't have heard of him—"

"It's a *pie,* Mrs A. A pie does not have bones in it. Not even an experimental pie."

"Well, you *would* say that ..." she trailed off as Deidre pulled a wedge of pie up and out, bleeding thick dark gravy and chunks of tender meat, and ... something else. The something else rattled as it hit the plate, a distinctly un-bone-like sound. Mrs A leaned forward, frowning, as Dierdre poked it with the knife, teasing it out of the pie. No one spoke, and the chair of the Women's Institute hooked the offending object, lifting it aloft so it hung between them, dripping gravy.

"Is this a *joke?*" she demanded, and Mrs A made some small noise that could have been a half-swallowed scream.

They were leaning against the counters, prep done, eating pasta and drinking pint glasses of what they all would have sworn was straight lemonade when Mrs A came pounding into the kitchen and thrust the pie at Simone, her face pale. The dog collar – rather less pink and missing some diamantes – rested on top of it, some ill-thought-out crown.

"What have you done?" she hissed, her eyes tight little dots of fury. *"What did you do?"*

Simone gave her a confused look and set her bowl down, taking the pie from her. She peered at the collar. "What's this, then?"

"You know what this is! You made it!"

Zack picked the dog collar up and examined it with some wonder. "Holy hell, Simone."

"Yeah. Don't know how that happened." Simone teased a piece of meat out of the pie and popped it in her mouth, chewing with relish. "Probably shouldn't really eat it. Some of those stones are probably loose in there."

Albert leaned over, stabbed a piece of meat on his fork and ate it, grunting in approval.

Zack shrugged, took the pie from Simone, helped himself then held it out to Freddy. "Seems a shame to waste it."

"I really do apologise," Simone said to Mrs A, who was watching the pie being passed around with staring eyes, the front of her dress twisted in one hand. "I don't know how the collar got in there."

"You ..." the woman whispered.

"This is really good," Freddy said, then winced. "I think I got a diamond."

Albert huffed laughter and took a swallow from his pint.

"What's wrong with you?" Mrs A asked, in that same breathy whisper. She backed toward the door. "There's something wrong with *all* of you." She hovered at the threshold, wavering, then added, "And you're all *fired!*" It came out as a reedy sort of scream, and she hurried away, almost running.

"Really?" Freddy said uncertainly. "Like, now?"

"Nah. Get your apron on," Simone said. "Service as usual."

Zack rubbed the back of his head and looked at the dog collar. "So how exactly *did* it get in there?"

"Wouldn't you like to know."

THE HEAD CHEF swanned in with a flush in his cheeks from gin tasting at the fête, and Simone handed him her notice, effective immediately. She'd been carrying the letter around since the first week, figuring it'd come to it sooner rather than later. And while she might have been able to put up with doggy dinners a little longer, wearing the by-products of a doggy dinner was going a bit far.

The head chef blustered a little and swore a lot, and she pointed out that if he gave her a bad reference, she had the numbers of three waitresses who had quit because he felt their duties should extend beyond serving diners. She also suggested he get his baby-soft hands used to slinging pans rather quickly, as they had a full house tonight. Zack, Albert and Freddy hid their grins and kept their eyes on their plates, and as she walked out Zack mimed *call me.* She nodded – she would. Probably when she needed a good sous-chef. She headed for her car with the shouts of the head chef ringing across the car park like the shrieks of an angry bird. Yeah, she was done with this. The next kitchen was going to be *her* kitchen.

She opened her car door and looked at the little dog. "Off you go. Go find Mrs A."

The dog stared at her with his bulging eyes, wagging his tail so hard it looked like he was going to fall over.

"Come on. I have a cat that'll eat you alive. Out."

Fabien yipped happily, and rolled onto his back on the passenger seat.

She sighed. "Seriously? Wearing cute little outfits and being fed a macrobiotic diet was that bad?"

Fabien wriggled, watching her.

"They can't get me for dog murder with a venison pie, but I'm pretty sure dog theft is a real thing."

He yipped, sat up, and watched her with liquid eyes.

"God." She grabbed the dog and deposited him on the driveway, where he whined unhappily. "Shoo!"

He darted past her and jumped back into the car.

"Crap." Cars were starting to arrive, people trickling in for dinner. If she left him out here, he'd probably get run over, brainless thing that he was. And she wasn't about to take him back inside now. "Fine," she said, throwing her bag in the back and getting in. "One night, okay? I'll bring you back tomorrow."

Fabien yipped, propping his paws on the dashboard so he could see out. Simone shook her head. The cat really would eat him.

HER PHONE BINGED a text in at one a.m. Zack.

The dog's back.

"What?" She looked at Fabien, snoozing by the heater while the cat regarded him suspiciously from the back of the sofa. *What're you talking about?*

She's just marched in here with him. The assistant found him. Lucky, right?

"Lucky," Simone said, and glared at the dog. He tapped his tail anxiously against the floor, and the cat growled. "I suppose one inbred mutt looks much the same as another, do they?"

Fabien scrambled to his feet and trotted to the sofa, trying desperately to pull himself up next to her, and she groaned. Bloody quick-thinking assistants. What the hell did she do now?

The dog whined, scrabbling madly with his back legs as he tried to get up next to her. The cat unwound herself with a snarl and launched an attack that sent the dog yelping and crashing back into the coffee table. He cowered under it, trembling, then recovered himself and lunged for the cat, and they tumbled across the floor, spitting and snarling at each other. Simone jumped up and flung a cushion at them, then found herself the subject of two sets of reproachful eyes.

"Stop it," she told them. "Seriously, I do not need this."

The cat sat down and started grooming her rumpled fur. The dog pattered to her and put his paws on her bare foot, tail whipping. She rubbed her face with one hand. So she had a dog now.

She poured the last of the wine into her glass and sat on the floor, the cat and the dog separated by the no-man's land of her lap. It had been a damn good pie. And that W.I. fête was going to be the stuff of legend. All in all, yeah.

Worth it.

All Wishes Are Granted

Ah, typos. The writer's constant irritant and the editor's hunting ground. The result of clumsy fingers, overzealous autocorrects, and that distracted moment when a bird flies past and your fingers type "bird!" instead of getting on about the actual business of writing coherent sentences. They're persistent little monsters, too. This particular one withstood three beta readers and an inordinate amount of self-editing before I spotted it.

But I can't hate typos completely. I'm fairly sure Mrs Smith tucking a brain behind her ear (rather than a braid) in the first Gobbelino London story led directly to the second Gobbelino London story.

And while the book this one came from may have called for bulging muscles, the typo itself called for this story.

The woman in the layered red top was sporting the sort of fixed grin that inspires sympathy jaw aches as she forced half a head of unchopped broccoli into the Super Magic Mind-Bending Bonanza Blender. Or whatever it was called.

"Broccoli rice!" she exclaimed, jabbing at the buttons, then clutched the glass jug with both hands as the blender screamed. Her arms shook violently as she tried to keep it on the table, the copious material of her sleeves shimmying like a flamenco dancer's skirt. The camera zoomed in on the contents of the blender jug, which looked remarkably similar to the stuff that kid from *The Exorcist* redecorated her room with. The woman stopped the blender and opened the lid, displaying the contents for the camera, while her smile stretched into a rictus and Ben thought any rice that looked like that would probably have attained consciousness. He took another mouthful of vodka as the woman jammed the lid back on.

"Broccoli puree!" The blender started screaming again. The woman's upper body strength must be quite remarkable, because it definitely looked like the Super Magic whatchama was trying to make a break for it. Ben's eyelids slid to half-mast, and he tried to hike them back up again. He wasn't at all sure he was drunk enough to sleep through the night yet.

Five easy payments! the text at the bottom of the screen screamed. *Don't miss out!*

Who *bought* this stuff? How was it even worth their while, paying the grinning woman with the unmoving hair to stand there with the painfully yowling blender? How desperate must she be to do it?

And how desperate was he, sitting here watching it?

He woke with a sticky mouth, but no pounding head. Not yet. That'd come later. But he was awake, which was annoying as hell. He'd fallen asleep too soon. He picked up his glass – there was still a good inch of vodka in the bottom – and shifted position on the sofa. The broccoli woman was gone, and instead there was a slight woman with drifts of white hair and a purple ... kaftan? Was that a kaftan? He wasn't actually sure he'd ever seen a kaftan. Weirdly, she was in the same kitchen broccoli woman had been in. She'd dimmed the lights and thrown a deep red cloth over the display table, but the same blank white walls and fake, empty windows loomed behind her. Ben could see a spill of crushed broccoli on the table where the cloth didn't quite cover it, the bright green rendered grimy in the low light. The woman adjusted her hoop earrings with a hand that was so heavy with silver rings and beaded bracelets that Ben was surprised she could lift it, then she squinted at the screen. Well, the camera. Although it kind of felt like she was looking at the screen. At him.

"Dani," the woman said, and Ben realised she must be reading off an auto prompter. "Dani, are you with us?"

A text box appeared in the top right of the screen. *Yes, yes, I'm here!*

Holy hell, was she pretending to communicate with ghosts via text message? Ben giggled. Late night television could get away with anything.

"Dani, tell me your wish. All wishes will be granted, but be careful. The old saying is true."

The text box didn't respond for a moment, the cursor

flashing uneasily, white against black. It looked like something out of a '90s chatroom.

"Dani, there are others waiting."

I want my husband back.

The woman nodded, lowering her head to look at the red cloth. It had gold symbols painted on it, and it clashed horribly with her floaty purple dress. "You must use the words."

Ben suddenly imagined a gang of goblins hiding under the table, holding the woman's hubby captive while David Bowie sang at them and flourished his crop. He almost spat his drink out.

I wish my husband would come back.

The cursor flashed violently at the end of the words, and Ben shivered, the laughter dusty in his mouth. Poor woman. She was grieving, and here was this mystic faker playing with her loss like it was a damn game show. Playing with it, and charging her, no doubt.

"Shouldn't be allowed," he whispered to the empty house, and wondered if he should turn the TV off. This felt greasy, voyeuristic. But he was too awake, the house too empty. He took another gulp of vodka.

"As you wish, so it shall be," the woman on the TV said gravely, and there was no flash of light, no puff of smoke, but Ben found himself leaning forward, shoulders suddenly tense under his ears.

When? When will he come back? How? the text demanded.

"Now she asks," Ben muttered, and dug through the sofa cushions until he found the vodka bottle. It was all so painfully silly. But grief makes fools of us all.

The woman shook her head. "I can't give you a time. But he's coming. I feel him. He will be with you."

The cursor flashed a few times before it said, *As he is now, or as he was before?*

Ben shuddered, although he couldn't have said why.

"I can't say. But you wanted him back, so back he comes."

Ben thought he caught a flicker of something in the woman's voice – malice? Amusement? Or was he imagining it, half-cut as he was?

"And now we must move on," the woman said. "If you'd like to text in, the number is on the screen. Texts cost 50p each. Please make sure you have the permission of the bill payer. Only one wish per person. All wishes are granted. No responsibility is taken if you make an unsuitable wish or change your mind."

All wishes are granted. Ben swallowed hard. What would he wish for? Would he wish her back? No, not after what she'd done. And with her personal trainer, of all people. Brain the size and complexity of a pink marshmallow, but of course all six-pack and bulging muscles. No, he didn't want her back. He was angry and drunk and miserable, but even so he could see it'd only happen again. Accounting and competitive rose gardening was a hard sell for someone who preferred triathlons and skydiving. He supposed he was lucky it had lasted as long as it had. Or unlucky, considering how it had ended.

So no, he wouldn't wish her back. But maybe he could wish flat bike tyres on her. Or that muscle boy would get a ravenous appetite for pies. That'd be pretty funny.

"Scott," the woman was saying gravely, "please tell me your wish."

I want to go to Mars, to be light years away from anyone.

The woman nodded. "If this is your wish, please use the words."

I wish I was on Mars.

"As you wish, so it shall be." The woman straightened the sleeves of her kaftan while the cursor blinked in its box. "Who do we have next?"

Ben stared at the cursor, willing Scott to say something, to ask when he'd get to go to Mars, to say thank you, anything. Anything except that ominous, hungry cursor, waiting to deliver the next texter to the Goblin King.

There was nothing. Scott was gone. Not to Mars, of course not, that was impossible, but he was *gone.* Mars would be cold. Cold and suffocating and lonely in the moments before Scott died. Would his blood vessels burst out of his unprotected skin? Would his eyes bulge like hard-boiled eggs? Would he have time to regret his wish? Would ... Ben drained his glass in two gulps, wondering if his mind would ever just shut up. Bet muscle boy never had that problem.

Mystical TV lady was asking someone called Glen if he would use the words to complete his wish of winning the office Fantasy Football league when Ben dragged his attention back to the screen. That was pretty innocuous, if a bit of a waste of a wish. The next person wanted a Rolex, and whinged a lot about how he wanted to know when it'd arrive, until Mystic Madge cut him off. Ben wasn't entirely paying attention. What *would* he wish for?

Maybe wishing terrible things on the gym bunny

couple was a bit nasty. Not that he felt above being a bit nasty, not after the way she'd ended things, but it wouldn't give him anything other than a brief, bitter moment of satisfaction. So what if he wished something for himself? Something to make her jealous. Not to get her back, just to show her that she'd underestimated him, perhaps. Something to make muscle boy feel a little inadequate. Yeah, that'd be good.

He grinned, leaning back and putting his feet on the coffee table. Not that he was actually going to text in, of course. He wasn't that desperate. Or that drunk.

"And we only have time for a few more wishes," the woman said, pushing her hair back with fragile-looking hands. Ben wasn't sure how many wishes he'd missed, but it didn't feel like that many. She was stopping already? Why so quickly? He leaned forward, frowning at the TV, wondering if he'd dozed off, or maybe even blacked out for a bit, although he didn't think he'd drunk enough for that. He wasn't Friday night drunk, just weeknight-damn-insomnia drunk.

"Please text in immediately if you would like your wish granted," the woman said, raising her eyes to the camera. Again Ben had the feeling that she was looking right at him, seeing him sitting there still in his work clothes, with the curry spill on the collar of his shirt. "Don't wait. This opportunity will not be repeated. Normal programming will resume. There will be no second chances."

No second chances. Although he didn't want a second chance. Not with her. No, he wanted ... what did he want?

The phone was in his hand, although he didn't remember picking it up, and he typed the number in with one eye squinted shut. It couldn't hurt, right? 50p on his phone bill, and this was probably cathartic. It was the sort of thing therapists told you to do, attain closure through writing letters that would never be sent, or cleaning and rearranging the house to reclaim it, or acting out some other ritual of farewell. So this would be his. He'd make a wish that would do nothing, but he'd be able to believe that if it *did* work, they'd both be jealous of him. Maybe she'd even regret leaving, but that had been her choice, just as it had been his choice to drink himself to sleep on the sofa every night for the last three – or was it four now? – weeks. And, most importantly, he'd know he hadn't wished for her back. And then he could be done.

"Ben," the woman on the TV said, and he froze. There really couldn't be many people texting in, if he'd got straight through. "Ben, tell me your wish."

I want bigger muscles than my ex's new boyfriend, he typed, feeling shallow and ridiculous. He hit send, and the text appeared on the screen immediately. That was risky. Imagine if someone sent something they needed to censor.

"Use the words, Ben," the woman said, and her pale gaze seemed to lock with his.

He swallowed, his thumbs lingering over the phone. This was ridiculous. He could dress it up all he wanted, but it was just some petty fantasy. Imagine if his clients heard of this? Worse, his *colleagues?*

"Ben. We're almost out of time. Yours is the last wish.

Normal programming will resume. There will be no second chances."

Well, what the hell. Even if anyone he knew was pathetic enough to be sitting up like he was, what were the odds they'd know it was him? And it wasn't going to work. He wasn't going to turn up tomorrow with muscles bulging out of his shirt.

He used the words.

Ben woke with a sore back, a mouthful of glue, and a brass band playing in his skull. He rolled off the sofa and staggered to the bathroom, the events of the night before muddled in his head. There had been a woman juicing broccoli to send to Mars? A blender that granted wishes? Someone's dead husband coming back? No, missing. Had to be missing.

Also had to be a dream.

He clambered into the shower and turned it as cold as he could stand, shivering in the deluge, and decided that this was the last week of moping. It was getting out of hand now. He needed to stop before he did something silly.

Some vigorous toothbrushing and liberal applications of Listerine, deodorant and cologne later, he made it into the car. He felt reasonably human, but not even a double dose of ibuprofen and paracetamol would stop the clanging in his head. He chugged a migraine pill before he pulled away, knowing he'd taken too much paracetamol already, but hoping the codeine would do the trick. His head didn't even hurt that much, it just sounded as if a high school trumpeter had taken up residence in there. He was never going to be able to concentrate if it didn't ease off. At least he didn't have any meetings with clients today. He could snooze a little this morning, and get down to work this afternoon. He'd be fine.

The noise in his head didn't abate, although it was a little quieter while he was sat in the car. Moving seemed to exacerbate it. He parked up outside his offices and got out, keeping every movement as gentle as possible. Even so, his head trumpeted in outrage, and he tottered straight to the back door without even diverting to the little cafe across the road for a coffee. He'd make do with the office stuff. He just needed to get himself sat down and he'd be fine. He'd be just fine—

"Ben?"

Why was Simon talking so *loudly?* He was just about shouting, and Ben's head was already reverberating with noise. "Morning."

"Morning. Is that a new ringtone? Can you turn it down?" Simon sounded uneasy, worried, and Ben supposed he had a right to be. It was after nine, for a start, and Ben was never late. It was one of those lead by example things. Plus he could feel sweat rising on his face, nausea not far behind, so he probably didn't look too good.

"Ringtone?" he asked, since Simon was still staring at him.

"The brass band thing you've got going on. Ben, are you okay?"

He put a hand to his head gingerly, and the noise changed notes. It really *did* sound like trumpets, but played by someone – or a whole group of someones – who had only the faintest idea of rhythm and had never looked at a sheet of music in their life. "You can hear that?"

"Of course I can." Simon left the reception desk and approached Ben. "Do you need to sit down?"

"I ... yes. In my office. I'll sit down in my office." He shied away from the other man and staggered down the hall, past the meeting rooms and his partners' offices and into his own, pushing the door clumsily shut behind him and groping for his chair with his eyes half shut. He sat down carefully, taking a couple of deep breaths, and the noise went from a band to quartet.

Ben considered this for a moment, then slid off the chair, ignoring a blare of experimental jazz as interpreted by toddlers, and lowered himself gently to the floor. The toddlers eased off, leaving just a couple of trumpets tootling softly, something you might hear a busker attempting.

He lay flat on the floor, staring at the ceiling, and noticed a cobweb in one corner. He'd have to mention that to the cleaner. He wondered how long this might last, this migraine, these auditory hallucinations. Auditory hallucinations Simon could hear. He closed his eyes and willed the trumpeters to stop.

THERE WAS a soft knock on the door, then it eased open, and Ben endured an enthusiastic blare of noise as he craned his head to look around the corner of the desk at Simon.

"Do you need a doctor?" Simon asked, his forehead creased with concern.

"I don't know," Ben whispered.

Simon blinked at him nervously, then ventured in. "I brought you some water," he said, and set the glass on the floor next to Ben. "Have you had breakfast?"

Ben's stomach turned over. "No."

"The noise is still there."

"I know." His words were all but swallowed by the horns.

"Would you like me to check your phone? See if it's an alarm of some sort?"

"Sure." Ben stayed motionless while Simon crouched down to fish the phone out of his coat pocket, then rocked back on his heels to check it.

"You'll have to unlock it."

Ben took the phone carefully and drew the unlock across the screen, his hand trembling as the trumpets upped their jagged tempo. The phone opened to a text screen, and he stared at it through watering eyes. Simon reached to take it, and Ben tightened his grip, the night before suddenly painfully clear.

All wishes are granted. No responsibility is taken if you make an unsuitable wish or change your mind.

All wishes are granted.

The black text on the screen stared back at him stolidly.

All wishes are granted.

Even those made on TV by white-haired women in kaftans, with not a Goblin King in sight.

All wishes are granted.

He let Simon take the phone and switch it off. He

didn't need to look at the text any longer. The words were burned into his mind.

I wish I had bugling muscles.

He closed his eyes and listened to the trumpets playing the ragged tune of his heart.

Plausible Deniability

I had read that the lockdowns of the last year or so (2020 and 2021) had sent the prices of house plants rocketing as everyone tried to bring a little outside in, a little breath of nature for those not fortunate enough to be able to get out in it.
But I hadn't realised this extended to ***all*** *plants until an article popped up about shrubs being stolen from a botanical garden in New Zealand. And a little further reading revealed that there was an absolute epidemic of plant theft going on, with the holes left behind sometimes carefully filled, but other times left bare, like a cartoon of a rabbit-infested field.*
So, naturally, I realised there was a story there somewhere ...

The patrol car was a cocoon of warmth against the sharp edges of the spring night, and Nadira took a sip of takeaway coffee, rubbing weariness from her eyes with her free hand.

“Quiet tonight,” Sam said.

“Quiet’s good,” she replied without much conviction.

“Quiet’s sending me to sleep,” he said, and she snorted agreement.

“Still better than a Friday night, though.”

“True,” he admitted, and held a hand out. “Hit me.”

“M&Ms or brownies?”

“Brownies? You made brownies?”

“Well, I *brought* brownies.”

He gave her a narrow look. “Tesco’s?”

“I like Tesco’s brownies. You don’t want them, I’ll eat them.”

“*I* bake when it’s my turn,” he pointed out.

“I baked once, remember?”

“Eh, good point. M&Ms.”

Nadira dug into the bag at her feet, looking for the family-size bag of M&Ms among the Tupperware containers her mum always dropped off for night shifts. Judging by the quantity, her mum held firm beliefs that dhokla and idli offered as much protection from the facets of humanity that always emerged in the wee small hours as their stab vests did.

“What’d your mum make this week?” Sam asked, once he had a handful of chocolate.

“She’s on a health kick at the moment,” Nadira said. “Or she’s putting me on one, I’m not sure.”

“What? So no cheese dosa?” he asked, sounding stricken.

“No dosa,” she confirmed, her gaze still doing the restless tick-tock across the streets and houses they were cruising past, constantly on the hunt for something that wasn't quite *right.* And just as she was about to explain that all was not lost, as her mum had apparently decided paneer didn't actually count as cheese, but was, in fact, a health food, something caught her eye. "Hang about," she said, as the car purred past the entrance to the new gated community that had gobbled up the site of the old retirement home. The home had been moved across town, after it had been decided it'd cost more to renovate the little independent living bungalows and apartments to a decent state than it would to just build new. That decision coming, oddly enough, at the exact time a developer had been looking for a nice slice of real estate on which to erect a bunch of fancy detached houses with pillars at their doors and hot tubs on the back decks.

All of which Nadira knew because her gran's bestie and old business partner had a bungalow in the retirement home. Mrs Davis liked the new place, but not the location – it was closer to walk to the shops, maybe, but there were no open fields or quiet woods bordering the property, only takeaways and pound shops.

"What?" Sam asked, his foot already on the brake.

"I spotted someone in the development there. Seems a strange time to be out."

"Let's take a look." He checked the empty streets and swung into a U-turn, heading back to pull up to the big double gates. There was an intercom in the middle of the drive, with a keypad and a little camera above it, to go with the cameras Nadira could see above over the gates.

"It's like a bloody prison," she said.

"Just in reverse," he replied, and frowned at the intercom. "What d'you reckon we hit to get security?"

"Think they've got security physically here, or just remote?"

"There's someone on site full-time, I think. I read about it when it launched."

Nadira made a face, leaning forward in her seat to peer down the dimly lit street beyond the metal bars of the gates. It was smoothly paved and illuminated by mellow lights set in low pillars on the edges of the houses' front gardens.

The speaker crackled into sudden life, and a woman said, "Can I help you, officers?"

Sam jerked his hand back in surprise, then grinned and said, "Ah, *cameras*."

He reached out to poke a button, and the woman said, "The line's open. I can hear you."

"Creepy," Nadira muttered.

"My colleague spotted someone wandering about as we went past the gates," Sam said. "Can you let us in so we can check it out?"

"Are you sure?" the woman asked. "It's almost two in the morning."

"That's why it seemed unusual," Nadira said, loudly enough to be heard on the intercom.

There was a pause, then the woman said, "It's likely just a resident with insomnia or something."

"Seems remiss not to check," Sam replied.

Another pause, and finally the woman said, "I'll be there in just a moment." There was a click as the intercom went off, and Sam and Nadira looked at each other.

"She's not letting us in, is she?" Nadira asked.

"Not unsupervised, anyway. We might make a mess on the carpets."

Nadira snorted, and wondered if the camera could see her hijab. That'd explain a lot.

They didn't have to wait long before a fancy little electric vehicle like a souped-up golf cart with a cabin on it zipped down to the gates, and a woman in khaki trousers and a soft jacket with *Security* printed on the back got out and trotted toward them. She opened the gates with a remote, and came out to meet them.

Nadira swung out of the car, and the woman raised a hand to her in an apologetic sort of wave. "Sorry, but I can't let you drive in. We have to minimise cars on the streets after nine p.m."

Nadira smiled and said, "I'll try to ensure my colleague doesn't do any boy racer stunts."

"Can't you just walk in?" the woman asked. "Or I can take a look around myself. No one but security and residents have access cards, and after nine p.m. you can't get in without one unless you're buzzed in by someone inside, even if you've got the gate code. So I don't think you can have seen anyone who shouldn't be here."

"No back way in?" Nadira asked, and the woman shook her head.

"Only via the admin entrance, and that's just as secure. And you can see climbing over is pretty unlikely."

Nadira looked at the razor wire topping the fence, where the top angled out over the footpath. "Attractive."

"Secure." The woman spread her fingers and shrugged. "It's what they pay for. And, honestly, I'd really rather you didn't come in at all. If someone sees police on the property, it'll be a whole thing, and my supervisor'll be on me about letting the residents get upset over nothing."

"Which is, of course, much worse than the possibility that someone *did* circumvent all your fancy security and actually got in."

They stared at each other for a moment, then the woman sighed. "I can't stop you, of course. But can you at least come in the buggy with me? Then no one needs to see you."

"Sure," Nadira said. "Why not?"

Sam parked the car on the side of the road so that no one could be horrified by the sight of a police car in the drive, and they climbed into the warm confines of the little security buggy. It was surprisingly spacious, with plenty of room for even Sam's long legs in the back. There was a tablet mounted on the dashboard between the front seats, and the woman – who'd introduced herself as Caitlyn – tapped a quick entry into it before pulling soundlessly away from the gates. They purred down the main street of the development, the near-identical houses set well back in their front gardens, curtains drawn against the night. Not all the houses seemed to be lived in – some had gnomes, or fish-ponds, or wind sculptures in the front yards, little stamps that declared, *this is my house*, but a lot stood silent and untouched, the lawns neatly mowed and the flowerbeds tended, but nothing to say anyone lived there. The front gardens were separated by low stone walls that merged into high wooden fences further back, where the houses almost touched each other across the plots. Each had an attached garage to one side that met the dividing fence line, and a gate plugging the gap between the house and the fence on the other.

"Do those gates lock?" Nadira asked.

"Yes. They've all got individual codes set by the home-owners," Caitlyn said.

"I can just feel the level of trust and security within the community from here," Sam said, and Nadira bit the inside of her cheek.

"What's that?" she asked as they purred past a cul-de-sac, and Caitlyn braked hard enough that Sam bounced into the back of Nadira's seat.

"What?" Caitlyn asked, and backed up a little so they could all see. Not that it helped. In the low light of the little street lamps, all that was visible was a bundle in the middle of the road. Caitlyn backed around and drove up to it, and they stared at the small bush lying in the centre of the smooth tarmac, its roots on show and dirt scattered around it. "That wasn't here earlier," Caitlyn said. "I do rounds every hour, and it wasn't here on my last one."

Nadira opened her door and climbed out, going to crouch in the wash of the headlights and examine the plant. Not that it gave anything away – it was a plant. Her gran would've been able to tell her what it was, but as far as she could tell, it was just a small bush of some sort, leafy and green and probably about a metre high, if it had been upright. She straightened and looked around as Sam joined her, and spotted clumps of dirt on the kerb to one side. She followed it, seeing more on the path that led to the gate on the side of the house beyond. She glanced at the letter box – number five – and then at the windows. Curtains stood open on the night, and there were no lights inside, or anything at the front door other than a plain mat. She looked back at Caitlyn, who was standing uncertainly next to the plant as if not sure if she should take it into custody for dirtying the streets or not.

"We need to check that back garden," she said. "Does anyone live here?"

Caitlyn looked at the house, then back at her. "No, this whole cul-de-sac was the last completed. Only those two are occupied." She pointed to the end of the lane, where one house had an elaborate water feature chuckling away in the middle of the lawn, and another had a basketball hoop above the garage door. Nadira would have bet good money *that* wasn't allowed to be used after nine p.m.

"What's the occupancy in here overall?" Sam asked.

"About sixty percent at the moment," Caitlyn said. "I don't think it sold quite as well as expected."

Nadira found herself wondering how it had even sold that well, but she just pointed to the house and said, "Can you get us in?"

"Sure," Caitlyn said, and then as Nadira started across the grass said, "Can you use the path? Only the grass ..." She trailed off as Nadira stared at her, then said, "Never mind."

"Stay *off* the path," Nadira said to her. "If there's been a break-in, there could be footprints we can pick up from it."

"Right," Caitlyn said. "Got it."

Caitlyn wouldn't let Nadira have the master key card, and Nadira wouldn't let her join them without gloves, so there was a moment's fuss while the security guard found some gardening ones in the back of the buggy, then followed them to the door. Nadira and Sam had already pulled blue latex gloves on, and as soon as the door was open, Nadira led the way into the bland cream interior, playing her torch along the smooth walls and polished expanse of wooden flooring in the hall. The door to her right opened straight onto a dining room, already furnished with a glass-topped table and stark white chairs, looked over by some cityscape photographs. An arch led from the other end of the room into a big open plan living area, and she saw Sam emerge from beyond the wall – he must have come through another entrance in the hall. The lounge area held a couple of sofas and armchairs, more beiges and whites, and nondescript art prints on the walls, and nothing looked to have been touched since the interior designer laid it all out, right down to the spread of lifestyle magazines on the coffee table.

Nadira turned to ask Caitlyn if it all looked right to her, and Sam said, "Dira?"

He was looking through the bifold doors into the garden, his torch pointed at the floor. There was more soft lighting out there, probably solar stuff designed to light up the plants, but as she hurried to join him, she could see that the lamps were just sitting in their own pools of illumination, unfiltered by leaves or branches. She blinked out at the garden, then Sam slid the doors open, and they stepped out onto the back deck. They looked at each other, and Nadira turned back to beckon to Caitlyn, who was hovering in the hall. She hurried forward, and Nadira said, "These houses are all finished?"

"All of them."

"Gardens too?"

"Oh, yes. The gardens are a big selling point. Native species and exotics, all landscaped by the well-known—"

She broke off as Nadira stepped aside and pointed out into the softly lit yard. Softly lit, but bright enough to see the neatly turfed lawn, the stepped flowerbeds, and the ravaged borders. There wasn't a shrub or a tree in the entire place. Nothing but raw earth and wooden fences, the razor wire that met the perimeter revealed without the disguise of plants, turning the back yard into a claustrophobic box as bland as the house.

"Huh," Sam said.

NADIRA LEANED back in her chair, scrubbing her hands over her face and wishing she'd bought another box of Tesco's brownies. The first lot was long gone, as were the M&Ms, and all her mum's food. A tour of all the streets in the development last night had turned up nothing except the one rogue plant in the cul-de-sac, and Caitlyn had refused to allow them to do anything else until she'd cleared it with the development management. Which had meant waiting until this morning, after she and Sam should technically have been off shift, before going back to check the other empty houses. And of the fifteen empty properties, eleven of them had very empty gardens, which the management company were currently having a meltdown about. Apparently the cost for replacing all the plants was somewhere in the six-figure range, which Nadira couldn't even get her head around. For *plants.* Posh plants, Sam had said, with a shrug, but as far as she was concerned they'd have to be gold-plated to be that posh.

And somehow Sergeant Lee had decided that it was a

compliment to Nadira and Sam to remain at the forefront of the investigation. Although Nadira suspected he just didn't want to spend the day looking through CCTV footage himself.

She yawned, and clicked through to the next file. There were cameras *everywhere* in the damn place, but so far they hadn't showed anything. She was concentrating on the footage from the cul-de-sac last night, watching cars run to the occupied houses and vanish into the garage at four-times speed, when Sam plonked a mug of tea onto her desk and snagged a chair to join her.

"Any luck?" she asked. He'd been watching the gate footage.

"Yes, but probably no."

She picked up the mug and frowned at him.

"No one in or out. *But,* just after we left the car, a van went past the gate. It might be nothing, but the timing's interesting."

"Traffic cams?"

"Requested." He leaned forward and said, "What's that?"

Nadira turned her attention back to the screen just in time to see a security buggy pull up to number five. She hit pause, and they both stared at it. It was towing a covered trailer, just a short stubby thing. She pressed play, and they watched the garage door rise, and the buggy vanish inside, sweeping into a tight angle to pull the trailer after it. The doors closed again, and she skipped forward until the buggy re-emerged. It scooted off down the street, and as it swung out of the cul-de-sac the back door of the trailer sprang open, scattering half a dozen plants across the road. The buggy stopped, and a figure in dark clothes with their sleeves pushed up to their elbows climbed out and hurried to collect the plants. Another person joined them, both of them rushing to reload, and a third leaned out of the driver's seat, gesturing at the street. The two on the road rammed the plants into the trailer and jogged back to the buggy, and Nadira checked the timestamp. "That's what I saw," she said. "It must've been them running to get the plants."

"Hardly running," Sam said. "A mild and non-urgent jog, I'd say."

"The driver's rushing them, though," she said, and pointed at the screen as the buggy pulled away again, "See, they missed that plant. I bet they knew Caitlyn'd be making another pass soon." She tapped away to a different window and checked the security route. "Yes, see – they arrived when she was at the far end of the compound, and left when she was at the same. They know the schedule."

"And have access to a security buggy and a trailer."

Nadira leaned closer to the screen, trying to see more detail. "We need to get this enhanced."

Sam grunted and pushed away from the desk. "See if tech can blow it up. I'll chase traffic again."

Nadira nodded, but she wasn't really listening. Because she wasn't tired anymore. They *had* something.

WELL, they almost had something. Every vehicle in the development was fitted with tracking devices, and the only buggy on the move last night had, apparently, been Caitlyn's. The trailer, which was used to collect rubbish from the houses daily, to be tucked away behind big double gates in the administration area where no one would have to see such common things, hadn't been out since the previous five a.m. run.

"So they disabled the tracker," Nadira said to Sergeant Lee.

"But left the security cameras alone?"

"They're not monitored all the time – when the guard on duty's doing rounds, no one's watching the screen. They're only reviewed if something comes up, and judging by how many gardens were cleaned out, they'd been at this for a while with no one noticing. If any resident happened to be awake, it was just the rubbish buggy doing its rounds. They wouldn't think twice about it."

"What did they do after, then? How did they get the plants out without being seen?"

"Tech's not sure, but they think there's a loop on the footage from the work gates, where the bins are. Those ones might've been tampered with. And considering they got in and out of the garage just fine, they must've had a master key from somewhere."

The sergeant rubbed his chin, then sighed. "Certainly not spur of the moment, was it? Anything else?"

Nadira pointed at an image on her screen. "Tech managed to get this. They kept their faces hidden, but it looks like this one's got a tattoo on their forearm."

He squinted at it. "Huh. Looks like an anchor, so that really narrows things down." He shrugged. "Well, good work and all that. Go and get some sleep. You look shattered."

"I am," she said. "But I was thinking of going back and talking to the other guards, see if anyone's misplaced a pass—"

He waved dismissively. "Leave it. Apparently, the management of the place just wants a police report so they can claim on insurance. They've already said they're tightening security, so that'll be the end of it."

"Tightening it? What're they going to do, put trackers in the guards?"

He snorted. "And truth serums every Tuesday, I suppose. But we're done. They don't want any of it getting out and making the residents uneasy, or putting people off buying."

"Someone still broke in," she insisted. "We can't just—"

"But, as you said, no breaking appears to be involved. So probably an inside job, and they'll deal with it. It's not like we don't have enough other stuff going on. *Plants*, for God's sake."

Nadira opened her mouth to argue, then shut it again. He was right. And it wasn't even as if she were a detective. Her job was to get back out there and do the hands-on stuff. Prevention, support in the community, and cleaning up the messes of humanity on a Friday night. "Alright," she said instead. "I'm out of here, then."

"See you later," the sergeant said, and she wandered back to clear the empty mugs off the desk so someone else could use it.

Sam was pulling his jacket on in the locker room when she got there, and he gave her a weary nod. "So much for that, huh?"

"Yeah. The company probably just don't want it getting out that they've had a security breach."

"Makes sense. Be pretty bad publicity when people are paying so much." He yawned.

Nadira took her bag out of the locker, empty Tupperware clattering together inside, and said, "Did you hear from traffic about that van?"

"Yeah, no go on that. It was from Sunrise Gardens – that retirement village."

Nadira blinked at him. "At two in the morning?"

He shrugged. "I checked, and the van's not been stolen. The woman I spoke to said it's used for group outings mostly, but also by the staff for various things, so maybe someone was on night shift and in dire need of a kebab."

"That seems weird."

He nodded. "Sure. But I doubt our esteemed elders are out robbing gardens, so I'm pretty sure they're in the clear."

She started to say something, but yawned instead. Even her bones felt tired, and she wasn't thinking straight. "I'm going home."

"Really? Me, I'm off for a ten-mile run."

She threw a napkin at him and wandered out into the thin spring sunshine, squinting at it as she let herself into her own car.

Sunrise Gardens. That was the place her gran's friend lived. The place that had been unceremoniously moved to make room for the new development. A weird sort of coincidence, but Sam was right. It wasn't like the residents would be out robbing gardens. And how would they have got in, anyway?

NADIRA SMILED at the woman behind the desk in the office. It was one of those portable cabin–type places, and although an effort had obviously been made to pretty it up with a profusion of potted plants and art prints and a couple of comfy armchairs with bright cushions, it still looked like a building site office.

"I'm here to visit Mrs Viola Davis?" Nadira said.

The woman blinked at her, and at the rather sad bunch of flowers she'd snagged from Tesco Express. At least she also had a box of pastries from an actual bakery. "You don't have to check in for the independent living residents," she said. "Only if you're going into assisted living, and they've got reception there."

"What do you do, then?" Nadira asked, and when the woman looked mildly offended she added quickly, "I just mean, I thought with the office right here you'd keep an eye on people coming and going and stuff."

"I do," she said. "But it's more just to direct delivery drivers, or if people don't know where they're going. My main job is organising outings and shopping trips and such. We do the supermarket and town centre daily, then there's the garden centre on Monday, bowls club on Tuesday—"

"Sounds busy," Nadira said.

"It is."

"Do you drive them, too?"

"No, I'm usually stuck here." She looked around the office, then shrugged. "We have a few volunteers who come and drive, and some of the residents still have their licences and do a bit of driving too. Viola does, actually. She normally does the garden centre for us on Monday. She says it means she doesn't get dirt in the back of her own car." The woman smiled, and Nadira returned it.

"So anyone can get the keys, then?"

"Yes." The woman frowned, tilting her head to one side. "Why?"

"No reason." Nadira had gone home, showered, put her pjs on, and an hour later got up and dressed again in civilian clothes. She didn't *look* like a cop, but she knew she still sounded like one. "Where do I find Mrs Davis, then?"

"Number fifteen. Straight on, and it's on your left."

"Thanks," Nadira said, and started for the door, then hesitated. "Nice plants in here."

"Thanks," the woman said. "They were presents, actually. The residents really love their plants. The garden centre's always the most popular outing. I swear they must be spending all their kids' inheritance, the amount they come back with sometimes. The place was so bare when we first got here, but now ..." She waved throughout the window at the packed flower beds in front of the office, and the trees and shrubs lining the little road as it headed deeper into the village.

"It's very nice," Nadira said, and went back outside, tucking the back of her hijab into her jacket to stop the wind grabbing it. Her car was parked in one of the visitors' parking spaces outside the office, but she ignored it and walked up the street instead. It was smoothly paved, and although there was no pavement to either side, it was wide enough for two cars to pass – or a car and a mobility scooter, she noted, as one zipped past her on the other side of the road, the driver waving cheerily. She waved back, her attention mostly on the buildings. They were little bungalows, mostly semi-detached, with a couple (the more expensive, she imagined) fully detached and standing stoically in their own gardens. She couldn't see into the back yards, of course, but the fronts were a mix of neatly tended flower beds, rock gardens, and the occasional short-shorn lawn.

Number fifteen was a semi-detached bungalow on a corner plot, the little road becoming a T-junction next to it and framing a riot of flowerbeds, early spring blooms popping up everywhere. Nadira could name the daffodils and tulips, but she was less sure about the rest. They were pretty, though.

She went up the front path to the ramp that led to a wide door and knocked lightly. There was a moment's pause, then a man opened it and peered at her over his glasses. There was a stoop to his shoulders, but his bare forearms were still muscled, the loose skin stained with the soft green of old tattoos, and there was dirt under his fingernails.

She gave him her best, friendliest, not-a-scary-Muslim smile. "I was looking for Mrs Davis."

He blinked at her, then returned the smile. "Oh, I thought you must be here for Fareeha. Sorry, bit presumptuous of me."

"Fareeha? My gran's here?" But then, why wouldn't she be? She and Mrs Davis had been best friends since they were Nadira's age. They'd met when they were both secretaries for a law firm, and had ended up starting their own IT company back in the very early days of such things, when that had essentially meant selling new-fangled electric typewriters. Nadira's mum and sister still ran the modern version of it.

"We're just having some tea. Come in." The man turned and led the way inside and she followed him, pulling the door shut and smelling toast and talc and a warm lavender scent. There was a hall beyond the door, and the man led her straight to the end, where light spilled through big windows that looked over a compact back garden, washing the open living area with rich colour. There were three people at the dining table – her gran, Mrs Davis, and another older man, and as she walked in, he shut the top of his laptop, and her gran turned a tablet face down.

"Hello, Poti," her gran said.

"Hello, Naani," she said, and went to kiss her grandmother on the cheek. "I didn't expect to see you here." She offered the flowers and the bakery box to Mrs Davis. "How are you?"

"We're just planning some gardening," her gran said.

"Oh, lovely," Mrs Davis said, sniffing the flowers. "I'll put these in some water."

"I wouldn't have brought flowers if I'd known how many you already had," Nadira said, nodding at the garden through the big windows. "This is lovely."

"One can never have too many flowers or plants," Mrs Davis said. "Tea?"

"Please," Nadira said, and watched the second man tuck some papers under his laptop. He did it casually, as if tidying a place for her to join them, but she caught a glimpse of a grid with times and locations on it. She held a hand out to him. "I'm Nadira."

"Oh, *sorry,* Poti," her gran said. "This is Mr Baker—"

"Kenneth," he said, taking her hand and shaking it. He was wearing a short-sleeved shirt with a cravat, and his moustache was curled neatly at the corners. "Pleased to meet you, Nadira. Your gran's always telling us you're the best police officer in the county."

Nadira snorted. "I'm glad someone thinks so."

"Roy Bennett," the man who had opened the door said, leaning in to shake her hand and placing his free hand on Kenneth's shoulder as he did so. Kenneth smiled at him.

"And it's past time you started calling me Viola, dear," Mrs Davis said, coming in with the pastries set on a plate and a mug of tea in her other hand. She passed it to Nadira. "You're far too old to still be calling me Mrs Davis."

"Um ... thanks?"

"You can still call me Naani," her gran said solemnly, and the little group chuckled with delight. Nadira smiled at them and took a sip of tea, turning to look into the garden. It wasn't large, but there was a small garden shed at the back, and a combination of raised vegetable beds and freshly turned flower plots filled the space around a scrap of lawn. Wooden trellis lined the fence, offering some privacy from the neighbours and waiting for some summer vines.

"Wonderful garden you've got," she said. "You must've done a lot of work to get it looking so good in, what? Eighteen months?"

"A year since we moved in," Kenneth said. "But, of course, one can buy bigger plants to hurry things along. We had to do quite a bit of that for the communal garden. It was so *bare*."

"Must be expensive."

He smiled at her. "Well, what else are we going to spend it on?"

"I suppose it makes up a little for not having the woods nearby," she said. "You know, having nice gardens."

"The less independent residents enjoy it very much," Viola said. "We've worked rather hard to make sure they have some nice grounds to enjoy. When one has so little in life, such things are terribly important."

Nadira looked at her, a tall, thin woman with knobbly wrists, waifish next to her gran's reassuring solidity. She took a sip of her tea and said, "That's a lovely thing to do."

"They needed it, after all the disruption of the move," Roy said, dropping into one of the armchairs and flinging an arm over the back. "Some of the residents aren't able to cope with such things so well. They should never have been forced to move in the first place."

"Roy," Fareeha said, her voice gently chiding.

"Well, they shouldn't. Damn companies coming along and just taking whatever they want—" He stopped as Kenneth clicked his tongue, and looked at Nadira. "We lost some friends. They were okay as long as things were familiar, but the move was too much for some of them. They never really recovered."

"I'm sorry," Nadira said. "I can see it being a really big adjustment."

"It was," Kenneth said. "But we've created a lovely place here, in the end. Would you like to see the park?"

"You have a park?"

"It's what we call the communal gardens. Come on. Bring your tea."

They trooped out into the sunlight and strolled down

the little road, Fareeha with her arm linked through Nadira's. There was a growing warmth to the sun, a promise of summer on the horizon, and when they stepped off the road onto a path that dived into a broad green space that divided the bungalows from the looming hulk of the assisted living building, the shade of the small trees was almost welcome.

Nadira could see why they referred to it as a park. *Garden* seemed small and controlled, a place for dozing in wheelchairs and staring at flower clocks. This space overflowed with exuberant life, with birdsong and sun and shade and the strong whiff of crushed grass and warming earth. It was pocked with benches and sweeps of bright grass, and the vegetation was lush and crowded, forming stands of variegated greens and interesting patterns of shrubs and flowers and little trees already working on filling their branches with spring growth. A lot of the earth around them looked raw and new, and they passed three women power walking with headbands on, as well as a man in his pyjamas feeding a squirrel and another in a wheelchair yelling at a pigeon for stealing his breakfast. The pigeon looked unconcerned.

Viola led a tour around her favourite trees, and Nadira made admiring noises, and complimented Kenneth on his choice of shrubs, and Roy on his koi pond ("Well, it'll be a koi pond as soon as I get some koi," he said, and Kenneth rolled his eyes, then winked at her), and her gran didn't even need to point out the insect hotels and bird houses for her to know who had made them. She agreed that it was truly a wonderful space, and just what the residents needed.

"Stops us getting bored, too," Kenneth said.

"And you did it all yourself?" she asked.

"For all the bloody money the village got for selling our old place out from under us, they somehow didn't have *quite* enough for anything more than absolute basic landscaping," Roy said. "Had enough for a bonus for all the shareholders, though."

"Honestly, aren't you bored of going on about that yet?" Fareeha asked.

"No," Roy said, and Kenneth poked him in the ribs. He sighed. "Alright, a *bit*. But it just annoys me. That eyesore of a new development didn't even make use of our lovely gardens, or let us dig any of it out to bring with us. Just bulldozed the lot and shoved a bunch of cookie cutter homes on top."

"It's called progress," Viola said, as they turned back toward her bungalow. "One can't stand before it, and there's nothing us old folk can do about it. We must simply accept it."

Roy grumbled, but didn't argue, and Nadira watched the centre's van rumble past on the road, the woman from the office driving. The woman waved, and they all waved back, and Nadira yawned.

"Ah, Poti. They're working you too hard," Fareeha said.

"I haven't been to bed," she said. "There was a theft on the new development."

"Really?" Roy said, crossing his arms. He wasn't wearing a coat, and Nadira watched the anchor tattoos on his forearms shift with the movement. "Imagine that, with all their fancy security."

"What'd they take?" Viola asked, her eyebrows raised,

and Nadira looked at her, then shook her head and handed over her mug.

"I'm going home to sleep." She hesitated, then added, "There's a traffic cam outside the gates, you know. It picked up the village's van last night."

The three residents and her grandmother looked at each other.

"Obviously there must be a good reason for it to have been going past just after a disturbance in the development, and as the development management don't want any publicity and are claiming everything on insurance, it *probably* won't be followed up. No more than I'm doing, anyway."

They all looked at her, and her grandmother smiled. "That's very interesting, Poti. I'm sure one of the night staff must've needed something from the twenty-four-hour shop. Things always run out at the most inopportune times."

"That's what I thought," Nadira said. "Do you need a lift home, Naani?"

"Oh, no. Your mum's picking me up later."

"Alright." She started toward her car, then stopped and turned back, to find them all watching her expectantly. Viola had taken Fareeha's arm, and her gran was the only one who didn't look worried. Nadira opened her mouth, shut it again, then shook her head and just said, "Thanks for the tea."

"Come back any time," Viola said. "It's lovely to see you."

Nadira nodded and went back to her car, starting the engine and plucking Caitlyn's card from the cupholder between the seats. It had still been in her pocket when she'd left the station.

Caitlyn Jones, it said, *Security Officer.* And under that was the name of the security firm. *Baker & Bennett*, it read, and she wondered if it was still in the families, or if it had been sold outright. She could find out, of course, just as she could find out exactly how many rather more modern computer skills her gran and Viola had picked up before they'd stepped back from the IT company.

But then again, the case was closed.

And the park really was very nice.

And she was sure the development company had plenty of insurance, and the funds to replace as many gardens as they needed to. Unlike retirement villages with more interest in shareholders than residents.

She pulled out of the parking space and headed for home, wondering if her mum would make her a dal for dinner. She could just go for a nice dal.

A nice dal, and a good dose of plausible deniability.

An Unconditional Rescue

I love walking by the sea after wild weather, as well as during it. As a kid I adored finding the treasures a storm would throw up, and I still do – even though these days it seems to be more plastic bottles and snarls of fishing nets than soft worn planks with mysterious fragments of words on them, and tortured scraps of driftwood like the limbs of sea creatures. But it's still fun to see what the sea returns to us. And sometimes you can stand on the shore and watch a log rolling in the swells further out, and think, what if…

"Thinking of going out?" Mrs Mallow asked Tim.

He looked up from his coffee, wondering why it tasted greasy, and nodded at the landlady of the B&B. "It looks like a nice day. I was thinking I'd go and rent a boat in town."

Mrs Mallow nodded, and whisked some crumbs off the

table next to him. They joined a fine carpet of older debris on the floor, and Tim regarded his full English breakfast suspiciously. The food *looked* fine, but the milk jug had congealed circles inside it, marking older breakfasts like the rings of a tree trunk, and his fork had someone else's egg stuck between the tines.

"Go and see old Fred," the landlady advised him. "Tell him Ruby sent you, and he'll give you a good deal. Nothing fancy about his boats, but you don't need fancy for a bit of fishing, do you?"

Tim agreed that he did not, and pushed beans around his plate with a piece of toast. He wondered if lifejackets were considered fancy.

THE SUN WAS high by the time he wound his way down to the waterfront. Fred, he'd been informed, kept his boats somewhere near the fishing docks, so he avoided that particular area and wandered into the marina instead, his fishing rods in a shiny new case over one shoulder and a half-empty backpack over the other. Mrs Mallow had offered to fix him a pack-up, but he'd told her he couldn't eat on the boat due to seasickness. He'd stopped off at Boots instead and bought sandwiches and crisps and biscuits, as well as a breakfast wrap that he gnawed on contentedly as he walked. The day was looking up.

The first boat rental place he found was shut, which he supposed was only to be expected. It was out of season still. He took a photo of the phone number, and ambled further along the docks. He found a second boat rental not far from the first – the office had the blinds drawn, but there was a young man with his shirt off scrubbing the floor of a rather flashy little powerboat moored just outside it.

"Hello?" Tim said. "Are you from the rental place?"

The young man straightened up and regarded Tim without much interest. "Yeah."

"Oh. Well, great. I want to hire a boat. For fishing," he added, when the young man's expression didn't change. "Self-drive."

"We do that," the young man said, not moving.

Tim looked at the logo emblazoned on the hull of the boat, which matched the one on the dock. *Self-drive and captained boat hire*, it said. "Yes. So I see. Do you have any available?"

"When for?"

"Today. Now."

The young man gave an exaggerated sigh and turned his attention back to the cleaning. "You should have booked ahead. We're full."

"Full?" Tim looked around the deserted midweek marina. The summer crowds, such as they might be, were still a month or so off.

"Full." The young man didn't look up.

"Well, where else can I try? Your neighbours there are shut."

The young man's expression finally changed. He frowned, as if Tim had asked him to solve for *y*, if *x* was shut fishing shops and *z* was a beautiful day in late April. "There isn't anyone," he announced eventually. "You'll have to call later and book for tomorrow."

"Can I book now?" Tim asked, although he didn't

really want to extend his stay in the B&B past tonight. He was worried the mould in the bathroom might be catching.

"No," the young man said, dipping the scrubbing brush in a bucket of soapy water. "You have to call. Talk to the boss."

"So I can call them now?"

"No." It was said firmly, in a way that suggested the young man thought Tim might be a bit slow on the uptake. "There's no one there, is there?"

Tim looked at the shuttered office, and sighed. "I guess not," he said. "When will they be there?" He wondered what small business owner didn't have a mobile these days.

"I dunno. I'm not the boss."

Tim decided that it was best not to answer that, and trailed off down the dock again, wondering if he should just give up and read a book on the beach instead. That might be nice. Have an ice cream. Take his shoes off and paddle in the sea, even. But he'd come here to go fishing. That had been the whole sort-of point. That he'd finished the latest contract, and he and Patty had agreed to do more of their own things these days, so they didn't become one of those boring middle-aged couples that had no life outside each other. And he hadn't been fishing in so long. So he'd decided that this, fishing, would be his thing. He straightened his shoulders, a small man with small hands and calm eyes and a gracefully retreating cap of fair hair. He was going fishing.

Fred didn't have a sign out. He didn't have an office, either. But he did have two small aluminium dinghies pulled out of the water by the fishing dock, and they had rod holders on the sterns, and the outboards were padlocked to a beam inside a rotting wooden shed that stank of old fish and tobacco.

"Sure you can take one out," he said to Tim, scratching his belly through a hole in his ancient green jumper. "You know how to use one?"

Tim admitted that it had been a while, but that he was pretty sure he remembered the basics.

"Course you do. Like riding a bike." Fred gestured the younger man to help him slide one of the dinghies into the water, and stepped into it in his wellies, making it bob violently. "Nice day, anyhow. Can't get into much trouble on a day like this."

It felt alarmingly quick, the speed at which Fred got the engine in and showed him how to start it, then ran through the controls, clapping Tim on the back and laughing when he almost fell over backward trying to get in. Then the old man was hooking a mildewed lifejacket over Tim's head, telling him to stay in the bay and clear of the rocks at the eastern point, and the painter dropped into the bottom of the boat with a painfully loud clang, and Fred pushed him off, and then it was just him and the growling motor. Tim stared at it, then back at the dock, then out to open water. *Oh,* he thought. *Oh, I'm doing this, then.* And he carefully pushed the gear lever to forward, and grabbed the throttle on the tiller a little too tightly, and puttered toward the sea.

OUT IN THE BAY, the water was as silken calm as it had looked from the shore, although a long, slow swell rode in from beyond the horizon. The little dinghy barely noticed it, cutting a slow V through the green water as Tim started to relax, the sun warming his bare head and face, and the wind of his forward motion tugging at the hood of his jacket and ruffling his hair. Out here, he could smell nothing more than salt and the not-unpleasant tang of outboard fuel, and the horizon looked bowed and close enough to touch. He loosened his grip on the throttle, tugged his lifejacket down, and smiled. This. This is what he'd been imagining. Not badly lit guest houses that smelled faintly of old porridge, or even the sleek modern boats like the one the young man had been cleaning. *This.* The vibration of the engine humming under his hand, the sound of the water sluicing past the hull, and the cries of the seagulls following him hopefully. His smile broadened, and he opened the throttle a bit further as the dinghy described an arc across the wide, empty bay, and the sun turned the spray to rainbows.

By the time he slowed the dinghy and started to think about fishing – reluctantly, because he felt he could have driven about all afternoon, just for the sheer joy of it – he was only barely within the confines of the bay, the town looking small and squished under the green hills. The water out here was deeply green too, sunlight forming shafts that ran down to meet in the depths below him, the surface pocked with floating mats of seaweed. There were bigger boats bobbing further out, no doubt fishing themselves, and he felt an almost uncontrollable urge to keep going, to just arrow out toward the horizon, past them and then further, seeing how far the little dinghy could take him. But that was silliness, so he turned the bow back toward the shore and tried to remember what the old man had said about fishing. That he should be near the rocks on the eastern shore? No, that he should keep clear of them. So which one was the eastern shore?

There was a compass sunk into the midships seat, but it was so yellowed by the sun that he couldn't see anything in it. He supposed his phone might help – would Google maps work for this sort of thing? Maybe, but he didn't entirely trust himself not to drop it, and there was an un-alarming but not insignificant amount of water sloshing around his toes. He tried to imagine the bay's orientation on a map of the country, but he couldn't, so he just motored slowly back in toward town and decided to stick himself somewhere in the middle of the bay. It seemed safest.

The afternoon passed pleasantly, to say the least. As the dinghy drifted in the centre of the broad bay, watched by the seagulls, Tim ceremoniously unpacked his fishing rods, baited the hooks, and dropped them over the side. Then he settled the rods into the rod holders and lay back in the bow, watching the birds wheel across the clear sky and trailing his fingers in the cool water. He knew quite well that this was not something he'd done as a boy, not where he grew up, but it felt like living a childhood memory anyway. He drank ginger beer and ate his sandwiches, and it was warm enough that he even took his jacket off and sat there in his blue fleece, the one Patty said brought out his eyes, with his sleeves pushed up to his elbows. Every now and then he reeled the lines in and replaced the missing bait, but he didn't move from his fishing spot, even though neither rod so much as bent in anticipation of a less stealthy fish. It was all too perfect to be ruined by actually catching something.

He was sitting comfortably astride the midships seat, baiting a hook, when he noticed a shadow. It ran under the boat and was gone, and he felt the back of his neck tighten. It had been big. He looked up hopefully, but the sky was still cloudless. A basking shark, maybe? They were common enough. And harmless, he reminded himself. Still, he hesitated before dropping the hook carefully back into the water. Whatever it was, it wasn't interested in the dinghy. And if he did snag it, it'd surely break the line. He stayed where he was, examining the dimpled green water around him. No dramatic fins cutting through the water, no menacing music. Whatever it was, it was gone.

He was just starting to relax when a swirl of turbulence caught his eye, just on the corner of his vision. He turned jerkily enough to set the dinghy rocking, but there was nothing to see except spreading ripples. His heart was pounding. He hadn't seen what caused the disturbance, not properly, but there had been *something*. Something big, and ... and green, maybe? Were basking sharks green? He'd never had to ask himself that question before. Or anyone else for that matter. He searched the water anxiously, half-standing with one hand on the sun-warmed engine cowling. Nothing, no shadows, no more turbulence. Maybe it was gone. Maybe it had even been a turtle, something like that, and he'd just misjudged the size—

One of the rods went. Not far, just an angry little rattlesnake hiss as the line was pulled out, then stopped. Tim sat down hard and started to reel the other rod in. He didn't want whatever it was to try this line too— The reel snarled suddenly, the line spinning out, and he gave a little yelp of alarm. It stopped just as quickly as the first, both lines hanging limp into the green depths, and after a moment Tim started reeling one in carefully. It didn't take long. He hadn't put much line out, and it came up quickly. He turned to bring the second one in, then sat and regarded them anxiously. Both hooks were gone. It wasn't strange, not with the size of that thing out there, but it made him uneasy anyway. The dinghy suddenly seemed very small and fragile, the town very distant. He stood up again, searched the water for more shadows, then tugged the starter cord for the engine. He'd had enough. The day had lost its joy.

The engine coughed, then fell silent. He tried again, and again, sweat forming on his shoulders as he tugged stubbornly on the cord, almost falling backward into the bow more than once. He played with the throttle, and the choke, and swore at it in a creative manner that would have surprised Patty. And finally, with the skin between his fingers raw from clutching the toggle on the end of the cord, he gave up and sat staring at the sea. No more ripples or turbulence, except those made from his own panicked movement. No shadows, either. He sighed, wondering if he'd imagined it, then unclipped the oars from under the seat and set them in the rowlocks. He could phone someone, he supposed, but he thought that maybe the engine would start again if he waited. He'd had an old car when he was younger that was like that. It seemed to sense urgency. He dipped the oars in the water and back out, and was gratified to feel the boat start slipping forward. Okay, so this wasn't so hard. Good. He put his back into it.

THIS WAS HARD. This was *so hard*. His back was aching, and his hands were sweating on the oars, and every time he looked over his shoulder (because that was how the professional rowers did it, with their backs to their destination, so he assumed it must be right), the town had slipped to one side or the other as he zig-zagged across the bay. Plus it didn't seem to be getting any closer. He tried the engine again, but it still wouldn't start, and he felt oddly determined not to call anyone. It wasn't as if he had Fred's number, anyway, so he'd have to, what? Call Mrs Mallow? He didn't like the idea. And what could she do anyway? He settled himself back down at the oars, then gave an involuntary little yelp as a shadow slid across his stern. Long and tapered, but hard to get any other sense of it from here. The size of it, it had to be a basking shark. But it was fast. Were basking sharks fast? All the photos he'd seen of them they had their cavernous jaws open, and they certainly didn't look as if they'd go very fast like that. He leaned into the oars. It wouldn't be interested in him, anyway. He didn't even have any dead fish aboard.

There was a bump from the bow, gentle but distinct, and Tim added a new level of creativity to his swearing. He never swore at home. It must be a sea thing, he thought, and craned his neck, hoping to see some debris bobbing away. There was nothing but a swirl of disturbed water that made his stomach contract. Just keep paddling, he thought, then remembered the kids' movie – although that was *just keep swimming*, wasn't it? A bubble of nervous laughter rode up from somewhere, and he tried to speed up.

Another bump, but it was more of a *tap,* wasn't it? Like someone knocking a walking stick against a door. *Tap, tap*, again, and he tried to ignore it, to paddle harder. *Tap. TAP.* A dent appeared in the bottom of the dinghy, popping up next to his foot, and he shrieked, and thrashed at the water with the oars. But now the boat wasn't moving forward at all, in fact it was *tilting*, the bow rising as if the sea had thrown a rolling wave out of the still water, but the wave wasn't moving, it was just sitting there and lifting the bow, or was it that the stern was sinking? No, that couldn't be it. Why would it be sinking? He must have run over a log, that was all it was, a silly log, and it had lifted the bow, or it was caught around the leg of the outboard and making the stern heavy. He should just go clear it, just lift the engine over it and he'd be away again, and maybe he should call Mrs Mallow after all, or the Coast Guard, or the bloody Natural History Museum, because whatever was drifting toward the surface behind the boat was no log, and no shark, and it was twice as big as the dinghy at least, and it had one paw ... claw ... something ... on the outboard, and as its head surfaced Tim screamed, then fainted.

He came to with the sun beating down on his eyelids, and a dull pain at the back of his head. He groaned, disoriented, and wiped drool from the corner of his mouth. For one foggy moment he was back on his stag do, passing out at lunchtime on a beach in Cornwall and waking up four hours later with a thumping hangover and heatstroke. Then he smelled outboard fuel and something fishy, and he sat straight up and screamed again. The large, scaly head peering over the side of the dinghy screamed back, blasting Tim with fishy breath so strong it made him gag.

There was a pause then, as they stared at each other. Tim could hear blood rushing in his ears, and the ... the *thing* at the back of the boat blinked at him with big silver-grey eyes. It had a ruff of fins sticking out just behind its head, little nubby horns, and a large collection of very sharp-looking black teeth. One heavy paw rested on the stern, and it had long grey claws. The rest of it was green and glossy and, admittedly, rather sleek and elegant. It cleared its throat, a gunshot of sound that made Tim flinch.

"Holy crap. What the hell. Holy Mary Mother of God. Bloody hell. Um ... Jesus Christ. Crikey. Holy cow." It bared its teeth at him, then continued, swearing enthusiastically in a BBC world service accent. It finally finished on an expression that Tim had never even heard before, but that sounded anatomically impossible, then peered down at him expectantly, teeth still bared.

Tim licked his lips, and wondered if he'd been out in the sun too long. But, imaginary or not, at least the thing didn't seem about to eat him. "Um. What?"

The creature stopped baring its teeth and its eyebrow ridges drew down in something that looked remarkably like concern. "Did I miss something? You all say so many different things. I'm never sure what the correct greeting is." It scratched its chin with one long claw, then, with a hopeful tilt to its head, added something that would have made even old Fred blush.

"Definitely not that," Tim said.

"No? Someone said that to me only a year or so ago." The creature looked so crestfallen that Tim smiled.

"They're more, ah ... expressions of surprise."

"Really? I do knock. You heard me knocking, right?"

"I ... I did. But no one expects a ... a ... what are you?"

"I'm a sea dragon," the creature said, and Tim could hear the *obviously* it had left off at the end of the sentence.

"A sea dragon?"

"Well, yes. What else would I be?"

"I was actually thinking a hallucination, possibly from toxic mould on the shower curtain. Or food poisoning from the coffee."

The creature looked puzzled, then shrugged. "Well, I'm not."

Tim looked at the scratches the sea dragon's claws had left in the aluminium stern, and thought that it really was a particularly vivid hallucination. "Okay, so, sea dragon—"

"Audrey."

"Audrey?"

"It must be an unusual name for you humans. You always have to repeat it."

"It's ... it's not an unusual name for sea dragons?"

"Not really. I mean, my aunt's called Fandance. That's unusual."

"Okay. Yes. Okay." Tim ran a hand over his head and noticed that his scalp was quite hot. Sunstroke, obviously. He should have worn a hat. "So ... Audrey. Are you ... I mean ... are you planning to eat me?" It was easier to ask than he'd thought. But then, she *was* a hallucination, so she couldn't really eat him. The teeth did look alarmingly real, though.

Audrey looked horrified. "Of *course* not! Why in the name of all good sea creatures would I do that?"

"Um ... you have big teeth?"

"That's a very personal thing to say." She actually sounded upset now. "I'm very friendly. And no one eats people, not anymore. Well, no respectable dragons do, anyway."

"I ... I'm sorry. I didn't mean to offend you."

Audrey sniffed, a little dramatically. "Well, I guess if you can't even recognise a sea dragon when you see one, you can't be expected to know these things."

"You are the first sea dragon I've met. First any dragon."

They regarded each other for a moment, then Audrey said gravely, "Pleased to meet you ...?"

"Oh. Tim."

"Pleased to meet you, Ohtim."

"It's ... um, yes. Pleased to meet you, too."

There was another moment's silence, and Tim could hear gulls crying further inshore. Audrey scratched her head somewhere in the vicinity of where her ears probably were, and bared her teeth at him, making him squeak again.

"Are you alright?" she asked.

"I am, yes. But I should probably be getting back to shore. I have to give the boat back."

"Yes, of course. You might want to use the engine, though. You won't get back against the tide, rowing."

Tim looked around in alarm, and added to Audrey's unsuitable vocabulary when he saw how far away the shore was. He was further away than he had been when he'd started rowing. "The engine's broken. I'm going to have to call for help."

Audrey sank down in the water and gave him an unmistakably disappointed look. "Humans. A few people get eaten by sea serpents, a few rogue mermaids dress up and sink some ships, and you just can't see past it. Why do you think I stopped by?"

Tim stared at her. "You'll help?"

"Of course. I thought you were some silly tourist, rowing for the fun of it, so I was just going to tell you to start the engine."

Tim looked at the rods, the line coiling limp and useless. "What about my hooks?"

Audrey dipped her nose like she was embarrassed, then said, "Okay, so I was hungry. Then I realised you might need help."

"Oh. Well, that's okay. I didn't want to catch anything anyway, really."

"Why did you have the lines out, then?"

"It was a reason for being out here."

Audrey lifted her snout out of the water and stared at him out of those silver eyes, then shook her head. "Humans," she said again, then put one paw on the transom and started to swim.

They stopped just outside the breakwater, Tim sitting in the stern with one hand on the outboard tiller for all the world as if he wasn't being propelled by a large underwater dragon.

"There you go," Audrey said cheerfully. "Home safe."

"Thanks," Tim said, still fairly sure he was imagining the whole thing.

"My pleasure," she said, and raised one paw to him. "Be more careful next time."

"Will do," he replied, but she was already gone, the water swirling in her wake. He put the oars back in the rowlocks and paddled back to the boat ramp, sheltered from the tide behind the breakwater. The sun was still warm on his head and the seagulls were fighting behind the fishing boats. It was all very normal, and very dragon-less, and he thought it was past time he got out of the sun. He'd be seeing dancing pink elephants next.

Fred met him at the ramp as the nose of the dinghy bumped into the green-stained mooring poles, and put one hand on the engine. He grunted. "When did she die?"

"Just outside the breakwater."

"Cooled down quick."

"I guess," Tim said, and gathered his gear together, leaving the old man to deal with the outboard while he clambered out of the dinghy and picked his way over the rough ground to a bench by the shed. He was just pulling his shoes gingerly onto his sunburned feet when Fred stopped next to him, the oars in one hand and the fuel can in the other.

"Used to be, mariner types made offerings to the sea," Fred said. "To ensure safe passage."

Tim looked at him, feeling a dehydration headache starting behind one eye.

"Before the voyage, after the voyage, and other times too. You know, an offering to Neptune as you cross the equator and so on."

Tim still said nothing.

"It's worth thinking about. No one offers thanks, why should the sea look after you?"

"So I should leave a fatted calf on the beach at full moon just because I went out in a dinghy one afternoon?"

Fred snorted. "You could. But I find some biscuits left on the end of the breakwater at sunset works a treat."

Tim summoned a laugh from somewhere. "I guess I could do that. Be in the spirit of things." He definitely had sunstroke – or the old man was a bit strange. Probably both.

Fred handed him something from his pocket, a hard flat scale with a filigree pattern of waves running through it. The sun turned the fine edges into emerald glass. "There you go. Little souvenir from the back of the boat. Enjoy the rest of your stay." And he stumped away in his wellies, the oars swinging over his shoulder. Tim watched him go, the sharp corners of the scale digging into his hand and the headache thumping insistently behind his eyes.

He'd heard of places playing tricks on tourists, but this seemed excessive.

Sunset was late, and Tim was tired, but he stayed out anyway. The B&B wasn't the most enticing place to spend time, and what else was he going to do? Sit in a pub and watch midweek football? No, that didn't appeal. So he sat on the end of the breakwater instead, flanked by his two toothless fishing rods, with a book open on his lap and a bag from the corner shop at his feet.

He *had* been planning to go straight home rather than risk the B&B again. Not that it was *terrible,* but, well. There was that mould. And he was fairly sure something had bitten him in bed last night, a thought which made the skin at the back of his neck go all funny.

But he'd had sunstroke, and a hallucination. Patty had wanted him to go straight to hospital, or at least to a GP. He'd refused both, but they had agreed he should stay on another night, and he'd bought insect repellent to treat the bed with. He'd also treated himself to a small can of beer, which he took from the bag now and cracked open as he watched the sun dip into the sea, spilling like molten glass over the smooth surface of the water. The can foamed onto his hand, and he shook the spill off with a little *tut* of annoyance, then settled himself more comfortably onto the rocks, smelling salt and hops and the peculiar tang of unseasonal days.

He wondered if sea dragons preferred chocolate digestives or hobnobs, and if he should have bought some bourbon creams. Everyone liked bourbon creams.

He waited.

The Lizards are Anxious

A second entry for the Twitter prompts. I quite love them, not necessarily as prompts, due to my aforementioned ornery-ness, but as strange little snippets that are almost a story unto themselves. A snapshot of a world set at just slightly the wrong angle.

And every now and then, one opens a door to something else.

I can't find the exact prompt again now, but it involved the ghost of a sous-chef who can only say, "the lizards are anxious!"

As they may well be.

Rachel ran her finger carefully down the listings in the *Ghost Hunter's Manual & How-to Guide*.

"Poltergeists and Restless Spirits," she read aloud. "Haunted Objects. Ek ... eko ... *Ec*toplasm and its Origins." She closed the book with a sigh and looked at the cat sat on the table next to her. "Laetitia, it's all just the same as the other books. Nothing new. Nothing *interesting.*"

The cat looked at her with cool green eyes, then rubbed her face on the edge of the book, almost knocking it from Rachel's grip. She giggled, and scratched the cat's head.

"Honestly," she told the cat, "we're not learning anything new here. I mean, the case studies are interesting, but it's just rehashing the same old stuff. If only Mum would let me sign up for that online course. I bet we'd learn *loads* from that."

The cat blinked lazily, then sat up straight, staring into the shadows of the library stacks. Rachel followed her gaze. She couldn't see anything unusual, but all the books said that animals had better perceptions of the supernatural than humans, so there could be anything out there.

Movement among the shelves, a soft scuff of feet on worn carpet, and the squeak and groan of old wheels. Rachel relaxed. Ghosts didn't scuff their feet. Or she didn't imagine that they did.

A librarian rounded the corner, pushing a trolley laden with returned books. He spotted Rachel at the table and gave her a loose salute.

"Morning, Ghost Hunter General. How goes it?"

"Well, I'm researching," she said, "but it's the same in all the books. You need crosses and holy water, but that doesn't seem terribly scientific, and Mum won't let me get holy water from the church anyway. She says it's rude."

"I suppose she has a point," the librarian said, unloading an armful of books. "You can't just be going around stealing holy water."

"I said that if I couldn't have holy water, then I needed

more scientific equipment, but she said I have to wait till Christmas to get an EMF. I think she thinks I'll have grown out of it by then."

The librarian gave her an amused look. "I'm sure she knows you better than that."

"Well. Maybe." Rachel closed the book. "But I don't know how I'm supposed to build my career without the right equipment."

"Indeed." The librarian put the last of his armload away and scratched his beard thoughtfully. His name was Angus, and as well as the beard he had tattoos, and a ring in his lip. Rachel liked him – he never tried to send her off to the kids' section like some of the other librarians, or do the "Are you sure, dear?" thing when she was checking books out. Now he selected a book from the Paranormal section and held it out to her. "What about this one?"

She slid off the chair and went to take it from him. "The Beginner's Guide to Spirit Communication." She glared at him. "I'm not some cheap medium. This is a scientific endeavour."

"Absolutely. But the nature of scientific investigation is to eliminate all possibilities. So you could set up a video camera and have a go at contacting the spirits, in order to disprove the practise of, of ... of spiritual charlatanry."

"You made that last word up."

"Look it up."

"You're a weird librarian."

"Thank you."

BEING a medium was a lot cheaper than being a ghost hunter. Rachel raided the candles from her parent's bathroom – the book didn't say anything about what sort of candles you needed, and she imagined that lavender and sandalwood scented ones would only make for more relaxed spirit communication. The crystal ball was trickier, but apparently it wasn't strictly necessary. You just needed something to focus your attention, and her old shooting star night-light did just fine for that.

She set everything up on the desk in her bedroom, wondering if the drama of things mattered. The desk was pink, and still had My Little Pony stickers emblazoned across it from that embarrassing phase a couple of years back. She pulled out her *Rachel Agnew, Ghost Hunter* notebook and wrote down her doubts about the unsuitable backdrop, then took a couple of photos on her phone. Thorough documentation was important.

She sat down, closed her eyes, and announced, "I am talking to those who have passed over! Come, speak to me!"

Perhaps unsurprisingly, the response was an overwhelming silence.

"GOOD MORNING, LAETITIA," Rachel said to the cat, who was sitting on the returned books pile.

"Her name's Miss Brontë," the librarian said. Rachel didn't like this one as much. She was young and pretty and sniffy, like she didn't think libraries were a place for young ghost hunters.

"It's not," Rachel said. "She told me it's Laetitia. It's really rude to keep calling her by the wrong name."

The librarian rolled her eyes and went back to the computer. Laetitia jumped from the counter and followed Rachel deeper into the library.

The library was an old building, nothing grand or particularly beautiful, but aged and solid and soaked in years. At some stage there had been a suspended ceiling and clad walls, hiding the grey stone, but sense had eventually prevailed, and now hooded lights hung suspended from the dark beams high above the stacks, and the walls were bare brick and beautiful. Well, Rachel thought they were. Except in the kids' section, where they were all primary colours and big-eyed animal posters. She skirted it carefully, as if afraid she'd be dragged in, and found a quiet corner between History and Nature.

She set out a black cloth (it was an old T-shirt that her dad never wore and she was fairly certain he wouldn't miss) and placed LED candles around its edges. Her mum had been less than happy when she'd walked into Rachel's bedroom to find all the candles burning. She'd confiscated the matches and given her a lecture about playing with fire, and hadn't listened a bit to Rachel's indignant assertions that she was *working*, not playing. But she had found the LED candles for her in a drawer in the kitchen, so there was that. Rachel supposed that lighting candles in the library would probably have got her in even more trouble.

Now she sat cross-legged on the floor in front of the T-shirt, closed her eyes and intoned, "Spirits, come to me. I am talking to those who have passed beyond. Come to me."

Silence. No cold drafts or whispering voices. Just the

muted clatter of keys from the internet stations and someone laughing toward the front of the library.

"Spirits, come to me," Rachel insisted, starting to feel a little silly. "I mean no harm. Reveal yourselves."

Still nothing, and she opened one eye a crack. Laetitia was sitting in the centre of the black cloth, staring off into the stacks.

"Laetitia! You're sitting in the middle of the summoning thingy. That's not going to help matters."

The cat didn't look at her, just kept staring.

"Laetitia?" Rachel followed the cat's gaze cautiously, feeling the hairs beginning to prickle on her arms. Was it colder? She didn't think so, but ...

There was a man standing in front of the History shelves, the books still faintly visible through his white jacket and checked trousers. Rachel stared at him, suddenly far too hot, almost feverish feeling. It was like when she'd been really sick that once, waves of heat and cold passing over her and black spots swimming in her eyes. The man lifted one hand uncertainly, then dropped it again, and his movement broke her paralysis. She scrabbled for her phone, the video already running, and turned it toward him. She could see him on the screen, a little faint and quite suddenly not that terrifying at all. She raised her eyes to him again, reminding herself that she was a scientist first and foremost, and she needed to act like it.

"Hello, uh, spirit," she said. "Can you identify yourself?"

The spirit took a hesitant step closer, and Rachel zoomed in on his feet. It *looked* like he was standing on the old green carpet, but it was hard to know for sure. She zoomed out again.

"I'm Rachel, and I'm a ghost hunter," she told him. A look of terror crossed his face, and he backed up, starting to fade into the shelves. "No, no! Not like a ... I don't kill ghosts, or anything. I just investigate them. Come back!"

The ghost stopped, a copy of *The Battle of Britain* protruding from his forehead, which was somewhat off-putting.

Rachel smiled encouragingly. "I'm not going to hurt you. I just want to find out why you're haunting the library." She'd never even heard of the library being haunted, and you'd think someone would mention it. But he did seem to be a particularly nervous ghost, so maybe he just hid all the time. "Come on," she said. "Look, we're friendly!"

Laetitia gave her a look that suggested she might not entirely agree, but the ghost re-emerged from the shelves and came a little closer. He didn't drift, exactly, but his footfalls were entirely silent, so Rachel supposed that the less keen-eyed observer might imagine he was drifting.

"Now," she said. "What's your name?"

The ghost whispered something, a rustling sound like pages turning.

Rachel frowned. "I'm sorry, I didn't quite catch that."

He whispered again, more forcefully this time. "*... lizards ...*"

"Lizards?"

"*... lizards are ...*"

"Lizards are what?" Rachel asked, bewildered. "What lizards?" This was not going exactly how she'd expected.

"The lizards. The lizards are ... "

"Rachel? What on *earth* are you doing?" the Unfriendly Librarian demanded.

Rachel gave a little shriek of surprise, almost dropping her phone, and the ghost let out a startled wail, spinning around and diving head first into the History shelves.

"Rachel?"

"No, no, come back!" She rushed to the shelves, ignoring the librarian, peering between the books, but there was no sign of the lizard-obsessed ghost.

"Rachel! I asked what you were doing."

She turned back reluctantly, and looked down at Laetitia, still seated in the middle of the electric candles. The Unfriendly Librarian obviously hadn't seen the ghost. Not that Rachel was surprised – grown-ups lacked the sensitivity of children and cats. All the books said that.

"I'm having a tea party with Laetitia."

The Unfriendly Librarian looked sceptical. "Really? Where are your teacups, then?"

Rachel snorted. "Since when do cats use teacups?"

The woman shook her head. "Honestly. Your mother shouldn't bring you to work like this all the time, expecting us to babysit."

"I don't need a *babysitter*. I'm a ghost hunter."

"Sure you are." She turned away. "Don't make a mess. And don't hassle Miss Brontë."

"Her *name* is Laetitia," Rachel whisper-shouted at the Unfriendly Librarian's back, but she didn't turn around, just gave a vague wave with one hand. Rachel looked at the cat. "Isn't it?"

The cat winked, which Rachel figured meant yes.

The ghost refused to come back, although Rachel tried summoning him several times through the afternoon. The Unfriendly Librarian had obviously frightened him off, not that Rachel was surprised. She'd seen small children reduced to tears by the Unfriendly Librarian, so it made sense that a timid ghost would have the same problem.

At home, she uploaded the video onto her laptop and watched it over and over, but she couldn't find out anything more from it, except to determine that the ghost was wearing chef's clothes. Still, it was excellent research material, and she entered the relevant notes into her logbook, remembering to highlight the bit where the Unfriendly Librarian had scared the ghost off. Honestly. How was she expected to work under these conditions?

The next day she set up her workshop – she couldn't bring herself to call it an altar, even in the name of scientific investigation – in the same spot, and called for the ghost once more.

There was no response, and eventually she had to give up when an elderly woman came to browse the war section, and kept stepping over the cloth, muttering "excuse me," and once treading on Laetitia's tail. They retreated together to the big sofas in the adult reading section, and curled up to read about the significance of lizards to ghosts, something that had surprisingly little documentation.

Rachel had dozed off over a copy of *The Layperson's*

Guide to Spiritual Symbolism, when she felt the cat shift and sit up. She petted her reassuringly. "S'okay," she murmured. "Go back to sleep."

The cat gave a soft, breathy mew, and Rachel opened her eyes.

The ghost was crouched in front of the sofa, his vaguely translucent and very worried face so close that she'd have felt his breath if he'd had any. Rachel gave an unprofessional yelp, pressing herself back into the sofa, and the ghost flinched backward, his eyes wide and terrified.

"No, no! Don't go! Stay, please!" She reached out to him instinctively, her fingers passing through his arm and setting an electric little shiver up her spine. They gawped at each other.

"The lizards," the ghost whispered. This close, she could see that his checked trousers were dusted with ghostly flour, and that he had a burn on one hand.

"What lizards? I don't understand."

He closed his eyes, frustrated. *"The lizards. The lizards are. The lizards are ..."*

"Are *what?*"

He shook his head, and drummed his fingers against his lips. Laetitia had been sniffing around his feet, and now she tried to rub against his leg. She stumbled sideways and through his trousers, an astonished look on her face, and Rachel stifled a giggle. That would be very unscientific, laughing in the middle of an actual ghost encounter. Which reminded her – she grabbed her phone and put the video on.

"The lizards are what, Mr Ghost? And what's your name? Do you remember?"

He opened his mouth, thought for a moment, then repeated, *"The lizards."*

"But what's your name?"

He pounded a ghostly fist against his ghostly thigh. *"Lizards! The lizards are! Lizards! LIZARDS!"*

"Okay, okay. I get it. The lizards are the important bit here." She supposed she should have been a little scared at least, but the ghost looked so unhappy. Obviously she needed to release him from his haunting, but she wasn't quite sure how she was going to do that. She'd not researched excess— exer— removing ghosts yet. "Okay, so I think I see the problem here. You have to tell someone about the lizards, then you'll be released from this earthly plane, right?"

The ghost looked puzzled. *"Lizards?"*

"It's okay, you don't have to understand. I do. I'm a professional ghost hunter."

"Lizards." He sounded suitably impressed.

"So sometimes ghosts are just an echo of our former selves, but you're interacting with me, so that's not it. Your spirit is actually here. Which means you have unfinished business. Obviously this unfinished business involves lizards."

"Lizards."

"Exactly." She frowned. "But how – oh, I know! Stay here!" She jumped up and ran toward the children's section, leaving the cat and the ghost sitting next to each other in the quiet library with matching expressions of bemusement.

She was back a moment later with a chalkboard. "There. Now you can write it out."

The ghost looked at the board dubiously, then reached out for the chalk. His fingers passed through it. *"Lizards?"*

"Well, not with your hands, obviously. You have to use telekinesis."

"Lizards?"

"Move it with your mind. You know, like a poltergeist."

"Lizards!" The ghost became markedly fainter, looking around nervously.

"No, no. There aren't any poltergeists here. You need to move the chalk like *you're* one, though."

The ghost frowned, then stared at the chalk, his face screwed up in concentration. Rachel and Laetitia looked on with interest. There was a long, tense silence, then the ghost sighed, and shook his head in frustration.

"Lizards."

"Really? You can't move it at all?"

"Lizards."

"Maybe you just need some practise."

The ghost shrugged, then pointed to the stacks, mimed opening a book, and shook his head again.

"You can't even open a book?"

He pointed at her and nodded.

"Wow. How long have you been dead?"

He turned his palms up and shrugged, then brought his hands together and pulled them apart again, eyebrows raised.

"A long time, huh?"

He nodded.

"Umm – so, have you communicated with anyone before?"

He shook his head, made a sad face.

"Okay. Okay, let me think." He was a bit of a rubbish ghost, really. Dead for ages, but he couldn't even haunt anything properly. Still, every ghost hunter has to start somewhere. "Alright," she said finally. "So maybe if you mime out the rest of the sentence, maybe I'll understand it, and then if I say the words, maybe you'll be able to as well. Then you'll be released. That'll be good, right?"

"Lizards!" He sounded suddenly excited.

"Okay." Rachel had a quick check around, but there was no one about. The library was always at its quietest in the early afternoon. "Off you go."

"The lizards. The lizards are. The lizards are ..." He pulled a gruesome face.

"In pain?"

He shook his head, tried again.

"Unhappy?"

He waved. Closer.

"Umm ... angry. Furious. Hungry."

He stopped, glared at her.

"Sorry. I missed lunch."

"The lizards are ..."

"Scared. Frightened. Worried. Anxious. Panicking—" But she stopped, because he was bouncing up and down, feet soundless on the carpet, one leg vanishing into a shelf. "Anxious? The lizards are anxious?"

He nodded eagerly, clapping his hands together. They connected, Rachel noticed, but made no sound.

"What lizards, though? And why would they be anxious?"

His smile faded, and he shrugged, looking worried.

"Okay, well, maybe that's not important. Say it. See if you can say the words."

"The lizards. The lizards are. The lizards are ..."

He stopped, and Rachel could see his throat working. "Come on! Come on, you can do it!"

"The lizards are. The lizards are ... an ... anxious! The lizards are anxious! The lizards are anxious!" The ghostly chef was jumping up and down again, shouting the words, and one of his out-thrust hands caught a book, sending it spinning to the ground.

"Ooh," Rachel said. "I thought you couldn't do that?"

He stared at the book, then at her, eyes wide. *"The lizards are anxious?"*

"Try it again." She kept the phone camera trained on him as he reached out carefully, and pushed a book with his fingertips. He didn't look any more solid, and his fingers sank into it up to the first knuckle, but then it moved, sliding out of place and teetering on the edge of the shelf before falling to the floor. Rachel winced as it flopped open, and she went to pick up both books. "Okay, so that's interesting."

"Lizards."

"Indeed. Why haven't you vanished, now you're been able to say your words? I mean, can you see a door, or a white light, or anything?"

"Lizards." The ghost picked up the piece of chalk gingerly, managing to hold onto it for a moment before it fell to the floor. *"Lizards!"*

"Yes, but this wasn't the point. You were meant to move on once you could talk, not turn into a poltergeist."

"The lizards are anxious!"

"Stop that!" Rachel grabbed a book before it could fall to the floor. "You'll scare Laetitia!"

The cat gave her a bored look from the back of the sofa.

"Lizards! Lizards lizards lizards!" The ghost spun in a circle, grabbed the chalk from the floor and flung it across the room. *"LIZARDS!"* Then he dived into the shelves and was gone.

Rachel looked at Laetitia. "This did not go quite the way I intended."

The cat gave a yawn that was uncomfortably close to laughter.

The ghost didn't appear again that afternoon, and when they arrived back at the library the next morning everything seemed normal.

"Are you sure you're okay hanging around here again?" Rachel's mum asked her. "You know I could get a babysitter some days."

"And what? Have to go to the park or the movies or something? No. I'm happy." Rachel was examining the shelves for signs of disruption.

"Are you sure? You seem a little anxious."

"*Anxious?* No! I mean, no. I'm fine. Is Angus working today?"

"Yes, he is. Don't be hanging around bothering him all the time, though."

"No, Mum."

"And please stop calling Angela the Unfriendly Librarian. It's not nice."

"Yes, Mum." Rachel was already heading into the stacks.

THE LIBRARY WAS QUIET. It was sunny outside, and not many people bothered with the library on sunny days. Rachel and Laetitia patrolled the shelves, the sound of footfalls and books on the counter making her jumpy. But all was quiet. No whispers, no supernatural activity at all. Maybe it had just been a bit of a delayed reaction. Maybe the door had opened for him during the night or something, and off he'd gone into the light.

"Rachel?"

She jumped. "Yes?"

"What're you doing? You've been walking in circles all morning." Angus stepped around one of the stacks. "You're going to wear poor Laetitia's paws out."

Rachel peered around him. The Unfriendly Librarian was on the front desk, ignoring them. "Have you noticed anything *unusual?*" she asked him.

"Other than you?"

She rolled her eyes at him. "Yes, other than me."

"No. Why?"

"Because I think the library has a ghost."

"Oh! You found one! Well done."

She scowled at him. "I'm serious."

"So am I. That's great ghost hunting."

"Well, the thing is, we may have a problem."

"What's that?"

"The lizards are anxious!"

The whisper came from right next to her ear, and she jumped, spinning around. The ghost grinned at her from among the books.

"Rachel? Are you okay?" Angus asked.

"Didn't you hear that?"

"Hear what?"

"Lizards."

"Shut up!" Rachel hissed.

"I'm sorry?" Angus folded his arms, frowning at her in a most un-Angus way.

"Not you, the ghost."

"The ghost's here now?"

"Lizards. Lizards. Lizards lizards lizards!"

"How can you not hear that?" Rachel asked.

"Humour me. What's it saying?" Angus still looked unimpressed.

"'The lizards are anxious."

"'The lizards are anxious?"

"Yeah. Or quite often just 'lizards'."

"I see." Angus scratched his beard. "Umm – do you think maybe you're spending a bit much time in here?"

"There's a *ghost!*"

"Okay, but Rachel—"

"Lizards! Liz-ards!" Three books spun off the shelf from behind Rachel and onto the floor.

"Rachel!" Angus was frowning again.

"It was the ghost!"

"Put them back."

"But it wasn't me!"

"Lizards?"

"Oh, *shut up!*" Rachel shouted at the shelves.

"Pick those books up, then go and calm down," Angus said. "Otherwise I'm going straight to your mother." He turned and walked away, and Rachel slumped against the shelves, her face hot and tight feeling. Laetitia sniffed the fallen books, then sat down and started cleaning a paw, unconcerned.

"Lizards?" A voice said, rather apologetically, and the ghost emerged from the stacks. He tried to pick up the books, accidentally putting his hand through the cat, who hissed. *"Lizards."*

THEY SAT ON THE SOFA, the girl, the cat and the ghost. Every now and then the ghost would forget he was meant to be sitting on top of the cushions, and would sink in up to his waist, which was disconcerting.

"I helped you," Rachel said to him. "I mean, I know the door and the white light didn't appear, but I *helped* you."

"Lizards," he said, rather disconsolately.

"Now Angus is angry at me, and thinks I'm a liar. *And* a book damager, which is even worse."

"Lizards."

"It's just no good. You're going to have to stop."

"Lizards!"

"Well, it's just too bad. You should have behaved."

The ghost pulled himself out of the chair and picked up a book carefully. *"The lizards are anxious,"* he said earnestly, and the book floated into the air, followed by a sofa cushion.

Rachel gaped, watching the book turn a lazy somersault, then land on top of the cushion, which was still adrift in the air. "That's *amazing!*"

"Lizards!" The ghost gestured toward Laetitia, who rose into the air, looking mildly astonished.

Rachel burst out laughing, then covered her mouth with her hands, still giggling. The ghost grinned, and another few books slipped off the shelves and headed skyward, circling each other like some complicated mobile.

"How did you learn that so quickly?" She'd quite forgotten to be angry at him.

"Lizards."

Rachel felt her feet leave the floor, then her bottom lift off the sofa, and she covered her mouth again, smothering a torrent of giggles as she floated past Laetitia, banging her knee on a bookshelf and rolling upside down with her hair in her eyes.

"Lizards?"

"I'm okay, I'm okay." She paddled wildly at the air, managing to right herself, still giggling.

"Lizards!" The ghost sounded happy, and she saw him smiling as she spun slowly on the spot, like a ball drifting in a pool.

This would all have to be recorded in detail, of course, but right now she didn't even care that her phone was still on the arm of the sofa below her. They'd do it again, properly documented, and then she'd write a ghost hunting – no, a ghost *befriending* book, and be world famous and— she was upside down again, and looking at a pair of pointy purple heels with green skulls on them.

"Oh, *no—*"

"Lizards!"

Then she was falling, everything was falling, and the floor was too close for her to get her legs under her, and she was going to break her nose or lose a tooth or—

The owner of the purple shoes caught her before she could face-plant into the worn green carpet (although it was a close thing), and helped her straighten up. Laetitia gave an indignant hiss as she plunged to the floor behind the sofa, and books rained down all about them. The Unfriendly Librarian caught one just before it could land on Rachel's head, and looked at the shelves.

"Ghosts," she said thoughtfully. "Has Angus been giving you books?"

"Umm … yes?" Rachel offered, her ears rushing with the adrenaline of the fall.

"Damn warlocks. I *thought* he was one." The Unfriendly Librarian shook her head, sleek hair shimmering over her shoulders. "That's a dirty trick, though, getting you working spells for him, to keep the stink off himself. Bet he was hoping for a demon. Never mind. I'll sort it out."

Rachel stared at her as Laetitia wandered out from behind the sofa and rubbed against the woman's legs.

"What?" the Unfriendly Librarian said. "You've never seen a witch before?"

Rachel made a very small sound in the back of her throat, and wondered how exactly she was going to work this into her Ghost Hunter's report.

A Demon of Small Frustrations

I loved living in France. It was a beautiful place of old towns curling into the sea and sprouting from hilltops, of crowded beaches and bulking, empty hills, of small streets swelling with tourists in the summer only to have them ebb away like the tide every autumn. Living there year-round felt like being let in on a secret, as life reasserted itself outside the busy season. It was fancy modern cars and brutally roaring motorways, crammed artisan cheesemakers and crowded markets, flash tourist shops and well-worn local tabacs, and always the beautifully fragrant, ubiquitous boulangeries. And, unfortunately, also home to some ferociously complicated bureaucracy.

Although I'm sure that writing this particular story in one sitting immediately after three days of being sent back and forth between two different towns' tax offices was purely coincidental.

ZOD, THE PERPETUAL IRRITANT, THE CONSTANT frustration, the leaker of pens and loosener of bottle caps, eyed up their latest victim. The human morsel was flopping around in that discomfiting way they had, with their four weird appendages and white-rimmed eyes.

"Ugh," the human said to no one in particular. "I'm going to be late. I'm going to bloody well be late again, and where is my damn *phone?*"

Zod snickered, and pushed the phone a little further behind the breadboard that was leaning against the wall.

"I just – *dammit!*" the human jumped back as the piece of toast they'd been holding snapped in two. Zod gave the falling piece a little flick with one of their tentacles, making sure it landed butter-side-down.

"Today sucks," the human said. "Today totally, totally sucks." It bent down – Zod was always fascinated by how they bent, all at funny angles, instead of concertinaing or oozing – and picked up the toast. It inspected it, sighed, and threw it in the bin. Zod gave the bin a tiny push, so the toast hit the edge, flipped, and landed on the floor again. The human gave a shriek and waved its funny arms about, then sat down on the floor and covered its face with its hands. Zod took the opportunity to scoot to the table and take the human's keys from the cloth receptacle sitting on top of it. It appeared humans didn't have proper, practical pouches, and instead carried all their various accoutrements around in external ones. It made them very easy to visit frustration upon.

Zod wrapped a couple of tentacles around the keys and was turning to stash them behind the fridge when the human said, "What the hell?"

Zod froze. The problem with using physical things to implement little acts of chaos is that one needs a physical body to affect them. While Zod could slip between the atoms of a wall and step from one continent to the other in their thought form, if they wanted to start a tap dripping, they had to take their corporeal one. Which was painfully visible.

They met the human's eyes with half a dozen of their own, the rest roving about wildly in several dimensions trying to see if there was a supervisor in the vicinity or if their slip-up had gone unnoticed so far. The human's eyes were even wider and more stare-y than usual.

"Are those my keys?" it said after a moment.

"I am Zod, Queen of Triplicate Forms and Lord of Pointless Delays!" Zod roared, flinging their longest tentacles wide and raising the ruff around their legs. "Bow before me, worthless meat-monster!"

Or, rather, they tried to roar that. The air of Earth and the aether of the Not-Quite are different, so what came out was a purring squall that made the human bare its teeth to show its amusement.

"Aw, look at you! Where did you come from?" it said, getting up off the floor and crossing to the table. There was water on its face, and it smelt of hideous things like soap and toothpaste. Zod tried to will themself back into their thought form, even though they knew it was impossible now that the thing had seen them. They had to wait until it looked away again.

"I am of the Other!" Zod bellowed. "I stride the demon realms! I am the caster of stubbed toes and the conjurer of slightly-off-even-though-you-only-bought-it-yesterday milk! Tremble before me!" *Prrrrrah-squeee! Prrrr! Grr-maow!*

"Okay, seriously, you are *adorable.*" The human crouched in front of the table, and Zod twisted themself into a taller and more terrifying shape, really putting the writhe into their tentacles. The human made a little squeaking sound and held a hand out toward them. "Where did you come from, little guy?"

Zod abandoned their efforts at communication, as the horrid thing was obviously clueless, and wrapped half their tentacles around its hand instead, putting vigorous effort into melting the flesh from the bone, even though that was a talent for the so-called lower demons. Zod wasn't sure how only being able to exercise your powers when summoned by a human (even if accidentally), then suffering through the inevitable exorcism that followed, qualified you to be a lower demon and enjoy all the status that came with the position. It didn't seem that special to them. Not when compared with inflicting splinters under nails and unexpected items in bagging areas.

The human giggled, a noisome sound. "Aw, are you hungry?" To Zod's horror, the thing *picked them up*. Them, Zod, King of Snagged Tights and Empress of Broken Zips! The revoltingly clean creature pressed them against its soap-stinking chest and carried them in an undignified bundle to the kitchen worktop. They squawked in horror, eyeballs watering with the shock, and the human laughed again. "Okay, I'm doing it. I just bet you're hungry. I wonder what you eat?"

"Your Tuesday gloom and Sunday boredom!" Zod screamed. "Your Saturday terror of not finding a parking space and Monday morning elevated anxiety!" *Prrah-prrah-prrrrrrah!*

The human took a jar from the cupboard, still prattling on in its horrible mouth-voice, and opened the lid. "I don't know what to give you," it said, sticking a finger in the jar. "Maybe— *whoa!*" Because Zod had flung themself at the jar, thinking that if they could throw it across the room the human's attention would be diverted, and they'd be able to make good their escape.

They'd have to report the incident, of course. There was no way around it. The human would need to have its mind scrubbed by lower demons, and Zod would be disciplined. They'd probably be relegated to the Mildly Troublesome But Expected Department, where they'd have to do things like put blisters in new shoes, or make sure people forgot their umbrellas on rainy days. Ugh. Or – oh, devils, *no* – maybe they'd have to bruise new bananas and stick chewing gum on seats in the Everyday Issues Department. Oh, what a devastating promotion that would be! That would be *unthinkable*. Surely it couldn't come to that. Maybe they could put a spin on this somehow. Maybe— They stopped, some of their tentacles still wrapped around the human's hand.

Prrah?

"Dude, I'm not at all sure you should be eating that," the human said, and Zod moved some more of their taste organs to where there was ... something. What was that? They made a little inquisitive noise, and when the human used its other hand to take the jar away, they didn't resist. They were focused on the taste of ... of ...

"Well, you sure like it." The meat-monster shook the jar

at them. "I'm getting a spoon, alright? Stop ... just stop whatever you're doing to my finger. It's gross."

"You're gross," Zod retorted, but without much heat. Not that the human noticed – the word still came out as a little squawk, and Zod went back to slurping the magic jar content off the human's finger. It tasted like a torn fingernail at the end of a too-long week. It tasted like takeaway coffee cup lids that don't seal on early mornings. It tasted like someone else eating the last piece of cake. It tasted like a small scrap of soul, less stolen than worn away.

"Here," the human said, and offered Zod a spoon piled high with the brown goop from the jar. "You weird little thing." Zod detached themself from the human's hand and wrapped themself around the spoon instead, humming with high-pitched pleasure. The human watched them for a moment then said, "I have to go. I can't be late." It sighed, took its keys from the table, and left. Zod barely noticed. They were lost in an ecstasy of taste.

WHEN ZOD CAME BACK to themself, the apartment was empty, as was the jar. They sat up, shaking themself off and rearranging their tentacles, shifting from an amorphous blob to their normal multi-limbed self. They felt a bit shaky, and their eating tubes had been drooling on the worktop. The jar lay on its side next to them, glass polished clean. They burped, loud enough to penetrate the layers of reality, and set about cleaning their tentacles.

They had a problem. Demons fell for earthly delights all the time, which is how they so often ended up exorcised, returned to the Not-Quite in bouncing glass balls that sang with on-hold music. Even for demons, that's unpleasant. And if they didn't get exorcised, but started getting too humanised instead, the real lower-downs dragged them back. Usually in pieces. Neither of those options sounded like something Zod wanted to experience. True, said earthly delights usually seemed to involve flesh of some sort, not – they checked the jar – chocolate-hazelnut spread, but they trusted the lower-downs no more than they did any other demon. Which was to say, not at all.

They investigated the lid of the jar, slurping a lingering smear of spread up just to check it really was as dangerous as they thought, and wondered how to play this. The supervisors wouldn't be aware of the incident until Zod resumed thought form, not unless one decided to pop in and see how things were going. So they needed a plan before they slipped back to the Not-Quite. A way to mitigate the fact that a human had not only seen them, but had engaged with them. *Touched* them.

They shuddered. Just the thought was hideous. Humans were so ... *dry*. And skin-clad. And, of course, there was the problem that the creatures weren't meant to know about demons because reality tears and crossover catastrophes and reality breaches and so on and so on. So what to do? If they could get the human's soul, of course, all would be forgiven, but soul-taking was really for much lower-level demons than them. Zod knew the theory, of course, but how were they meant to strike a deal when the human only heard squawks and purrs? It would have to be a written contract.

They rolled off the worktop and slithered to the table,

where there was any amount of paper piled up, as well as some pens stuck in a chipped mug. Zod resisted the urge to stop two of the pens working and make the other leak all over the table, and instead grasped one in a few of their tentacles and began to write laboriously on the back of a delivery note. Human writing was so unpleasant. All curls and swirls, no nice stabs and brutal slashes. But they could do a passable job.

And then all they had to do was get the human to bleed on it.

ZOD WAS HALFWAY through clause twenty-three and, having run through all the paper, was writing directly on the table, when a key in the lock made them freeze. They almost took on their thought form, and stuttered on the edge of dimensions for a moment, hoping no supervisor was nearby. They settled back on the table as the human let itself in with a bag in one hand, filling the room with the smell of grease and vinegar.

"Hey!" the human said. "You're still here. Cool. I almost thought I'd imagined you, you know?"

Zod wondered if they really needed all ninety-six clauses written out in full. Even using the floor, they were going to run out of room.

"I went to the shop and got bananas." The human inspected Zod with its funny round eyes. It had dark hair that looked soft, but only on its head, and the rest of it was covered with cloth except for its skin-clad face. Zod wondered if it got cold. "I thought you might like bananas.

But you liked the spread, so then I thought maybe you ate nuts, so I got some of those too, and I got fish'n'chips, because I wanted them."

Zod shrugged. They didn't know. They were mostly hoping for more of the chocolate-hazelnut goop.

The human opened a cupboard and got a plate down, and Zod barely managed to resist the urge to knock the creature's head against the open door, just enough to sting.

"I hate my job," the human said in a tone that suggested they'd said it before and never expected anyone to listen. "I had to call a woman and tell her we were repossessing her car today. She's sick. Really sick. It's not her fault, but I can't help. It's the worst." It unwrapped the greasy pack of fish'n'chips and tipped them onto the plate. "Then I had to tell someone else that I couldn't give him finance for a car, even though he can't afford to fix his, and he's going to lose his job without it." The human sighed, and ate a chip. "I wish I could do anything but this."

Zod leaned on their pen, considering the idea of hating what they did. It didn't make sense. Zod *loved* what they did.

"But it's like, leave and be broke and miserable, or stay and be able to live, and still be miserable." The human took a can of something from the fridge and crossed to the sofa, where it did that weird folding thing again and sat down. "You're lucky you're a ... whatever you are. Being a human really sucks."

The demon watched the human push a chip around on its plate. There was water on its face again. It looked like every frustration Zod could conjure, every broken pen and red light and petty, power-hungry official, had been visited on it in one day, and that it expected to wake up tomorrow to more of the same. And the day after that. And the one after that, too, for all eternity. It should have been beautiful.

Zod looked at the contract, dotted an *i*, and put the pen down. They oozed off the table, scuffling across to the sofa on the tips of their tentacles.

The human looked down at them. "Hey."

Prrah-aw?

"And the worst of it is, I know I should leave. That it's better to be broke than be this unhappy. But what if it's not the job that's the problem? Not really?"

Prrah.

"Dude, I think it's me. I think *I'm* the problem. It's all me, but I don't know how to fix it. How do you fix unhappy? *Can* you fix it? Is that even possible?"

The human was leaking from its eyes at an even greater rate, which was alarming. Zod didn't want it to desiccate before they could get the contract done. They clambered onto the sofa and sat next to the thing, waving their tentacles in a conciliatory manner.

Prrah-oop, they advised it. *Prrap-aow*. Which was as close as they could seem to get to, "The limitless void awaits your death, but if you sign with me on this limited time offer I can guarantee you an eternity of those annoying little bits of skin that come loose by your nails and hurt a completely disproportionate amount, tempered by the occasional bout of out-of-season mosquito bites." That should make the futility of mortal existence a little easier to bear.

"Yeah," the human said. "*Prrah* to you, too." It bared

its teeth in that alarming way again. "You're a good listener."

Prrah-nah-nrra. "I can throw in a few aeons of being passed around marketing departments on hold, if you want."

The human shuffled itself around so it could get its whole awkward body and angle-y legs on the sofa, taking care not to knock Zod off, then it offered them a chip. "Dinner?"

Zod doubted anything could come close to the glory that was chocolate-hazelnut spread, but they wrapped a tentacle around the chip and moved some mouth organs into place. Grease, yes. And heat and earth and, oh, devil, *vinegar*, cutting through it all and sinking the whole thing into a glorious euphoria of taste! They squawked, rolling half a dozen eye stalks, and entirely forgot their distaste of all things human. They scrambled onto the creature's lap and curled themself around the plate.

"Hey! Don't get greedy." The human bopped them between a few eye stalks, making them squeak in alarm and pull back. "Share, okay?"

Zod was not at all sure what this *share* was, but the human was offering them another chip. They took it, and let the human push them around gently so they were only leaning on half the plate, quite ignoring the natural revulsion the thing raised in them.

"There we go," the human said, and tore off a piece of battered fish. "Eat up, little dude."

Zod purred, gobbling the fish and the chip at the same time, their whole body trembling with delight. The human chuckled and turned the TV on, and Zod wondered if one could have chocolate-hazelnut spread with fish'n'chips. They'd have to try.

THE HUMAN HAD SLID FURTHER DOWN on the sofa, and Zod, full of glorious, greasy food, was on its chest, slowly becoming a blob.

"I need to give you a name," the human said.

"Zod, Empress of Small Torments," Zod said, feeling horribly tired. They'd heard of this, that sometimes if one stayed in physical form too long one periodically lost consciousness. It had sounded implausible, but now it made a strange sort of sense.

The human chuckled. "That almost sounded like you said 'Zod'. Okay, Zod. It's bedtime."

"Zod," Zod agreed, eyes half-closed. They didn't even flinch when the human put its horrible clean fingers in among their tentacles and scratched them in a gentle sort of circle, the way succubi sometimes did with demonlings. It made their locomotor tentacles go all limp and exhausted.

"Zod," they mumbled again, aware that they were starting to drool and managing to hold onto themself enough to hope it gave the human a nasty rash. Then they were gone.

Zod, father of tiny crises and mother of niggling annoyances, snored musically, smelling of fish'n'chips and a lingering whiff of chocolate. The human watched them for a while, a smile creasing its lips. It was still smiling when its eyes closed and it drifted off, the demon curled in the curve of one arm.

Somewhere, reality shivered. Flowers bloom wasteland, and missing socks found their match. A cat vomited on the tiles instead of the rug, and someone caught a mug before it smashed.

On such small foundations are good days built.

Sometimes even the best.

Organ Thieves

I very clearly remember where this story came from. I was stop-starting my way down the Bord de Mer from Nice airport to Antibes, on the Côte d'Azur, and there was a segment on the car radio about organ thieves. Which was an entirely unpleasant thing to be thinking about, but I wasn't really listening, to be honest. I was mostly concentrating on not hitting any of the delivery drivers on mopeds who evidently believed cars were nothing more than fun obstacles, to be dodged by the finest margin possible. By the time I tuned back in, the radio was talking about a Christmas concert in a church. A few days later, my subconscious flung up this story. It's a weird place, my subconscious.

"*How much?*"

"Well, it depends on the organ, but £50,000 or so."

"Agnes, that's crazy. And risky."

"No, it's not. We only take those that won't be missed, anyway. Abandoned, if you like."

There was a pause, then Ralf said, "What would we do with the money?"

"Put it in the fund to get this place done up." Agnes gestured across the roof, where chunks of missing tile gave it the patchwork look of a balding snake. "No one else is coming up with anything."

Ralf scratched his chin. "I think it'd need more than that."

"So we get some more from somewhere. It's a start, right? This damn place is going to fall down around our ears, and there's not a building in the city I like enough to move to."

"All the decent ones already have gargoyles, anyway," Ferdinand said. "We can't *move.* We've been here forever."

Agnes nodded. "Not to mention Bertram's not moved for a hundred and twenty-three years. We're hardly going to be able to shift him now."

"Cecily?" Ralf asked. "What do you think?"

She shrugged, shaking the damp mist off her wings. "Personally, I think our Aggie's onto something. And if no one's going to miss them, well ... at least the money'll be put to good use."

Ralf ticked his claws off the tiles. "Alright," he said finally, and Agnes gave an enormous, toothy grin. "But if we're going to do this, let's do it right. Let's round up a few. May as well make as much as we can."

The man in the expensive jacket frowned at the woman. She was unclear, somehow, as if he were looking at her through someone else's glasses, and he took his own off, giving them a little polish on his shirtfront before putting them back on again. She still seemed a little out of focus, and he supposed it must be the cold. There were days he really wished he had the sort of meetings that were conducted in heated offices.

He adjusted his fedora – it gave him a little extra height and a touch of sophistication, he felt – and asked, "Can you be more specific?"

"Not as yet." Her voice was rough. She sounded like she smoked a couple of packs a day, but it could be just the flu or something. Jesus, it was cold enough out here to freeze the spit on your tongue.

"Then I can't give you an exact price," he said, thinking longingly of the deep seats of the car, and maybe a tipple to warm up with. "It's going to depend on condition and quality. I'll have medical staff examining them on pickup."

"Oh," the woman said, and she sounded confused. What, had she thought he'd just hand the money over without checking the product? But then she nodded and added, "Yes. Of course." She was wearing some voluminous black dress that made the man in the jacket think of period dramas and bonnets, although she wasn't actually wearing anything on her head – was she? He pinched the bridge of his nose, eyes watering in the sharp edges of the night air. It was oddly difficult to look at her directly. His eyes just seemed to lose interest, wandering off again, choosing to focus instead on the brickwork beside her, or the stained tarmac at her feet.

"Fifteenth," he said. "Two a.m., here. If you're not here, I'm gone. Anyone else is here, I'm gone. And if you've been jerking me around with all this crap about 'quality organs' – well, there's more than one way to get them, if you catch my meaning."

There was movement at the edge of his vision, and he knew the man who had been lounging against the side of the car with affected disinterest had straightened up in anticipation. He was a big man, employed for the breadth of his shoulders and the impressiveness of his scowl. Although the man in the jacket also knew that his large employee harboured dreams of appearing on a certain well-known baking show. No one else needed to know that, though.

"I'll be here," the woman said, sounding unimpressed.

"Well. Good." He wanted to say something more, to impress on her the seriousness of the situation, the seriousness of *him,* but it was too cold, and she was ... well, weird. So he just nodded, a sharp, dismissive movement, and turned back to the car. His cake-loving bodyguard had already opened it, and warmth swelled out toward him. He slid into the embrace of the smooth leather seat and listened to the reassuringly heavy *chunk* of the door shutting out the night.

The car barely dipped as the bodyguard got in, and the engine gave a hungry rumble as it started. All was as it should be. So why did the woman seem so very much not as *she* should be? He watched her, rendered still more indistinct by the tinted windows, as they backed out of the alley, tyres hissing in an early frost. She didn't move, just watched him go, and as they purred away down the shuttered high street, he had the uneasy feeling that she was standing there still, in the city-dark shadows between the old buildings, immobile and silent and not quite real. He shivered and took his hat off, then plucked the whisky from the well between the seats. Seriously, the weirdos he met in this business.

"Boss, did you see the showstopper challenge?" the bodyguard asked as they paused at the lights. "Bloody marvellous, it was."

Never mind the ones he worked with.

"Ferdie! Gods, don't *break* it!"

"Sorry, sorry." He lowered his corner of the box gingerly to the ground.

Agnes scowled at him and took a moment to look around the abandoned church. It had become a bolthole for the broken and the lost, abandoned bottles and discarded rubbish pocking the lurching, derelict pews like the droppings of some heartbroken creature. The stained-glass windows were long-shattered, and the graceful loft of their frames were patched with soggy cardboard. It was cold, the wind slipping through the gaps in the walls and roof to play amid the dust and leaves and debris. Not that the cold bothered the gargoyles, but Agnes could have wept for the building. It had never been grand, but it had once been beautiful, with its vaulted ceilings and fine stonework on the columns. Now it was just another piece of rotting masonry, walls defaced with graffiti by the kids who came in on dares, smelling of rats and damp and filth.

Ferdie sniffled, and Agnes blinked at him. "Don't do that."

"But—"

"Ferdie." She kept her voice as level as she could. Him and his bloody romanticism. He'd never fully recovered from seeing Byron visiting the graveyard once. And she could see it already – in a moment he was going to want to try and save this church as well as theirs, and this one was a lot less pleasant. The gargoyles had been gone from here too long. They'd slept too deep and fallen as their roof rotted, perhaps, but more likely they'd been smashed by the ignorant in the name of progress. Agnes had seen it happen to more than one clan, when the gargoyles were too old or too stubborn to move. Time moves on, things fall out of fashion and out of knowledge, and everyone forgets gargoyles are protectors, the fierce soul of a building. Humans would declare them ugly, broken, old-fashioned, and tear them down, smash them on the earth, then wonder why the building became something haunted and broken after. But once it was done, it was done. It was rare you could save a building whose soul had been taken.

"Ferdie," she said again. "We've got a lot to do tonight. Can we move it along?"

"Yeah, yeah." He sighed, then picked up his end of the box again. "It just upsets me, you know?"

"I know." She wished she'd paired up with Cecily instead, or even Ralf. Lectures on the history of each building, including architects, builders, techniques and materials used were still preferable to listening to Ferdinand do his dramatic sighs. If he started crying, she was going to drop the damn box on his tail. Just see if she didn't.

Dusk was undecided, heavy clouds pressing the light out of the sky so that dark grey afternoon gave way to darker grey evening. The street lights were swaddled in mist, and the pavements were filled with people who walked with their heads bent and their coats pulled tight at the collar. On the roof of the church, a winged gargoyle with a ridged spine shook herself, then yawned and stretched. It was still early, but unless there was a service, they didn't bother about the people passing by. No one ever saw them. Well, no one *noticed* them, to be more accurate. The odd kid might, of course, but adults are so keen to rub the magic out of young minds that the gargoyles would just wave at them or pull faces. It kept both parties amused.

Agnes groomed herself while she waited for the others to wake up, dislodging the day's grime and pigeon droppings. Foul birds. Her mind wasn't really on the job, however. Tonight was the night of the deal. She thought of the boxes stacked in the crypt and felt a little worm of unease. It wasn't *right*, selling organs. But then, neither was allowing this beautiful old church, one of the last in the city, to fall still further into disrepair. She'd heard the vicar praying for money to fix the leaking roof as often as she prayed for more attendees. And it wasn't like the owners of the organs had any use for them anymore. She just hoped they were in good enough condition for the small man in his big car.

THE BODYGUARD HELD the car door open for the small man in the expensive coat, who settled his hat on his head as he got out. The van with the medical team pulled in behind them, and the two sets of headlights lit the alley like a stage set, washing over the woman in the strange black dress.

"Good evening," the woman said in her rasping voice.

"Good—" the small man started, then stopped, his attention caught by the pile of boxes stacked next to her. They looked like they'd been put together by twelve-year-olds in a rush to finish art class, all splintery and uneven. "What the hell are *those?*"

She inclined her head slightly. "The organs, of course."

"What?" The boxes certainly weren't refrigerated – although he supposed they *might* be insulated – and they were the roughest bloody things he'd ever seen. Even that guy in the early days who had turned up with his own kidney, chopped out by his cousin, had at least put it in a proper cooler box, even if it had been one with strawberries printed on it. The boss strode forward, shadowed by the bodyguard, and rapped on top of one of the boxes, unconsciously choosing the one furthest from the woman. It sounded empty rather than insulated, and they were all *far* too big. Some of them were as tall as he was.

"What *is* this?" he demanded again.

The woman tipped her head again. It was odd how she

still seemed unclear, difficult to see even close up, and with the two sets of headlights on her.

"Open it," he snapped at the bodyguard. "Hurry up!"

The big man grabbed a box and pried at the top ineffectually. "It won't open, Boss."

"Then get some tools, for God's sake." He shook his head as the bodyguard hurried to the car. The size of these boxes ... could there be whole *bodies* in them? *Drugged* bodies? That'd explain the lack of insulation, too, but man. That was messed up. That was ... well, he could still take them, he supposed. As long as there weren't kids. He wasn't dealing with kids. And he wasn't paying full price if he had to dispose of bodies as well. He glanced sideways at the woman, but she just stood there serenely, arms hanging loose at her sides as the bodyguard hurried back from the car with a tyre iron in one hand and the medical guys in tow.

The boss waved at the boxes imperiously and took a step back. "Get them open so I can see what we've got."

The bodyguard raised the tyre iron, ready to jam it into the top of one of the boxes, then gave a yelp as it was pulled from his grip, as effortlessly as a parent takes a toy from a toddler.

"No," the woman said. "You might damage them."

The bodyguard made some wordless sound as she gripped his shoulder and moved him away from the box, then handed the tyre iron back to him. He stared at it as if he'd never seen one before, and the woman took hold of top of the box in one hand and ripped it off in a screech of nails.

The man in the expensive coat looked from his bodyguard to the woman, who gestured at the box invitingly. He didn't actually want to look. He wasn't a stranger to unpleasant things, but he felt very firmly that this night was not going his way, and had maybe got a little more weird than he was comfortable with. He wanted to go home. But if there really were bodies in all these boxes, and they were usable ... well, he couldn't walk away.

So he stepped forward and peered into the box, bracing himself for the sight of a corpse, or a comatose body, or even – God knows – a jumble of bloody organs just all sloshed in there together. But what looked back at him were pipes packed in loose leaves and old newspaper, discoloured with age but still smooth and straight and true. He reached out and poked one with a hand that trembled just slightly. The pipe was cold to the touch, a little dusty, and very, very un-organ-like.

"What the hell is this?" he whispered, looking at the woman finally.

"Organs," she said. "We found four, all complete, all in good condition. They just need a bit of a clean."

"Organs," he repeated, looking back in the box. *"Organs?"*

"Or-gans," she said, drawing the word out. "For music? In churches? Yes?"

"Yes." He straightened up, suddenly understanding. It was a scam, some madness set up by the bloody Southerners most like, to distract him from ... from what? They must have a massive deal going down, damn them. Moving into his territory, trying to make their mark— *"Organs,"* he hissed at the woman. "Hearts and lungs and livers and kidneys, not ... *this.*" He kicked the box, setting the pipes clanging. "But you know that, don't you? Bloody Danny set this up, didn't he?"

"I'm sorry," she said, and the rasp in her voice was more pronounced. "Hearts and lungs?"

"And livers and kidneys and eyes and all the rest." He pointed at her, feeling a vein throbbing in his forehead. "But that's okay. I'll not have my time completely wasted. Yours'll do just fine."

"*Bodily* organs. *Human* organs."

She didn't even sound afraid – didn't she realise he was going to gut her right here, in front of her bloody boxes? Gut her and send her ears back to Danny as a warning. "Grab her," he ordered the bodyguard. The big man took a tentative step forward, tightening his grip on the tyre iron.

"Humans *need* those," the woman said, and casually shrugged the bodyguard off as he grabbed her shoulder, sending him spilling to the ground with a look of panic on his face. "You nasty little man." She addressed the last to the man in the expensive suit, and another rasping voice called from above her.

"Told you it was too good to be true, Agnes." The man looked up, startled, and saw three ... three *things* climbing ... no, climbing suggested effort, and they seemed to be *walking,* walking down the walls on all fours, tails curling and whipping behind them like cats in a mood, wings casting shadows on the stone behind them.

Which was one weird too many. He bolted for the car, his hat spinning to the ground behind him.

"Dammit, Ralf," Agnes said, and pulled the dress over her head, dropping to all fours and unfurling her wings in a snap that knocked over one of the men from the van. His friend didn't even stop to help, just turned and fled. She glanced at the bodyguard, who had sat up and was staring at her with the tyre iron still clutched to his chest, then said to Ralf, "How was I to know? What kind of degenerate goes around buying bodily organs from strangers in a dark alley?"

"Maybe you should have thought of that first," Ralf replied, and took an easy leap from the wall, landing on top of the car before the small man in the expensive coat could reach it. The suspension creaked alarmingly, and glass shattered as the sunroof gave way. The man screamed, and Ralf said, "Oops."

Agnes growled at the back of her throat and stalked over to join them. The bodyguard scrambled to his feet and ran for the medical van, flinging himself in as the driver slammed it into reverse. There was a solid sounding crunch, followed by the belch of an exploding tyre, and Ferdie said, somewhat indistinctly, "Ouch."

Cecily prowled up to the man Agnes had knocked over with her wings and sniffed him. He had both hands over his eyes, pretending he couldn't see them, and was muttering to himself in a panicked monologue. "I think you broke him," she said.

"I didn't hit him *that* hard," Agnes protested.

"Not bones. But he keeps saying he's in his happy place."

"Huh." Agnes turned her attention to the small man at the centre of all this distastefulness, still cowering by the car, and said, "Human organs? Why?"

"People need them," he whispered. "It's just supply and demand."

She nodded. "I rather had the impression that sort of thing was done through hospitals, not back alleys."

"Too many people need them. Not enough people give them." He was shaking so badly she was surprised he didn't just fall over right there.

"And you don't ask where they come from."

"People need money."

"They do." Agnes looked at Ralf. "What d'you reckon?"

Ralf took a swig from the bottle he'd fished out of the car through the sunroof. "I've got an idea."

"Hey, George! Check this out."

"What?" It was warm behind the duty desk, and George had no desire to go and peer out into the night-time streets.

"Just come here."

He groaned, got up, and let himself out of the office, then went to stand in the police station door next to Deva. In one of the visitor parking spaces outside the station, sitting cross-legged and looking both terrified and humiliated, were four shivering men in underwear of varying degrees of cleanliness. Their hands and legs were bound to each other, so that they sat in a little circle, facing outward. There were some scratches on their shoulders, but otherwise they seemed unharmed. Someone with uneven, jagged handwriting had printed in permanent marker on the chest of the man closest to them, *I deal in human organs*. Their clothes were piled in front of them, crowned with two sets of car keys.

George looked around for either the missing cars or the culprits, but, other than the sad little huddle of men, the street was three a.m. empty. He rubbed the back of his head. "Batman?" he suggested.

"No idea," Deva said, and took her phone out. "But I'm totally getting this on camera."

IN THE COLD chill of early morning, Reverend Valerie Scott let herself in the side door of the church, then went to unlock the main ones from the inside, the drafts from the cracked windows and unsealed walls chilling her even through her thermals and heavy boots. She pushed one door open just far enough to peer out and make sure no poor soul had been sleeping in the vestibule, and was about to let it close again – for all the good it did against the weather – when she spotted a box in the corner. She frowned at it, then pushed her way through the doors and poked the thing with the toe of her boot. It didn't scream or explode, so she picked it up and carried it into the kitchen while she put the kettle on. It was probably some sort of donation for the charity shop. She could drop it off in the afternoon.

A little later, she absently opened the top of the box while she waited for her bread to toast, and spat tea over £200,000 in neatly stacked, unmarked bills, then had to go and lie down for a while.

And on the roof, the gargoyles crouched unmoving and weather-stained, their faces lifted to the thin winter sunlight as it filtered through the trees in the graveyard, just as they had since the days when the church was young, and just as they would until the walls fell beneath them and the world moved on.

One was wearing a rather jaunty fedora.

The Water Hazard

I do not play golf. I don't play any ball sports, actually, as I have the coordination of one of those dogs with hair so long it can't see where it's going, and which only stay upright because four legs are better than two. I take it as inevitable that I will fall off any bike I get on, probably sooner rather than later, and have fallen while running more times than is reasonable. I currently have a large scar on my shin where I apparently tried to run ***through*** *a stone stile in Yorkshire, for reasons that are still unclear to me.*

Which is why I tend to stick to water-based sports, given the choice. The landing's usually a little softer. And also why I am apparently a little hazy on what exactly a water hazard is.

But I do know people should listen to their spouses.

"No! You're doing it all wrong."

"Am I, dear?" Laura asked wearily.

"Yes. You're not following through on your swing properly."

"I see."

"And your stance is terrible. Maybe you need new shoes. We should get you new shoes."

"I like these shoes." Laura rested the golf club against her shoulder and peered down at the footwear in question. They were – or had once been – canary yellow, and were comfortably scuffed.

"We'll get you new ones," Saul declared, and gave her a little hurry-up gesture. "Well? Are you going to play, or what?"

Laura had a brief but satisfying vision of smacking the golf club straight into his carping, whingeing mouth, but then there'd be blood to clean up, and dentists to go to, and complaining, complaining, complaining. And also assault charges. So she settled her stance, tried to ignore her husband huffing and *tsk*-ing next to her, and swung the club in a smooth, relaxed movement, hearing the satisfying clunk of connection as she twisted into the follow through.

Saul *hmph*ed. "I'm amazed you get the distance you do. Your form's awful."

Awful enough to know her handicap was one of the best in the club, but there was no point mentioning it. There was never any point mentioning things like that. She took her water bottle from the buggy and had a sip as he fussed, windmilled his arms to stretch out, set his ball on the tee, moved it half an inch, shaded his eyes to peer down the fairway, moved the tee another half inch, and finally started to settle himself in position. She swallowed a sigh.

"What was that?" he asked her, straightening up. "Did you say something?"

"No, dear."

"I thought you said something." He peered at her suspiciously, and she wondered if she'd ever actually found him attractive. Handsome, yes – even now, newly retired and carrying a little belly, he was handsome. But attractive was something else entirely.

She waved the bottle at him. "I was having some water."

"Huh. Well, be quiet. I'm concentrating."

He turned to the fairway, and she gave his back a mock-salute. Such a pity she hadn't had anything else to do today, and he'd cornered her before she could come up with a plausible excuse. She hadn't played golf with him for at least ten years, and she was starting to remember why.

"So why couldn't you play at your club, dear?" she asked as they followed the trail of their balls down the fairway. Hers was on the edge of the putting green, she noted with some satisfaction. Even with the distraction of Saul's comments, she'd still hit further and more accurately than him.

"Well, now that I'm not in the office every day, your club's much handier."

"I didn't know you were thinking that." She tried to keep a small note of panic out of her voice. "I thought you liked your club."

"Well, I also had a falling out with a few members of the committee. They didn't want me on it. Can you imagine?

The skills and experience I could bring to that place, and all I got was, oh, we're not looking for any more board members right now, Saul. When that doddery old Alfred should have been made to retire ten years ago!"

Laura made a small, commiserating noise, and wondered where the next nearest club was. She'd miss her regular golf buddies, of course, but it was better that than having to put up with Saul on the green as well as everywhere else.

"And isn't this nice? Spending time together?" He gave her a gentle, one-armed hug, and smiled down at her. "We haven't done this for years."

She smiled back in spite of herself. It was true, they hadn't done it for years. Between kids, and work, and just *life*, time together had been hard to come by. Which, over the years, she'd decided was no bad thing. Saul's presence seemed to throw her off balance, to undermine her foundations and make things shaky. In theory, he was a wonderful person to be with. Maybe he even had been, once. In practice ... well, in practice, living separate lives out of one house turned out to be by far the best option. Divorce seemed excessive, and like such a hassle besides. Especially as her investments had shored up his business for so many years, so the settlements would be complicated, and then there was alimony, and one of them having to move, and ... no. It had worked. She examined his face as they walked together, his arm snug around her. Maybe it could still work. This ... yes. This was nice.

"There's your ball," Saul said.

Laura frowned. "That's *your* ball. Mine's on the green."

He laughed, a hearty *aren't-you-cute* laugh, and patted

her bottom. "You're so funny, love." And he left her there, marching over to commandeer her ball without even the smallest glimmer of remorse. She scowled after him, and swung her club a few times. No. She'd been right the first time. This was not going to work.

Ten holes down and she had a pounding headache. She'd taken a couple of paracetamol, but she could still feel the tight bands of stress across her forehead, forerunner of a migraine if she wasn't careful. And she knew why. The silly sod kept stealing her balls and acting like she was the one trying to cheat when she protested. She wondered if she should just throw her golf club across the fairway, like tennis players sometimes did, and storm off. Only then he'd probably say something condescending about "ladies' problems", and she'd end up throttling him with that ridiculous tartan bandanna he was using to keep the sun off his neck. Prison would certainly give her a break from him, but it wouldn't be her first choice for a solution.

"Are you alright, Laura?" a new voice asked, and she lowered her hand from over her eyes to give the golf pro a half-hearted smile. He had two women in tow, both of them bright pink with sunburn and effort.

"Hi, Giles. Just a bit of a headache."

He followed her gaze to Saul, chest puffed out over his chequered green trousers as he fussed on the putting green. At least he couldn't steal her balls on there. That was going too far even for him, and by her count he'd taken three shots and still hadn't sunk the thing. "So I see," Giles said. "Not helping your handicap today, then?"

She smiled, properly this time. "Not today."

"Ah, well." He touched a hand to his forehead in mock-obsequiousness, tipped her a wink she just glimpsed behind his sunglasses, and turned to shepherd his students away.

"You there, wait! You work here, yes?" Saul had hurried over while they talked, sweat beading on his cheeks.

Laura resisted the urge to cover her face with her hand again.

"I'm the golf pro, yes," Giles said.

"There's something wrong with this hole. The ball won't go in."

Giles looked at him, his expression carefully blank, and repeated, "The ball won't go in."

"No. I think there's a ridge around the hole, or something. You need to look at it."

"I'm actually giving lessons right now—"

"I pay to use this course! I expect things to be in working order!"

"I see. Well, I can get someone from maintenance—"

"We're playing *now.* It needs to be working *now.*"

"Saul—" Laura tried.

"It's okay, Laura, I've got this under control." Saul puffed his chest out in his pale pink polo shirt and glared at Giles like an enraged parakeet. "Just take a look, can't you? These ladies look like they could use a break, anyway."

The ladies in question looked slightly bewildered, and one of them gave Laura a sympathetic look, but Giles shrugged. "Fine. I'll take a quick look, then call maintenance if I find anything." He selected a putting iron from his bag and crossed to the green, sparing Laura a sly sideways grin as he went. She followed the two men.

"I tell you, the ground's rough close to the hole. Or there's a slope."

Giles crouched down, running tanned fingers over the close-cropped grass. "Huh. Maybe." He straightened up and looked at Laura. "Care to try?"

"Sure."

"Well, you won't have any more luck," Saul told her. "There's something wrong with it."

"I'm sure you're right, dear," she said, lining up the shot. She gave the ball a soft little just-so tap, and it scooted across the ground, hesitated, then dropped neatly into the hole.

No one spoke for a moment. Then one of the women said, "Did you teach her? Because that's amazing!"

"She's a natural," Giles said, and gave Saul the full benefit of his smile. "And now we've got a lesson to get on with."

Saul was still staring at the hole, the ball nestled inside like an uninspired Easter egg. "Sure," he said. Then, when the trio had left – not without Giles tipping Laura that conspirator's wink again – he looked at her and said, "That's still my ball."

"Of course," she said. "Why not."

THE FOURTEENTH HOLE, and Laura's headache was spreading, turning to tight knots of tension in her shoulders that made her swings uncomfortable. She'd run out of water, too, because they'd been out here for so damn long. They'd even had to let four groups play through, and that hadn't improved her mood.

"Dammit," Saul snapped. He had sweat stains under his arms, and his nose was painfully red. His ball had overshot the green and vanished into the long grass just before the water hazard. He'd stopped stealing her balls after the fiasco on the tenth, and mostly stopped talking, too. Laura sighed. She shouldn't have taken the shot. She should have just told Giles to do it himself, but there was a mean little part of her that wanted to rub her husband's face in the fact that she was a better player than him, that wanted him to feel small for once. She was ashamed of it, but ... but. It had felt good.

"Take another one," she said, her voice mild.

"No." He gave her a sulky look. "I'll hit it back."

"Not from there. Not by the water hazard."

"Why on earth not? It hasn't gone in."

"We just ... we don't. Not within two metres of the water. See? There's a sign." She pointed to the neat *Do Not Enter* placard anchored at the edge of the long grass, between them and where the ball had disappeared. Beyond it, the water of the mini lake was placid and dark, a gap in the brightness of the day.

"Why? Is the bank unstable? That's very unsafe. Health and safety—"

"I don't know, Saul. It's just club rules. No one goes in." Not even the mowers.

He *hmph*ed. "Well, I'm not losing a ball for an *I don't know*. It'll be fine." He stomped off toward the water hazard, his posture very clearly that of a man hot, thirsty, and fed up with Nonsense.

"Saul, wait!" She jogged after him, catching his arm just before he stepped off the shorn grass of the green. "Don't. Just get another ball and go from here." This close, the water seemed to be watching her, and she didn't want to look at it directly. Reeds formed strange shapes on the edge of her vision.

He shook her off, mouth twisting into a sneer. "You'd like that, wouldn't you? Something else to laugh about with your golf crones and that creep of a golf pro?"

"Saul—"

"No, I'm not *stupid*. I know you don't want to be out here with me. Think you're some hot shot in your pathetic little club, don't you? All special?"

"Saul, don't go near the water." She could smell it now, boggy and stagnant, and she imagined the corpses of birds sinking into the thick mess of mud and silt somewhere in the depths, nesting among the lost balls.

"Don't go near the water," he mimicked her in a sing-song voice. "I really thought we could have a nice day, but no. You and your eternal superiority, your headaches, your sighs. I don't know why I bothered."

"Just leave the ball," she said. "It's a game. It doesn't matter."

"Of course it *matters*. Everything *matters*." He pulled away from her and strode into the long grass, then started digging through it with his hands. "Where is the damn thing? And I'll hit it out from here, Laura. See if I don't."

"Saul, please! We don't go in there!" She hovered on the edge of the green, on the edge of safety, smelling that festering stink and seeing the way the still water refused to reflect the sky.

"*We?* Who's *we?* You and your girlies making up stories and simpering about some over-the-hill golf pro who never made it big and wouldn't look twice at any of you anyway?" He was still digging through the grass. "Where *is* it?"

"You're not going to find it. Just come out." Her headache was well into migraine territory, and she couldn't even muster the energy to feel properly offended at being called both a crone and a girlie in the space of one conversation.

"Jesus, it stinks in here. No wonder they don't want anyone going anywhere near it. They can't have done any maintenance on the bloody thing for years."

"Saul, just *listen*, would you? Come out!"

"Oh, *shut up*, Laura!" He straightened up, and they stared at each other in shock. "I'm sorry," he said, his shoulders slumping. "I'm being an arse, aren't I?"

"Yes," she said.

"Look, I'll just get the ball—"

"Leave the Goddamn ball!" The peaty, boggy smell was so strong she was almost gagging on it, and she backed away, trying to find fresh air. God, her head hurt. And her eyes were swimming, even behind her sunglasses.

"Well, there's no need to talk to me like that." The old Saul, glimpsed for an instant, was gone again, and the sulky lip and furrowed brow were back. "But if you're going to make such a bloody fuss— wait. It's there!" He waded through the grass to the edge of the water. "It almost went in."

"*Saul!*" The shout made pain splash across her forehead, but her vision was clear enough now. Clear enough to see the ripples in the lake arrowing toward the shore, spilling off the movement of something unseen in the dirty water.

"Yeah, yeah, I've got—" He straightened up, waving the ball at her, then stopped and stared at the water with a frown. "What— Is there something in here? Laura, I think there's an alligator in the water hazard!"

"It's not an alligator," she said wearily, and too quietly for him to hear. He'd know soon enough.

"Laura? Laura – oh my God, what *is* that?"

She turned away and walked back to the golf trolleys. There was nothing to be done now. She'd tried. "We don't have alligators here."

"Ohmygodohmygodohmygod—"

"Mine," something said, the word raspy but unmistakable, and Saul's voice rose into a scream that was rapidly cut off by a splash. Just the one. Then there was silence. There were no frogs in the pond, but there were plenty of birds to fill the quiet. Laura took Saul's water bottle and had a sip, rolling her shoulders. The tension seemed to have eased somewhat.

Giles slid onto the bench seat next to Laura. "Did you survive the game from hell?"

She smiled, and sipped her G&T. "I did."

"No more trouble with faulty holes, I hope."

"Only with the water hazard."

"Oh. Oh dear." He gave her an uncertain look. "Ah – condolences? Felicitations?"

"He should have stuck with his own club. There was never any trouble when he was at his own club."

"Well." Giles drank from his water bottle and rested his forearms on the table. "Retirement changes relationships, they say."

"So they say."

They drank their respective drinks in companionable silence for a little longer, then Laura nodded to Saul's clubs, propped up next to her own. "Can you put them in the shop? No point having them lying around, cluttering up the garage."

Giles nodded. "Sure. Do you fancy a late lunch?"

She gave him a disapproving look. "The water hazard just ate my husband."

"Right. Sorry."

"Maybe tomorrow." She got up and went to check Saul hadn't left his house keys in his golf bag. That would be just like him.

That Time of the Month

A French friend asked me once if there was romance in my books.
I said absolutely not, as I have the romantic sensibility of a month-old cabbage.
She then asked if there was friendship in there.
Oh, yes. Lots of that, I said, and she gave me a puzzled look.
But that's still romance, she pointed out, and I don't think I've ever heard anything so French or so beautiful.
Because romance is simply love, and love is a strange creature.
It takes many forms, and we express it in many ways, and we find it in many places. And it can be young or old or complicated or simple, but as much as it's always different, it's always the same, too.
So this is a story about love.

"Have you seen my glasses?" Ted asked.

"On your head, dear," Dorothy said, slicing mango into neat, almost identical chunks.

"You didn't even look," he grumbled, reseating them on his nose.

"They're always on your head, dear." She tipped the mango into the bowl and mixed it in with the sliced strawberries and kiwifruit and the waxy dark moons of the blueberries. "Don't eat it all before tonight. I want some for my dessert."

Ted grunted, already absorbed in the newspaper, and Dorothy put the bowl of fruit in the fridge. He'd eat most of it. He always did. Then he'd feel guilty and confused and want to go out and buy flowers. But that was alright. He needed the vitamin C, especially at this time of the month.

Besides, she always left a generous serving in a Tupperware behind the cabbage. One had to look after oneself, even in a marriage. Sometimes, she thought, particularly in a marriage.

IT WAS A BUSY DAY. First was volunteer duty at the library, where she gently explained to a man with heavy bags under his eyes that no, all the books on how to sleep-train children were out, and there was a three-month waiting list on most of them. She also extricated a small girl who got stuck behind the shelving in the horror section, and convinced a young man that yes, she could hear him with his noise-cancelling headphones on, even if he couldn't hear her.

Then there was the tall, floaty woman dressed all in

shades of green who wanted books on Wiccan practices for the full moon, and the rather shorter woman in a large floppy hat who (loudly enough for the young man in his noise-cancelling headphones to take note) told the tall woman she'd burn in hell unless she was saved right this minute, and kept trying to exorcise her in the children's section. The tall woman retaliated by burning sage sticks (and who carried such things on them like that?) and shouting earthy blessings, and while Dorothy tried to shoo them both out before the fire alarm went off a small dog appeared and wee'd on the bottom of the self-help shelves.

Dorothy was starting to think that hell would look a lot like certain Wednesday mornings in the public library, but she kept that to herself as she gave up on shooing and called security to escort both women out. Well, she called Frank, who was large and tattooed and looked alarming, even though he was the library accounts manager and kept prize-winning guinea pigs. He was convincing enough for most people.

At lunchtime she pulled on her coat and picked up her bag, and hurried out before anyone else could complain at her. It always seemed to be *at* her rather than *to* her. No one really wanted a solution. They just wanted to complain. If it wasn't that retirement was terribly long and somewhat uneventful, she wouldn't bother with the library at all.

She ate lunch on a park bench in the patchy spring sunshine, watching the ducks squabbling in the pond and the fluffy puffs of ducklings struggling against a considerable amount of wind resistance to stay clear of the fracas. Moor hens were fighting on the grass, and dogs snapped at each other, tugging ferociously at their leads while their humans snarled just as irritably. The only exception was a very old Labrador watching the ducklings with sleepy eyes while their owner dozed on the bench next to them.

After lunch it was bridge at Sophia's house, where Louise cheated even more blatantly than usual and Eleanor flounced out after losing three hands in a row, knocking a vase over and scaring one of the cats as she went. The cat bit the nearest person, who happened to be Ethel, and she screamed so loudly that Wendy jumped up and knocked a whole plate of cream buns to the floor. Wendy shouted at Ethel, Ethel shouted back, and then they got into such an argument that Sophia kicked them all out. Dorothy couldn't say she was sorry. She'd been getting a headache from all the cat hair anyway.

Plus it meant she was earlier to the supermarket, and didn't have to deal with the post-school rush. There were, however, two older gentlemen hitting each other with umbrellas and wrestling over the last imported raw milk Camembert, and a very well-dressed couple hissing insults at each other over conflicting brands of pesto. And that was all before she got to the checkouts and was confronted by aggressive bag-packers collecting for charity. One of them dropped a four-pack of baked beans on top of Dorothy's eggs, then glared at her as if she'd been the one to do it. She just sighed and put two pounds in the collection bucket. It was for a good cause, after all.

The altruistic feeling didn't last long. She was unpacking her shopping trolley when a woman in a gleaming SUV honked her horn and shouted something about it being excursion days from the nursing home. Dorothy wasn't sure why, as she wasn't blocking the way and the woman wasn't even trying to park next to her. So she just gave a cheery (if rather sarcastic) little wave and kept on with what she was doing.

"That time of the month, isn't it?" a young man in a yellow jacket said, taking her trolley from her and attaching it to the train he was towing across the parking lot.

"*Excuse* me?"

"You know. Full moon. Everyone goes bonkers, I swear it."

"Oh. I see." She nodded and found a more sincere smile somewhere. "I don't think that's actually a real phenomenon."

The young man laughed. "Trust me, it is. Worse than Christmas, sometimes." He headed off, towing the trolleys and nodding sedately at a man who almost hit him with his fancy car. The driver made rude gestures through his closed window, and Dorothy supposed the young man had a point. Misguided, probably, but still.

She saw three near-crashes before she got out of town, and once she was on the main road a young man in a dark blue car overtook her dangerously close to a blind rise, screaming something he probably thought she'd never heard before as he went past, and almost clipping an oncoming caravan before he pulled in again. And that was quite beside the cyclists throwing drink bottles at a post van, and the tractor refusing to move into a lay-by to let anyone past, and the two women blocking the road outside the school with their people carriers while they expanded the children's vocabulary in unusual ways. Dorothy could barely wait for the countryside to rise up around her, for the houses and traffic to thin out and fall away, and the smaller roads to wind their way up to the little cottage nestled in its garden in the hills, separated from its neighbours by a slow roll of fields.

Yes, home sounded good. Home, and a cup of tea, and then they just had to get through the night.

"DOROTHY? DOROTHY!"

Dorothy sighed and put the shopping bags down, rubbing the small of her back as she called back, "Yes, dear?"

"I just ... dammit, I seem to have ... um ..." Ted appeared in the hallway, his hand wrapped in a tea towel and his wellies tracking grass and mud across the floor.

"Ted," she said, pointing at his feet.

"Oh! Oh, sorry." He stared at his boots as if unsure who they belonged to. "Shall I take them off?"

"Just go back into the kitchen. Carefully."

"Yes. Okay. I'll do that." He retreated, and she took her own shoes off, sliding her feet into slippers and following him.

She found him at the kitchen table, still with one hand in a tea towel and a slightly woebegone look on his face. "What happened?" she asked.

"I was cutting the hedge, and ... well, I don't know. I was just very clumsy, I suppose."

Dorothy sat down next to him and unwrapped his hand carefully, squinting at the bloodied fingers. "Pass me your glasses."

"I don't—"

"On your head, dear."

He sighed, and handed them to her. "What would I do without you?"

"Buy lots of specs, I imagine," she said, and smiled at him, then put his glasses on so she could see a little better. "Oh dear. Yes. It's not very pretty, is it?"

"Do I need stitches?" he asked, staring fixedly at the photos on the fridge. He'd gone a strange waxy colour.

"Hmm." She glanced at the clock on the microwave. "No. I think you'll be fine." She rewrapped his hand in the cloth. "Keep that elevated."

He did, holding it above his head with the other hand so he looked like a high diver about to leap into an unseen abyss. "Are you sure? I feel a bit funny."

"Blood always makes you feel a bit funny. Remember when I stubbed my toe in Spain that time?"

Ted made a gagging noise and went even paler. "Your toenail was hanging off. It was awful."

Dorothy smiled and went to wash her hands. "Tea?"

"Ooh, please."

It didn't take much to get the grass and dirt off the floor – Dorothy was happy they'd opted for wood laminate rather than carpet all those years ago. It was scratched and a little scruffy these days, but much better for staining. The blood was trickier, as Ted had managed to drip it all over the cushions on the kitchen bench seat, as well as the curtains at the windows over the sink somehow, which was annoying. She left those until after dinner to tackle, taking them down once the dishes were safely out of the way.

"But why did you touch the curtains?" she asked again, running them under cold water for the fifth or sixth time and wondering if they were dry-clean only. "There was no need to touch the curtains."

Ted waved his mug vaguely, splashing tea on the table. He'd given up on holding his arm overhead and had it propped on a saucepan. He'd tried to use cushions until she'd scolded him. "I was trying to get to the sink."

Dorothy looked from the window to the sink and decided there was no point trying to clarify the issue. Either he'd climbed in the window or had just been panicking, and she rather thought it was the latter. Poor man. He really did hate the sight of blood.

"Are you sure I don't need stitches?" Ted asked again. There was a steady rivulet of blood working its way out from under the sodden tea towel and down to his elbow.

Dorothy checked her watch and nodded. "Quite sure, dear."

"It's bleeding rather a lot. And I do feel most odd."

Dorothy dropped the curtains in the sink. They'd keep until morning. She topped her mug up from the teapot and set it on a tray, then added a few pieces of shortbread off the plate on the table. "That's to be expected."

Ted sighed. "I suppose you know best. You usually do in these things."

She set a mug in front of him and kissed his cheek. "I do indeed. Now why don't you pop outside and have your tea out there?"

"It's almost dark," Ted objected. "I'll be cold!"

"I think it'll clear your head admirably. And I can clean

up all this mess." Dorothy nodded at the bloody smears on the table.

"I'm sorry," Ted said. "I can clean them if you want?"

"You'll just make more mess." She pushed his mug toward him and clapped her hands together. "Off you go!"

He sighed and got up, picking up his woolly hat and jamming it down over his ears. "Alright." He took his tea and let himself out into the garden, and Dorothy waited until he was halfway to the shed before she quietly turned the lock and shot the deadbolt across. With no curtains, she couldn't stay in the kitchen. She'd learned a long time ago that it was important not to be seen.

She picked up her tray and switched the lights out as she headed for the stairs, stopping to check that the front door was locked before she climbed up to the bedroom. She drew the curtains on the last of the sunset, folded the bedspread back carefully, plumped the pillows up, then went to brush her teeth. She could hear Ted banging on the door over the insistent buzz of the electric toothbrush.

The banging had stopped by the time she went back into the bedroom, and she checked the time on the little alarm clock on her side of the bed as she changed into her nightie. Yes, that seemed right.

She slipped between the sheets, shivering a little at the coolness on her legs, and settled herself comfortably, her cup of tea steaming softly on the bedside table and her book open on her lap. Outside, a dog was barking in the distance, a dog-walker forgetting the time or a farmer bringing in a last recalcitrant sheep, and she hoped they'd all be indoors soon. It wasn't a night to be out. Not at this time of the month.

But there was nothing to be done about it now, so she just took a sip of tea and put her ear plugs in, in case of howls. They always unsettled her, the howls.

THE MORNING CAME in pale and timid, the sky a white dome scorched on the edges with the beginning of the dawn. Dorothy checked the curtains in the sink (they still had a faint shadow of blood on them, but she thought that once they were dry it'd be barely noticeable), checked the time, then unbolted the back door. Ted was curled on the step, entirely naked. Scraps of clothing and tattered slippers littered the lawn.

She bent over and patted his shoulder.

"Ted, dear?"

He moaned, and hugged himself into a smaller ball.

"It's morning, dear," Dorothy said, and shook him a little more firmly.

Ted gave a sudden harsh, hungry gasp, like a free diver surfacing from the depths, and uncurled enough to look up at her. There were smudges of blood around his mouth. "Dot?"

"Yes. Come along. I've started the shower."

He sat up and stared down at himself, pale and gently saggy and smeared with mud. "Oh, no. Did I sleepwalk again?"

"You did. But it's okay. Let's just get you warmed up."

"I'm sorry," Ted said, taking the dressing gown she offered him. "I don't know what happened. I can't even remember going to bed."

"It's quite alright," Dorothy said, plucking some feathers from his stubble. "You just get in the shower and I'll make you a nice big plate of bacon and eggs. How does that sound?"

"That sounds good," Ted said, and looked at his hand. "You were right, too. Look – the bleeding's all stopped."

"Of course it has, dear," she said. His hand was smeared with so much mud and muck it could have stopped the bleeding all by itself, but she knew that underneath would be nothing but the pale silver lines of old scars. The change healed everything. "Now, shower. Before you catch your death."

She shooed him to the stairs and watching him stagger up, trailing one filthy hand along the wall and leaving handprints she'd have to scrub off later. She didn't mind. They'd used the hard-wearing paint. Wipe clean, it was, and very useful.

She turned back to the kitchen and popped the kettle on, giving the curtains a final swirl and draining the water from the sink.

"Fifty-three years of it, and the man still thinks he's sleepwalking," she said to the empty room. "Honestly." Then she switched the computer on so she could check the local groups on Facebook and make sure no one had seen anything untoward, or lost any livestock they might have to be compensated for.

Someone had to keep an eye on such things.

A Significant Debt

I'm not sure if Baz is the same baking-fixated bodyguard as in Organ Thieves, *or if baking is actually quite a common (if secretive) pastime for hired muscle. If the former, I can see why he would be craving a change after that particular experience.*

I do, however, know why he's called Baz, and his dad's called Barry. And that is simply because I have a strange compulsion to call every side character Barry, and at one point promised the wonderful Lynda of Easy Reader Editing (who has to catch all these recurring Barries and get me to change them) a story in which everyone was called Barry. That seemed a little confusing, so instead we have just two. Lynda, I'm sorry. Hopefully that's all the Barries out of my system now.

Maybe.

As for the story itself – well, we all know many things can be raised by repeating their names in a mirror. Which always made repeating self-affirmations in them a little risky, in my mind. ...

THIRTY SECONDS.

That's all it needs for scrambled eggs to go from silky to dry, and less time than it takes for caramel to burn.

It was also, Baz thought, if one were to be particularly picky – and he was – the difference between a tender crumb in a Victoria sponge cake and a subtle, sneaking dryness that not even the buttercream could completely disguise. Not to a connoisseur, anyway.

It was also a good length of time to hold someone's head in a toilet bowl. Not long enough to drown them, yet more than long enough for them to realise that you *could*, then to tip into the conviction that you *might*.

Baz pulled the man back up, ignoring his flailing hands. They weren't aimed at him, anyway. They were peddling with the same frantic helplessness that a ladybird's legs have when it lands on its back, until some decent person tips it back upright again.

"Now then, lad," Baz said conversationally, keeping a firm grip on the back of the man's jacket. It was some shiny designer thing, and the collar had ripped like cheesecloth. "We were discussing the importance of keeping to payment schedules, and the generosity of my employer in even allowing you such a thing. All due to you being such an excellent customer, like."

"I *am!*" The man gasped. "I will, I'm going to pay! It was just this week—"

Baz returned the man's face to the toilet bowl before he could get his arms out to brace himself on the rim. The timing was the trick of it. The less chance people had to gather themselves, or to mount any sort of resistance, the more disoriented they became, and the less chance anyone was going to get hurt. Well, accidentally hurt rather than intentionally. One just had to know when to let them rest and when to keep working them. Rather like a good bread dough.

He kept an eye on his watch as the man kicked and bucked in his grip, and dimly heard Scotty at the bathroom door say, "Nah, I wouldnae. It's occupied, mate."

There was a muttered response, probably someone saying *what, the whole thing* and Scotty repeated, "*Occupied,* mate."

There was nothing after that. No one wanted Scotty getting emphatic about anything.

Baz pulled the man back up, and he gave a high, helpless, screaming intake of breath.

"So when can my employer expect your next payment?" Baz asked pleasantly.

"Next week! Next week, I promise!" The man was almost sobbing.

"That would make you three weeks late," Baz said. "Obviously there will be penalties for such egregious breaching of the terms of the loan."

"What?" the man managed, twisting to peer at Baz. His eyes were wide and reddened, and there was toilet paper stuck to his cheek. Quite an effort, considering how often club toilets seemed to be *out* of paper.

"You pay later, you pay more. Right now, we're just talking monetary penalties being incurred. But I find myself concerned that you're not taking your commitments seriously, considering you're out flashing my boss's cash in fancy bars and cruising around in a truly hideous car."

"It's an RA8," the man protested.

Baz ignored him. "If I don't hear that the three weeks of missed payments, plus a twenty-five percent penalty, have been paid by the end of the week, the penalties will move from fiscal to physical. Understood?"

The man stared at him blankly.

"I will start breaking things," Baz explained, and the man flinched.

"Okay, okay. Twenty-five percent of the weekly payment on top. I'll do it, I swear."

"No. Twenty-five percent of all three missed payments, plus the payments themselves, plus let's get a fourth week in advance, so that we can all rest happy knowing I won't have to pay you another visit."

The man blinked at him. "But that's—"

"A substantial amount, but I'm sure you can start on it by returning your eighty-eight."

"It's an RA8."

Baz just looked at him, his hand tightening on the back of the man's neck, and the man wriggled.

"Okay, okay! I'll try!"

"You'll try. Well, then. That's just fantastic. I suppose I'll see you next Saturday, in that case?" Baz grinned, fully aware that the scar which twisted his cheek hiked his lip up into quite an unnerving grimace when he grinned. Everyone took one look at that scar and the size of him and became startlingly helpful, and the man in front of him was no exception. He started nodding so hard Baz thought he might give himself whiplash.

"Okay, yes! Yes, I'll get it paid, I will, I'll take the car back, I'll—"

Baz let go of him and straightened up, pushing out of the stall and letting the door swing shut on the man still huddled over the bowl. He washed his hands carefully, examining himself in the grimy, poorly lit mirror, and wondering why places that could charge twenty quid for a beer still had the same bathroom standard as the local boozer. He met his reflection's gaze and mouthed, *You are more than your job. You are more than your every day. You are all you believe yourself to be.*

Then he straightened up and shook the water off his hands, and went out into the shadowy hall, almost bumping into Scotty.

"Sorted?" Scotty asked. He was watching an animated film on his phone and barely looked up.

"Sorted. Let's get out of here and get a proper drink."

"Bloody hell, aye. I could murder a pint."

They hulked their way out of the club, the crowd parting before them like startled sheep, two big men with hard faces and harder hands, one of them thinking he'd prefer a decent glass of rosé and an artisan cheese platter, if he was being honest about things.

Baz leaned against the clean, well-lit sink in his own bathroom, dabbing cream gently around his eyes. He leaned back, picked up the dental floss, and reminded himself, "You are all you believe yourself to be."

Which, at the moment, was a little reflux-y after six

pints and a kebab from some hole in the wall that Scotty insisted was the best kebab shop outside Glasgow. Baz hadn't realised Glasgow set the world standard when it came to kebabs, but he'd kept that thought to himself. Suggesting to Scotty that Glasgow wasn't the world standard in anything was liable to earn him a smack. The man was almost endearingly proud of his heritage – he'd even *introduced* himself as Scotty, rather than wait for anyone to bestow the painfully obvious nickname on him.

Baz had tried, on occasion, to introduce himself as Bartholomew, as Bart made him feel like a cartoon character (and American to boot), and Barry was his dad, may the vicious old sod rest uneasy. But once he expressed his displeasure over being referred to as Barry, Baz it was. He supposed it was better than some of the names his dad had used for him, particularly when he'd found Baz in the kitchen helping his mum.

He touched the scar on his cheek reflexively, then dropped the floss in the bin and set about with his interdental brush. He needed to call his mum, come to think about it. She was in a rather nice home down south, one equipped to deal with people whose pasts were quietly eclipsing their presents. Sometimes, when he visited, she'd grab Baz and whisper, "Your father's not home yet, is he?"

Baz would pat her hand and say no, he wasn't coming home. They were safe. Her face would get all soft and dreamy then, and she'd give Baz five pounds for the bus. He was never sure where she thought he was taking the bus to, but he'd just wait until she was asleep, then tuck the note back into her bedside drawer where she could find it next time. Then he'd tiptoe out, trying not to smile at anyone on the way. He'd made one of the residents cry once, by smiling.

He swapped the interdental brush for his electric toothbrush, and reminded himself as he looked in the mirror, *You are all you believe yourself to be.*

There was a *flicker,* a sudden dimming or brightening of the lights, like a power surge, there and gone so fast that he frowned at his reflection. Had he seen that, or was the kebab messing with more than his guts? He blinked around the room, but everything stayed steady. Whatever it was, it was gone. He put the toothbrush down and rinsed his mouth out, thinking of the parcel that had been waiting on the mat when he got home. It was the new piping kit he'd ordered, a fancy one with three reusable bags and thirty stainless steel tips, rather than his old plastic one which only had ten and used disposable bags that tended to split if he was using it for choux pastry or a thick buttercream. He wondered if he should try it out tonight. It was late, though.

He was still considering whether he should start with cupcakes tomorrow, to experiment with the different tips, or with biscuits so that he could do some really fine work with the icing, when he wandered into the apartment's little open plan living area. He was leaning toward biscuits, but as the bathroom door swung shut behind him the thought vanished, and he stopped short.

"What the *hell?*" he demanded.

The small woman sprawled in his armchair, one leg hanging over the armrest and a copy of *Delicious* magazine open on her lap, looked up at him and grinned, showing neat white teeth. "Well, hello there, big guy."

"Where the hell did you come from?" he demanded, trying to see if she had any weapons under the magazine.

"You called me," she said.

"I most certainly did not." She didn't seem to have anything on her lap, but maybe behind her? Or maybe this was the boss's idea of a bonus. He got weird ideas about such things sometimes, even though Baz had made it clear he was only interested in the sort of bonuses he could use to pay for expensive rest homes. "How'd you get in?" he asked.

"You invited me."

"I didn't call *or* invite you," he said, examining her. She was wearing jeans that had seen better days, and some sort of dark, faintly glossy, goth-ish T-shirt that was all printed with tentacles or something. At least she had her shoes off, considering her feet were up on his armchair.

She chuckled, a delighted sound, and said, "You did call me. Three times, in the mirror. Well, two mirrors, but near enough."

"What? What're you talking about?" He could feel a hot flush of embarrassment starting around the base of his neck. Had Scotty heard him doing his mantras, maybe? Was this some joke of his?

The woman tipped her head on the side. "You look in the mirror, and you think of your deepest desire, then you say my name three times, and *boop*, here I am."

"Boop?"

"Boop." She laughed again, and the light in the room must've been a bit strange, because her teeth looked not just white but *pointed,* and Baz could've sworn the tentacles on her shirt moved.

He opened his mouth to ask how the hell *boop* worked,

then realised it was blatantly impossible and he potentially had some delusional housebreaker in his favourite armchair, so he just said, "I didn't call anyone."

"Did you look in the mirror?"

"Well, obviously, everyone does, but—"

"Did you think of your deepest desires?"

"Um. Maybe sometimes. But look—"

"So you summoned me."

"*Summoned* you? I'm not some school headmaster!"

She indicated herself. "Must've. Wouldn't be here otherwise."

"I absolutely did not. And you said I had to say your name three times, and I don't even know it."

"Eh, I'm sure I heard it." She glanced around, as if she were in a dark alley rather than the confines of the apartment, then said, "D'you have any whisky? I could really go for a whisky."

"Look, I didn't summon you, okay? That's not a thing. You're obviously not ..." He hesitated, then continued, "Not *right.* But you've broken into my home, and if you don't leave right now, I'm calling the police."

She chuckled at that. "Ah, but you won't, will you, Baz?" She swung herself off the chair, a disturbingly *fluid* motion, as if she didn't bend where she should, and wandered across the room to stand in front of him. He had to resist the urge to step back, even though she barely came up to his chest. This close, her teeth were definitely pointed, filed or fake or something, and in the low light her eyes took on a disturbing non-colour that he supposed could have been from contact lenses, but he had an unsettling feeling wasn't. The tentacles on her shirt still seemed to be moving, shifting minutely, and he could smell her, a hot dank scent that scratched the back of his throat.

"No, you won't call the police," she repeated. "You stay well away from them, don't you, Baz? Always have, ever since your dad *ran off*." She made air quotes around the last two words, her fingernails cropped almost to non-existence.

Baz kept his face blank. There was no way she could know. No one knew, not even his mum. She'd been in the hospital at the time, and when she came out, Baz's dad was just *gone*, run off, never to be seen again. Maybe he realised he'd gone too far this time, done too much damage to deny it if the police got involved. Not that they would, after all, considering old Barry senior *had* been police. But not popular police. They hadn't looked too hard for their esteemed colleague. His home family weren't the only ones who carried his scars.

But even if this woman couldn't *really* know, she obviously had some sort of knowledge about him. And what if she went and tried to stir his mum up? So Baz just said, "What do you want?"

"To help you achieve your heart's desire," she said, and gave that quick, wary look around the room again before she smiled her sharp-toothed smile at him. "And a whisky."

THE WOMAN SAT at Baz's breakfast bar, her legs swinging from the stool and a tumbler of single malt in front of her. Baz stood on the kitchen side, the bottle between them, but he'd opted for a mug of tea and some lavender shortbread he'd made the day before. He put some napkins next to the biscuit tin and helped himself, frowning at the shortbread as he examined it. Getting the right balance of lavender was tricky. He'd gone with storing some stalks in the flour for two weeks before he used it, plus grinding up some flowers and blending them into the butter and sugar. Extracts were always too intense, in his mind, but the blending hadn't worked as well as he'd hoped. He kept getting chewy bits of flower.

She – the woman who knew what she shouldn't, the woman with tentacles on her shirt and pointed teeth and weird eyes, the woman who'd appeared from nowhere – took a biscuit and bit into it, ignoring the napkins and scattering crumbs all over the bar. "Nice," she said, her mouth still full. "Tesco's finest?"

He scowled at her and she laughed, but he didn't miss the way her eyes kept darting around the room. He knew that look – and the feeling behind it, too. The feeling of always watching for pursuit, even when you weren't sure you were being hunted. Even when you were big enough to be the hunter yourself.

"Who're you running from?" he asked.

"I'm not," she said, too quickly.

"Look, I can accept you're not ..." He hesitated, staring at her. *Not human* was what he wanted to say, but he couldn't *really* think that. And he certainly couldn't *say* it. That was impossible, and even if he did think that (he did, because her tentacles were moving again, *definitely* moving, and one was uncapping the whisky while another lifted the bottle to top up her glass, he was seeing that, and all the time she was holding half a biscuit in each small hand, and licking the crumbs from the broken edges with a long pale tongue), that was the sort of thing you didn't admit to. If it got out that he believed in tentacled women who lived in his mirror it'd be even worse than it getting out that he had a subscription to *Delicious* magazine and had once queued for three hours to get Mary Berry to sign his copy of her *Baking Bible*. She'd been very nice, too, and had patted his hand.

He considered it. Actually, no. The baking thing getting out would be worse. There were plenty of paranoid, unbalanced people in his industry who probably believed the CIA were peering out of their bathroom mirrors (even in the UK), and aliens were living in their TV, so the woman wasn't as much of a problem. And he wasn't actually entirely convinced yet that this wasn't some elaborate prank set up by Scotty or someone.

Tentacles, his mind pointed out, and he ignored it, saying instead, "I accept you didn't break in, and that you think I called you somehow, and you know stuff you shouldn't, so I'm going to play along for a bit here. See where we go." He gave her his best, twisted grin, but she just smiled back, unperturbed.

"Good," she said. "I can't be bothered with this believe me/believe me not dance. It's so boring."

"You need to tell me who sent you, or who you're running from, though. That way I know who to punch when they turn up."

She snorted. "You would too, you great lump." She extended a hand. "I have many names, but you can call me ... Bee."

"Bee?" Her hand was hot and dry and *itchy* when he

grasped it, as if he were holding a fistful of woodlice, and he dropped it quickly.

"Sure. Bee and Baz." She chuckled. "So when you did the whole, *you are all you believe yourself to BE* thing, you called me. Which, cool mantra, B-T-W. Very self-actualise-y thingy. But the problem being, of course, that you still believe yourself to be a messed-up kid who sentenced himself to a life he never wanted, just because he looked out for his mum." She clicked her tongue and shook her head.

He blinked. "No, dropping out of school did that. And this." He indicated the whole slope-shouldered, big-bellied mass of him, hard but unpicturesque before one even got to the scars.

She tipped her head to the side. "Sure, can't see you in an ad for family cars, but the rest sounds like some self-limiting bollocks to me." She pointed at the double-stacked bookshelves that took up one full wall of the apartment, spilling onto the floor and encroaching on the coffee table. "School's not everything. You might not get to uni without it, but there are other options. Go do a course. Start your own business. Invent a bloody app. Stop believing what you *were,* and start believing in what you're going to be." She glared at him, and took a sip of whisky, then waved a shortbread at him. "Plus you make bloody good biscuits. These are epic."

He folded his arms. "So I should just quit my job? Reinvent myself? I need money for that."

"You've got money."

"Only enough to ..." He didn't want to mention his mum, so after a moment he continued, "Pay the bills."

"Get a loan."

"You think I can just walk into a bank with no credit history, no legit employment history, and get a loan?"

She swirled her whisky. "Get a better job, then."

He snorted. "My employer isn't the sort you walk away from."

She took a sip of whisky, holding his gaze with her unsettling no-colour eyes. "See?" she said. "You are what you believe. Stuck."

He spread his fingers, suddenly not trusting himself to answer.

"I can help," she said after a moment, and he chuckled.

"Oh? And what'll that cost me? My soul?"

"More or less," she said, and grinned.

BAZ WOKE up late the next morning – or later the same morning, he supposed. Although *morning* wasn't actually accurate, either. It was afternoon when he checked his watch, which meant he was late to feed his sourdough starter. He rolled out of bed and pulled his T-shirt on as he wandered to the bathroom, his head foggy with beer and weird dreams. Or was it the whisky? Had he drunk whisky, or had he dreamed that too? Although the feel of his head suggested the whisky had been quite real.

He brushed his teeth, grimacing at the sticky film on his tongue, then rested his big hands on the edge of the sink and peered at his own reddened eyes in the mirror.

"You—" he started, then stopped, frowning, and his expression went from exhausted to horrified faster than cream curdles. He charged out of the bathroom and into the living area, staring about wildly. The whisky bottle was still out on the bar, next to the empty biscuit tin, along with two glasses. *Two.* He covered his face with both hands, scrubbing at the stubbly skin in something close to panic, then wheeled around to check his bedroom. But unless she was under the bed, she wasn't in there either.

"Dream," he said to the empty apartment. "Has to be."

The two whisky glasses offered a silent rebuttal, and he almost screamed when his mobile went off. He clutched his chest as if anticipating a heart attack, then lurched to the coffee table to pick up the phone, fumbling to answer.

"Yes?" he managed, in something like his usual tones.

"Baz – Jesus, are you okay?" It was Scotty, his voice so thick with panic that Baz could barely understand him.

"Yeah, fine. Why? What's going on?"

"You don't know? Holy hell, man, it's all gone off."

"What?" Baz demanded.

"The boss. His ... his house. It's all burned. Some massive explosion this morning and it's all gone. Like, there's just a crater."

"The boss?"

"He was there. Whole family was there, and now ... nothing. Everyone's gone, man. What do we *do?*"

Baz shifted his grip on the phone, aware his palm was sweating. *My employer isn't the sort you walk away from,* he'd said. And she, the woman with the tentacles and the strange eyes and all her *knowing*, had answered, *I can help.*

My soul? he'd asked. And ... and what? He looked at his free hand. There was a plaster wrapped around one finger, and he could feel it smarting faintly.

"Baz? *Baz!* What do we *do?*" Scotty sounded like he was close to tears.

"Has anyone claimed responsibility?" Baz asked.

"Nah, no one. News is saying gas leaks, but no way. Not the *boss.*"

"And there's no one left? No one other than us, I mean?"

"Everyone was there. Friday morning meeting. *We* were meant to be there, but I was waiting for you, and you were late, and—"

The door to the apartment opened, and Bee walked in barefoot, a paper deli bag swinging from one hand and a cardboard tray with two coffees in the other. She kicked the door shut behind her and set the bag on the bar counter. Baz could smell smoke and chaos on her, and one of her tentacles waved at him.

He took a deep, slow breath, and said, "Take a holiday."

"*What?*" Scotty demanded.

"If everyone's gone but us, we're going to need to look for some new employment. But first we need to make sure no one's doing a clean sweep and wants us gone too."

"Sod *that.* We can take them, we can—"

"No," Baz said, his voice sounding far away to his own ears. "Take a holiday. Go out to Spain or something, get some sun. Lay low. Once everything settles down we'll have a better idea of the new order."

"I can't go to Spain," Scotty said uncertainly. "I've got me dogs."

"Get them pet passports."

"Aw, hell. Nah. I'll go to Skegness. Don't need passports for that, right?"

"Not when I last checked."

"That'll do. I like the seaside. All the donkey rides and stuff."

Baz hoped Scotty left the dogs behind when he went donkey riding. "Sounds good. And lose your phone. Clear out your contacts. Usual thing."

"But how'll I get hold of you?"

"I'm sure we'll work it out," Baz said, as convincingly as he could.

"Alright," Scotty said. He sounded calmer now that someone had told him what to do. "You'll be in touch, though, right? You won't just leave me in Skegness?"

"I'll be in touch," he promised, and didn't bother feeling guilty about it. If he'd already sold his soul, what was the odd lie? He hung up and broke the phone apart, taking the battery and the sim out, then looked at Bee as she offered him a coffee. "What did you do?" he asked.

"I got breakfast. Or lunch." She shook the cup enticingly. "I went to that place down the road with all the unfinished wood and pipes everywhere, and half a dozen different kinds of milk. Looked like your sort of spot."

"I'm going to have to clear out," he said. "If anyone from the family's left, they're going to come knocking wanting to know how come I didn't get killed along with everyone else."

Bee set his coffee on the bar and picked up the other one, taking a noisy sip. "Boring old flat white for you, caramel syrup, quadruple shot latte for me. Not bad."

"What the hell do I *do?*"

She licked her lips. "There's a nice little apartment just come on the market not far from your mum."

He scowled at her, deeply unsurprised that she knew about his mum. "You leave her out of this."

"I intend to," she said, surprisingly sharply, then pointed at the bag. "Bacon butty with red sauce. I mean, sorry – hand-crafted breakfast sandwich on organic sourdough with hand-reared bacon, fresh churned butter and homemade ketchup. It's a very good price, that apartment."

"There's no way I can afford it."

"Oh, you'd be surprised."

He sighed, and finally snatched his coffee from the bar, taking the lid off to peer at it. It appeared to be a regular, well-made flat white, and he took a sip. "So, what – I toddle off down south to this surprisingly affordable apartment and sit there waiting for you to take my soul or whatever?"

She had a mouthful of her own sandwich, egg yolk decorating her chin, and her tentacles produced a wedge of A4 papers from somewhere and waved them at him.

"What's this?" he asked. "My contract?"

She snorted and swallowed. "This is the bit I don't help you with," she said. She took another bite while he examined the papers.

Entrant Application, they said, and there were curls and cakes on the edges of the words, a whiff of cinnamon and promise.

Baz looked from the papers to Bee, who was peering at her coffee suspiciously, then sat down next to her and retrieved the bacon butty from its bag, taking an enormous bite. It tasted of grease and sunshine and everything possible.

Baz held the plate aloft, the heavy muscles of his arms shaking from something other than the weight, the cheers of the crowd on the eye-wateringly green lawn outside the marquee roaring in his ears like the surge of the sea. Hands patted his shoulders, and someone was hugging him, more than one someone, and everyone smelled of flour and sweat and triumph, even if he was the one holding the trophy. *Him.* Him with the scarred face his dad had put a bottle into, and the twisted fingers his dad had broken with the rolling pin when he'd found ten-year-old Baz using it to roll pastry for his mum. And which Baz had rebroken not many years later on his dad's jaw. Him, with his jutting belly half the internet called the sign of a good baker, and which another half wanted to squeeze, much to his astonishment. He was crying, and he didn't even bother to wipe the tears away when the camera zoomed in on him and he gave a stumbling speech about how amazing and inspiring everyone had been, and how important it was to just believe in oneself, because if he could do it, anyone could. Then he staggered over to his mum where she was sitting in a wheelchair on the edge of a picnic blanket, wearing a sunhat and giant sunglasses.

He deposited the bouquet of flowers in her lap and collapsed to the blanket.

"For me?" she asked, and petted the lilies like a cat's back. "Oh, Baz. You're such a good boy."

"I won, Mum," he said. "I did it."

"Of course you did," she said, and swapped petting the flowers for patting his head. "I always knew you could do anything."

Bee crouched next to him, cream smearing her mouth

and two bottles of beer in one hand. She flipped the caps off with a tentacle and offered him one. "Nice work, Big Man."

He took the beer and had a long swallow. "I suppose I have you to thank for that."

"Nah. I merely gave you a kick to get started." She licked cream from the corners of her mouth. "Excellent crème pâte, by the way. Tastes like the forbidden fruits of heaven."

Baz poured his mum an elderflower cordial, then let himself be pulled away by the crowd, shaking hands and tasting food, laughing in the long, magical hours of an English summer afternoon, and wondering who this Baz was, because it was a different one to the one he'd known before.

It was later, as the shadows grew longer and the crowd thinner, as blankets were pulled over knees and cardigans over shoulders, that he said to Bee, "How long have I got?"

"Mmphf?" she asked around a mouthful of sausage roll, then managed, "Are these yours? Venison?"

"Yeah. Venison and black fig jelly."

"Damn. I shouldn't have put ketchup on them."

"You shouldn't," he agreed, with feeling. "How long have I got, Bee?"

"Got for what?" she asked, pulling her sunglasses down her nose so she could look at him properly. He wondered why no one else seemed to notice the tentacles curling over her, but maybe they just thought it was a fashion choice. There had been a woman in the tent who wore a different stuffed toy on her shoulder every day, after all.

"You know."

She shrugged. "A bit yet. Go drink your champagne and

eat your cake, Big Man. You've earned it." She turned away from him, cutting a sausage roll into bite-size pieces and sitting next to his mum to feed them to her. Baz wondered if he should pull her away, if it was *wrong* on so many levels to let a creature like that near his poor confused mother, but his mum was petting Bee's tentacles with as much delight as she'd petted the flowers, so he supposed it was okay, in some strange way. He let himself be tugged into the crowd by a young man who made excellent profiteroles and who had christened Baz Uncle B.

Baz didn't mind. It was still better than Barry.

Baz sat at the coffee table, staring over it to the churning winter sea across the road from his apartment, and ignoring the recipe book proofs he was meant to be making notes on. Bee lounged on the sofa, her bare feet up on the back and her head hanging off the seat so her hair pooled on the floor, reading a *Delicious* magazine. It had his interview in it, the one about mental health and overcoming adversity and a difficult start, and the joy of baking for healing.

"This is good," Bee said. "I like this: *the act of creation in baking is open to everyone. It doesn't matter if you're good at it. You just have to love it, and that's enough to heal.*"

"It's utter bollocks," he said. "All the stuff about working toward your dreams. But I couldn't exactly say, *Just summon a demon in your mirror and get them to sort it out for you.*"

Bee sighed. "How many times do I have to tell you – I just got you out of a rut. You're the big scary dude who cried on national TV when the nice judge lady said his scones were better than hers, and who heroically saved his competitor's cake by jamming it in the oven with his own when her oven was playing up, even though it almost lost him the competition. *And* who became a national hero when he gave the nasty judge man such a dirty look when he was being rude about old Ethel's prune slices that he apologised to her. You are the nation's gnarly sweetheart."

He snorted. "But I couldn't have done it without you sprinkling demon dust everywhere."

She looked at him, a couple of tentacles making flowers and loops in her hair where it lay on the floor. "Go to Manchester local news," she said.

"What? I'm working."

"Go to the news," she insisted, and when he didn't move, she sat up and swung his laptop toward her, clicking through a few things and muttering to herself. Then she spun it back to face him. "There."

He stared at it. It was a photo of the boss, leaving a nightclub with two young women flanking him, all of them smiling at the camera like toddlers that have got away with something particularly messy. "When's that from? I don't recognise the club."

Bee tapped the screen. "Last Friday."

"But—"

"*You'll be in touch, though, right? You won't just leave me in Skegness?*" Bee said, her voice suddenly deeply Scottish and rough at the edges.

Baz stared at her. "But you were in the room with me when I was talking to him!"

"I'm multitalented, me," she said. "And time and space are a bit more fluid than you'd expect."

"But—"

"You were so sure you couldn't leave, you didn't even try. But first chance you got, *bam*. Phone smashed, apartment empty, you were *gone*. You didn't even bother to check if there really had been an explosion." She chuckled. "I thought for sure I'd at least have to fake a funeral, but you were out of there, Big Man. I like your style."

"But—" He pressed one hand to his face, suddenly queasy. "But I've been on *TV*. What if they come for me? For *Mum?*"

"Oh, no. They won't come after you. And certainly not for her. I won't allow it." And her smile was suddenly so toothy that he didn't ask for details.

"Alright," he said. "Okay, so you didn't actually kill them. That's good, I suppose. But you still did all this." He waved at the cookbook proofs wearily. "You've been doing it all along. Making me win and get these deals."

She blew air over her bottom lip. "Why do you insist on believing this?"

"Well, I signed a deal, didn't I?"

She blinked at him. "What?"

"You know, that night. I ... my finger was all bandaged up when I woke up the next morning. And then this. So you got me drunk and made me sign a deal, didn't you? I get my heart's desire, or whatever, and you get my soul."

She stared at him for a moment, then burst out laughing. "Oh, *dude.* No. You started slugging whisky, and about halfway down the bottle decided to make cucumber sandwiches." She thought about it. "Cucumber *finger* sandwiches. Ha!"

He didn't laugh. "What?"

"You cut yourself. I put a plaster on it before you could redecorate the kitchen with claret."

"But then ..." He waved vaguely at the little but perfectly placed apartment, the beach across the road, the magazine and the cookbook and the pale sunshine riding the waves.

"All you, Big Man. I keep telling you."

They were both silent for a moment, listening to the gulls calling and the wind outside.

"Really?" he asked. "You didn't help at all?"

"Not after the little push to get you out of where you were. And, yeah, okay. The apartment was all me. You're totally right that you wouldn't have been able to afford it otherwise."

He thought about it. "But what did you think I meant when I asked how long?"

She scratched her jaw. "Something else."

"And why are you here in the first place?"

"Reasons."

He tapped his fingers on the table, and said, "What reasons?" His voice was dangerously calm, and she gave him a wary look. "Tell me."

She sighed. "Do you have to know?"

"Yes."

She shook her head. "Your mum."

"What?" He was on his feet in a breath, lunging for her, and she rolled off the sofa with sinuous grace, tentacles flar-

ing. "What do you want with Mum? Have you taken her *soul?*"

"Obviously not," Bee snapped, trying to soothe her tentacles and keeping a wary eye on him. "But she did make a deal."

"*When?*"

She sighed and pointed at the sofa. "Sit."

He scowled at her, hesitated, then sat. She sat as well, on the end of the L, out of reach, and examined him. "Alright. When you were young, she called me up. Well, not me specifically, but I took the call. She wanted to trade her soul for you to have a better life. She wanted to stick around until you were happy and successful, and she wanted your dad gone. I agreed, but you got there before me on the dad thing."

"What?"

"I almost stopped you, do you remember? You shouldn't have had to do it." She shook her head. "I was too late, though."

Baz rubbed his mouth, his stomach churning. "But ... she *sold her soul?*"

"She did. For you. But I kind of gave her a bit of an open contract, with the whole waiting till you were happy and successful thing. No time limit, see. And you two had a pretty tough time of things." She shrugged. "I kept putting off collecting. The lower-downs kept saying, come on, your soul quota's down, but I kept saying, nah, he's not happy and successful yet, so I'd go and ask your mum if I should nudge you, and she'd say no, so I'd go back and report in that our side wasn't fulfilled yet."

"And now?" he demanded. "You can't take her. You *can't.*"

She made a *calm down* motion at him. "Let's say management were unhappy with the lack of progress, but it was my deal, so they were stuck with it. Deals aren't transferrable unless a demon's terminated, which is extreme and unusual and generally pretty gross. And then we hit a complication. We can't take souls that aren't fully present." She glanced around. "Do we have some chocolate cake or anything? I could just go for some chocolate cake."

Baz ignored her, thinking about it, then said, "The dementia."

"Exactly. Early signs were there. So I said, no, can't take her, because there's no point tormenting someone like that. They check out too soon." She scratched her jaw. "There were some consequences, mind, due to the fact that if I'd taken her on time, her soul would've been fine. Management were displeased."

"What sort of consequences?"

"Nothing you need to think about. But debts are passed on." She pointed at him.

"*My* soul?"

"Your soul. Do we have biscuits, at least?"

"So why haven't you taken it?"

"Fine, I'll get it myself." She got up and wandered into the kitchen area, taking the cake tin from the shelf. She carved two large slices, scattering crumbs all over the worktop and the floor as she took them out of the tin. "Is there cream?"

"What are you waiting on?" he asked.

She poured cream onto the cake and brought both

plates through, leaving everything out on the worktop. She handed a plate to Baz, and he took it automatically. "Your mum was willing to trade her soul for you to be happy. For love. But you've done everything you can in your life to make *her* happy, including something that, by your human morality, made your soul forfeit already. But you did it anyway. Again, for love. You're weird little creatures, humans. And yes, I put off collecting her soul until it was too late, which I really have no reason for, and now you have that debt, and I'm sorry." She took a bite of cake. "But this is *my* deal, and as long as I'm here they have no way to claim you."

He blinked at her. "But at some point—"

She waved. "Never mind *at some point.* Aunty Bee is here to keep the nasty demons away. Well, other nasty demons," she amended, and flexed her tentacles. "All the rest comes later, if it has to come at all."

Baz poked his cake with the fork. "How bad were your consequences, really?"

"You're not prepared for that level of nightmare, Big Man."

"Why risk it again?"

"Who said I was?"

"You still check the corners of the room sometimes."

"And you still flinch when a door slams," she said, and they looked at each other for a moment, the room silent but for the cries of the gulls.

"You put so much cream on this I can't even taste the cake," Baz said finally.

"It's better that way. Your cakes suck. Those judges know *nothing.*"

And their laughter pushed the dark a little further back for both of them. Maybe not forever, but for now. Which is as much as anyone can hope for. That the dark stays back for now, and that there is laughter, and there is friendship.

And that the cake is good – or the cream at least is plentiful.

Spandex Always Fits

Twitter has much to answer for. I don't spend as much time on there these days as I used to, simply because I'd intend to juuust check in, and find myself four hours later rating mythical beasts on a scale of floofiness.

But at some point, when not distracted by floofy mythical beasts, I saw a post bemoaning the fact that superheroes tend to fit a very restricted age demographic. Which seemed rather unfair, if you ask me.

And I totally call that sort of Twitter usage research.

DANNY DROPPED HIS BACKPACK ON THE passenger seat as he swung himself into the car, an alarm still yowling two streets over. He straightened his tie, adjusted his cuffs, and started the engine, pulling smoothly away from the kerb. He stuck to the speed limit as he drove away from the town centre, pausing as two police cars careered across an intersection ahead of him with lights and sirens blaring. He hesitated, as anyone would, checking for more emergency vehicles, then pulled onto the main road and headed in the opposite direction.

He settled back into the seat, rolling his shoulders. He had another rental car booked at the train station, using a different company and driver's licence to this one. He'd return this car, walk to the other, then drive south for a couple of hours before making another change. He wasn't meeting the buyer until the day after tomorrow, in London, so he had plenty of time. That was always the key: time. Never hurry. Never be rushed. A flicker of movement in his rear-view mirror caught his eye, and he looked away from the road, frowning, but there was nothing there. Eleven o'clock on a Sunday night, and the streets were all but deserted.

He looked back at the road just in time to see a skip looming in front of him, half-blocking the previously clear road, piled with building debris and shattered panelling and with an old toilet balanced precariously on top. He yelped and jerked the wheel over, the little car skittering wildly. For one moment he thought he was going to spin straight into the bloody thing, then the tyres gripped, and he shot across the road. If there had been anyone coming the other way it would've been a hell of a mess, but the road on the other side was empty. He started to swing around the skip, then the headlights caught a ... a *barbecue*? One of those enormous ones you could put a whole cow in, if the fancy took you. He didn't take the time to figure it out, just spun the wheel back again and carried on straight across the road into an alley on the other side, wondering where in hell the skip and barbecue had come from, and why there were no road closed signs anywhere.

Danny's hands tightened on the wheel as he followed the low beams of the headlights down the alley. It was nothing more than a poorly lit stretch of patchy tarmac, flanked by the backs of pubs to one side and a row of garages on the other. There were no windows lit in the buildings or security lights on the walls, and the street lights didn't reach far down here. He wondered uneasily if it was a set-up, some sort of half-baked trap by kids trying to carjack unwary drivers. He touched the gun in its shoulder holster. If it was, they'd be in for a shock.

He looked up just in time to catch movement ahead, there and gone again, quick as a promise. The headlights caught a flash of metal on the ground, and he slammed the brakes on, but it was too late – he bumped over something unpleasantly solid, there was a horrible ripping sound, and the little car's nose dipped sadly toward the tarmac as it stumbled to a halt.

Danny swore, grabbed the backpack, and swung out of the car.

"What the hell was all that about?" he bellowed. "I'm calling the police!"

Only silence answered him, and he swung in a circle, peering into the shadows. He itched to grab the gun, but if it was just kids he might not need to. No one was going to mention a small and irritated man who'd taken a wrong turn. They would definitely mention the small and irritated man waving a gun at them, even if they'd been planning to mug him in the first place.

"Anyone there?" he tried, shouldering the bag.

Still nothing. He couldn't see anyone, and after a moment's hesitation he crouched to inspect the car. The front tyres were shredded, as if someone had taken a knife to them with great enthusiasm. He touched one, frowning, but in the dim light it was hard to see what had done it. Not that he could do anything either way – the rental would have one spare at most, and he wasn't about to call the AA. He was going to have to walk. Give it a couple of miles to get clear of the area, then grab a bus. He sighed with more resignation than irritation. This was why you gave yourself time. There was no telling what the universe would throw at you.

He straightened up and turned toward the road, meaning to leave as he'd arrived, and found five figures blocking the alley, the streetlight behind them rendering them as shady silhouettes. They stood with feet wide apart and firmly planted, hands on hips, except for the one clutching a walker, and another who was bent over with their hands on their knees, panting noisily.

"You're not going anywhere," the tallest said, her tone imperious. The light turned her fluffy white curls into a halo.

Danny shaded his eyes. "Excuse me?"

"Thief," the bent-over figure panted. "Ooh, I've got stitch."

"I did tell you to go a bit slower, Hilda," one of the others said. "He wasn't exactly making a speedy getaway."

Hilda waved a dismissive hand, straightened up and took a puff on an inhaler. "One can't let standards slip like that."

"Who the hell are you?" Danny asked.

"*Language,*" four of the figures chorused.

"Is that how you'd talk to your gran?" the one with the walker added.

"What's he say?" the shortest asked.

"He said, 'Who the hell are you?'" the tallest one shouted.

"Don't scream in my ear, Moll," the other snapped back. "I'm not that deaf."

"She is," Hilda said, as if confiding in Danny.

Danny shook his head. "Are you alright? Should you be out on your own?"

The women looked at each other, and as the light caught their faces Danny could see masks decorated with embroidery and beads obscuring the tops of their faces. He wondered if they'd wandered out in the middle of some sort of rest home masquerade ball.

"Are we alright, he asks us," Moll said.

"He should be asking himself that," the woman with the walker agreed.

"Damn straight, Lou," the fifth woman said, which Danny thought was a bit off, considering they'd just objected to his use of "hell".

"What?" the short one asked.

"Hand over the bag," Moll said, waving at Danny.

"Are you *mugging* me?" Danny asked.

"We're not letting you walk away with those diamonds," Lou said, shaking her walker at him for emphasis.

"Look, I don't know anything about any diamonds. I'm late home from a business trip, I've taken a wrong turn, my car's been damaged, and I'm not in the mood for any of this." Danny spoke smoothly, but his face had gone cold and tight. How the hell did they *know?*

The woman who'd said *damn straight* giggled and elbowed Hilda. "Says he's not in the mood."

Hilda snorted, and Moll said, "Stop that, Lorraine."

"Oh, come on, he walked straight into it!"

"Can I call someone for you?" Danny asked, with no intention of doing so. Dotty old women roaming the streets were not his problem, and still less were dotty old women who somehow knew about the diamonds. "The care home or something?"

"The *care home?*" Hilda said, planting her hands on her hips. "The cheek!"

"What?"

"He suggested we should be in a care home, Doris," Lorraine shouted.

"The cheek!"

"Well, it *is* a retirement village," Lou pointed out.

"That's not the same. And it's still rude," Hilda said.

"You should really apologise," Moll agreed.

Danny settled his bag more firmly on his back. "What I'm doing is going home. And you should too." He skirted the women, heading past them for the street, feeling absurdly sure that one of them was going to try to grab him. Not that a bunch of old women in arts and crafts masks were any danger, but ... but they knew about the diamonds. That was impossible. They *couldn't* know about the diamonds. Not even the *buyer* knew where Danny was going to get the diamonds from. And even if this lot had somehow seen him, there was no way they could have followed him from the store without him noticing.

"Why do men never listen?" Lou asked.

"To be fair, it does seem to be a failing for criminals in general," Hilda said.

"Men are the worst, though," Moll said, and the others clucked agreement.

Safely past the little group, Danny slowed. He shouldn't just leave them out here. They obviously weren't *right*, and must've wandered away from somewhere. They likely didn't even know how to get back. And the diamonds thing had to be a coincidence, something they'd watched on TV and got all confused about. He was just being paranoid, because it was his profession to be paranoid about such things. He glanced back at them. God, it was like imagining his gran roaming the streets unsupervised. It didn't bear thinking about. He wasn't going to risk calling the police, but he had to do *something*. Anyone could just come along and mug them, or worse. There were bad people out there.

He turned back, thinking he'd offer to get them a taxi, and stopped dead, staring. The light from the street had been behind them before, turning them into nothing more than silhouettes with fluffy halos of hair. But now it washed over the little group, flushing them like stage lighting as they glared back at him. And while the hair was just as thin and white as he'd expected, the rest was ... not. In addition to their beaded masks, the women were clad in a startling array of bright spandex leggings and figure-hugging tops printed with large teacup logos on the chests. Lou was wearing a cape that had got itself tangled around her walker, and Hilda was doing little squats, bouncing in very orange trainers.

"Um," he said, and they looked at him expectantly. He

couldn't find the words. Wherever they'd got away from, he was starting to think it was probably more high security than your average care home. Doris *hmph*ed and took her hearing aid out, fiddling with it. She had a pink cardigan buttoned over her canary-yellow suit, and it was making Danny's eyes hurt. Moll took a step forward in knee-high blue boots, levelling what looked an awful lot like a spatula at him.

"Give us the bag," she said.

It took him a moment to reply. "No," he said finally, and decided he wasn't going to offer to get them a taxi after all. He turned away again, shaking his head and thinking that old people should really be better looked after, and at that moment a whistle pierced the air. It was so shrill, so loud, that it seemed to be drilling into his skull, and he howled, clapping both hands to his ears and spinning back to the women.

Doris looked at her hearing aid, smiled, and tucked it back into her ear.

"Give us the bag," Moll repeated.

"No," Danny said, bracing himself for a repeat of the squalling hearing aid. "What're you lot playing at? Go home!"

Moll shrugged. "We gave you the chance to cooperate. Remember that."

"Whatever. You lot need some help." He started to turn away, and she hurled the spatula at him. It spun through the air with an ominous snarl, and slapped his cheek hard enough to make him yelp.

"*Ow!*" Right, that was it. He had a schedule to keep, and this was ridiculous. With a whisper of apology to his gran, he pulled the gun from the holster. He made sure they could see it, but kept it pointing at the ground as he said, "You try anything like that again—"

There was a snap of sound, and the gun was gone. He stared at his empty hand, then at the women. Doris twirled the tea towel – which shouldn't be long enough to even reach him, surely, but it had – with a self-satisfied look on her face, and Hilda patted her on the shoulder.

"You—" Danny started, then blinked, because Hilda was gone, just gone, and someone tapped him on the back. He spun around to find Hilda grinning up at him, then someone else grabbed him by the neck of his shirt and the back of his trousers, lifted him like a WWF wrestler and slammed him face-first to the ground. His chin bounced off the tarmac, setting a firework display of pain off behind his eyes, and the air was forced out of him in a yelp.

He wheezed, gulping like a stranded fish, tasting blood on his lips and wondering who had hit him. Someone pulled his bag off and he tried feebly to catch it, then he was rolled roughly over onto his back. He stared up at five powdered, smiling faces, and when he tried to move Lou planted her walker firmly over him. He squirmed, huffing and pushing ineffectually at it. It should have been light enough to fling across a room, but it appeared to have not only anchored itself to the ground but shrunk to trap him underneath it.

"Ooh," Lorraine said, rubbing the small of her back. "I can't lift what I used to. Good thing he's not any bigger."

"Nonsense," Moll said. "That was wonderfully done. But maybe bend your knees a bit more next time." She returned the spatula to her belt among an array of other kitchen tools. Danny regarded the potato peeler with something like horror and whimpered.

"Has he confessed?" Doris asked loudly, shaking the tea towel at him.

"No, Doris. We already know he's guilty," Lou shouted, and patted her walker. "He's not going anywhere, though."

Danny wriggled, hoping to prove her wrong, but if anything the walker seemed to be pushing even tighter against his chest and sides. "What's going on?" he managed, still struggling to get his breath.

"What do the kids say?" Lorraine asked. "You got owned?"

Hilda frowned down at their prisoner. "Do they still say that? I can never keep up."

"You have to let me up," Danny pleaded. "Unlock this thing!"

"Oh, it's not locked," Lou said. "It's melted. I used to remember how to reverse it, but my memory's a bit dicky these days. Once it's done, it's done."

"What?"

"Get comfortable," Moll said. "You're not going anywhere till someone cuts you out."

Danny thrashed wildly, but all he got was a sore head when he banged it on the tarmac. He stilled, panting. "The diamonds. Have them. I won't even try and get them back. Just let me up!"

Moll patted the bag. "We've got them anyway."

"Yes, but I'll come after them if you don't help me!"

The women looked at each other, then burst out laughing. Lou had to hang onto Hilda for balance, and even

Doris was snorting with laughter, whether she'd heard anything or not.

"*Please!* I have money!" How had this *happened*? He always planned so carefully, never used accomplices, never left any aspect of the job with less than three contingency plans, each as flawless as the other. He'd never been so much as a suspect for a *parking ticket*, let alone for any of the actual jobs he'd done. And now he was lying in some crappy northern alley, trapped by a bridge club? He strained at the walker frame again, achieving nothing but a warning pop in his shoulder. "I won't tell anyone!"

Moll leaned over and patted his face. "No, you won't, will you, dear? After all, who'd believe you?" This earned another bout of laughter, and as Danny struggled, light washed into the alley, along with the low rumble of a powerful engine. The laughter faded, and the women looked at the car, hands shading their eyes against the headlights. The engine died, and the car door opened.

"Help!" Danny yelled. "Help, these crazy– Ow!" He couldn't tell which one had kicked him. *"Help!"*

There was the clip of hard boots on tarmac, then a new face joined the circle, this one younger but no less amused.

"Hello, hello," the newcomer said. "What do we have here, then?"

"They attacked me!" Danny said. "Jumped me from behind!"

"Did they now?" The woman smiled. She had a ring in her nose and small, neat teeth, and didn't look exactly like the police, but it was hard to tell sometimes. Who else would be investigating doings in dark alleys at this hour?

"They did! They've stolen my bag! Arrest them!"

"Your bag, huh?" the woman looked at the spandex-clad ladies, her eyebrows raised, and Moll handed it over. The woman opened it, turning toward the light to inspect the contents.

"Sample phones," Danny babbled as he heard the half-dozen pay-as-you-go mobiles clanking together. "I'm a phone salesman."

"Even I don't buy that," Lou said, and patted her belly. "I could murder a cuppa, you know."

The young woman found the slim neoprene pouch and shook it gently. "SIM cards?" she suggested, a smile curling her lips. Danny closed his eyes, dropping his head back to the tarmac.

A siren wailed not far away, and the women looked at each other. "Let's go," Moll said.

The young woman nodded, and closed the backpack. "Load up."

"What?" Danny pushed at the walker. "Wait, you can't let them go! Aren't you going to arrest them for assaulting me?"

The young woman smiled. "Oh, I'm not the police. We are ... what would you say, ladies?"

"Redistributors of wealth," Lorraine suggested.

"Oh, I like that," Hilda said, hitching her control pants higher over her pink leggings. "It sounds very official."

"Which charity gets this one?" Lou asked.

"What?" Doris said, but no one responded, and she took her hearing aid out to frown at it.

"I think this'll cover quite a few," the young woman said, and gave Danny a finger wave. "Thanks," she called as she led the way to the car. He considered shouting after her, but he clung to a final shred of dignity and just watched them go instead. The older women in their capes and masks were silhouetted against the headlights for a moment, then were gone. He looked away, staring at the sky silently. The car left, casting the alley into deeper shadows. He tested the walker, but it wouldn't move, so he gave up.

After a while it began to rain.

Much later, so much later that Danny thought he might have dozed despite the cold and discomfort, a car pulled into the alley. It came to a stop not far away, and a man clambered out and ran to crouch next to him.

"Are you okay?" the man asked, breathing coffee and toothpaste into Danny's face.

"Not really," Danny said.

The man tugged at the walker, which looked less like a walker now, and more like the rusting bones of an old ship. "How the hell did this happen? I can't budge it. I'm going to have to call the police to get you out."

Danny sighed, and nodded. It wasn't like he had many choices. He closed his eyes and tried to think of any story that didn't include being robbed by geriatric superheroes. The possibility of being arrested and identified as an international jewel thief was one thing.

Being laughed at was quite another.

Autumn's Done

I lived for a while in a tiny village that nestles between two of the Yorkshire Three Peaks. It's a little bleak and a little wild, and a lot beautiful. I ran there a lot, and often found myself on the fells either before dawn or just after dusk. There would be the sheep and the crows and me, racing down the empty tracks as I either tried to beat the dark home, or the sunrise to the peaks. Sometimes, especially if the clouds were low or the mist was out, hiding the village, I felt like I'd stumbled into another world, one where unknown things hid just out of the corner of the eye, and humans were small and insignificant and unnecessary. Somewhere magical. Somewhere I could breathe.

And there was also, not far off the track, a sinkhole ...

It was raining, and the hole was growling.

Everyone stood well back from the edge, shifting uneasily as the rain got in their eyes and the wind burrowed through the grass to throw muck and shed leaves at their feet, then ran off around the hole to raise that terrible growling sound. An early dusk had come in with the lowering clouds, and there was something hungry and insistent about the way both wrapped the peaks.

"No one's coming," Arlene whispered.

Patricia shushed her, shuffling a little further back from the hole. "There's still time," she said. "It's not dark yet."

"But no one's going to be out in this. We should've done it last week, when the weather was better."

"It wasn't time last week," Marilyn said, glancing over her shoulder at them. "You know if we do it too soon it only wants more."

Arlene subsided. She did know that, but she also knew that if no one came along tonight, it'd be one of their bodies lying broken in the bottom of the hole tomorrow morning. It was that, or risk the hole feeding its hunger the old way, sinkholes opening in unexpected places, the ground vanishing beneath trusting feet, the earth itself betraying them. Waiting wouldn't help them then.

"Someone's coming!" The hiss ran around the group like an echo of the wind, and they busied themselves looking casual, trying not to make eye contact with whoever was crunching down the lane. Arlene heard the gate click over the complaints of the hole, and lifted her head to watch. A few of them always did. Because they had to know if this was who they were waiting for.

Now she sighed inwardly, because it was a runner, moving fast in the fading light, muddy water splashing off the track with every stride. He never even glanced toward the hole or the little gathering around it – just ran for the next gate, let himself through, and kept going. A mutter of disappointment rose in the dimness, and the rain grew heavier. The ground shivered, and Arlene found herself trying to look everywhere at once. Not that she'd have any warning if the hole did reach out. The soggy grass beneath her feet would just be gone, and she'd drop with her eyes rolling and the scream caught in her throat, waiting for the snap of her limbs as she crashed to the bottom, hoping she hit her head on the way down, because if she didn't she might just starve down there with her shattered bones, licking desperately at the drops of water that trickled down the rocky sides of the new gorge. And no one would help her, because someone has to fall. Someone *always* has to fall.

Someone has to feed the hole.

The clouds, no longer content with gobbling the peaks, were drifting down the slopes and pressing their fat bellies against the path, not even the keening wind able to tear them away. It felt a lot later than it was, but the path was still clear before them, rolling down the slope wide enough to walk two abreast. Amy tightened the cords of her hood and glanced at her watch. They couldn't be much more than half an hour off finishing, and bollocks to a pint. She was ordering a pot of tea for two – which she had no intention of sharing – and if there was a dog asleep in front of the pub fire, she was kicking it out and taking its place. Her hands were frozen, and her waterproof boots had sprung a leak about two hours ago. They sloshed with every step.

"Alright?" Toby asked. His nose was red from the cold. "British weather, eh?"

She scowled at him. Why they couldn't have just changed plans she didn't know. It wasn't like this hadn't been forecast.

"Want a protein bar?" he offered.

She was rather satisfied to see that his bare legs looked as cold as her hands. At least she'd dressed for it.

"Almost there," he said. "Great walk, right?"

"I'm sure it would have been, if we'd been able to see anything," she said, and picked up the pace, her little toes rubbing uncomfortably against her sock seams in the soggy boots.

"SOMEONE'S COMING, SOMEONE'S COMING." The whisper, the rumour, running through the group again, and Arlene swallowed hard. This was their last chance. At this time, with this weather, no one else was going to be coming down the path from the peak. And then they'd have to choose. Because if they didn't, the hole would, and it was indiscriminate. No targeting of the sick or the old. Anyone was at risk. *Everyone.*

They emerged out of the murk, a woman with her head down and a man swinging his arms enthusiastically to stay warm. Two. Two was dicey, and Arlene glanced at Stella. She was peering down the lane that ran to the village, but it was impossible to say if there was anyone coming. There could have been an army of walkers on the way up and they'd never have spotted them.

Stella looked around finally. "Block the gate," she said, and Arlene took a deep breath, not sure if she was relieved or horrified. Both, she supposed. Always both.

"Hey, Ames," Toby said, closing the gate behind them as she pushed on through the rain. Ahead, the path split in two, one branch running straight ahead while the other turned to the left through a second gate which would take them to the village. "There's a really cool sinkhole just over there. Want to take a look?"

Amy tried to convey with a glare just what she thought of that idea, but the effect was ruined somewhat by the rain blowing in her face and making her squint. Instead she said, "I'm wet, cold, and completely over this, Toby. I do not want to go look at some hole."

He rubbed the back of his head. "I'm sorry. I didn't think it'd be this bad."

"Forecast. This was on the *forecast*."

"Yeah, but weather people get it wrong all the time."

She wondered briefly if she should try pushing him into a ditch, but he'd probably just think it was hilarious. That was who he was. "I'm going to the pub," she said. "Go look at the hole if you want."

"Alright," he said. "I'll take pictures for you."

"Can't wait." She marched to the next gate as he veered down a sheep track to the right, splashing through puddles with all the enthusiasm of a five-year-old. Sheep watched him pass with that odd mix of boredom and alarm that seemed to be their perpetual outlook on life, water dripping from their ears and bellies. There were a few sheltering from the wind in the lee of the wall, and a couple blocking the gate. "Shoo," she told them, and they stared at her. Poor sodden creatures. She hoped their wool was doing a better job than her thermals.

"LET HER GO," Stella said. "He'll do."

Arlene and Patricia ran stiff-legged away from the gate as the woman pushed through and latched it behind her. Arlene turned to watch as she stomped along the path, head down against the wind. The woman didn't pause or look back, her hands stuffed in her pockets and her shoulders a stiff line of fury.

"Come on," Patricia called. "He's almost there!"

Arlene broke into a trot, squinting against the wind. They had to get this right. If they didn't, there'd be no second chance. The light was all but gone, the rain stealing the day, and the man was slowing as he neared the hole, peering into the dimness and picking his path carefully. The long grass washed right to the brink, to where the earth crumbled to nothing and the rain ran in mini waterfalls over the edge to join the stream that washed the bottom. There were plants down there, clinging precariously to the sides, and piles of stone like dragon treasure, and bones. Always plenty of those. Arlene never liked to get too close. It made her stomach swoop and her head spin, until she wasn't sure if she was frightened or exhilarated by the idea of the plunge to the bottom. She supposed that was all part of the hole's magic.

Now she joined the others, shoulder to shoulder, forming a rough half-moon around the man as he peered into the depths and tried to shelter his phone from the worst of the rain.

"Awesome," he mumbled, and crouched down to take another photo.

They edged closer, no one speaking, a wall of warm bodies with their eyes on the man.

"Amy would have liked this," he announced to the late afternoon, and stood up, still looking at his phone as he turned. He took a step forward, and bumped into Stella. "What—?"

He lowered the phone and stared at them. They stared back, yellow-eyed and silent, feet planted firmly on the sodden ground, bodies round and unmoving.

"Shoo," he said.

No one moved.

"Go on, get out of here!" He clapped his hands.

They were still.

He looked at the tiny space of grass around his feet, then tried to push his way through them.

They pushed back.

Amy looked at her watch and shook her head. She'd tried Toby's phone three times already. He might have no signal, of course, but the odds were he'd dropped it in a puddle or down his silly hole. Still, he should have been here by now. She got up and went to the bar.

"Hi," she said to the landlady. "Do you know of some sinkhole up near the last gate?"

"Of course," the landlady said. "It's only a few hundred metres off the track."

Amy sighed. "My ... friend went to take a look at it, and I left him to it. Is there another way down from there or something? It's just he shouldn't have been far behind me."

The landlady looked at a man sitting on one of the bar stools, his fingers wrapped around a large mug of tea. He looked back at her, expressionless. "There's another track," she said eventually. "He could well have gone that way. Takes a wee bit longer, but comes into the village all the same."

Amy tapped her fingers on the bar. "Maybe I should go back up."

"No, don't do that," the woman said. "You'll just get wet and cold, and if he's taken a different track, you'll miss him anyway. I'm sure he'll turn up, and if he's not here in an hour I'll get one of the boys to take a quad bike up."

"Thank you," Amy said. "I'm sure he's just gone on some detour."

"I imagine so," the landlady said, and went back to stacking glasses.

The man at the bar said, "Autumn's done, then."

"Sounds like," the landlady said, and Amy wandered back to her table by the fire.

Autumn's done? It was only September. She supposed it was a local thing. She took her phone out and tried calling again, but it went straight to voicemail. Silly sod had the car keys, too.

Products of Unknown Origin

There are two parts to the story of this story, and possibly some anecdotal evidence regarding genetic predispositions to not entirely thinking things through when it comes to small, mysterious creatures.

I've lived and worked in the tropics for a lot of my life, so when, while working on a catamaran in the Caribbean, I discovered a small caterpillar on the saloon table, I didn't think much of it. Food would often come with passengers, whether it was weevils in the flour or small inhabitants in the fruit. Sieve the flour, wash the fruit, and as long as you don't let any ants or cockroaches aboard, it's all good.

So I popped the caterpillar in a jar with a lettuce leaf inside and a tea towel over the top, and decided to put him ashore at the next bay.

And then there was another, so he joined his buddy.

And then there was another.

And another.

And another half-dozen, by which point I realised that, unless I planned on switching profession to become a home for stray caterpillars, I needed to find where they were coming from. I waited until the guests were ashore and pulled all the lockers out, eventually finding a bag that had once held muesli, but now held a thriving metropolis of moths and caterpillars. Which was ... not ideal.

I did get them all cleared up before the guests got back, but it was a near thing.

I told this story to my dad and his girlfriend not long after, only for her to burst out laughing and tell me, over Dad's protests, about how he had just recently rescued a stray caterpillar and kept it in a jar until he could take it ashore and set it free.

He chose a nice tree to do this, and wished the caterpillar a happy life.

The next time they went back to that harbour, the tree was no more.

Let this be your lesson, lovely readers.

Never trust a caterpillar.

"OH, THAT BLOODY SHOP," NORA SAID, PEERING into the muesli packet. "Look at this!"

"What?" George poured boiling water over the tea leaves and turned to look at his wife. She was glaring at the cereal quite furiously.

"There's only a caterpillar in it."

"A caterpillar? Really?" He leaned over her, one hand on her shoulder. "Aw, there is too."

"Don't 'aw' it. What am I supposed to have for breakfast now?"

"He won't have eaten much."

"Oh, ha. I'm not eating caterpillar leftovers."

"Toast, then?" George suggested, and pulled the loaf out of the cupboard.

They drank their tea as they watched the caterpillar exploring the top of the muesli box, lifting himself up on his back legs to wave his fuzzy head around.

"I'm not shopping there again," Nora said.

"You say that every time," George replied, passing her the jam.

"It keeps happening, though! I don't know where they get their stock from. Weevils in the flour, a slug in the lettuce – I'm just going to have to stick with Sainsbury's."

George made a face. "How boring. I like that little shop. It's got all sorts of odd things that you can't find anywhere else. And it's good to support smaller businesses."

"I know, but we can't keep throwing stuff away." Nora stood and picked up the cereal box. "When I tried to take the lettuce back, they said the slug must have been living in our fridge. The cheek!"

"What're you doing with him?"

"It's an it, George. I'm throwing it out."

"Don't do that. I'll take him down to the park." He held his hand out, and she glared at him.

"It's raining. You're going to take him down there in the rain?"

"You can't just put him in the bin. Poor wee fellow." George plucked the caterpillar off the cereal pack, and it immediately started exploring his hand. "It's not his fault, is it? I'll just pop him in a jar with some leaves or something for now."

Nora shook her head and dropped the cereal box in the rubbish. Whatever kept him happy.

THE RAIN CONTINUED ON and off for much of the week, that drizzly spring weather that always threatens to brighten into something lovely but never quite does. It was Friday before it was nice enough to go out for a decent walk, and a sharp little breeze played with the trees that lined the road and tugged at Nora's coat as they strolled arm in arm toward the park.

"We should go up to the gardens for lunch," George said.

"It'll be crowded."

"True. Do you fancy an ice cream in the park, then?"

Nora looked up at the scrubbed sky, feeling the first hints of warmth in the sun, and smiled. "That would be nice."

They took their usual route through the park, treading carefully on the muddy paths that wound through the wooded area, nodding at joggers and dog walkers. There was spring growth everywhere, struggling up after the rain, and everything seemed breathlessly alive, from the birds flinging themselves across the sky to the spring flowers flooding the ground.

Except for one small tree, standing where the path from the woods split, carrying one either through the fancier area straight ahead, with its gazebos and vine-covered pavilion, or out to the playground and mini-golf on the right, or off to the botanical garden-style area on the left, with the little planting areas representing different countries, and lichen-encrusted information plaques nestling in the foliage.

"Oh," Nora said, peering up at the tree. Every leaf had been torn from it, and its branches slumped forlornly toward the ground, dry and cracking under their own weight. "That looks rather poorly, doesn't it?"

"Hmm."

"Virus, do you think?"

"Hmm," George said again. He let go of Nora's hand and went to inspect the tree a little more closely.

Nora watched him go, tucking her hands into her coat pockets. "That's not the tree you put our little friend in, is it?"

George turned back, looking shifty. "Of course not."

"I told you we should have put it in the bin." She linked her arm through his again and they ambled on toward the ice cream shop.

The sunny weather held, and the next day they started down the road toward the park again, agreeing that this time they should have a coffee, because it didn't do anyone any good to have ice cream every day. It stopped feeling quite so special if one had it every day. As they approached the path through the woods, they slowed, then stopped altogether, staring at the trees that yesterday had formed a reaching, spring-green canopy over the footpath.

All the leaves were gone. Not a single tree had been spared, and the trees themselves looked diminished and shrunken, their limbs twisting in ways Nora was certain they hadn't the day before. As they watched, a branch detached itself with a brittle snap and crashed to the pavement ahead of them, shattering with the finality of a broken figurine. They looked at each other.

"Shall we go the other way?" Nora suggested.

"It might be wise," George said, as another branch fell in a pained chorus of tearing and cracking.

The rest of the park seemed unaffected, and they drank their coffee while watching children and their parents – well, mostly their parents – driving remote controlled boats around the pond, framed by lush dark foliage dripping with life. There were a lot of park workers about, and they saw some stringing yellow caution tape along the edge of the woodland area, much to the frustration of the dog walkers. Occasionally a crash could be heard over the sound of the coffee machine.

"I did put the caterpillar there," George said.

Nora had her cup cradled in both hands, and looked at him over the rim. "You don't say."

"Should I tell them?"

They both looked toward the taped-off woodland. A man with a poodle was arguing with a workman and waving his arms wildly. The poodle was peeing on one of the new sculptures the council had installed, and Nora rather thought she approved of the creature's evaluation of it. "I don't think so," she said finally. "It was a caterpillar. Even if it was exceptionally hungry, it can't kill trees."

"I suppose," George said. He was fiddling with the sugar packets, and Nora sighed, then leaned over and squeezed his arm.

"If it'll make you feel better. But I doubt they'll even pay any attention."

The workman with the warning tape paid no attention whatsoever. The woman driving the park's golf cart listened gravely, then patted George's hand and thanked him, telling him she'd be sure to pass it along, before driving under the tape and up the hill toward the woods.

"She's not going to pass it on, is she?" George asked once they were out of earshot.

"I did tell you," Nora replied.

The next day they packed sandwiches and a thermos of tea, and drove out to the Dales to walk in some wilder spaces.

Neither of them mentioned the caterpillar.

Monday was a little grey and fragile feeling, as if spring had worn itself out over the weekend and wasn't sure just what to do now. Nora had books to take back to the library, so they bundled themselves against the cold and ventured out, their route taking them past the park, although it wasn't a day for sitting outside with coffee.

Not that they needed to worry, as the coffee shop was shut. The entire park was shut. The big iron gates at the main entrance were closed for the first time Nora could remember, and the smaller entrances were strung about liberally with more warning tape, and guarded by soldiers with tight faces. Beyond them, they could see nothing but grey and broken trees, stark against the green spring grass. They stopped in front of the main gates, and asked one of the soldiers what had happened. She examined them with a flat expression, and must have found them harmless, because she relaxed and said, "Biological event."

"A biological event?" George said. "What's that when it's at home? A birthday party for amoebas?"

The soldier grinned, her cheeks dimpling. "No, sir. But that's all the information I can give you. There's no danger to people or animals. Just the trees." A roar punctuated her words, the sound of a glacier calving, and they turned to watch as the great oak tree that had stood at the centre of the park folded in on itself like so much paper.

"Oh dear," Nora said. "Now that's a real shame."

The soldier looked back at them, her smile fading. "I know. It must have been really pretty."

"It was," George said, and took Nora's arm. "Well – good luck, then."

"Thanks," the soldier said, and watched them walk away along the rain-damp street, a small woman and a thin man, dusted grey around the edges with age.

"NORA," George called from the little balcony that gave onto the street.

"What is it?"

"Come and have a look at this."

Nora frowned at her crossword. *Something strange (7).* "Is it important?"

"Yes."

She sighed and put the paper on the side table, then

padded over to the balcony. The rain had stopped, but the night still felt damp and chilly. "You're letting the cold in."

"Come and see." He put an arm around her as she tightened her cardigan, looking down the street toward the park. In the dark the dead grey trees were pale as old ashes, and there were searchlights punching through them, and silently rolling red and blue lights on the roads at the entrance.

"What are they doing?"

"I can't tell," George said. "I think they're looking for something." As he spoke, a sudden rash of shouting broke out, accompanied by the crash of falling trees. More shouting, and then a sound that made them clutch each other in instinctive fright. It was the snap of guns, familiar from too many TV shows and movies to name, but never heard in earnest. It was flat and hard, both less impressive and more frightening than either had imagined. They stared out toward the park as the searchlights began to congregate by the gates. The shooting had stopped, but there was more shouting going on, and the thunder of falling trees was building to a crescendo.

"Do you think—" Nora started, and George interrupted her.

"Look!"

The trees were falling in a clear-cut line, bearing down out of the woodland and toward the main gates, exploding in clouds of silver dust that spun the light back to the watchers and obscured whatever was within it. The noise swelled as the tidal wave of falling vegetation roared across the park, drowning the shouts of the soldiers and police, who had withdrawn beyond the gates. Big searchlights mounted on the jeeps were still shining into the park, but the all-pervasive dust of the dead trees fractured it as surely as mist, and the closer the thing – because there had to be *something*, didn't there, the trees weren't falling like that just by chance – the less that could be seen. And the unseen thing was almost upon the gates.

George and Nora stood with their arms around each other, wide-eyed and astonished, on their neat little balcony at the front of their neat little terraced house, and watched the gates of the park blow open, and the police and soldiers scatter with a soundtrack of belching gunfire. The thing plunged down the street, oblivious to the shots, moving with a muscular, ungainly speed that reminded Nora of a charging hippopotamus. It bounced off a few cars and set the alarms shrieking before it steadied its course down the centre of the road. It had so many legs it barely humped up as it ran, and Nora thought she could hear its sucker feet peeling eagerly off the pavement and planting back down again. It was like hearing the world's biggest Velcro strap being opened and closed rapidly on the street below them.

They leaned forward to watch it pass beneath the balcony, and as it did it seemed to tip its head toward them, so tall that it was level with their feet, and they could see themselves reflected in one round dark eye. Then it was gone, Velcro-ing down the night-time street, taking up so much of the road that a car coming the other way veered in panic and ploughed into a parked moped. A moment later the first of the army jeeps roared after the creature, shouting soldiers hanging off it in all directions, followed by screaming police cars and more jeeps. Nora and George stayed where they were, their bodies still pressed together, trembling with the excitement of it all. Then the street was empty again, the car sirens still yowling, doors and windows opening and shutting anxiously.

Eventually, Nora looked up at George. "Cuppa?"

"Please," he said, and they retreated to the warmth of the living room, settling themselves in their chairs and looking about cautiously, as if expecting something to have changed.

Nora put the kettle on, and took a packet of biscuits from the cupboard. "Digestive?" she said, offering them to George.

He took one, then hesitated. "Where are they from?"

"Sainsbury's," she said, putting the packet on the coffee table.

"Ah. Good." George settled back into his chair and put his feet on the footstool. "I rather think you're right about that other shop."

"Of course I am," Nora said. "And Sainsbury's does some quite nice biscuits." She picked up her crossword, read the clue again, and thought, *Ah. Anomaly. That's it.*

Outside, the car alarms had finally stopped.

A Memorable Cruise

Anyone who spends any time on boats, especially offshore, gives at least a little thought to what might happen if they go overboard. Partly out of necessity, as thinking such things through is part of maintaining safety, and partly out of the same stomach-churning fascination that makes us peer over cliff edges. Because what if…

So I suppose it was inevitable that I'd write ***something*** *about it one day.*

PHIL TROD WATER, WATCHING THE LIGHTS OF THE cruise ship recede in a stately manner, the bulk of the vessel silhouetted against the star-crowded Caribbean sky. It was rolling slightly as it went, like a rotund duck hurrying hopefully along a riverbank.

This, Phil considered, was less than ideal.

Although, he reminded himself, it could have been worse. He could have hit his head on the way over the rail, rendering himself unconscious before he even completed the plunge into the unexpectedly cool waters. Or he could have survived the fall, but been sucked down into the maw of the enormous propellers, which wouldn't have even hesitated as they chewed him up and spat him back into the sea. Well, he didn't think they would have, anyway. He was hardly an expert in such things.

He paddled in a slow circle, his sandals already discarded and his socks slowly slipping down his calves to join them. He couldn't see land, no matter which way he looked. Not that he'd expected to. They were in the middle of a night passage from Saint Lucia to Barbados, which, apparently, was quite a long way. Not that it looked a long way on the map, but he'd never been good at such things.

That night passage was one of the reasons he'd been on the otherwise deserted deck at one in the morning.

Which, in retrospect, may not have been his first mistake, but it was certainly one of them.

THE WOMAN HAD BEEN at the bar all that evening, fiddling with a succession of frozen drinks in primary colours, fishing out pineapple leaves and paper umbrellas and strawberries on toothpicks to discard next to the frost-beaded glass. Her dress, like all the others he'd seen her in on the trip, looked new but faintly uncomfortable, as if someone else had chosen it for her, or she'd chosen it while thinking she was someone else. She smiled hopefully at anyone who drifted into her vicinity, blinking a little too quickly in the not-quite-flattering halogen lights, adjusting her hair, her skirt, the way she sat. There was still ridged skin on her ring finger.

Phil had seen her elsewhere on the trip, too. Sometimes she'd be half-reading a book by the pool while she watched the other passengers over the top of enormous glasses, an equally oversized hat flopping over her ears. Her toenail polish almost matched her swimsuit, but not quite, and sunblock smudged her nose. And she'd been on the same tour as them in Grenada, the one that had taken them to the spice gardens. He'd dutifully carried a basket as his wife filled it with jars and bags of spices, exclaiming over them in excitement. They'd languish unopened in the back of the kitchen cupboard with the za'atar from Morocco and the saffron from Spain and the dried mushrooms from Italy, brought home from other trips.

The woman had laughed a lot, he remembered. Laughed at the commentary of the guide, at the sweet bite of the chutney, at the polite smiles of the other guests. Phil had watched her as she stood alone for a moment in front of a display of jars, the rest of the group melting away from her as if she might be catching. She was swathed in a dress full of rich greens and purples, her bare arms soft and vulnerable looking. Her smile slipped, became crooked, then she looked up and caught his eye. The smile returned immediately, wide and urgent.

"Jerk seasoning," she said, pointing, and laughed again. "Jerk!"

He looked away, embarrassed, and trailed after his wife, feeling rather than seeing the woman follow them back out to the bus, adjusting her hat against the sun.

BIOLUMINESCENCE TRAILED IN THE WATER, sparking off his fingers like fairy dust in a children's movie, turning the careful, economical sweeps of his arms into glowing halos. He wondered if the ship was far enough away now that he didn't have to worry about any sharks that had been following it. He'd read that they did that, sharks. Followed ships to eat the rubbish that was thrown overboard.

Were they still allowed to do that these days, though? Throw things overboard? It seemed unlikely. But that didn't mean the sharks had stopped following the ships. It might be some sort of instinct by now. Or memory. Hope, even.

Phil lay back in the grip of the sea and let his feet float up, his belly a check-print dome before him, a tiny island bulging out of the ocean. He watched the stars.

ONE LUNCHTIME, on the deck that looked out to the pool, his wife said, "Maybe we should invite her to join us."

Phil followed her gaze and saw the woman, in a blue and white dress this time, the straps thin on her pinkened shoulders. She was slowly carrying a plate of salad from the buffet to a table in the corner, shooting hopeful glances around the room. Phil looked away, patting his wife's hand, feeling the looseness of her skin under his fingers.

"This is our holiday, dear," he said. "And it's her own fault. It's a couple's cruise."

"Hmm." His wife slipped her hand away and picked up her wine glass. "Maybe she booked it as a couple, but something happened. We don't know."

Phil glanced at the woman again, perched alone at the edge of a room full of matched sets of thinning hair and expensive dye jobs, tropical shirts and flounced sundresses.

"It's not our problem," he said. "We should leave well enough alone."

His wife didn't answer.

He wondered now, as he examined the excess of stars, why they had been on the trip in the first place. It wasn't the first cruise they had been on, but it was by far the most expensive. The others had been in the Med, little week-long jaunts with only a couple of hours to fly at each end.

It had been his wife's idea. Something different. When had she suggested it? Christmas? Just after?

He remembered agreeing, because things had felt *unsettled*. Had been feeling unsettled since just before the Christmas drinks party, when he'd been late. He'd had to pick up the catering-sized pork pie from the organic butcher in town, but his other, more private engagement had run late, and in his rush to get showered before the guests arrived he'd left the wine in the boot of his car.

His wife had gone to fetch it.

And hadn't she been a little odd, after that?

She hadn't even asked why he'd been so late. Or mentioned the small stain on his trousers, even though he'd had the papercut on his finger to explain it.

WHEN PHIL and his wife had left to go to their cabin after dinner that night the woman had still been at the bar, dangling one sandal from her toes as she shredded a napkin into soggy confetti. The bar staff were alternately avoiding her or smiling too brightly. She didn't look up.

Phil led his wife hand-in-hand down the mellow-lit corridors and into the cabin, which was small and a little too warm, almost claustrophobic, but the porthole looked out on the sea. It had cost more for that tiny glimpse of the outside world, and Phil wasn't sure it was worth it, but his wife had insisted.

"If we're going to do this," she had said, "we should do it properly."

And he had agreed, because he wanted things to feel settled again, and it seemed that might help.

He let her use the bathroom first, just as she did at home, and while he listened to the *burrrrr* of the electric toothbrush he popped a pill out of a blister pack and dropped it into her water bottle. It fizzed softly, turning slow flips as it sank, and by the time she came out of the bathroom it was gone. Phil had changed into his pyjamas, the pale blue ones with the dark blue piping that she had given him for his birthday.

"All yours," she said, and sat on the edge of the bed – or bunk, he supposed, it being a ship – to pull her shoes off.

Phil thought that the water really was cooler than one would have expected, given that it was the Caribbean. It was certainly cooler than the top-deck pool, or the beaches they'd paddled at briefly during excursions. He supposed because it was deeper out here. He rolled onto his belly, attempting a clumsy doggy paddle as he wondered just how deep it was.

The swells were long and lazy, lifting him toward the stars then easing him back down again. There was no wind to speak of. When the sun had set that evening it had lit the entire ocean on fire, pouring molten across the swells and rendering it even more alien. Now, the sea might have been tar, thick and dark and drowning.

Phil stopped paddling and craned his head out of the water. He'd already lost sight of the ship. There was nothing in any direction but endless swells, rising to meet the dark dome of the sky.

He swallowed, his throat clicking on salt.

When his wife's breath was slow and even, and she didn't even stir when he whispered her name, Phil got up again. He exchanged his pyjamas for shorts and a checked shirt, and pulled his socks and sandals back on. Then he let himself out of the cabin and retraced their steps to the bar.

The woman was still there, and she looked up with a hopeful smile as Phil took the stool next to her. Recognition flickered, and the smile faded to a shadow of disappointment, or even distaste.

"Where's your wife?" she asked.

Phil gave her a polite smile, pushing his glasses up his nose. "She's sleeping."

"So what're you doing here?" Her tone was flat, unfriendly.

"Insomnia," he explained, and ordered a hot chocolate from the bartender. "Sometimes there's just no use trying, but a hot drink can help a little."

"Oh," she said, and for a moment neither of them said anything else. Then she added, "I thought … oh, never mind."

"That I was coming to proposition you while my wife slept?" Phil gave a little, restrained laugh. "Oh, my, no. I mean, you're very attractive, but I love my wife."

The woman laughed as well, a relieved sound. "That actually makes me feel better. It's hard being here alone. Everyone either feels sorry for me or thinks I'm some sort of man-eater."

"Why are you here alone?" Phil asked, sipping his hot chocolate.

"I wasn't meant to be." She touched the raised skin where a ring had been reflexively. "Long story. I should have cancelled, but I thought it might help, somehow. Getting away."

"I'm sorry," Phil said.

She shrugged, and pressed her fingers to the soft skin below her eyes. Her hands were shaking slightly.

He offered her his napkin. "Shall we get some air? I find a little fresh air does wonders for, well, everything."

She dabbed at her face with the napkin, looked at him carefully, then nodded. "Alright."

Phil wondered if he should be able to tell what direction land was in by the position of the stars, or the angle of the swells or something. Not that he supposed it mattered if he was swimming toward it or away from it, not at this distance. And there would be currents, among other things.

Now he thought about it, the cruise really had been out of character. The extravagance of it. Two weeks aboard, sailing out of Florida.

"It'll be memorable," his wife had said. "Something to treasure."

And he'd agreed that it was time they started treating themselves. Mostly because things had still felt unsettled after Christmas. Because she had been *odd*.

But there hadn't been anything to see in the car, when she went for the wine. Of course not. He was too careful.

Although he had been pressed for time. The butcher shut at five.

And hadn't he wondered if things had been slightly out of place at his work office the next week, when he went to put his souvenir away?

But they'd had a temporary cleaner. He remembered that, because they'd put the mugs back in the wrong order.

So maybe his wife had just been odd for some woman's reason, something to do with age or hormones or her sister's endless problems. There had been nothing for her to see.

Nothing.

PHIL and the woman from the bar leaned together on the rail, cradling their drinks and looking across the endless sea. She named some of the constellations, but he wasn't listening. He was looking at the skin of her neck, just beginning to gain that glorious looseness, and at the beautiful lines creeping up to her chin from her décolletage. Her arms were softly sunburned, but her neck and face were pale. She must use good sunblock.

He put his cup down on a table by a sun lounger and made a polite noise as she pointed out a planet, still burbling on about Greek myths or some such. He pushed his hands into his pockets, his eyes on the dimple at the base of her throat, on the hollow where her jaw met her neck. In the dim lights of the deck he couldn't see the blue veins under her skin, but he traced their path with his eyes anyway.

She turned away from him to put her own glass down, and his hands floated after her almost of their own accord, the tie of his dressing gown hanging loosely between them. He looped it over her neck in one swift, sure move, jerking it back fiercely, cutting off her scream before she could draw breath. She scrabbled at the tie, but he kept the pressure on with the conviction of long practise. He had her. His heart was louder than the sea in his ears, his breath quick and elated, and he braced himself to force her to her knees.

The pain was so sharp, so unexpected, that he was falling almost before he registered it. For one moment he wondered if he was having a stroke, spots flaring over his vision as his head reverberated in agony, the tie slack in his hands. The woman in front of him reared up, twisting away, and he stumbled to all fours. He touched a hand to the base of his skull, and the fingers came away wet.

Then his wife was in front of him, and he stared at her in astonishment. She was holding a hand-carved walking stick she'd bought in Saint Vincent.

"Quick," she said. "While he's still groggy."

Phil tried to ask her what she was doing there, but the words wouldn't come.

"Don't you want to hit him again?" the woman from the bar asked. "I do."

"No. Stick with the plan." His wife grabbed his ankles, and he mouthed a protest at her. She should be comforting him. He was hurt. She met his eyes for a moment, her gaze cold and hard. "Grab his arms," she said.

"Are you sure there aren't any cameras here?" the other woman asked, and he felt her hands under his armpits. It was uncomfortably intimate.

"There won't be any," his wife said. "He's too careful. Aren't you, dear?"

He wanted to ask her why she was acting so oddly, wanted to explain that he hadn't come out here to cheat on her, not at all. He'd never cheated on her, not once.

The women hefted him into the air with matching grunts of effort. For a moment he felt the smooth wood of the railing under his back, digging into his buttocks, and it confused him. What were they doing? He was hurt, they should be calling a doctor, or putting him on a sun lounger at least—

He was falling. There was no countdown, no signal. They just let go, and then he was plunging past the sheer sides of the cruise ship, suddenly much taller than it had seemed before, their faces rapidly receding white ovals peering down at him. He had time to glimpse the walking stick falling after him, and to have the sudden panicked thought that it might hit him, then he slammed into the water and was swallowed by it entirely. All was roaring confusion, with no sense of which way was up, and the powerful throb of the ship's engines boomed through his bones, and he discovered that the walking stick really was the least of his worries.

HE STOPPED doggy-paddling and tried floating again. Paddling was starting to feel like hard work, and his head was still pounding insistently. He touched it, finding a large, tender lump. She could have cracked his skull, he thought, outraged. He could have concussion!

He stared at the smooth flanks of the swells, wondering if he was still bleeding. Sharks could smell blood from a mile away, he'd heard. Or read, he wasn't sure. A sneaky little wavelet slapped his face, and he spat salt water, his heart suddenly painful in his chest.

The temporary cleaner at the office had only done one evening, the evening before he'd thought things had been out of place. It had been a sudden sickness that called the usual one away, a migraine or something. He hadn't paid attention.

The temporary cleaner had been in the office the evening his wife had gone to her sister's because ... what had she said? He couldn't remember. It hadn't seemed important. Women's stuff.

The mugs had been in the wrong order, but his souvenirs hadn't been out of place, had they? The rug might have been moved, his chair not pushed back properly, but the floorboards had been firmly in place. The folder had been nestled safely in the recess.

The locks of hair in their individual sleeves, soft and lovingly labelled, had glowed in the light just as before, untouched and only for him.

Hadn't they?

It was impossible. She wasn't that smart. *He* was smart. He'd have known something was wrong.

She wouldn't have been able to keep this secret.

Would she?

A memorable cruise, she'd said, and handed him the brochure, smiling in her small, neat way. *The trip of our lives, perhaps.*

The sea rolled smoothly around him, and his nose dipped below the surface. He pushed himself back up, spluttering, a cold hard pain digging into his ribs as he tried to lift himself clear of the water. His heart felt tight and small.

He sucked in as much air as he could.

"Help!" he screamed. *"Help!"*

The ocean didn't return so much as an echo.

Stay Tidy

Sometimes, I can point at something – a picture, a tweet, a story half-lived or half-heard, and say, "There. That's where this idea came from."

Other times? Well, let me put it this way: I wouldn't go into my subconscious without a guide (and if you find one, let me know, because I don't mean me), some breadcrumbs, a whole lot of rope, three escape plans, and possibly some weaponry. It's a strange place in there.

THE DOOR WAS LOCKED.

That wasn't supposed to happen. It had never happened in the practice runs.

Del tugged at the handle, as if by denying its locked-ness he could change it. The door didn't budge, just stood there looking bored and featureless. A whimper caught in the back of his throat, and he scuttled back down the steps, sprinting for the house across the street.

Locked.

"No," he whispered. "No, no, not all of them. They can't be." He jumped off the step into the flowerbed beneath the window and tried to squint through a gap in the curtains, but the early morning was dark and the room behind was darker still.

Which was why it should've been safe. *They* couldn't range far without solar or a docking station to top up their charge. He should have had time, but he'd just had to go further, hadn't he? Had to try this one last street, even though his dad had told him when he left, *Don't get creative, Del. Follow the plan.* And now he was too late to get back to the pickup point on the river before *they* started stirring.

He knocked on the window lightly, flinching at the hollow, demanding sound of it echoing across the empty street. No birds, of course. He remembered them, in a vague sort of way. He hadn't paid much attention when they'd been around. Pigeons in town, mostly. Fat things with the self-satisfied strut of a well-fed cat. They'd lasted longer in the cities and towns than the sparrows and other birds, partly because they were big and partly because they were even more stubborn than the humans had been, slower to leave their familiar, trusted spaces and tuck themselves away in desolate pockets of the countryside. Now all the birds were scarce and scared, and you counted yourself lucky if you could get your hands on a scrawny grouse – or anything else. They'd been too messy to survive.

No movement beyond the window, not that he'd really expected it. It had been a knock of desperation, not hope. The pigeons weren't the only ones that couldn't survive in the cities anymore. Too many of *them*. Del ran back to the road, heading for the next door along the row of terraced houses as the sky steadily lightened above him, streaks of orange and rose blushing the clouds. His breath coiled in the chilly air ahead of him as he hurried up the steps, his trainers all but soundless. If he couldn't get in here, he'd head to the end of the row, find a way into a back garden and hope there was an empty shed or something he could hole up in. He had to get off the street. *Had to*.

The door was locked, as he'd half-expected, given the rest of the row. Some people had done that, had turned off the power and water and locked up their houses like they thought they'd be back again in a month, when Someone Sorted Things Out. The government, maybe, but they'd been among the first to go. Too many of *them* roaming the halls and the streets, stolidly doing their duty, keeping things clean and tidy. It had been a statement, Del's dad said, for them to be introduced in the capitals and the seats of power before anywhere else. Prove they were safe and show everyone the way forward. Well, they'd done the second bit, for sure.

Del abandoned the door-knocking and sprinted for the end of the row, the tiny paved patios in front of the terraced houses immaculately clean, not a weed or drift of leaves decorating the corners. His rucksack bounced on his back, mournfully empty. It was why he'd gone further – he'd found almost nothing worth taking in the houses he'd been allocated to check. A long-expired tube of antiseptic cream and a half-used packet of paracetamol in one, a bag of sticky miniature shampoo bottles in another. Nothing much useful at all. They'd all been cleared out ages ago.

A high brick wall ran down the side of the last house in the row, then turned sharply onto a path of clean tarmac with neatly trimmed edging. Wooden gates gave onto the alley from the terraces on both sides, and Del peered through the small gap at the side of the first one. No good – the grass was trimmed perfectly, the flowerbeds taken down to a flattened, uniform size. He ran to the next. This one was partly paved, the stone flags immaculate and a small garden gnome by the shed polished until it was all but colourless. His head was starting to swim, and his breathing had gone all ragged at the edges. He could feel a sick sweat soaking through his T-shirt, too. He couldn't stay out here. He was going to have to risk trying a gate.

The gnome gave him the creeps, so he chose the next gate along, scrambling up the wall next to it when the latch wouldn't lift. He balanced on the top for a moment, aware of the strengthening light around him, the sky lifting blue and broad far above and the clouds already losing their flush. But rushing was what got you caught, so he stayed where he was a little longer, his hands braced on the top of the wall and his trainers pressed into the red brick. The garden was all grass and ruthlessly trimmed flowerbeds, the heads of the flowers lopped off to keep all the plants at the same height. A small fishpond was fish-less and clear enough to drink from. Del swallowed hard, his throat clicking, then boosted himself up and over the wall, dropping as softly as he could to the cropped grass. He stayed where he was, eyes on the door of the garden shed. It was slightly ajar, the crack a glimpse into a bottomless dark.

He hurried to the house, keeping to the grass and avoiding a little gravel path that snaked from the gate to the door. He put his hand on the handle, took a deep, steadying breath, and turned it.

Well, tried to. It didn't move, and he had to bite down on his lip to stop himself crying out. He went to the window, testing it, his hands shaking. It was full light now. The window didn't move, and he strained to hear beyond the confines of the garden. Nothing. He was still safe.

Not for long, though.

Even as he rushed to the window on the other side of the back step a gate or wooden door clanged open further down the row. There was a breath of silence, and for one irrationally hopeful instant he wondered if the still day had found a breeze somewhere, then the smooth *mmmmph-hhrrrrr* of blades on short grass started up.

A sob was building up at the back of his throat, and he threw a panicked look over his shoulder at the shed. No movement, not yet. He wiped his mouth with the back of his hand. If he smashed a window they'd be on him in an instant. *Stay quiet. Stay tidy.* He looked back at the shed. The roof. If he were quiet ... the drones probably wouldn't patrol somewhere like this, somewhere so obviously under full compliance. Or not too much, anyway.

Don't run, don't run. He started back across the grass, keeping his steps soft, tremors racing through him, eyes fixed on the door. He couldn't see the opening from this angle, couldn't tell if anything was waking up in the depths. *Stay calm.*

He was almost there, two metres to go, maybe three, when the door started to swing open. He stopped, a rangy boy in old, clean clothes that mostly fit him, head freshly shaved so he couldn't drop any hairs, frozen in the act of stepping forward. He watched the shed door inch its way slowly wider, heard the soft whisper of oiled hinges, and thought, *well. That's that, then.*

Not that it'd be able to deal with him itself, of course, but the signal would go out, and backup would be here in no time. Others would come from the neighbouring houses. Maybe a sweeper, if there was one close. Even if he ran, they'd be on him before the morning was over. The drones would spot him if he was outside. Listening ears and prying eyes would find him inside. He was too untidy to be ignored, with his breathing and his sweat and his soft, continual shedding of skin cells and hair and scent. They'd cleaned up every city in the world, just as they'd been designed to. Every town, every village. Only the furthest places were safe from them, the places where the mobile signals didn't work and the terrain was rough and jagged. Up high or down deep, that was where humans lived now. On the edges, with the last of the animals and birds and insects and other untidy life.

Del wondered how he should finish this. Just sit down, maybe. Take the rough sandwich his dad had given him last night and sit on the grass to eat it, flinging scraps at the thing to keep it occupied for a bit, perhaps. It was better than spending his last hours running for no good reason.

He was already unclipping his pack when there was a soft pop from behind him, and multicoloured streamers shot past his shoulder, almost reaching the gate before they drifted softly to the ground. A second pop, and more streamers, landing closer to the shed door this time, and a third, a fourth, until the area between the shed and the gate was an exuberant tangle of flimsy paper strips and scraps, an eyesore of disorder in the perfect garden.

Del froze, watching with wide eyes as a flat black disc emerged from the shed. It nosed toward the paper, not even turning to check the rest of the garden, and a low, busy hum rose in the still morning as its cutting blades started to turn. It ran over the first lot of streamers, tearing them to pieces and scattering the scraps, sending them raining down around it. Without pausing, it turned to try again. And again. And again. Every attack on the streamers only created more mess, and the disc ran back and forth more frantically with each pass, its business-like hum rising to an infuriated buzz.

A hand grabbed Del's arm, and he almost screamed. He jerked around to find a young woman glaring at him. She tipped the bare dome of her head at the house, and ran softly to the front door. For a moment he couldn't move, his heart too loud in his ears and tears pressing at the back of his eyes, then the whine of another machine started up in the garden next door and he lurched into motion.

He sprinted after her as she ducked through the front door, pausing to take her shoes off on the hard floor inside. He pushed the door softly shut behind him and copied her, then followed as she led the way through another door to the left. He closed and locked that one behind him, too – not that it'd help. They couldn't use door handles, but if they wanted to they could get through doors just fine, locked or not.

There were stairs leading down, and a warm light shone faintly below, enough to see by. He trailed after the woman to the smooth floor of the cellar, passing a wide desk stacked with electronics below glass windows that looked into a small room. She headed into the room, its sides panelled with grey foam, and pushed the door shut once he was in. The door was covered with foam on the inside too, and she threw her shoes down next to it and said, "That was close."

"Shh," he hissed. "What if the house hears us?"

She shook her head. "This whole room's soundproof, and all the electrics are gone." She waved at the paraffin lamp on the table. "No smart speakers, no smart lighting, nothing."

Del looked around warily. He hadn't even known you could get rid of them. To hear his dad tell it, the smart electronics had been as wound into the buildings as his veins were into his body, spying on you through the very walls. "Are you sure?" he asked.

She nodded, dropping onto a bean bag in the corner. "I wouldn't still be here otherwise."

"How long have you been here?"

She shrugged. "Since The Cleaning."

"You *stayed?*"

"Didn't know what else to do."

He hadn't thought anyone who stayed had survived. His dad had walked in one night when Del was nine and told him to pack up. There had been a whole group of them, families and couples and singles, all heading for the remote valleys and high hills of Scotland. They'd gone before it happened, leaving the cities and towns to what was to come.

It had been inevitable, his dad said. It had started with bins that knew when you mixed the recycling, with fridges that scolded you for wasting food. Heating that ran on the best setting for the environment (so mostly off), and TVs that only played documentaries tailored to your personal sins. Then cars that had to be told where you were going, and refused to start if you could walk it instead. Litter drones that obediently picked up after everyone, then suddenly started tracking litterers. The software engineers said it was just a glitch, but tell that to the people finding their litter returned to their front doors. Which everyone (except those embarrassed individuals) thought was actually a great idea, so the engineers didn't bother fixing it. Technology would save us, everyone said. It was for our own good. Humans couldn't be trusted.

By the time the machines had decided how to fix litter and pollution for good, it was too late for the engineers to do anything. Or anyone else, for that matter.

Del sat down on the floor and opened his bag. He took out his sandwich and passed half to the young woman, who looked at it in surprise, then accepted it. She took a can from a box on the floor and handed it to him.

He stared at the red can with its flowing white writing, and thought he could almost remember the taste.

"To the batteries running out," the young woman said, raising her own can.

"To being out of warranty," Del agreed, and cracked the can open. It was a little warm, but sweet and still slightly fizzy and almost exactly as he'd expected.

They ate in companionable silence, while above them the city purred with electrical life, with ovens cleaning and streets being swept, carpets cleaned and tiles polished. Drones flicked through the streets, empty except for the trundling automatic disinfectors, and plucked leaves from gutters, noting repeat offenders for destruction. Bird-repellers and cat-deterrents screamed their shrill tunes, and in the garden of the little terraced house the automatic lawnmower ran desperately through the tattered, drifting remnants of the paper streamers, over and over again.

A Risk of Sexy Armour

This story was not meant to be in here. But I sat down to start editing the stories I had, and it just sort of turned up. And it seemed a very appropriate story to end a collection with, so I let it stay. Because we never know where stories go. We may know where they start, but that's always a little nebulous, too. Sometimes they just are.
Just like life.

HOWARD ADJUSTED HIS ROBES A LITTLE, TRYING to get the pleats to flow a little more subtly over his stomach. Robes shouldn't really have *pleats,* of course. It brought to mind the practical but ridiculous-looking metal skirts favoured by a certain kind of well-proportioned soldier, and which were almost entirely out of fashion now. However, decent robes were expensive, and there was plenty of wear in these ones yet. It seemed rather wasteful to replace them simply due to a little personal expansion.

The bell above the door tinkled, a dry little sound that rattled around the tiny, crowded store, and Howard straightened up behind the counter, tucking his *World's Best Pet Sitter* mug out of sight (it was slightly scorched where the pet in question had expressed its own opinions about his pet-sitting abilities). He couldn't see his customer immediately, not with the tall banks of shelves in the centre of the shop, all packed with softly humming crystals, and bundles of dried, sweet-smelling herbs, and floating things in jars and bottles that gave off a whiff of *intent.* But a moment later a woman in worn-down boots and travel-stained trousers emerged, trailing one hand along the books crammed into the shelves on the wall to Howard's left. Her eyes were mostly on the counter beneath the books, though, which held an assortment of charms worked in twisted wire. Howard was quite proud of them – protection and fashion statement, all in one.

The woman looked up finally, fixing him with a glare that was probably meant to be friendly but had seen too many people say things like, "What's a pretty girl like you doing on a battlefield like this?" Probably immediately before being run through with one of the two long knives strapped to her back.

"Welcome to Howard's—" he started, and she cut him off with a wave of her hand as she dropped a gold coin on the counter.

"Yeah, yeah. I'm in a hurry."

"Chosen one, perilous quest, or star-crossed lovers? Or we have a special on mistaken identity—"

The look was definitely a glare now. "Do I look like I'm in the market for star-crossed lovers?"

Howard shrugged. "Everyone needs a change now and then. Might be fun."

"Might be that someone loses their head."

"That's often a risk with star-crossed lovers anyway, I believe. It's the star-crossed bit, see."

She shook her head. "Give me a perilous quest. I don't trust mistaken identity not to end up with me having to fight in heels, and once was enough on that."

"No chosen one?"

"Ugh, they're such a pain. The last one was adorably clumsy as well as being able to save the world as soon as they learned to believe in themselves. I mean, the angst for a start ..." She grimaced. "But do you know how problematic adorably clumsy is when they drop your last waterskin down a fiery warthog hole in the desert? Or when they trip and fall into a pine dragon nest and break *three* eggs?"

"Ouch," Howard said sympathetically.

"Ouch is right. My hair's still growing back."

"Perilous quest it is, then," he said, and came out from behind the counter, trotting to the front of the shop to lock the door. The woman eyed his robes as he came back, her eyebrows raised slightly, but she didn't say anything about the pleats.

Howard returned to the counter and faced the machine that took up the entire back wall of the shop. It was all gleaming copper pipes and dark metal surfaces, dials and valves and vents and the rich scent of oil and steam and other worlds. He flexed his fingers, then grabbed a big, circular brass valve in both hands, turning it exactly one and three-quarter turns anticlockwise. He moved to the valve next to it and turned that one four and one-third times in the opposite direction. He tapped a couple of pressure dials, then examined a bank of enormous breakers and forced three to the right with grunts of effort. That left one sticking straight out in the centre, and he jammed the final one to the opposite side, then watched a series of bulbs light up in a warm gold glow. He nodded in satisfaction, grasped a handle that looked like it had come off a hand-powered sewing machine (it had – the original, beautifully carved wooden one had come to an unfortunate end in a separate pet-sitting incident) and churned it wildly.

A whine started, growing in volume and intensity as he kept winding the handle, then the machine leaped into life with a roar that shook the wall. Howard let go of the handle and stepped back as dust sifted from the old beams above them. He covered his tea with one hand and looked at the woman, who was staring at the machine with undisguised admiration.

"Never gets old," he shouted over the clamour.

She blinked at him. "Well, you're going pretty grey, actually."

Howard opened his mouth to clarify, then gave up, adjusting his robes. Some people just aren't good at small talk.

The machine whined and groaned and thudded hard enough that Howard could feel it in his chest, the lights flaring in urgent sequence and gears churning deep within the wall. He finished his tea. The woman examined some throwing knives and a jar of skin-clearing lotion. They waited. And, eventually, the machine wound down to silence. They both looked at it expectantly. The lights went off, all except one which flashed thoughtfully as the quiet settled over them, ringing in their ears after the cacophony of a moment before. Howard could hear the tavern across the road getting started – someone was singing rather beautifully, and the stomp of booted feet drifted through the windows.

Then the machine *ding*-ed and spat a small strip of paper out of a slot in the middle of the wall. The light went out.

Howard tore off the strip of paper without looking at it (but not without wondering, as he did every time, how it never ran out of paper, and how the paper itself was so smooth and shiny, and not at all like the paper he was used to) and tucked it into an envelope made of heavy parchment. He reached for his wax seal, and the woman gestured at him impatiently.

"Let me see."

"You can't," he said. "You only get to ask for the adventure you want. After that it's up to the machine."

"It's *my* perilous quest."

"You know it doesn't work that way." He heated the seal and dipped it in the wax, then pressed it to the back of the envelope, sealing it shut.

"I should be able to know," she insisted. "What if it goes wrong? I started off with a decent quest last time, couple of rivals, tavern brawls, treasure to be had – good times, you know? Then next thing you know I'm wearing sexy armour and lopping the heads off orcs for no good reason. I *like* orcs. They make great ice cream."

"Sexy armour?" Howard asked doubtfully.

"Yes! It chafed."

He sighed, and put the envelope on the counter

between them, keeping his fingertips on it. “I’m sorry. That does sound most unpleasant. But you know how it works. You ask for the general adventure, the machine does the rest. None of us get to know the details, otherwise ...” He hesitated. “Otherwise, we don’t know. Maybe the door won’t open. Maybe it’ll open on something more terrible than we can imagine. Maybe it’ll never work again.” He shook his head. “But we can never know the shape of things until we’re in the midst of them. Adventures may start one way but take an entirely different turn as we go along. There are no guarantees.”

She scowled at him. “Sexy. Armour.”

They looked at each other, and eventually he turned and took a jar from the corner of the counter, holding it out to her. “For the chafing,” he said.

For a moment he thought she was going to start lopping off heads again, but instead she said something about what he could do with his sexy armour, snatched the jar and strode to the wall to Howard’s right. Half of it was taken up by a heavy tapestry that looked like it should’ve hidden the stairs to the private rooms above the shop (it didn’t – he had to go out the back door to go upstairs, which was inconvenient in the winter). The tapestry itself was hardly the best example of the art form, although its colours were rich and deep. A black and red border twisted around it, and sometimes it looked like words that were just a little too far out of focus to make out, and other times like nothing more than blips and blobs of spilled mud on a clean floor, a random almost-code. In the centre, surrounded by something that might’ve been a starry night sky, or a stormy one, depending on what angle one viewed it at, was a door. Or a door of sorts, as stitched by someone who really hadn't got the hang of this whole tapestry-making thing just yet. Or doors, for that matter.

The door was ajar, and there was a glimpse of a room behind it, although Howard was never sure, when the stitching was so rough, how it conveyed the idea of the room so clearly. Sometimes he thought he could see a chair and a desk, as in a wizard's study (or an accountant's, one being much the same as the other, in his view), and other times he thought there was the suggestion of a wild sea, or a torn, blasted heath, or a forest glade. It was all suggestion, though, he suspected. Shapes in the clouds, meaning given to nothing.

"Come on, then," the woman said, and gestured at the tapestry. "Let's see what you've landed me in this time."

"I do apologise if there are armour issues," Howard said, joining her and tugging the drawstrings to pull the tapestry aside. "I really have no control over such things. I just run the machine. I hope it won't stop you returning to Howard's Emporium of Adventure for future excursions."

"Sure," she said, but Howard didn't think she was really listening. She was staring at the heavy wooden door revealed behind the tapestry. It was unassuming, maybe marginally bigger than an interior door should be, but no bigger than an average exterior one. The wood was smooth, unpainted and unstained, and there was a single stone step leading up to it. A brass knocker hung in the middle, simple and un-ornate, and above that was a slim metal slot with a flap over it.

Howard handed the envelope to the woman. "Put it through the slot. Make sure it goes all the way through, but don't look in. Knock four times and wait. You must walk through immediately when the door opens. If you delay, the adventure may move on, or not be as requested. Once the envelope is posted, the contract is in place. You cannot choose not to go, even if you delay and miss your adventure. If you try to refuse to go through, there will be undefined consequences. Do you understand?"

"Yeah, yeah." She waved the envelope at him. "Step back, old man. I'm not looking after your sorry self as well as dealing with whatever else waits in there."

"Good luck," Howard said, and retreated to the safety of the counter.

The woman squared her shoulders, checked her knives, then stepped forward and slipped the envelope into the slot in the door. She grasped the knocker, giving a little, alarmed shudder as she did so. They all did that. Howard didn't know if the handle was hot, or greasy, or if the power of it shook through their bones like the echo of a lightning strike. He'd never dared touch it himself to find out. The machine was enough for him.

The woman knocked four times and stepped back.

They waited.

SOMETIMES THE DOOR OPENED IMMEDIATELY, other times it took a while. Once he'd had six dwarves, a goblin wedding party, and one highly inebriated faun camped out in his shop for three days before the door finally let them through. It always seemed to take longer for groups than it did for individuals, though, as if it needed time to find places for them all. But it did always open.

Howard was just considering another cup of tea, and the woman was sitting cross-legged on the floor, painting her fingernails a vibrant purple, when a high, keening note started to float around the shop. It wasn't unpleasant so much as *quickening,* setting the heart thumping a little faster and the hair rising on the back of the neck. A sense of something drawing close, unseen worlds and undreamed riches, wild chases on impossible plains, roaring fights through inexplicable cities, crashing seas and roaring storms, magic and glory and pain and love and a thousand, thousand *possibilities* spinning past the door, crying out a siren song of *what if?* It made even Howard's old hands twitch.

He stood up from his chair behind the counter as the woman scrambled to her feet, a grin blossoming across her face. The noise built and built, filling the store and stealing his breath, and he pressed both hands to the counter as much to stop himself running to join her as to stop the pages of his ledger book being ripped away in the sudden wind that was funnelling its way out of the gaps around the door. It smelled of salt and night jasmine and open fires, of rocky shores and sweat and desert blooms.

There was a *clunk* that echoed in the heart, and the door popped open, resting on its latch. The woman stepped forward, smiling as if she were meeting an old friend, and pulled the door wide. It opened away from Howard, so he couldn't see beyond it as the woman crossed the threshold without looking back. The door shut immediately behind her, with a final, heavy clunk, and the shop was suddenly still, and darker than it had been, although a whiff of something wild and floral remained. Howard sighed. There was always that slight loss, a *bereftness* about being the one left behind, alone with the machine and the tapestry. But it was as it should be. Someone had to mind the door. And he was no adventurer. Besides – sexy armour?

He shook his head and went to pull the tapestry back into place, straightening a few things on the cluttered shelves as he went. Then he went to the front door and unlocked it, peering across the road at the tavern. It sounded like things were well under way over there, even if it was only mid-afternoon. Which would likely mean good business for him later. Nothing motivates a certain portion of the population to seek adventure like an excess of home-brewed beer and liquor of dubious origin. By the time they sobered up they were either already through the door or the envelope had been posted and the whole thing was underway. There was no going back then. The door had ways of ensuring that, although it did mean he occasionally had to barricade himself behind the counter with a few defensive spells to stop any reluctant adventurers enraged with regret and hangovers from skewering him.

A squeak at knee-level drew his attention, and he looked down to see four rats staring up at him. Two were dragging a gold coin between them, and one had lost half its tail.

"Good afternoon," he said. "How may I help you?"

The one with the stubby tail sat back on her hindquarters and squeaked at him, gesturing at one of the rats dragging the coin.

"Star-crossed lovers. Excellent choice. There isn't

enough rat representation in such things, if you ask me." He stepped back to let them into the shop, then locked the door again and followed the rats to the counter, where they'd already dragged the coin up to sit on his ledger book. He picked up the coin up and examined it, although he didn't bite it. Not because they were rats, but because it was a coin, and with all the pockets, hands, paws, and taverns it had no doubt travelled through, he had no intention of getting it anywhere near his mouth.

"Do you know how it works?" he asked, and the stub-tailed rat nodded. "You need to understand that while you can request star-crossed lovers, adventures always have a life of their own. How they start is not necessarily how they go on. Once you're through the door, everything may change."

Squeak.

"Well, then. Just checking. Let's get you started." He turned to the machine, then looked back at them. "Also, I've recently learned there may be a risk of sexy armour."

The rats looked at each other, then at him, and the stub-tailed rat shrugged.

"Alright." He started to adjust the valves, and an uncertain little squeak stopped him. He turned to look at the smallest of the rats, who was sitting up on his hind legs, front paws pressed together earnestly and bright eyes fixed on the machine.

"It's called the Story-O-Matic," he said. "No one knows where it came from, or the others like it. They've just always been here, as long back as anyone can say. So have the doors, and the keepers."

Squeak.

"Oh, there are plenty of theories. Parallel worlds,

different dimensions, time travel, other planets." He shrugged. "There's even a school of thought that says we're all just figments of someone's imagination, but I don't buy it. Too far-fetched, if you ask me."

The little rat nodded and dusted his paws off, and Howard turned back to the machine, adjusting the valves and resetting the breakers, then grasped the handle to power up the Story-O-Matic. It shuddered into thundering life, sifting through worlds and dimensions and possibilities, shaking the walls as it pulled the threads of story together. And in the end it didn't matter where they came from, although they did come from somewhere. Nothing comes from nothing.

It only really mattered that they were.

And that the armour wasn't sexy.

Thank You

Lovely people, thank you so much for picking up this book. I know you could as easily have just read some of the stories online, or skipped them completely, as short stories are not everyone's catnip. So thank you trusting me enough to step into this strange and slightly murky world. I hope that you enjoyed the ride.

And now I have one request, plus a little extra story for you. Because it's Christmas as I write this, so we shall have presents. Although maybe a little more creeping unease, a little less sparkly lights, in this case ...

But, first, the request! Reviews are a bit like magic to authors, but magic of the good kind. Less *send in the chicken, it's all gone wrong,* more *get more readers and so be able to write more books* variety. More reviews mean more people see our books in online stores, meaning more people buy them, so giving us the ability to write more stories and send them back out to you, lovely people. Less vicious circle, more happy story circle.

So it would mean the world to me if you left a review at your favourite retailer, on Goodreads, or at any other website of your choice. It doesn't have to be long – "liked it" or "would rather deal with the mysterious caterpillar" will do just fine. Of course, if you'd like to leave a longer review, that would also be wonderful!

Thank you once again for being so entirely wonderful. And jump over the page for an introduction to cats and your free bonus story!

Read on, lovely people!

Kim

Meet Gobbelino London, PI

"What've we got?"

"Tigers. Snakes. Alligators. Tears in the skin of the universe." Susan shrugged. "I think I saw a kraken in the sink, too."

We were only hired to find a book. No one said anything about void-monsters, sink-krakens, or saving the world from a plague of niceness.

And there was *definitely* no mention of dentists ...

Scan above or head to https://readerlinks.com/l/2373712/oddbm to discover Yorkshire's premier magical PIs today!

MISTLETOE & SNEAKING UNEASE ...

No one asked questions. Not with that vague threat of reindeer hanging around ...

Christmas isn't all mince pies and chocolate oranges, you know. *Someone's* got to stuff all those stockings.

And even the best job in the world wears a little thin after a few hundred years ...

Grab your free copy by scanning the link below!

And if this is your first visit to my newsletter, I'm also going to send you some *more* story collections - snarky cats and modern dragons included!

Scan above or head to https://readerlinks.com/l/2374680/oddbms to claim yours!

About the Author

Hello lovely person. I'm Kim, and in addition to the Beaufort Scales stories I write other funny, magical books that offer a little escape from the serious stuff in the world and hopefully leave you a wee bit happier than you were when you started. Because happiness, like friendship, matters.

I write about baking-obsessed reapers setting up baby ghoul petting cafes, and ladies of a certain age joining the Apocalypse on their Vespas. I write about friendship, and loyalty, and lifting each other up, and the importance of tea and cake.

But mostly I write about how wonderful people (of all species) can really be.

If you'd like to find out the latest on upcoming books, as well as discover giveaways, short stories, blogs and more, jump on over to www.kmwatt.com and check everything out there.

Read on!

amazon.com/Kim-M-Watt/e/B07JMHRBMC
bookbub.com/authors/kim-m-watt
facebook.com/KimMWatt
instagram.com/kimmwatt
x.com/kimmwatt

Acknowledgments

First and always, thank *you,* lovely reader. Without you there would be no writing, and no dangerous golf courses or superannuated superheroes. You make all this possible, and you are all entirely wonderful.

Thank you to my wonderful editor Lynda Dietz, of Easy Reader Editing. I hope very much that all the Barries are out of my system now, for her sake if not mine. All good grammar praise goes to Lynda. All mistakes are mine. Find her at www.easyreaderediting.com for fantastic blogs on editing, grammar, and other writer-y stuff.

Thank you to Monika from Ampersand Cover Design, who's some sort of writer-whisperer. I have no idea how she came up with such a wonderful cover from: "There's, I don't know, a chicken? And demons and tears in the universe and stuff. Oh, and I like blue." She may be magic. Find her at www.ampersandbookcovers.com

And thank you to all my wonderful friends and family, online and off. It's been a long, strange year, and it would've been a lot longer without you. Less strange, possibly, but definitely longer. And I like strange, anyway, every bit as much as I like you.

Also by Kim M. Watt

The Gobbelino London, PI series

"This series is a wonderful combination of humor and suspense that won't let you stop until you've finished the book. Fair warning, don't plan on doing anything else until you're done ..."

- Goodreads reviewer

The Beaufort Scales Series (cozy mysteries with dragons)

"The addition of covert dragons to a cozy mystery is perfect...and the dragons are as quirky and entertaining as the rest of the slightly eccentric residents of Toot Hansell."

– Goodreads reviewer

Short Story Collections

Oddly Enough: Tales of the Unordinary, Volume One

"The stories are quirky, charming, hilarious, and some are all of the above without a dud amongst the bunch ..."

- Goodreads reviewer

The Tales of Beaufort Scales

A collection of dragonish tales from the world of Toot Hansell, available at www.kmwatt.com as a welcome gift for joining the newsletter! Just mind the abominable snow porcupine ...

The Cat Did It

Of course the cat did it. Sneaky, snarky, and up to no good - that's the cats in this feline collection, which you can grab free via the newsletter (you can use either this link or the *Tales* one to sign up. You'll still get both books). Just remember - if the cat winks, always wink back ...

Printed in Great Britain
by Amazon

41237834R00229